COLOR
OF
SALT

Grateful acknowledgment is made for the use of the following songs:

"If I Fell": Words and Music by John Lennon and Paul McCartney. Copyright © 1964 by Northern Songs. All rights controlled and administered by MCA Music Publishing, a division of MCA Inc., New York, NY, 10019.

"Hey Bobby": Written by K.T. Oslin. Copyright © 1988 by Wooden Wonder Music. Administered by PolyGram International Tunes, Inc.

"I Can Help": Written by Billy Swan. Copyright © 1974 by TEMI Combine Inc. All rights reserved. International copyright secured. Used by permission.

AVON BOOKS
A division of
The Hearst Corporation
1350 Avenue of the Americas
New York, New York 10019

Copyright © 1992 by Noreen Ayres
Published by arrangement with the author
ISBN: 0-380-71571-6

Published in hardcover by William Morrow and Company, Inc.; for information address Permissions Department, William Morrow and Company, Inc., 1350 Avenue of the Americas, New York, New York 10019.

First Avon Books Printing: November 1993

AVON TRADEMARK REG. U.S. PAT. OFF. AND IN OTHER COUNTRIES, MARCA REGISTRADA, HECHO EN U.S.A.

Printed in the U.S.A.

RA 10 9 8 7 6 5 4 3 2 1

A WORLD THE COLOR OF SALT

NOREEN AYRES

AVON BOOKS NEW YORK

> **J Gary Brazelton**
> **1947–1990**
>
> - Professor of Administration of Justice
> - Recipient of the Medal of Valor
> - Simi Valley Police Officer

Through Gary's personal commitment, integrity, humor, energy, and caring, we who were privileged to know him are vastly enriched. It is in this spirit and to his memory that I dedicate this book.

"And may you never be dispossessed, forced to wander a world the color of salt with no young music in it."

—RICHARD HUGO, from
"Places and Ways to Live,"
in *What Thou Lovest Well, Remains American*

CHAPTER
1

First they shot him in the mouth. His tongue split down the middle like a barbecued hot dog. That was from the .22. Of course, we didn't know that until the autopsy. Usually with stop-and-robs it's a quick, "Hand me the money"—"No, I won't"—*BOOM!* And it's done. But there was something different here. Because first they shot Jerry Dwyer in the mouth, and *then* they went back for a bigger gun.

What was it Jerry did or said that made them so vicious? The boy was a cool head, would have laughed it off if he could. Would have thought, because he was trained to, Give them the frigging money, let them book; then call Dad, who knows all about that insurance stuff. Go on to the party and find some way to make the story funny. But Jerry Dwyer wasn't going to the party that night, or any other night.

They say about cops that there are cops' eyes, and your eyes. I could say the same about this work too. I'm a criminalist, job title Forensic Specialist, for the Orange County, California, sheriff-coroner's office. I work out of the crime lab in Santa Ana, about an hour's drive from L.A. What I do is collect, protect, analyze, and store evidence. A copper can have a guy cold—dead bang, as they say—and miss out sending the dirtbag to the gray-bar hotel if the evidence is not rightly collected, analyzed, and secured, and we at the lab help him and the DA do it.

I've been doing this work for more than five years, seven if you count cop work in Oakland. Friends call me Smokey. I'm female, five-five, bland blonde, the right weight. And I was pretty untouchable before this. I could do babies and not cry.

But this case got to me. The blasts of blood. The hopeless trail to the back of the store, where Jerry Dwyer ran to get away from his killers. The awful skid marks, like experiments in new paint.

Before the murder, I would stop at Dwyer's Kwik Stop on my way to work and grab a coffee and a doughnut, and with a couple of turns, be on the freeway heading for the lab.

He was a big kid, Jerry was. Twenty years old. Two-hundred-nineteen, six-one, blond/blue. He worked in his father's store two hours in the morning, then attended Saddleback College for computer classes till noon, and returned to the store afterward to work some more until his evening auto-shop class. How could you help but like a kid who worked like that? Here in Orange County it's real easy for kids to have a free ride, affluent even when they don't think so. Not Jerry. He knew, maybe from first eye on the world, that this wealth was an accident. While other people were counting on lottery tickets or their parents' various insurance policies, he'd say, You got to have a *plan*, man. He'd say yuppie scum were everywhere building/buying/busting, and someday it was all going to come down, and they're going to be looking stupid at each other like they all wet their pants the same day. Now Jerry's stretched out on a steel tray in the coroner's cooler, and my eyes tear up about four times a day.

Joe London Sanders was investigative team leader this time, and in better hands we could not have been. Team leaders are rotated. I'd been off having one of those surgeries you don't like to talk about; but before that, I'd led most of the investigations for several months.

Things had already begun to change for me. At thirty-two the fire shouldn't have been out. But the number of crimes was increasing almost exponentially, it seemed, and I admit the work does it to you. You go in wanting to fight the good fight, wanting to make a tiny ripple of difference. Before long you think everything counts the same, all murders are equal, everyone has to die sometime. Then a Jerry Dwyer wakes you up.

CHAPTER
2

Billy Katchaturian was standing around waiting for the blood to dry. By four-thirty the deputy coroner had come and gone and the techs were about ready to remove the body. Billy had taken preliminaries already, the panoramas and then the thorough pictures showing every relationship to every piece of evidence, but he always shot black-and-whites afterward. Forty-five minutes or so after being spilled, blood begins to coagulate, forming deeper contrasts. An hour later, it decoagulates again, gets pink and uninteresting, Billy says. Black-and-whites look sharper, though the coloreds are what the prosecutors depend on for jury influence. I never knew what he did with the black-and-whites.

He was standing, all six-three of him, at the east end of the store, over by the ice-cream machine, looking at I don't know what.

Jerry's father, Mr. Dwyer, had painted the outside of his store eggshell white and added a blue awning. The magazine rack was the first thing you'd see on entering, the girlie mags in blinder racks on the bottom, covering everything but the titles, the sports mags and gossip rags in the top row. In the back of the room by the ice-cream machine were the counter and cash register, and off to the side was a little alcove where Mr. Dwyer or Jerry had sat when there were no customers. The cold cases were on the right. Some of the food racks ran across the store, horizontal to the north-running aisle that led to the counter, the aisle the killers had taken.

Trudy Kunitz stood ahead of me midway into the store facing the counter, glancing down at her sketches, back up to the

11

points of reference, checking to see if she got them right. When her glasses slipped down on her nose, she pushed them up with the top of her tablet but kept her eyes locked on the wall behind the counter anyway, and didn't see me.

I moved out of Billy's line of sight. Billy didn't like me at all. Or hardly at all. It gets complicated. Our history goes back to when I was an FNG—fucking new guy—and he thought he could run me down the alley. I knew when I walked in that day five years ago that Billy Katchaturian, with his hunched shoulders and soulful eyes, took one look at me and said, Unh-hnn, fresh meat.

But I was older than I looked. I'd already spent two years on the Oakland force and a hell-length of time with a husband who was dying and didn't have a right to, didn't have the right to get zapped in the liver by a hepatitis B bug and leave me when we hadn't even worn out our deep welcomes yet.

So from day one, Billy K. was over me like a shark on a minnow, leaning over, leaning close, leaning on, and I'd look at him and say, "Whatcha doin', Billy?" and then, "I'm old enough to be your mama," even though I wasn't. One time he said, "It's 'cause I've got dark skin, isn't it?" Well, Billy's looking better to me as he ages, but not that good and never will, and let's say it's got nothin' to do with skin color.

Avoiding him, I followed the inside perimeter tape on the floor down an aisle away from the avenue of escape. Someone would already have done a grid search, mentally dividing the room into squares or, better, cubes, and then searching for evidence top to bottom in a methodical fashion. Still, as I moved down the aisle, I surveyed left and right searching for something different from the way the store looked every morning at a quarter to seven, when I normally came in.

I heard Billy's voice. "Welcome back, Smokes," he said. He'd moved to the ratty black office chair in the tiny alcove near the start of the cold-drink case. That was where Jerry Dwyer's dad sat to do the bills. I'd be stirring sugar in the coffee and glancing at magazine headlines along the rack, and Jerry's dad would give me a wink or a tight nod-and-smile and then bore back down on the checkbook. Now the chair was pitched back against the wall, Billy's legs grasshoppered up, one hand resting on the eight-hundred-dollar camera lens that protruded nose-up in his lap. It didn't seem right for Billy to be in that chair. Now Billy, grinning at me, saying, "Smokey, lovely as ever," in his ain't-I-a-dude voice.

I'm polite. He knows I'll close my eyes and sigh, and I do; even smile as if to say, I'm glad you're still Billy, Billy. What I said was, "Joe S. still here?"

It took him a second to answer because he had to get done shaking his head, telling me how rude. "He's here. In the fridge," he said, nodding behind him.

There was no going through the doorway to the back—too much blood. Let the coroner's guys mess it up. I wondered where Mr. Dwyer was, if he'd seen the blood. Not good.

At the southwest end, I could see the floor behind the counter without stepping over the tape. Two very big blasts of blood hit the beige tile between the middle of the counter and the door to the back room. They formed an odd pattern. What went on here?

The smell of nitrocellulose, gunpowder, was still in the air. Mix that with spilled body fluids, and if you could *taste* a smell, it was like a tooth you sucked on telling you you better see a dentist. It wasn't decomp yet and it wasn't that strong, but I still felt queasy. I told myself it was because I'd been away too long.

Trying for a better vantage point, I leaned against the stacked rolls of paper towels to see the white door that led to the storage area in the back where the cooler would be. Heavy spatter marked the door near the hinge side. The spatter had lots of spines, almost like somebody tossed shakers of paint. The bold blasts on the floor and the wall were not arterial spurt. The elegant theory of arterial spurts—elegant, that's what Joe Sanders calls it—is linked to the rhythm of the heart, the spurt forming patterns in weaker and weaker parallel arcs across a wall, say, if it were coming from a victim's neck. But this spatter was not so linear, and it was higher than neck-high, even Jerry's, who was football-player–sized. I'd seen this kind of spatter pattern before—where? Lots of force. To the right of the middle of the door were smeary handprints where Jerry had jammed on the door as he fled.

I leaned in. Close up, the discrete drops looked like Pac-Man ghosts—Winkies, Inkies, Blinkies, and Clydes—tipped on their sides. That is, wavy on the east, showing they planed in westward, from the direction Jerry would've come. Then some dripping down, red exclamation points like tadpoles heading north. I remembered then: esophageal varices. Our Physical Fluid prof had shown us the slides, told us how alcoholics sometimes burst the arteries in their throats, leaving so much blood it looks as if a crime's been committed. And in a way, it has.

In the back of the room there was more mess, and I could see Joe Sanders framed in the far rear door, talking to an officer, probably the patrol cop. Trudy Kunitz glided by in the back now too, measuring the room with a metal tape that zinged as she flipped it to lay it flat. Trudy is good at her job, reliable. Our department mostly works like good music. Few people fuck up. I lost sight of her as she drifted behind a stack of boxes, and I went back out the front door and around.

At the side of the building, a yellow crime-scene ribbon formed an inner perimeter within the larger outer one that extended into the parking lot. I noticed that one end of the ribbon nearest the building drooped to the asphalt near the ladies' room, but it didn't register then. The men's had masking tape on the door across the door frame. This meant someone closed the men's off for later checking, maybe because it was hot-hot, requiring further inspection.

Paper cups and taco wrappers from next door were piled against the wire fence in back. Behind the fence, eucalyptus trees caught the last rays of the sun and glowed red where the bark had split into stretched triangles, evidence of the Australian long-horn eucalyptus borer that's been feasting on thirsty trees from San Diego to Santa Barbara since 1984.

In the back of the store, standing near the door, Joe S. He saw me coming and motioned me forward. He had on the good suit. I thought he must be going somewhere this evening, speaking to some group or other. Maroon tie and a rich brown jacket, pale pink shirt, and shoes shined as though they'd never walked in murder.

When I was halfway to him, Joe said, "Sign the Order of Entry?"

"Are you giving me a bad time?" I smiled a whit.

He smiled back the same whit and said, "Just asking."

"I had a belly-cut, not a lobotomy, you tub."

Joe turned his head to answer somebody, then stepped just inside. When I reached him in the doorway I should have brushed by quickly, should not have let my clothes electrify, the field get set between us. I had hoped it all went sleepy bye with the rest of my consciousness in the hospital, but no. One look in those pink-blues and I was gone again. "How you doing, Joe?" I said.

All of a sudden he got shy, all business. I moved ahead of him into the back room. With the light the way it was, his hair seemed grayer since I last saw him. Joe's a fit forty-eight, proud of his waist, and that's why when I get the chance I have to mention the slight convexity just above the place he likely takes the measure. The better to hug, if he only knew. Looking over my head, he told me, "Point of attack was up front." Then, "You knew him," said not like a question.

"I stop here for doughnuts on the way to work, is all. Once I went to a party with him and his friends, but it was too young a crowd for me. But yeah, he was great, Joe. A great kid. This is a rotten thing."

He looked at me, listening to this, sorry to hear that from me. They're not all great, the victims.

He said, "Were you here this morning?"

"No."

"You okay?"

"You mean should I be back at work?"

"Should you?"

"Thanks a whole fuckin' lot." We'd stepped inside. He was too close now, standing so near I could smell his after-shave, but he wasn't looking at me.

He said, "I wouldn't ask if you didn't know him. Sometimes it makes a difference. You know that."

"Well, it doesn't," I said. Subject over. "Jerry Dwyer was a friendly, talkative, open kid. He knew his customers' names and could remember what doughnuts they liked." Joe shook his head.

My gaze went to the back of the room and took in the back side of the white enamel door. The only blood there was along the door's edge. Off to the left, nearer the cooler, is where I knew the body would be. I stood there looking frontward maybe thirty feet away, Joe quiet behind me, and the question no one ever has an answer for must have spelled itself on my back, because Joe placed his hand on my shoulder for a moment and then moved away: Why this one?

Dull fluorescent lights cast a filmy gray coat over everything. Crates of S & W foodstuff and cases of motor oil built verticals everywhere. The corner to my right was clogged with an old pinball machine, four boxes of Friskies cat food stacked on top. High windows along the wall let in the waning November light—Joe S. was going to have to shut the scene down pretty soon, safe the area with a guard, come back tomorrow. Fluorescent is good but not like daylight. Always there is a war with yourself in a homicide. If you're serious about justice, you must take whatever time is required to investigate thoroughly. But the more time you take, the more possibility the scene could be compromised—authorized people coming in and out, unauthorized people trespassing the scene. Not the least of the worries is budget and manpower, extending an investigation too long. We all knew this, but it was seldom mentioned.

While I stood there not really wanting to go forward to the cooler entryway, off Joe's left an anemic-looking young man with zits, government-issue black horned-rims, and milky hair placed his elbow up on a case of cans, the better to study his notes. This had to be a rookie.

Joe said, "Hey!"

"Sir?"

"Your shirt on the box."

The rook stared, his neck turning rosy.

"Dust," Joe said. "Did your shirt disturb the dust?"

The rookie turned to look. "I . . . I don't think so, sir. I don't see anything."

Joe's voice was slow, fair, not overbearing. "Take your flashlight," he said. "Hold the beam across the top of the box. Make sure there are no prior disturbances, no finger or palm prints." Joe glanced back at me. Actually, we all have sympathy for rooks; we were all there once.

"Yes, sir," the rookie said, and struggled with the flashlight attached to his belt.

Joe took me by the elbow and turned me toward the door.

He said, "Do you think it's too late to go into real estate?"

"Take me with you when you go."

Joe was talking as we walked back to the cooler. He told me how his son, David, was doing his first year in college. Midway, he stopped, turned back to the door. "You don't have to do this, Smokey."

"I know I don't."

"We have enough people here."

"If I didn't want to be here I wouldn't have called to ask to be in on it, Joe."

He swept a finger under his eye. I knew the gesture: He did it when he needed a moment to think. And then we walked the rest of the way, his left hand lightly holding my elbow. He handed me a mentholated stick, the kind you rub around your nose when you have a cold, and the kind some idiots boil down and inject for a cheap but complicated meth hit. Bodies don't smell that bad this early, but the distraction of a strong smell helps bring you back to yourself. The touch on the elbow, the quiet voice, and now this gesture of concern: These are some of the reasons he does what he does to me and my grown-up self.

I was looking down on an awful red mess. I couldn't see Jerry's face yet, the hips rolled to the side, the head away from the door opening, and I didn't want to; I stepped back. "He should have been safe here."

Billy Katchaturian appeared behind me. Even with the menthol, the sharp smell of mothballs leaked through. Billy was from the East. People from the East smell like mothballs. I looked over. He was examining the Polaroids, about three feet from me. Joe saw this and said, "You need more, Billy?"

"No, sir, go ahead. These are good." He held the pack of them out like a sharpie showing cards to an audience.

I moved closer in toward the cooler. A square of butcher paper was laid down where Billy K. had lodged a step stool to get overhead shots; I saw the stool's rusty black impressions on it. For some reason, I didn't want to step on the paper.

Right away I saw bone in the bubbly stew above the knee that was once Jerry's leg.

"Jesus," I said. "They used heavy stuff."

Joe said, "You can see bits of the slug at the top of the wound there." He pointed with a pen.

"Almost looks like a Glaser," I said.

"Crooks don't have them," Joe said.

"You and I can't get them, is all." Leaning farther in, what I could see of Jerry's head told me the downside would be worse. I'd seen Glaser safety slugs demo-ed at the range, but I'd never shot one myself. They're mean pieces of devastation with thin copper sides, designed to burst on impact.

The air in the cooler wasn't cold, the door open for so long, and I could hear the motor cycling. Moisture shone on the walls. It was a tight place, lots of open food boxes there containing the stuff Jerry or his dad would put in the microwave for us. White boxes marked "Hamburg." In one corner, the soft-ice-cream makings. Jerry Dwyer's father was going to lose more than a son here. More than his heart, I mean.

Joe said, "We know they had a twenty-two auto up front: six casings on the floor. One slug in the Lotto machine, one in the post by the register. Three in the wall. One slug must have caught him, and then he ran."

He paused, pulling his hands onto his hips and talking down to the floor, a move he makes when something's got to him. I knew .22's could do funny things—kill you in an instant, if placed in the right spot, or merely drill a hole in you like a paper punch, swell the tissue like an allergic reaction, and that's about it. One case I knew of, the victim took a round in the top of the heart, in and out. He ran two blocks home, lay on his sofa for fifteen minutes before paramedics arrived. Today he sells health insurance down the street from my bank. You can get whapped with a .22 round in the back of the head, the shell will fly apart, the pieces burrow under your scalp like worms trying to find the sun, but you live.

He said, "The one in the head, if I had to guess, would be a five-seven."

My throat went tight. I started to walk to the back door, and then felt Joe beside me. The rook was staring at us as we passed, as if he wanted to ask Joe a question.

Joe said, "The kid was holding the door, trying to keep them out. Looks like he was a big guy. Was he?"

"Yes."

"He might have been able to do it, except he kept slipping in his own blood. You can see that, with the smears. I think with that first shot they must have got him somewhere in the face or head, the amount of blood there was. See the spatter inside the door?"

I had. Blood on the cooler door, like on the door up front, only more of it, and lots at the bottom.

"It runs down on the floor while he's trying to keep them out," Joe said. "He slips, keeps sliding, can't hold it. See the skids?"

I nodded.

Joe went on. "Victim's pushing, pushing. They get the pistol barrel in—there's tool marks on the edge and frame; Billy's got shots of it—they get the gun in, shoot him in the leg. He goes down, *whoom!* It's all over."

Joe stepped closer, lightly leaned his shoulder against mine. I didn't move.

He went on. "We know there were two."

I managed to say, "There'd be blowback from where they got him in the head."

"Somebody's sailing around with dirty clothes. Shoes'd be good, too. We got definite sole prints."

"Transfers anywhere?" I asked. This would be blood transferred from clothing, say, to another object. Often there are identifying fibers or other trace evidence to be found.

"We got five red fibers off the outer-door frame near the floor, don't know what they mean, could be old. We got boot-heel and sole prints. A half-palm transfer on the register. I think it's got some gunpowder residue in it. We've done about half the latents." Latents are fingerprints not readily visible to the naked eye.

He looked around him and said, "It's going to be tough in a place like this. And no video, of course." Video cameras in the regular chains might have captured something. Dwyer's Kwik Stop was a mom-and-pop without the mom, the mom doing something or other in the Midwest after a divorce. I remembered Jerry saying once that his mom was a good businesswoman.

"One more 'we got,' please," I said. "Say we got a witness."

"Don't I wish," he said.

"You say it happened when?" How could there be no witness, a store near a freeway? We were outside now, and the late November chill was taking its toll. I wrapped my arms around my waist.

Joe gave me his freak-of-time speech. I'd heard it a million times applied a million ways. A freak of time kills people. A freak of time makes people fall in love. With the wrong people. A freak of time sometimes puts two and two together to make a case; a freak of time puts the right judge or the right prosecutor on it to get a conviction. This freak of time bore no witness. Sometimes it works for you. Mostly it doesn't.

"Jerry Dwyer deserves these guys on a stake," I said.

"Have at it, baby."

"Joe . . ."

"Nobody heard me."

"That makes it worse."

"Sorry."

The sky was a darkening purple because of the haze and the dying sun, and the traffic light at the intersection glowed a raw red. Next door, a tanker at the Texaco station was backing up, making dinging noises. Car engines whined up the on-ramp to the 5 South. Life was going on.

I half smiled at Joe. My third knuckle touched the back of his hand when I stopped for a second.

"What time will you be back?"

"Early."

That meant seven. Joe was not really an early guy. Early is like five, six at the latest, but it's still dark then, and besides, most of us, unfortunately, are, I hate to say it, government workers. Look at our paychecks. I know people who work in aerospace, and those people get up *early*.

"I'll be here." I started to head out to my car when I had to ask, "How's Jennifer?"

"Fine, fine. She got a promotion."

"She's happy, I guess?"

He shrugged.

I followed his gaze to the same ribbon end fluttered down at the stand near the ladies' restroom. The door was cracked open, something I hadn't noticed before. We looked at each other. "Somebody used it," I said.

"Damn," Joe said.

Joe was turning the corner, ready to scare the bejesus out of the rookie, I guessed, by the time I got my key in the car door. When I opened it, the interior light shone on something in the grass under the hedge I parked near. I reached down and picked up a roundish, gold metal object about the size of a walnut. It had a small hole in the back and flanges around the rim.

I didn't want to go back in when Joe was doing his thing, didn't want to fuss with Billy K., didn't want to find a bag-and-tag for something that probably wasn't even evidence. The metal thingy had been over too far in the grass, a long way from the outer perimeter tape. In a moment of doubt, though, I pushed my car door closed and took one or two steps toward the store and Joe. And then I returned. Why distract him now, when he had some chewing out to do? Once in the car, I pulled out a Kleenex from the box on the console and set my gold gadget in it, twisting the top of the tissue for a handle, and put it in my right pocket.

On the way out of there I was thinking about the FNG and feeling sorry for him. I thought, If the rookie took a wee in the ladies' because the men's was taped, maybe no harm. At least it wasn't the taped one. Maybe. Tomorrow. We'd see.

CHAPTER
3

I could get silly with Patricia. She'd be good for me now. I called and asked if we could meet at Chi-Chi's in Huntington Beach, near her house. How she and I ever became friends is beyond me. We're so different. Nearly six feet of pretty, all legs, Patricia has deep red hair bottle-streaked with blonde, and a child's voice. The first time I heard it, I thought she was putting me on, but it's hers. And the men just love her. She jokes about her lack of frontal topography, but if so, it sure doesn't interfere with the number of possible dates one woman could have in a lifetime.

The day I met her I was in the parking lot at Alisos beach after some breathless jogging—whose idea was that anyway, I asked myself, swearing off it forever. I was putting gear back in the car when she came up from the sand, walking on the side of her foot, saying "Ow-w!" and laughing at the same time. The small guy with her danced in front of her, holding her at arm's length around the waist as he kept saying, "Bummer, man." With one hand she clutched at the top of his head, and with the other grabbed up her ankle to inspect her foot, the blood on the bottom bright and shiny as an open tomato and the sand like white salt around the rim. To the rescue I came. I gave her a minipad from my purse, told her to stick it in her shoe till we could get her someplace. The little dude split, saying he'd be in touch. I said I knew where there was an emergency hospital. On the way to ER, she kept telling me how nice it was of me to do this, and then she'd convulse with giggles. I thought, What we have here is a certifiable loony, until she told me that the little dude had been following her around all afternoon so she wound up smoking dope with him in a cove. She hadn't been able to figure out how she was going to tell him she wasn't going home with him, and that made her nervous, which started her laughing, and he just thought she was having a good time.

Sometime during our drive to the hospital she asked me if I was home on spring break, meaning, was I a college student? No-o-o, I said. But I didn't mention what I did. I just said thanks for the compliment. I said I worked for the county. Later, by months, I told her precisely how.

At Chi-Chi's, six overhead TVs were tuned to rock video, as always. Go to the restroom and you get piped-in KROQ, as in K-Rock. Food servers sing those annoying songs on your b-day, and I suspect people pretend they have birthdays when they don't, for the free dessert, because you can't get through a meal without at least two attacks of happy singers interrupting your conversation. But the thing is, voices and laughter shoot off all the hard surfaces, and you've got two choices: Drink and join in, or curl up and die.

I walked in, the food smelled wonderful. Broiled everything. Cilantro and lemon. Good green things. Patricia wouldn't be there yet. I waited for the hostess. Someone forgot to write the special of the day in the smeary center of a blackboard. At the top, painted words read, "What Foods These Morsels Be." When the hostess came, she was wearing a blue-and-white flowered island dress pinched high up one leg. I asked for a certain table facing the water, even though it was night. In the daytime, you can see a square foot of Pacific Ocean with a shadow of Catalina Island behind it. I just needed to know it was there. Through fake fig leaves I watched the men at the bar. Red faces, heads whonked up out of their shoulders as they waited for a football moment on the TV. Two big guys. I thought of Jerry Dwyer. He would have been watching the game, Rams losing to the Forty-niners; a Rams man nonetheless.

"Hi," Patricia said. She sat down across from me. Over a deep-purple skirt she wore a hot-pink nubby-silk business jacket, which was frankly stunning with her red hair. Big glass purple-and-pink earrings glinted at her jawline. Her face is round and soft-looking, as if it doesn't belong to her lengthened and considerably sinewy body. It's a voluptuous face, if you can say that about a face, and it sports two dimples: one where you might expect, by the mouth; the other in an odd place I still find myself wondering at—the muscles pull in to form a little hole just under her right eye, riding the crest of her cheek. These twists of muscle make her look twice as happy. She smiles, you can't help smiling back.

"Guess what," she said.

"What?"

"I passed my real estate exam."

"Congratulations. You can buy dinner."

"I will."

"No, you won't."

Leaning in, she said, "I can quit my friggin' job now." She worked at a small import electronics firm in Laguna Hills, performing everything from minor sales to inventory control, but basically she was a clerk. I remember when she started wearing jackets with her dresses so she'd be taken more seriously. "When I sell my first million-dollar home, that is. Till then, tote that barge."

"Next week," I said.

"Next week," she agreed. "We're in a recession, right? Well, they are just *not* going to quit building homes, no way. I was driving up from San Diego last week and could *not* believe my eyes." Her red curls swung. It was not hard to imagine her telling a potential buyer, Have I got a dollhouse for *you*.

Any fool could have sold houses two years ago, and though this year's market collapsed for the ritzy ones, there was still potential in the more modest homes, she said. And she was right. Hills everywhere are shorn and scraped to white bone. Rows and rows of pink, peach, white, sand, and buff structures cut across the horizon in layers, with about twenty feet between them and no visible trees. Whole communities spring up virtually overnight. First you notice the giant water tanks rising like stacks of beige poker chips on the brown hills. Later, quick-growing trees will hide them. On the freeways pickup trucks with illegal aliens in the beds, their hats pulled low, arms dangling on their knees, travel to the new sites to work landscaping and any other back-breaking labor. Above it all float the dislocated ravens, circling, perching on light standards or scavenging cast-off lunch sacks, always with their mates, but sometimes in congregations of four or six, croaking, saying, What the hell is going on here, folks?

Though I live near the beach and work inland, I drive south often with my neighbor's dog just to feel I'm getting away. I walk the washes or park on a hill, take out my binoculars to look for birds, and see instead the methodical scouring of Orange County. Especially in the spring, you can't escape the steady *pock* of carpenters nailing roofs, shirts off and muscles gleaming in the sun. Or the low rumble of earth movers. Once, in a sort of valley, the sun had pinked the sky to the west, the workers had gone home, and there, in the blue shadows of a horseshoe-shaped set of hills, I counted thirty-one beige hulks, gathered like insects settling in for sleep. It was scary.

I said to Patricia, "You realize there's going to be no more room for marines or illegal aliens anymore? They might get rid of Pendleton," referring to a base down the coast.

"Won't *that* be too bad," she said. She'd been staring at my hairstyle for a long time without saying anything. I'd had my hair cut three weeks before, readying myself for my return to work. Ever since, I'd been feeling like a victim of a Carol Burnett skit. With the sunny part clipped off, the hair was definitely blah, more brown now, but not a pretty brown. She finally said, "Your hair looks good."

"You're full of shit. Thank you."

"No, really. I'd go even shorter. You got the ears." She pulled her own hair back to show off flaps, I will admit. I smiled. It's not often you get a compliment like that. Then, changing subjects by making a funny wince, she said, "I'm sorry I didn't get by."

"No problem. I wasn't crazy about seeing people."

"I hate hospitals."

"So do I."

She'd already waved down the waitress and told her what I'd drink, ordering for herself a vodka Collins to my Bud. Patricia used to kid me about Colorado Kool-Aid when I drank Coors. What I really like is whiskey. The reason I like it is the reason I stay away from it.

I said, "We got a serious murder my first day back."

"Aren't they all? I couldn't handle it, I really couldn't." She was holding her glass with both hands, wagging her head at me. She rested both thumbs on the side of her nose and peered at me over the glass.

"You think I'm bad. You should meet a coroner."

"No, thanks."

"There're some cute marines working autopsy."

"What?"

"Yeah. Big, handsome guy the week before I left. You would've loved him. He's cuttin' skulls and clippin' ribs with the best of 'em." She was looking at me with the silent fascination and repugnance most people show on their faces when I get feisty and talk about it. I said, "Of course, the reason he was there was because he was on detention. One too many DUIs, so they put him on morgue duty for a week. No indoctrination. Just, wham! Here's the hedge clippers, here's the saw. You'd think that would deter the stupid shits, but it doesn't. Last year they had a guy doing cut-ups one week, two weeks later he's back, only this time through the rear door. Stubborn."

Patricia took a drink, then her voice dropped low. "I still can't match you up with that . . . stuff. Police work, yeah, maybe, but even that. . . . I mean, cops are so often jerks. You're not. Except when you're trying to gross me out."

"It's science. Mental."

"What bothered you about the one you said—?"

"This was close to home, sort of. An acquaintance of mine. A kid, twenty, a college student. He worked at a store near me. He has no face this morning. They did a true number on him."

"I don't want to hear about it," she said quickly. But she did. She always did. Until the stuff got too grisly, and then she'd begin her nervous giggles. Usually I'm careful not to enhance the gore, unless I'm feeling bitter. It was hard for me to restrain myself, but, with very few details, I told her about the Dwyer case. Her attention held until I said the creeps got only about two hundred. Say it was a hundred thou and people's interest picks up. That's cynical of me, I know, but it's true. Like, Don't bother me with fifty-cent murders.

A distraction at the bar saved Patricia from hearing more:

Some dude with muscles up the wazoo telling a red-faced blond guy to go for it, the other guy saying sure, sure he would, right after you. Had to be they spotted Patricia. Nobody else around, to speak of.

Patricia poked a hole in the air in my direction and said, "We got to get you a guy, Samantha." She looked over at the pickings along the bar. The dark-haired guy smiled. Then the blond. Yep. Patricia. Patricia doesn't know me as Smokey, doesn't know anything about my reckless days. I was going to tell her sometime, if it seemed right. She always uses my full name—not Sam; not Sammi, as my family does; not Mandy, as a few in high school tried to—because she doesn't like people to shorten *her* name.

I said, "Don't worry about it, please."

"A guy is what you need, my friend. And look, you're lucky, you got no worries now. No pills, nothing."

"There's just forty kinds of disease around," I said. I really didn't want to get into it.

She whacked four fingers on the edge of the table. "Girl, we're having a party, we're getting you laid."

"This is giving me a headache," I said, and she screamed at this. It unglued the ice in her glass. She leaned in and said, "Poor baby. Eat two men and call me in the morning."

I love that girl.

CHAPTER
4

Santa Ana, the seat of Orange County's government, is cut through by one of the ugliest and most clogged freeways in the world, day or night. I-5 tries to ride on top of the city, but signs for motels, service stations, RV rentals, and U-Haul yards peep over its shoulders. Down the median, a concrete wall topped with fencing separates the drift of cars going the other direction, and in front of you, always, is a huge semi with mud flaps bouncing the silver silhouette of a woman resting on her laurels.

I should have gone home. When I left Patricia I said I was going to. My condo's about seven miles down the coast from Chi-Chi's, on a bluff overlooking the Upper Newport Bay Ecological Reserve, called Back Bay for short, a place I've learned to care about because it's teaching me about birds. The bay is an estuary holding some kind of distinction for having been created by an earthquake rather than by erosion. That should impress somebody, but they keep building, and we keep moving in. Housing prices are sky-high for anything in these parts. I am incredibly lucky to live there. An aunt I don't even know very well rents it to me.

But there's nothing so bleak as going home to a house with no lights on in it. The small brass weight I picked up from the ground at the Kwik Stop was excuse enough—I went to work.

The crime lab, or the barn as some people call it, for reasons I'm not sure about, is a gray-and-green structure in downtown Santa Ana, otherwise nondescript; in the county-office scheme of things, Building 16. On the south side of the

lab is OCTD—the Orange County Transit District bus line.
Across from the lab is the Santa Ana Police Department, and
just over one street is the sheriff's headquarters. Still, I'm
careful driving there at night. The juries in the courthouse
have gone home, the IRS clerks cleared out, the library patrons thinned. But moving toward Civic Center square, like
fragments in a mass centrifuge, are the homeless, the disen-
franchised, the ambulatory alkies seeking spots on concrete
benches, or, if they're lucky, under the gazebo near the city
library. Recently there was a roundup of dozens of homeless,
the assignment called Operation Civic Center by Santa Ana
cops but dubbed Littergate by the homeless. Arrests were
made for committing such violations as sailing a paper airplane, picking a leaf, or dropping a "snipe," as the vagrants
call cigarette butts. They chained these serious bad guys to
benches in Eddie West Field, the small stadium where city
cops play ball against county sheriff's deputies, and marked
an identifying number on their wrists with felt-tip pens. Imagine, correctly, how lawyers swarmed all over that one. The
sheriff's office—not the Santa Ana Police Department,
granted—has about five men on the gang task force, yet Santa
Ana deployed twenty-three coppers on the homeless. Some
things do get cocked.

Then there're people like the shoeshine man with a heart
of, pardon me, gold, who brings discarded food from the
markets and distributes it to the homeless. Wonder what my
copper neighbors think about that. But I must say I've come
to work at night or gone home late more times than I
should've, maybe, on my paycheck, and to see a phalanx of
black-and-whites across the street is vaguely comforting; so
what is right, what is wrong? Though nothing has happened
to alarm me yet, I'm still on the alert until I get up the back
steps, ring the buzzer, and somebody lets me in.

Paula, the maintenance person, did. No one else there I
could see. The radio hooked over the trash cart let me keep
track of her. It played a minister's voice. "Friends," the voice
kept saying, "friends, *this* is what it's all about, *this* is God's
plan. This is what we're here for. . . ." I wondered if Paula felt
assured she was where she was supposed to be.

I took my brass whatever to my desk, opened a drawer, and

retrieved a brown bag to put the thing in, Kleenex and all. I stapled the bag closed and rummaged in the back of the top drawer amid the half-used label sheets and wayward pens and pencils for the yellow evidence tag. Filled it out: Dept. No.; Case No., which I didn't know right then; Crime Category— "HOMICIDE." I wrote in black felt pen. Name of Suspect . . . nope. Name of Victim—"JEROME ALPHONSUS DWYER." On the last lines, I entered the location from which the evidence was obtained, and by whom. Just above that, under Description, I wrote "UNKNOWN GOLD . . ."; crossed that out: "BRASS OBJECT, APPROX. ONE IN. DIAM."

Pulling out the big drawer on the left, I put the bag in front where I usually kept my lunch. I'd take the thing to Property in the morning.

And then tell me why I did it—went into Joe S.'s office and grabbed files off his desk. Not always known for my good sense, I lifted Jerry Dwyer's file, Case 90-03284 HW, right out of Joe's bin and started going through it. At least I had the case number for the evidence tag. I'd remember it without writing it down because I'm good with numbers: I'm 32, and 32 is 8, 4 times. HW standing for the attending coroner on the scene, Hiro Watanabe, a man I didn't particularly like. This is what I was thinking. Not about protocol.

Billy Katch's photos of Dwyer's Kwik Stop Liquor and Grocery were thorough, to say the least. The outside, with the blue awning. The front door, magazines just ahead. The aisles. The counter. Palm print on the register, though palms won't usually give us anything, so that's more than likely useless. Lotto machine. The six shell casings on the floor, with bright ID cards next to them.

Before turning over the others, I went to the coffee room. Maybe somebody forgot to turn the coffee pot off. Who was I kidding? I wasn't ready for the shots of Jerry yet. About three ounces of hot, putrid black stuff lay in the bottom of one carafe. I flipped off the power switch, poured the coffee into a plastic cup, and sat there on a table for a moment. I'd forgotten that the beige linoleum floor gleamed so highly from earnest waxing you could see the waves in it, rolly waves, like the contractor put them there for some decorative effect. At my left shoulder, the same cartoon was on the bulletin board as before I went on leave: a man holding an ax behind his back, saying, "I love you to pieces, Ethel." Still wasn't funny.

Joe S. was in the doorway when I looked back. My face burned. He didn't say anything, just looked at me.

"Joe," I said. "I'm sorry. I know I shouldn't have gone in your files."

"You're right, you shouldn't," he said. "What're you doing here anyway? Didn't you just get off medical leave?" Not loud. He was furious.

"I said I was sorry."

"You should be." He had his hands on his hips, throwing the wings of his jacket out. His maroon tie was loosened, and maybe he had more of a shadow under his eyes, but otherwise he looked the same as he did six hours ago.

I got up and went back to Joe's office to get my purse. The pictures put away, the file nowhere in sight. Joe stood in the hall and watched me.

"Good night," I said, heading for the door.

"Miss Brandon," he said to my back.

I stopped. I didn't *want* to look him in the face. Understand, here was a man I'd been in love with for three years. Understand that I'd do things to gain his approval I wouldn't do for other people—work harder, work smarter, work when others would give up. And now there he was in the middle of the perfect, clean, and wavy hallway, lowering his head at me like a school principal.

I cinched the belt on my new leather jacket and said, "Fuck you, Joe."

CHAPTER
5

Raymond Vega, my CHP buddy, was at Dwyer's first thing the next morning, standing in front of his hot-shit Saleen SB/S 350, blowing on his coffee. That black Mustang's slick and mean, narrow eyes. Officially, it's a Law Enforcement Specialty Vehicle, and your captain has to have a lot of stroke to get one. The beefed-up suspension is what Ray brags most about. *Mogambo,* he says, meaning hot sex.

I parked my five-year-old white Toy by the hedge again. The sun shanked off the blue tile roof of the taco stand next door, dew brightening everything. Seven in the morning and I needed sunglasses. Raymond hauled out of the car when he saw me. Highway Patrol wears a tan uniform, and Raymond's dark hair and mustache set it off. His is the skin I'll have when I come back the second time around, and I'll borrow the deep brown eyes instead of these gray. City cops and sheriff's deputies make fun of CHP officers, calling them Triple-A With a Gun. They say their cars should have tow hooks. If anybody is likely to fuck up a crime scene, according to cops, your local handy CHP is. But Ray was not here for the investigation, I knew that.

His smile brought one to me as I was walking up. The man can fill out a shirt so it doesn't need ironing, just a sweet hunk of manhood. When I was recuperating, he'd call me from his field cellular, talk shop, and make me forget whatever hurt. Then end up with some salacious remark to remind me I was a woman. Raymond and I could, I suppose, get serious, but it would be made, not found.

"Look who's duded out," he said, casting his eyes up and

down with approval. The week before, I treated myself to a charcoal leather jacket on a credit card. Under the jacket, a red shirt he could see only the collar of, tight black pants, ye olde black tennies.

"Sheena Easton, here I come. To what do we owe the honor, Raymond?" I looked at his clipboard on the hood of the car. "You'll put a scratch in Sweet Thang there you don't watch out."

"No way." He picked up the board in elaborate slo-mo without sliding it, no etching on *his* rooftop. "And what I'm doing here is looking after my lady."

"Get up there on the freeway and nail some speeders." I nodded back over my shoulder and said, "Look at 'em, eighty miles an hour," because you could see the whole Southern California line of them shooping past until they'd come to a dead stop up ahead about a mile, I knew, and they knew, but that's how you drive it anyway or you're a wimp from Minnesota. "And here you're sipping coffee and flirting with me. Where's the doughnuts?"

I'm not as callous as this sounds. Sixty yards away there's a bloody crime scene and I'm talking doughnuts where a boy just died. You do that, that's all.

He tossed an arc of coffee alongside the curb and made a face. "Oily this morning. You want to go to Denny's?" Asking, but knowing I'd say no. Watching, I guessed, to see how ready I was to go inside. Joe must have called him. And then he said, "Your general told me."

I said, "I guess the saying goes for forensics jocks too."

"What saying is that?" Ray tucked his hands in his jacket pockets; his gaze flicked often to the street, to see what was passing by, which car carried the people who might come back to check what carnage they'd been responsible for yesterday.

"Telephone, telegram, tell a cop. What's all this fragile shit, he thinks I need my hand held?"

A sheriff's car pulled up. In it was Sergeant Gary Svoboda, with Bud Peterson, from the lab, beside him. "I gotta go," I said.

"Don't take it personally," Raymond said. "Joe just looks after his crew."

"Have a nice day, Raymond." It sounded sourer than I

meant it. I turned back and said, "Hey, I got a phone in my car now."

"A phone? My, aren't we fancy."

"Listen, I've got a ton of miles on my car. Who wants to get out on the shoulder of a freeway with a million cars whizzing by and hunt for a box to ring up help? *Even* if the auto-club cop who comes to help has perfect dark eyes and the buffest bod?" He smiled, and then I made him take down the number.

The tape was still up at the front door of the store. The lock was thrown, and no one was around. I saw Joe's blue Chevy parked way at the end on the right side of the building, under a tall eucalyptus.

Svoboda caught up to me. Svoboda can be an ass, but a harmless one.

"Gary, what are you doing here?"

"This is a little strip of county area people don't know about. There's a Costa Mesa patrol officer here. He was first on the scene."

Several cities in the county contract with the sheriff's department for law-enforcement services, but Costa Mesa wasn't one. The scene officer does the call-ins, the preliminary investigation, and the safeguarding of the area, but as soon as the sheriff's guys get there, activity is supervised by them if it's in county area. Bud Peterson, who got out of the car with Gary, was from our lab, the print section called CAL-ID I wasn't thrilled to see him.

Svoboda said, "This should bring the number of two-eleven's right up to around nine hundred for the year, don't you think?" I could hear him panting up the slight incline of the driveway. He's not that fat—he just pants. He said, "But robbery-homicides, maybe, what, twenty-five?"

"You keeping track, Sergeant?" I said. "Is there a pool? I want in, if so."

Bud Peterson was behind us a few yards, not panting.

"No. No pool. Nine hundred so far. And that's your dopers doing our job for us," he went on. "Two tacos blew away two more tacos Saturday come to collect a buzz right out there near Burger King." Svoboda doesn't hear himself. Someday somebody else is going to, though, and there'll be a flurry of public apologies. Some cops who use racist language mean it; Svoboda doesn't.

When Svoboda was talking statistics he was talking Santa Ana only, not Costa Mesa, where we were standing. I reminded him of that. I can be an ass too. If this were school, let's say Svoboda'd be a C, C+ student. Costa Mesa abuts Santa Ana, but it's got a much lower crime rate, maybe one to ten. His eyes were scouting as we walked, like all good cops. C+ doesn't meant not good, exactly.

I asked him if he'd talked to the people at the taco stand yesterday, or at the florist's in the next lot. The two stores nearest Dwyer's had been empty a few months now, the recession taking its toll. One was a tanning salon and the other a fake-nail place. I guess fast food and fake nails don't make the best business bedfellows.

"We got something from El Cochino, matter of fact."

I held the back door open for him, glancing into the storeroom toward the cooler. Joe was there, his evidence kit resting on a fold-up field table. The cooler door was still open, the blotches on it brown now. Ordinarily you come to a crime scene once; you do your job and get out. But we'd all worked together before, knew it would be okay. Gary made me sign in, of course, before we stepped in.

Svoboda said, "You know El Cochino? It means *pig*," proud of himself for that.

"I know, Gary."

You couldn't miss it. There's a happy pig you talk into at the drive-through. Pigs are on the paperware.

"Somebody over El Cochino's saw a pickup. Sort of a light green. Older, maybe fifteen years. Driver had a ponytail, he saw that. Another guy had a baseball cap, red or orange. The manager over there heard several pops—that woulda been the double deuce in the front there—but didn't connect it with anything. Only reason the little Mexican guy saw anything—not the manager, now—he's taking the garbage out. He hears the truck leaving rubber. No shots, though, just the truck peeling out."

"Green pickup and a ponytail," I said.

"But all we got is vaporware here so far." Gary likes talking computerese. He's fifty-five and just found Mac-heaven. "Let's see." He thumbed over the first few sheets on his FI pad—FI for field interrogation—as he was talking to me. "I also questioned two people who came in soon after commission—a housewife wheeling a stroller, who freaked, and an Iranian potato chip salesman. Both of them pretty shook. Did not see a soul. They just walk in, there's blood all over the place. They go hollering next door."

"They touch anything?"

"Would you touch anything, you see blood all over? The door was open, they see blood the first thing."

"That doesn't make any sense."

"Why not?" Then he was settling into his belt, ready to defend himself, taking a modified form of the stance, astraddle something invisible.

I said, "I'm coming into a store with something on my mind, okay? Something I want to buy. Twinkies, whatever. I'm not looking up toward the back of the store. I'm looking at *things*, checking which aisle my Twinkies are in."

"Well, that's the deal. They're a few feet in, they smell something," he said, coming loose again. "Cordite, only they don't know it. The Iranian looks up. The woman, she's looking over the top of the stroller easing in the door." He planed his hand out, eye level, to show me. "She looks up. Straight on. The stains don't register at first. She's pushing the kid down the aisle. All of a sudden the tire skuds on a shell casing. She fingers it out, looks up, starts screaming."

I asked him how much time he was going to give this case. He shrugged. These days, plain old robberies just don't get much attention, burglaries less than that. Crimes of property have to wait: bike thefts, forget it; car thefts, mmm, maybe you'll get a second phone call from an investigator, but not likely. Crimes of person—assaults, rape, murder—get manpower despite the fact that the numbers are increasing in alarming proportion. On murder the case never closes till it's solved; because murder, to civilized minds, is still unacceptable.

Joe walked up, and Svoboda said, "Unless you guys do your magic, we don't have much."

"We'll do what we can, Sergeant," Joe said, and looked at me a millisecond. Probably still mad.

I said, "Can't you do an NCIC pattern check for stop-and-robs?"

"I don't think it's refined down that far," Svoboda said.

"You doing the sergeant's work now, Smokey?" Joe broke down a Styrofoam cup, one piece flipping onto the leg of his pants, and when he leaned over to pluck it off, his eyes leveled out over the store. Checking, where he'd checked before. And then he grinned a little, and that's all that counts.

Bud Peterson came up behind us. Joe said hello. Bud's always nice and polite, respectful. He's thin, with a stoop to his shoulders that makes his chin jut out when he walks. His green tie this morning sported a miniature golfer in backswing. Most lab folks don't wear ties; they wear knit shirts and look like they've been out shopping with their wives in the mall. Joe wears suits, because Joe's been management. Bud aspires, and I wish I could say he'll never make it.

After Joe and Gary went off, Bud said to me, "I'll tell you what you could do. You could go back to the coroner's and pick up the autopsy report."

It was almost a shock, hearing the word *autopsy*. Maybe I thought the procedure wouldn't be over so soon, yet I know how proud the coroner's office is of how they shove them through. They do their work on a contract basis; piecework, you could say. The more bodies, the more pay. I didn't want to think of Jerry Dwyer on the table, because the worst thing is, the dead have no privacy. Pretty woman, ugly woman; shy person, bold; the dignified and the dirtbag, it doesn't matter: Once they wheel nude into the semipublic room, all is seen, all is known, and it isn't done with the finesse you might imagine. I did not want to attend Jerry Dwyer's autopsy, no matter that I saw him a mess on the floor. Most people avoid autopsies on their friends. Most people avoid them, period, unless they must be there.

I thought about what the report would reveal—the type of slugs that would be dug out, the bullet trajectory—and knew it was important to get the report for Bud, but it irritated me. Bud Peterson is like a few people I've met. He seems to be passive, but underneath plays games. I think it bothers him that I'm team leader sometimes, because he's got the seniority and hasn't been yet. What Bud was saying was, Take a hike, will you? Give me a chance to buddy up with old Joe, maybe I can take his place when he retires. How do I know this? Bud'll tell you. He thinks you'll think that because he confided in you, he won't be after your frijoles.

"Will the report be ready so soon?" I said.

"Only takes a couple hours, Watanabe on it. That guy can sling the guts."

Bud plays bridge with Dr. Watanabe, noons, in the morgue conference room while they eat lunch. Nothing wrong with that, I guess. The thing is, Dr. Watanabe's running for mayor this year.

"You're so couth, Bud."

"That's me. Couth youth. By the way, you want to join Toastmasters? A guy dropped out."

"I'm not good at giving speeches."

"That's what it's *for*. People exactly like you."

I said, "Listen, I'll check with Firearms and Trace when I'm at the lab. What about your print run, how long will it take?"

"At least a three-day wait."

"Why does it take so long, Bud?"

"That's *fast*. You know how long Tox has been taking? Six to eight *weeks*."

I looked away from him, fiddling with my hair, which felt too short to me again.

Fingerprint identification is still tricky. There has to be a print on file to check against. Though I volunteered a check with Trace on the fibers found on the door frame, we both knew it would be wasted motion. Fibers is tough duty—too many brands, and the manufacturers don't like to reveal information that might help their competitors; we all live in our small worlds. On cases involving cars, we sometimes have to go take a test drive with a dealer in order to swipe a few carpet fibers.

Bud said, "Put whatever you get on my desk, if you will, okay?"

"Isn't Joe going to want to see it first?" I needed him jumping all over my case again. I could go ask Joe if I should be getting the report for Bud first, but that seemed chickenshit.

Bud said, "Joe's taking tool-mark impressions now off the door, where they forced it open. Then he says he's got a dentist's appointment."

"Good," I said, uncharitably. Bud loosened up then and tried to grin, though it fell off at one side.

I moved away and went up to the cooler where Jerry's body had lain.

The mess, now darkened, reminded me how quickly the molecules of change take over, how the earth urges itself onward, into more change, and then again. By now, not even twenty-four hours later, Jerry Dwyer "was," not "is." Still, the face was there in my memory. The happy, friendly face with child-sized teeth. I could see him smiling at me, in the eyes as well as at the mouth. And I did not want him to be dead.

Off to the left of the cooler, Joe was putting the plastic molding gunk used for impressions back in the kit. The light from the high windows made his hair shine silver.

I asked him about the restrooms, remembering the tape that fluttered down.

"Yes, somebody used it."

"The women's?"

"Yep."

"The new guy?"

"Nope. Billy."

"Billy? He knows better." I said, under my breath, "Much as I don't care for Billy K., he's smarter than that. How do you know?"

"He told me yesterday. After you left."

"Christ."

Joe glanced at me. "Not a problem." Dismissing me. Joe gives everybody the benefit of the doubt, likes to think good thoughts, even if they're not reasonable, about everybody in police or forensics work. I, on the other hand, keep track of jerkhoodness. Born in late August—that makes me a Virgo, highly critical—what can I say?

He said, "What we did find was in the men's."

The little devil—I knew him well enough to know he couldn't wait to tell me. Until eight months ago, Joe had been two notches up the ladder from me. Then he had a heart attack, a bad one. When he came back to work and into Crime

Scene Investigation, he was atwinkle-twinkle, saying no more red tape, no more wall-to-wall meetings, and freedom, man, freedom.

Joe removed a brown bag from his satchel near the table, tugged open the staple, and held the bag open for me to see into. Inside was some kind of tool, shaped like a T. Electrical tape was wrapped around the crossbar to the vertical. He read the question on my face and said, "It was in the restroom, and no, we don't know. The victim's father said he doesn't know where it came from either."

"When did you find this tool?"

"After you left."

"When did you talk to Mr. Dwyer?"

"Last night."

"Joe . . ."

"What?"

"Why didn't you tell me last night instead of getting all over my case? Although I admit I was wrong—I admit that. But you've been grouchy with me even before I went on disability."

He rubbed the side of his thigh and looked away.

I said, "This thing is probably just some repairman's. Why would the creeps come in, go toity, leave an identifying tool for us, and then hit the store?"

He said, "It was on the paper-roll rack, right across the roll. But you know what?"

"What?"

"Criminals are stupid."

CHAPTER
6

"Svoboda says he talked to a worker from next door," I said, walking along with Joe as he was leaving.

"That's right."

"You satisfied?"

"Not really."

"Well?"

"I've got a dentist's appointment."

I stopped. He stopped too, turning to look at me.

I said, "The tooth hurt?"

He grinned at me. "Guess I could reschedule." After putting the evidence kit and satchel in the trunk of his car, he slipped the keys in his pocket and we headed back toward El Cochino. Police investigators do the field interviews, but Gary wouldn't mind us double-checking, I was sure. Like I say, he's not a *total* ass.

We cut between the end of the chain-link fence and the scrubby bushes separating Dwyer's from the taco stand, past the round pink tables to the front. "They serve breakfast," Joe said as he opened the door. A whiff of heavy sweetness took my breath away. He nodded toward the overhead menu straight ahead. "Early, too. Scrambled eggs, sausage-gravy." His eyebrows lifted as he said, "You should try it sometime."

I wondered just how early he'd gotten there, anyway. Or was he here other times, near my house? No. Couldn't be. He lived in the upscale part of Tustin, where lately million-dollar homes were popping up like movie sets. Who owns all those castles? All the rich people in the world must be moving to Orange County. The time I asked who all these people could be, out loud, near Joe, he said with disgust, "Drug dealers and cops on the take." This came on the heels of front-page stories about six L.A. cops busted for buying land and houseboats, using recovered drug money, a skim here, a skim there.

As Joe held the door open for me, his face shut down, so that I knew he'd become official. Behind the counter, a square-faced girl looked our way as she turned to fill an order for a car at the drive-through window. Her rose-colored uniform pulled tight across the back, creating pillows under her arms. A heavy kid, Samoan-looking, with a bad case of purple acne dotting his yellow skin, filled up the window in her place. He leaned forward on the counter as he said, "May I help you?"

"I'd like to talk to your manager, please," Joe said.

Then a worried look ran across the kid's face as he passed the tortilla oven and headed to the back.

A white man in his sixties, dressed in a white shirt and light gray pants, opened the door into the eating area. Joe told him who we were.

"I told you people everything yesterday. I got a business to run here. It won't run itself."

"This won't take long," Joe said. "My name is Joe Sanders, this is Miss Brandon. We are forensics personnel."

"You cops upset the help. They're all the time jabbering after you been here." He lowered his voice then because a woman with two toddlers entered, herding them, as they stumbled forward with fists in their mouths, nearer the order window. "I got one didn't come in today because of this. You know how these people are."

We followed him to one of the tables in a corner. Joe slid into a molded pink bench and, before we'd even settled, had the first word. "Are you working with illegals, Mr. Smith?" We could read his name tag now, the letters barely visible, incised on a white wooden background: WILLIAM SMITH, MANAGER. "Is that why they're upset?"

"I do things *right* here. The boy who saw anything is Emilio. Your deputy already talked to him, right?"

"Sergeant Svoboda, from the sheriff's department, did talk to him. But we may have to ask the same questions more than once, of everybody. You understand that investigations take time, particularly for a homicide, don't you, Mr. Smith? We have to do as thorough a job as possible."

"Sure, sure, a homicide." Red blotches formed on his nearly translucent skin. "I got Emilio washing dishes. But how do I know I'm talking to you he doesn't just hang up his apron?" Mr. Smith shifted to see behind us into the kitchen, where I imagined tortillas were being painted with refried beans and tacos slopped with filling. He shifted in his seat and rested both hands on the table, rolled into one-potato, two-potato fists. "Could be me next time. I mean, I watch myself when I'm taking receipts. I watch myself all the time."

Joe was nodding. He said, "That's a good idea."

"It's just I invest a whole lot of time in these people and I don't want them spooked. A lot of them can't, see, handle more than one thing at a time. You can understand that, sure. They're what you call simple."

I said, "What are you paying them, Mr. Smith, an hour, I mean?" Maybe I shouldn't have interrupted the flow of things. Then again, it seemed to me the man needed to play defense awhile.

"You want a job?" he answered. The voice was low enough but the stare told me it was hostile. His blue eyes were so pale they were almost white, with dark rims at the edge of the iris, hard to look into because they make a guy look crazy. He immediately turned his attention back to Joe. Dusted her off, he'd be thinking. In my career, I've been put down by experts.

"No, thank you, Mr. Smith. I have a job." I took out my notepad and pen, started writing and talking at the same time. "Let's see now, you've got how many employees here? Six? Let's say six, I can see." I twisted around to look over my shoulder. "And they all have their green cards, you say. You have your regular health inspection, too, I suppose. Say, every couple of months?" I started looking around, checking how clean the place was. "How about grease disposal, Mr. Smith? You conform to EPA guidelines for grease?" I kept my head down, writing, waiting for an answer. These issues have nothing to do with us. When I looked up, there was a changed expression.

"Emilio's English is not that great. Talk to him. Go ahead.

But ten minutes, okay?" He wasn't asking me. He was asking Joe.

"Let's get to that later," Joe said. "Right now, am I to understand you yourself saw nothing yesterday around the time of
the robbery and murder?"

"Nothing. I heard—I think I heard—some popping sounds,
real fast together. I was setting some rags out back." He
glanced at me with his spooky eyes, said, "We can do that,"
meaning put the rags outside to dry without an inspector
jumping him.

Joe said, "What time would you say that was?"

"Maybe one-thirty."

"Not a car? You didn't hear a car backfiring?"

"No. Popping—like firecrackers." His hands slid forward on
the table, body English for, I have nothing to hide. He said,
"I didn't know those people over there. I saw the young one
once, twice, maybe. That's all. Big blond kid, right?" He
looked at me then. I nodded, along with Joe.

"Can we talk to Emilio, then?"

"Would you go around, talk to him out back? We don't need
everybody stopping their work now to listen, do we?"

At the rear of the restaurant we stood waiting for the door
to open, looking, I guessed, at the same stiff rags Mr. Smith
draped over blue plastic crates a day earlier. I said to Joe, "I
hope this isn't a waste of time."

"You never know."

The door sucked open and a tiny little person in a black
shirt emerged, Indian facial structure, sunken cheeks, a
slightly horsey mouth, but a softness in his expression nonetheless. He was maybe thirty-five, and his skin bore a yellow-
brown cast, except for his hands, which were as pink as if he'd
been scalded. He stepped out, looking back and forth at us
while rubbing his palms up and down on his thighs as if they
never could get dry. Mr. Smith was behind him in the doorway. I acknowledged him and said, "Thank you," and he shut
the door.

Joe's tone was respectful. Straight off he told Emilio we
weren't police, just from "the office." I don't think Emilio understood *office*, but I think that since Joe wasn't a uniform,
and he had me with him, Emilio relaxed. Joe asked him if he

saw anything yesterday concerning what happened next door.

Emilio looked at me for help. "You understand? You understand what he asked you?"

"*Sí.*"

"You saw a truck?" I said. "You told the officer—"

"*Sí. Verde.*"

"Green."

"*Sí.*"

"Where was it, Emilio?"

He pointed over toward the store. "*Allí.*"

"Where, exactly?" Joe said.

He pointed again.

"Not in front? In one of the parking places?"

"No."

"You saw it leave in a hurry?"

"Bery hurry, *sí.* Yes."

"What were you doing when you saw it?" I asked.

He glanced around to the side of the restaurant as if he could see himself there, and told us he was taking out the trash, the sack, as he said, demonstrating then with two hands clutched higher than his shoulders, and I realized that at about five feet he'd have a struggle all right, not dragging it along the concrete.

"They bery hurry," he said.

"About what time was that? " I asked, tapping my wrist.

"One o'clock. I do one o'clock."

Joe asked if Emilio could tell what kind of truck it was and he said, "Like my father. Chebrolet," heavy on the *ch.* I grinned. I liked him. He smiled back, one tooth at the side missing, nice long crow's feet at his eyes.

"Your father has one? Same kind? About how old? What year?" Joe said.

"Sixty-seben Chebrolet, half-ton." Emilio's face lit up. He seemed very proud. "Half-ton."

"That's what your father has, right?"

"On farm, half-ton. Big focking half-ton." He was nodding happily now, pleased Joe understood, rubbing his palms again on the front of his thighs.

"A half-ton is still a big truck in Mexico, I guess," Joe said for my benefit. "If you get your four-by-four stolen around here, it winds up in Mexico pulling a plow." He asked Emilio, "On the farm, what's your father grow?"

"*El algodón.* Uh, cotton."

I looked at Joe. Cotton in Mexico?

"By Durango our farm," Emilio added. "Cotton." He was smiling as if he were proud, and a light came to his eyes.

I said, "The men, Emilio. You saw these men?"

He reached high over his head to indicate height, said, "Big. Bery big. Hat. Red bazeball cap. One habe"—hooking his hand behind his head in a motion to indicate the pony-tail—"tail," he said. "He dribe."

Joe said, "What color was their hair?"

Emilio didn't know the word for *brown.* We worked with him. He also said one of the men wore a Lebi jacket. Good. He couldn't remember what shirt the other had on. Both of them wore boots. Better. How many people in SoCal wear cowboy boots? I asked if he could tell the men's ages, how old they were. He shook his head but then said, "Nineteen?"

Before we left, Joe asked if he could show us exactly where the truck was parked. He led us to a break in the hedge and we stepped through. I expected him to lead us down to the front, nearer the marked parking places, but he didn't. He walked straight along the hedge a few feet and then stopped. "Back here," he said, squashing one hand downward as if he were bouncing a basketball. "Front here."

"The back was here," Joe said. "Then, you mean the truck was headed out toward the street."

Emilio nodded. "I see twelve-fifteen, too. Truck here twelve-fifteen."

"It was here at twelve-fifteen, and then it came back?" Joe asked.

"No. I see at twelve-fifteen too. It here long time, long time. That's why I say, "Oh! It go out . . ." and he blew a whooshing sound into the air above his scooping hand.

Joe and I looked at each other. I said, "That truck was here a long time, then, forty-five minutes. *Then* it decides to book out of here? Why the hurry if it's been there already forty-five minutes? I don't know, Joe. We probably don't have anything. Vaporware."

Joe asked him what hours Emilio worked. He said someone

else might have to talk to him, and would that be all right? Oh, yes, Emilio said, assuring Joe with a big smile, and then he gave us his home address, which was probably the same address for sixteen other illegals, or false, or would change next week. "And how old are you, Emilio?" I asked, jotting this down.

"Nineteen," he said.

I was back in the Kwik Stop parking lot when Joe left me to go talk to two more of our people who'd just arrived—Billy K. again, and it looked like the rookie too. I thought of Billy K. explaining to Joe why he violated scene integrity by using the restroom. And then something else flashed on me and my stomach began a slow twist. Because I stood there thinking, If Emilio could eye the pickup through the divided hedge, if the front was there and the back was here, then that meant, picturing my car the way it was parked last night, the truck would have been nosed into mine, driver's side to the store. Close enough so that when the truck swung out sharply toward the driveway, a small, brass round thing could theoretically drop out, hit the asphalt, and roll into the grass.

Joe was coming up the incline, the sun bringing out the coral shade of his shirt and the brown of his wool suit.

"Joe," I said. "You're going to hate me."

"What else is new?" he said, a smidgen of a smile in his eyes.

I was suddenly sweaty in my gray leather jacket, thinking how bad-ass I thought I had been last night telling Joe off. Picturing the brass object sitting in my desk drawer instead of Property, the custody of a potential piece of evidence compromised. Jerkhood, never forget it, cuts both ways.

I said, "I think I maybe have something for you."

CHAPTER
7

Ass-chewing is always harder on me than it should be. I do stuff, then get surprised when the consequences turn out different than I expected. Naïve I am not, so what's the problem, except maybe a case of terminal good intentions. Because I *mean* well.

Joe gnawed rather than chewed. Here, he says, here's my lawyer's number. He wrote on the back of his own business card in black ballpoint while I stood there. "Tell him he can take that trip to Cancun." I looked at him, not getting it. "Soon as he sues your surgeon for excising your brain."

Not nice, not nice at all. People told me Joe could get sarcastic—but in three years working with him I hadn't myself seen it. Maybe I wasn't paying attention. Funny how things roll off when it's not your back. Or, I don't know, maybe Billy Katchaturian pissed him off again when Joe went over to the car.

Now I was on my way to the coroner's, and hardly paying attention to my driving. I must have done something wrong, because a guy in shades and a blue baseball cap turned backward flipped me off when he passed me. I was going sixty-two, but he must have thought I was going too slow for the second lane. And before I knew it, I was on Santa Ana and Shelton.

Set into the ivy ground cover next to the sidewalk is a low stone block with unobtrusive letters: SHERIFF-CORONER FORENSIC SCIENCE CENTER, which spells *morgue* if you know how to read it. A few yards away is the building itself, a narrow belt of glazed orange ceramic tile coursing around its middle. Opposite, a four-story fiercely white building glares like a glacier in a tar pit: Building 42, the jail. North of 42, a smaller structure, Building 44, houses the women. I have not been in either one, since I am not a cop in Orange County and I've never had reason to go there. But whenever I come to the morgue, I imagine the prisoners looking down from cell windows, seeing their buddies hauled out of the vans and wheeled in through the automatic doors in the back, and later their buddies' families walking out the front all squeezed together, hands cupped over their mouths.

I crossed the red pavers at the entrance and went in the front door. Janetta, the records clerk, and pretty, was cloaked in her two cardigan sweaters, a white over a pink, and under those a navy blue polka-dotted dress. Janetta caught a glimpse of me and said, "Hi," a big smile looking pretty on her Hispanic features. "It's always cold in here," she said, and hugged herself. I smiled sympathetically, and wished she wouldn't dress that way. A Beatles song was playing on the intercom: "If I give my heart"—thump-thump—"to you-oo-oou . . ."

She walked to one of the antique wooden cabinets that still held the records not yet converted to the automated system, pulled open a drawer, and started flipping through files. In the back of the room a woman I didn't know sat working at a desk, asking Janetta, "Now, what do we do with the Does? File 'em by number also? Or do they go in a separate file?"

Janetta said, "Just a minute, Smokey," and tucked something down in the drawer. She's as nice to women as she is to men, and knows her job. Going for her degree in business administration. That's why I wish she wouldn't dress the way she does. I *want* people to take her seriously. I leaned on the shelf of the customer window. I always felt strange here, at the window, because it's got a foot-wide lip to it, as if anyone might at any moment slide a hot apple pie onto it and invite me to wait for dessert to cool down, there'll be coffee later.

Glancing at the sign-in sheet, I saw a long list of names. I said, "Who are all these?"

"Student tour," she said, smiling. "You know how Jack tells them, 'Don't faint. Anyone faints, we put 'em on a tray'? This girl excuses herself right then. She left out the door looking green, I mean seriously."

I pictured the student, sitting in her car in the parking lot, trying to get up the courage to come back in. They usually do, embarrassment or curiosity bringing them back. Once when I was witnessing an autopsy of a man who seemed to die of nothing, a student tour came through. The coroner's clerk walks the line of students each time, intoning, "Don't stare, don't lock your knees. Don't stare, don't lock your knees," until they get used to the sight of the bodies in whatever stage of the procedure they might be in at the time, some already split open, some with the scalp pushed down over the face so the techs can get at the brain. One student didn't take the advice. He fainted three times, kicking a metal-utensil cart into the middle of the room, on which lay the shears and turkey baster used for gathering urine. At least the techs don't have to worry about sterilizing the instruments here.

I must admit I wonder about the people who work here. Cops, at least, have moments when they know they *have* protected and served, and rarer moments still when victims and bystanders actually express gratitude. But here, these processors of flesh are another breed. Some seem flat-out ghoulish. It's not the jokes that bother me—humor keeps us all sane. It's something weirder I have not figured out yet; something that delights in the repellent. I'll say to Joe that this one or that one is a creep. He says, Hey, the guy has found his niche, don't knock it. Then there are the students, and the doctors from foreign countries who can't find other placement yet; the English majors who couldn't either. As in all workplaces, the good, the bad, the indifferent.

Janetta's high heels croaked over the tile floor, ending with a sound like a little *sput;* I marveled at how well waxed all our floors are, wavy or not, as if to say, Death doesn't happen here, no siree. We chatted awhile. She asked how I was doing. She asked if my operation was painful, screwing up her face; then backed up and showed me a fist-sized bruise she picked up on her shin from an open drawer.

"Dangerous place," I said. "You could probably find dead people here if you looked hard enough."

She laughed a rich sound, rolled her head as if she had a kink in her shoulder, and said, "Geez, it's cold in here, isn't it?"

I requested the Dwyer file, and she went to the back of the room and lifted up folders in a wire basket near the door that leads into the lab. "You know, I think that's still in the back. You want to go in, Smokey? I think it's in Dr. Schafer-White's."

She buzzed me in the door at the side.

"Ask Barney for it, will you?"

"Sure."

"And sign for it, okay, before you take a copy?"

A few of the laser techies were fussing around with the bench laser in the back, trying to get it to work. I didn't say anything to them, didn't want to bother them. I passed through one lab area looking for Barney, feeling a little strange, as though coming into an old grammar-school classroom. Six weeks off the job could be a decade. The smell of formalin, which is formaldehyde gas mixed with water, was strong today. There were two nude bodies on trays in the hallway, having been wheeled in from hose-down outside. I looked in at one of the workrooms and noticed, probably for the first time, that the wooden bar stools at the workbenches were orange. The cabinets orange too, an old color, chosen no doubt when Orange County had real groves. In that early enthusiasm, city fathers decided to paint street signs orange with white letters, virtually ensuring no one would be able to read them after a year of sun-baking, and in the city of Orange they remain to this day. As if for the first time too, I saw the clean yellow Formica countertops, rubbed nearly white in the centers. And I felt out of place, not sure of where I belonged, but maybe not here.

A big healthy girl with blushing cheeks and brown hair to her shoulders came through the back door, a McDonald's lunch sack in her hand. The smell of French fries wafted in with her. She told me through a mouthful that Barney was outside. I walked by the big floor scale—orange, of course—where the corpse and cart are weighed together, the cart's weight subtracted. On the wall in red crayon were the words HEAD HERE, with an arrow pointing down.

As I approached the automatic doors, the yellow reflective sheeting on them squinched my figure into flat waves. Outside, there's a three-sided shower stall for washing off corpses after autopsy—or staff, if they've gotten something especially contaminating on them. Vagrants used to take showers there until management fenced it off at the driveway.

Barney was tipped back on an orange stool by the shower wall, face laid to the sun. His lab coat covered a green knit shirt and rock-washed blue jeans. Rubber beach shoes rested on the concrete apron beside him. "Barney," I said. "You don't hear about the bad things sun does to you?"

He squinted over at me and rocked the stool down. "Hiya, stranger, how ya been?"

"Oh, good, good. Listen, not to disturb, but Janetta said I could sweet-talk you into getting me a file."

"You can get it yourself. Nobody's around. Just sign for it." Ordinarily, the charts go directly up front, but sometimes they land in a pathologist's basket for a while.

"I wouldn't think of pulling you away from the rays," I said, smiling, but wishing he'd seen some of the young patients I had seen when Bill was in the hospital, one guy just twenty-seven with holes in his shoulders and neck where cancers were plugged out, and a continual look of fear in his eyes.

I did what I was supposed to, signed for it, then took it up front to Janetta. On the way up, I glanced in the autopsy room at students lined up more or less against the wall. One held a Kleenex over her mouth and nose. Another leaned her head on a male companion's shoulder. They tucked their hands under their arms or into their pockets, or fingered their own faces. These people would one day be cops: The first time they have to pull a body out of a crushed car or out of a burned bathtub, they'd better be able to take it, but I was glad to be reminded of an almost palpable compassion people feel when they first see the dead so helpless.

Out front, a busload of light-custody inmates were waiting to spend the day picking up trash along the freeways. Some of the prisoners looked at me as I passed, their faces, what I could see of them, noncommittal. But I felt for them, maybe some of them dying to whistle, to inject some fun and normal-ity back in their lives; some of them thinking of families and bosses and how those people would handle it all, thinking of what screw-ups they'd been and how if they ever get out of this they'll never mess with so-and-so or such-and-such again;

some of them saying to themselves, Fuck this noise, I'm doing it right next time, no goofs. Because most of them, like it or not, were there for reasons serious enough that they couldn't escape even the cite-and-release program the sheriff had in place, and most of them, whether the average citizen wants to recognize it or not, had been jerks for a long time.

Another bus waited just beyond the sliding white-iron gate at the Intake/Release Center, the gate topped with rolled razor wire, and the bus no doubt destined for a return trip to outlying housing facilities after the prisoners' day in court. Business as usual.

My car was out away from the buses, deep into the packed parking lot, so I could sit there a moment, the folder in my lap. The sun on the seats felt good on the back of my thighs, the small of my back.

I looked at the label. "JEROME ALPHONSUS DWYER," it said, and the case number beneath. I sat in my car a long time before I opened it.

"We got a party at Bob and Dollie's tonight you want to come," Raymond told me. I'd called Raymond from my car phone, one of the first times I'd used it. I was able to do this because his hot-shit Saleen got installed with cellular. Most coppers just have the radio. He asked me if that's how I spent my disability money, on my new phone.

"Now, don't you be calling me every half hour, Raymond. It costs me money incoming as well as outgoing."

"Then what fun is that?"

"You're good at harassing. You a cop?"

"Listen, come on to the party, I'll buy you a beer."

"I need a party."

"Sure you do." It was good to hear his mellow voice. Voices get me. His is brandy-nice. Why wasn't I in love with him?

This conversation was taking place while I was on the Costa Mesa Freeway, the 55, headed home after an afternoon spent going over and over again the details of the autopsy report. The smaller-caliber bullet caught Jerry in the mouth; rolled apart the tissue like the Red Sea, then lodged in the meaty part at the back. That would account for the torrents of blood.

He'd be choking on it; yes, and slipping—failing in his desperate effort to keep the killers out.

When I returned to my desk after retrieving the report, I tried to work on old paper, go through all the bulletins to read and toss that had piled up while I was gone, all the medplan updates you never know what to do with and end up putting in a binder, unpunched, so they fall out the next time you pick it up.

At lunch I walked down to one of the nice restaurants on Santa Ana Boulevard, trying to get the pictures out of my head. Lawyers sit at cozy tables at this certain restaurant, talking lawyer stuff. I could tune them out. I pretended interest in the abstract paper sculptures framed on the walls in mauve and green, and made a good deal of small talk with the waitress, who'd heard you can still get homestead land in Alaska.

But I couldn't get Jerry out of my head. Walking back to the office I thought of that last time I saw him alive, how he waved and said, "So long. Take care now." And as I thought these things, the silica in the sidewalk swam together through my sunglasses, and I was finally actually glad to be back in the office doing routine things again.

Afternoon went better. Then getting on the freeway at fourteen miles an hour at the end of the workday kind of screwed things up again. The drivers were doing things deliberately just to piss me off, and yes, by God, I needed a party, please.

A man in a white Ford veered from his lane into mine and nearly clipped my right front fender. I didn't even beep. I said to Raymond, "Whoa, some guy just cut me off. Did not see me at all."

"Has he got his Old Fart plates?"

I laughed because yes, he was an old guy in white shirtsleeves, staring straight ahead through thick glasses. Some of the Leisure World types are out of it, but a lot of them are as aggressive as any gang member out there. They push ahead in lines as if they don't see you, stomp on your foot and never bat an eye; I guess they figure they lived this long, they got privileges.

Back on the subject of the party, I asked, "You coming with Yolanda?"

There was silence a moment because though Ray flirts with any woman as if it were his job, Yolanda's his steady, more like a live-in. But they fight. She's Mexican too and jealous of anyone he knows who isn't, and he uses that to tell her why she's not worthy of him. Relationships are way too much work, I think.

"Hey, Ray?"

"What?"

"Can I bring my friend Patricia?"

"Sure. You been telling me about her long enough."

"You won't like her."

"So why?"

"Too tall." Raymond was sensitive about those things. "She's six feet."

"Oh, well, as long as she doesn't *have* six feet."

"No, Raymond."

"Has she got two big, you know, eyes?"

"I haven't counted. Three, I think."

"Oh, shit."

"Calm yourself."

There was silence a minute. "You readin' your *Playboy*? Raymond. Hey."

"No, listen. I'm looking for . . . I forgot to tell you . . . oh, here it is. Robbins and Delco deposited two creeps in lockup about three-thirty. I meant to tell you. Two brothers. They do stop-and-robs. Name of Dugdale. Phillip and—"

"You shittin' me, Raymond?" I could feel the tension leaving my forehead.

"And, let's see . . . how much for the other one?"

"What?"

"One teeny-weeny kiss tonight, huh, under the table?"

"Come on, Raymond. This is costing me money."

"Oh, money is it? Oh-ho-ho. All right, here it is: Phillip G. and Roland G. Dugdale. Both *G*'s. Um, looks like they been in a whole rack o' shit from robberies to . . . assault. Some possession—the Roland guy."

"You've got a copy of their sheet?"

"Right here in front of me. On my MTV." He meant his MDT: mobile data terminal, a computer he can use to tie into the county database. His substation was chosen for the user test base. "The stuff's old," he said. "Looks like six years, the last. I'm surprised it comes up even. Oh—possession, no, it's like eighteen months."

"And they got them for what this time?"

"Bunch of traffic wants, rack o' fines. Gonna cost 'em a fortune, looks like. Your pal Svoboda was all over it, though. I saw him at the ATM half an hour ago. We bank at the same place, that's how I know. He'd been in on another arrest of these boys and does not like them at all."

"They could hold them, then, couldn't they, even on just the citations?"

"They'll be outa there like shit through a chute on just a traffic want. You know that, Smokes."

Yes, I knew. The proliferation of drugs makes for a housing shortage. Burglars, car thieves, and the like breathe fresh air scant hours after they're arrested. In by six, out by midnight, still enough time to steal a car to get home. "Hey, Raymond, where are you anyway you're reading me this? Why aren't you out here in your *mogambo* wheels getting some of these assholes out of my way?"

"Well, where are *you?*"

"Barely past Edinger."

"That's a tricky section there."

"Tell me."

"Listen, you want to come by take a peek at the boys? I'll escort. We can go in one car to the party, you want."

I felt myself sit up and take notice. "By the jail? Sure. Sure."

His tone was gentler now, more serious. "I know you got a thing about this case, right?"

"Right."

"Don't say nothin', don't do nothin'. Just peek."

"I could love you, Raymond. You're great."

"I know," he said. So cute.

The freeway opened up like a fist unfolding. I said good-bye to Raymond, my mind racing. They grabbed two guys who'd done stop-and-robs. So what? What they boxed 'em for was traffic cites. But you never know. Why not take a look? What's to lose?

The traffic stalled again. I was creeping by the Crazy Horse, the big-time country-western club just off the freeway where performers whose names get recognized by people who don't even know country pack 'em in in spite of tickets costing more than a good pair of shoes.

Lifting the handset on the car phone again—hell, I could afford it: How much worse is it than all the dollars blowing out my exhaust pipe to do a keratotomy on the ozone?—I reached Patricia.

"You wanna go to jail and a party tonight?" I said.

There was a short pause, and then: "Sounds like love to me," she said, and giggled.

CHAPTER
8

The Dugdale brothers did make an impression. The tall one's voice sounded like a steel drum dragged over gravel.

This was Roland Gene. He did not have a ponytail. Neither did the other one. I thought, These must be the wrong guys.

Thirty-one and "little brother" to Phillip, Roland reminded me of nothing more than a good-time boy, a man who makes his living in the sun, his fun in the dark. Maybe a carpenter or a cowboy—anything but a robber and a killer. I looked for boots. Emilio said they wore cowboy boots. But Roland Gene had on black running shoes and a gray quilted vest over a light-blue shirt. Didn't look like anyone but a Southern Californian to me.

We were at the sheriff's station, not the jail, and the Dugdale brothers were not in custody, only detained. I learned this after going to the jail with Patricia and talking to the gate deputy, who had not signed any Dugdales in. Raymond had it wrong. And Raymond didn't escort me after all, because at the last minute he called and said he had to take Yolanda somewhere. He said, "Call Svoboda, he'll get you in." So I did. Gary's shift, I knew, was over, so it surprised me when he told me he was on his way down to the station. He could be off cashing in on double-dinner coupons, feeding on spaghetti with his wife, who enjoyed food as much as he did. Raymond said Svoboda was all over this, and I guess he meant it.

On the way over, in Patricia's car, she said, "Wow, people are going to ask what did you do on the weekend, and I'm going to tell them I went to Club Jail. Neat, huh?"

She was dressed in party clothes: black bolero jacket over a

58

hot-pink dress, high heels and black stockings—and on those antelope legs, the combination would make men run into walls. I worried a bit about her, that I shouldn't have brought her here. Then thought better of it. What could it hurt, and it might just let her understand some things.

The watch commander let us go down to the observation room after okaying it with Svoboda, who'd answered the phone down there. While the deputy was making the call, Patricia hung back, flattened against the wall where both cadets and deputies manned the counter and telephone bank, and that was good, I suppose; but she could hardly be invisible.

Gary was waiting for us, to usher us into the room with the two-way mirror.

"Hello, ladies," he said, back to the door, twisting the door handle with his left hand. "The movie has started."

Patricia slid into the room ahead of us. We took seats in the folding chairs in front of the window. Patricia hugged herself under her bolero.

"Don't be nervous."

She made a face. "How can I not?" and gave a little laugh.

The interview room was plain, a table, some chairs. Two detectives in street clothes. Normally, suspects and witnesses are interviewed separately, so they won't automatically match stories, but the brothers were pulled in only on traffic wants. It was sort of an exploratory, and I was sure the brothers knew it if they'd been around at all, and apparently they had.

Svoboda leaned in from a chair behind us. He said, "The guy at the table—he look like a guilty little shitter to you?"

I whispered, "After a while they all look like guilty little shitters."

"Lovely business we're in, ain't it?" He looked at Patricia, but her gaze was glued to the window.

I wanted to hope these were the perps, but so far things just didn't fit. Emilio had said a ponytail; there was no pony-tail. He said the suspects were both big; the Roland guy was, but the seated one, his brother Phillip, was five-eight, by the sheet. I wondered what they'd been driving when they were picked up. And what about a red baseball cap—had they found one? As far as weapons, I knew it'd be too much to hope for, and if they'd had weapons, their asses would be in a holding tank right now.

The big one's voice: "When you boys gonna let us pay up whatever we owe, get something to eat? We told you, we been working, we got the money. We been clean. Regular square-bones citizens now. Ain't we, Phillip?" Roland stood against the wall facing us, one leg kicked back, arching his back every once in a while as if he'd just got off a long haul. At the end of the table, on the left, Phillip slowly nodded in agreement. Down two chairs on Phillip's side was a detective in a pink shirt, and across from Phillip another detective with a puffed rim of dark hair beneath a mound of smooth pate.

Patricia whispered, her eye on Roland, "How come they let him walk around like that? Aren't they afraid he'll do something?"

"Like jump somebody?" I shook my head no. They do, sometimes, but this pair didn't seem likely, not with this little informal get-together.

Phillip George was slender, but with a squarish, puffy face, as if he were on cortisone or something. He was thirty-seven, had darker hair than his brother Roland, almost black and slicked straight back, like Michael Douglas in *Wall Street*. Emilio had said the men in the truck had brown hair. Did Phillip's hair qualify as brown? Roland's you could call brown, but there were light edges. Phillip wore a plain white shirt and black pants. I couldn't see his feet to check for boots. When he talked, it was softer—and scarier. What sent a chill through me I don't know, even now. It was just a thing that, even through a crackly mike and behind a trick window, told me these two were bad company.

Roland said, "So what about it? You checked us out, where I been workin'. I give you my goddamn travelogue where I been the last six months. I even mail the postcard to my probation officer, right on time, every month. Ask her. I'm a good boy now." He smiled a slow, crawling smile. He dragged on a cigarette, tilting his head up, and I thought just then he looked like the actor who used to play in *The Rifleman*, high cheekbones, boxy jaw. The voice kept coming, like a dog beginning to growl. "I'll tell you who I been ballin', that what you want—she don't cost much," Roland smiling now.

"Clean it up, Dugdale. Tell me this: You're on probation, you're such a good guy, why don't you pay your traffic fines?" the detective said. "That could irritate the system just a little bit, don't you think? We could push you on that one quite a bit, bud."

"When's the last time you slammed, Roland?" The detective in the pink shirt was talking now. "Hm? Or are you just snortin' these days?" The detective in the pink shirt stood up and came toward the mirrored window, looking at himself, or seeing if today you could peer through, see who was there or wasn't.

Patricia reflexively pulled her shoulders in and nudged her chair backward.

The man in pink was nice-looking, eyes at a slant the way they make some people look kind. He turned to face the brothers, waiting for an answer.

Roland gave a swing of his head, pushed off from the wall, and said, "Man, you assholes gonna keep us up all night, aren't ya? I got commitments, man. I gotta be places." Stepping over to where his brother sat, he pulled a chair away and slid it near the wall and sat down, swinging his head some more, propping his right arm on his knee. Then he squinted at the pink detective as if he just thought up a truth: "You all need to get a life," he said.

The bald detective at the table pushed a coffee cup slowly away from him with the back of his wrist, leaned forward across from Phillip, and clasped his hands together. He said, "You got commitments too?"

Phillip stared back. His shirtsleeves were rolled three turns up. Beneath the right one I saw blue-green scallops peeking out.

I said, "Peacock."

Patricia's head turned to me, her eyes asking if I'd slipped a gear.

Svoboda nodded.

I said to her, "Peacocks. They get peacock tattoos so the eyes of the feathers hide the needle marks. Dragon eyes or spotted snakes are good too."

The bald detective kept at him. "Did you win the Lotto, Phillip? Where you get your money? Your brother here's been working. Where you get your money? Nice shirt. Nice ring. Buy that on credit?" He waited for the man with the slicked-back hair to answer. The man in the slicked-back hair held his gaze.

Roland was rocking now, front chair legs grazing the floor. "Lady pays him for his pretty face." He grinned. He was the only one.

Phillip, seated sideways facing the bald detective as if he and the detective were going to table-volley a wadded-up piece of paper to pass the time, slid his thumbnail over the lip of the table and stared as if he'd as soon put the guy's head down a toilet.

"Who says he got money?" Roland threw in. "Hell, he's into me five hunnerd and I know I'm gonna have to kick his Okie ass to get that."

The bald detective ignored Roland, just held the gaze on Phillip. I was looking at Roland's neck, where the light-tipped hair brushed across the high collar of his vest. Long enough for a ponytail? I didn't think so.

The detective asked Phillip, "What kind of primer you use under enamel?"

Phillip looked up at the ceiling and wiped his whole face with both hands. I wondered how many times he'd been asked the question before we got there.

"You know," the bald detective said, "I could use some painting done. My kid's room. Wife tells me she can't find a painter to do the room, the one room, nothing else. Must be a million women can't find a painter to do one room, huh?"

Phillip said something I couldn't make out. With Svoboda's heavy breathing, I almost didn't hear the rest. Then: "I said I found work. I did two jobs."

Svoboda practically in my ear now. "Guilty as hell," he said. "If he thinks he's stare-crazy now"—meaning *stir-crazy*—"wait till I get through with him." He glanced at Patricia, but Patricia's gaze never trailed off the tall handsome dude behind the glass.

I whispered, "What's the story on him? You busted these guys before?"

"He's a hype, a two-piece-a-day hype. He's been doing crime since fifth grade. I gave him a bunk in Theo Lacey for a year. I bombed him on *two* robberies, one he yanks an old lady's wig off and pulls her around the store by the hair at the bottom of her neck, right here." He pointed to the top of his collar. "Then he gives her the shoe. She falls, breaks her hip, two months later she dies, but the DA don't want to bring up murder charges, the asshole's doing time already for some other shit thing and the two-eleven not even calendared yet." His mouth twitched in disgust and then he settled his arms on his knees.

Patricia looked over at me now. She'd glanced back before too, listening to this, listening to what was going on in front of us, as if learning something new about me, and I wondered how to tell her it's okay, I'm still me. Bad things go on, good people clean it up, and most of us even lead normal lives.

While Svoboda was talking, other things we didn't catch were said in the room, and then the bald detective said, "You don't know the names of the contractors, and you don't know where your jobs were. Now, how do you expect us to treat you nice when you *bullshit* us, Phillip?"

Phillip was quiet for a time, then he said, "I don't remember."

"Where'd you get those jobs?"

"Off a bulletin board."

"Off a bulletin board. Right. Where's the bulletin board?"

"I don't remember."

Roland Gene slapped his legs and said, "Jesus, I'm starvin', I got a headache. You guys don't ever eat? I want a goddamn lawyer. I want to see the goddamn *judge*, you keep us here any longer. My brother's back hurts him—he told you—his *back*. Phil's sitting there being a hero, pain crawlin' up his spine, what do you care? Let us the fuck out of here or book us, for Christ's sake. Be a sport. Sport." He dropped the chair down with a thunk and locked eyes with baldie, and baldie's weight rested on his forearms as one hand went over the other and a game smile grew on his face.

Phillip said, "I been having a drinking problem."

The bald detective nodded, thoughtful, repeating back what Phillip told him, then saying, "You're pissin' on my leg, Phillip."

Roland again, saying, "Aw, shit. The man's having a rough

time. I told you, we were *not* in Costa Mesa yesterday. We were in L.A., man, seeing about our mom. Traffic's a bitch and we don't even find her. Then you guys come along and make our lives miserable just for the hell of it. What's with you all, anyway? Don't you have enough to do?"

"You don't own any kind of firearm, now, do you, Roland?" the pink guy said.

"Moth-er-fuck." Roland dropped his arms down between his legs. "Why don't you boys send out for a pizza? Jesus. I got a blood-sugar problem here."

I saw the man in the pink shirt, still standing, nod to the bald detective; then he walked around to the end of the table, playing with something in his pocket. He stopped, like he was thinking, then said, "Well, pizza sounds good. You haven't been as cooperative with us as maybe you could be. But I guess we can call it a night."

Roland laughed out loud. You'd think he'd just won at poker. He stood up and made a motion as if to pull a comb from his back pocket, then remembered and dropped his hands and moved toward the mirror. He stopped at the corner of the mirror near where I was sitting, and stared straight in. He had eyes the color of ocean in winter—deep, cold green. Then he ran all ten fingers through his hair. He said, squinting his eyes, "Who you got back there, Ralph? Anybody we know?"

If Patricia hadn't had to go to the bathroom, or if we hadn't gotten hung up by a bag lady who was sitting in the front lobby of the station all alone, asking for a quarter and looking as though she were used to sleeping there, cops coming and going nonetheless, we wouldn't have been at the car when the Dugdale brothers came out.

Patricia gave the bag lady a dollar. Standing there, her toes turned in, she dug in her purse for the woman. I watched her and thought, Patricia, you innocent. And then: I remember when I would have stood there and done the same thing.

At her car, Patricia had a hard time finding her keys, and when the lock on my side clicked open, I looked up to see Roland not twenty feet away on the sidewalk, with his thumbs in his jeans and a cigarette angled up out of his mouth, smiling at us; and Phillip turned sideways but ahead of Roland and still in motion, looking back to size us up also.

A shot of fear went through me. I got in the car and said, "Don't turn your lights on right away, okay?"

"Huh? Why not?"

"I don't want your license plate to light up."

"Huh? Why?"

"Just somebody I saw over there made me nervous."

"Who? I don't see anybody." She'd turned around to look. The parking lot was not that crowded, maybe thirty cars in it was all, no movement anywhere. I'd already seen in the side mirror that the brothers had crossed the street, were in shadow now. From their angle on the sidewalk, I didn't think they'd seen her license plate. Even if they had, it would be unlikely they'd get a fix on it. They wouldn't have DMV access. But you never know. Being single makes you cautious. Being in my work makes me nervous.

I said, "Oh, it's okay. Go ahead. I guess there's no problem now."

She started the car and eased out. "Jeez, Samantha. You trying to scare me or what?"

CHAPTER
9

Driving away from the jail, I thought about the slow way things change us. I thought about the bag lady and tried to imagine ways she might have changed from, say, a thirteen-year-old full of gossip, hope, and promise to a thirty-year-old, close to my age, who'd been around the block but was still looking forward to things, to a fifty-year-old with maybe a dead kid or a bad one run off with her money, no husband for any one of a number of reasons. I thought about my apartment by the bay, how pretty it is, decorated in green and wine, and wondered how it was I'd be here in this car, at this moment, with this friend, and why. I thought about Jerry Dwyer. Wondered how his father was getting on; if he'd ever be able to watch TV or sell magazines without his eyes going red and swimmy.

Patricia was quiet, but she didn't seem upset. At a stoplight, a car pulled up next to us on my side. It was a beast from before the oil crunch, dull yellow, with a crumpled front fender and the word *Elite* in metal letters on the side. The boy driving it wore a black weight lifter's glove on one hand. His window was down, and I could hear the heavy thump of rock music. I cracked my window a bit, to see what he was playing. He looked over. He gave us a look that said, Yo babe, and maybe he turned the music up louder. Patricia punched on her radio. The same station, the same song. She looked at me, not him, and smiled. "Why not?" she said, and then the light turned and we plunged off, the boy trying to match speeds, surging ahead, then falling behind, until another car came between him and his effort. He hugged the bumper of the car in front of him as he moved up, the back of his arm grown taut and muscled, and as we surged ahead I saw him smack the steering wheel with his gloved hand.

The lyrics on Patricia's radio hit me the wrong way I guess. At first I thought I didn't hear it right: something about waking up dead with blood on the guy's hands, but then it came again, and I asked her if I could change the station.

Ray was with us. We were admiring Bob and Dollie Anderson's hanging fuchsias near the edge of the patio, looking past the people we didn't know for someone we did. The tequila tasted good, but we'd said all we could about fuchsias.

Ray kept glancing at Patricia, who was on the other side of me. She made him self-conscious, I could tell. He turned to me and said, "They should run that Bronco for stolen first off. They should have K-nined it for drugs too."

"They let them go, Raymond. They weren't the ones. They checked the ownership or those two would be in jail."

"You can find drugs in your popcorn bag, in your shirt it comes back from the cleaners, you hear what I'm sayin'?"

"That wouldn't help any in this case." I couldn't figure why he was making a thing of this.

"Alls I'm saying is a little dust could shag off onto the upholstery from mysterious sources. Make 'em cool their heels overnight."

"Ray," I said. Okay. He was trying to impress Patricia. "They don't put people in jail for traffic cites, and you're not going to leave Patricia here thinking that police plant phony evidence."

"Oh, I have no doubt of that," Patricia said, and I looked at her with curiosity. She's not given to cynicism.

The patio was crowded. Raymond craned his neck around to me—talking to Patricia but looking at me. "Hey, listen, I saw a baby in a tree once. Parents spilled all over the place, deader'n hell. The baby's in the tree, not a peep out of it, wavin' its little arms. We almost didn't know it was there. It would have fallen right onto the street eventually. Guess what else we found? Coke in the diapers, I'm not foolin'."

I said I was going to get another drink.

"I'll go with," Patricia said.

A nearly panicked expression crossed Ray's face. "No, no—the *guy's* supposed to go get the *girls'es* drink." He said "girls-es." He was acting drunk, but he couldn't be yet. He squeezed in front of Patricia and smiled at us both, taking our glasses from us. "Whoopsie," he said, bumping into a tall man in a brown suit, then scooting off, a big silly grin on his face.

Patricia looked at me and said, "Whoopsie?"

"He's trying to impress you."

She smiled. "I wish he'd try some other way. Those stories"—giggle—"were making me sick."

"You'll hear lots of talk like that if you hang around coppers. Better go for a stockbroker."

She turned to me and said, "I don't know how you stand it, what you do."

"It's like any other job. Most people don't wind up in the job they think they will."

"What did you think you'd be?"

"In high school I was going to be an artist. Act precious and wear funky clothes."

"Oh, you did not. I mean, not you." She was watching the dancers now, twisting her body in small movements as if she'd do anything to be asked.

"I did too," I said, but I'm not sure she heard me.

Raymond was coming back. "I like him," she said under her breath, "even if he is a little strutter."

"He likes you too."

"I sure never thought I'd like a cop."

"Coppers."

"What?"

"Sort of an affectionate word cops use on themselves. And, by the way, neither did I." She raised her eyebrows at me and laughed, kept the smile there as Raymond threaded his way through to hand us the margaritas.

"Talking about me again? I know you were."

"Talking about cops," I said. "A special breed."

"That we are. Primo." He took a long sip of my drink before handing it to me. "Yum."

I said, "And auto-club boys are something else again."

"Be nice," he said, and drank from his own drink now.

"You driving tonight, Ray?" I said.

"I'd rather be drunk than driving."

"Pinch his little cheek for me, will you, Patricia?"

Instead, she leaned over and gave him a peck on the cheek. I was glad she was there with us. My drink hit, and I was happy my two good friends were with me. I looked at handsome Raymond and I thought, It would be good to work with cops again, shoulder-to-shoulder. Sometimes, in forensics work, as Gary Svoboda would put it, you get to be just a cog in the machine.

One time I asked Joe L. Sanders for job advice. I told him Raymond was saying I should wear a badge again. He said, Nobody can tell you what's best for you but you, but we wouldn't want to lose you, and that was a warm-fuzzy that kept me happy quite a while. Orange County has its share of women cops. They don't need me. Granted, they're not universally loved, but where are we ever?

The fact is, the reason I'm not a cop now is that I got shot once in Berkeley. It was my own damn fault for not paying attention. This woman pulled a miniwheelie on me—a minirevolver, tiny little shit of a thing; you can't control it. We were busting the house for meth. I saw her in a bedroom. She started to come out. I told her to get down on the floor, put her hands behind her neck. She looked kind of heavy but young, and I thought she was just the wife of the primary. I was more concerned about him and his buddy in the front room, two buzzed-out, meaty guys with stomachs that showed under their T-shirts. I turned my head to say something to my partner, *phoot!* She shot that thing at me. Whizzed right by my waist. Then another one caught me in the shoulder, burrowed along to my fifth vertebra. She jumped the hell out the window. I chased her, but I knew something bad was wrong. My back went numb, I sat down on the sidewalk, and I thought I wasn't going to slow-dance anymore.

My partner ran by me and plunked that lady's tushie down in the street with a .38 in the thigh, then performed some other unfun things upon her person.

Later I learned the woman's gun was a Freedom Arms boot gun, one of the smallest ever made, firing .22 longs. Add that much hypervelocity—about nine hundred feet per second—in a teeny-weeny gun with a grip like a bird's head, it somer-saulted right out of her hand or she probably would have popped me again.

For a while after that, back on the job, I John-Wayned it, a behavior a lot of cops experience after they've had some rough duty. Unkind to the suspects, you could say, and my partner didn't mind at all. The senior officer called me on it, though. My husband, Bill, said that I'd get over it, that I should just ignore the reprimand and do what I had to do. He was right. Time took care of the John-Wayneism. But it bothers me to think I was so stupid. I could have gotten a copper killed. Someone like Raymond, someone like Gary Svoboda, a good, honest man.

Six months after the shooting incident, Bill died, and the heart went out of me for toughness. That kind of toughness, anyway. I don't want to be pushing and shoving anybody. I don't want to use violence. Somebody has to sometime. But not me.

And so when I saw Raymond needling his way through the crowd, raising the drinks up over his head, I thought, Good for you, Raymond, that you did that kind thing, getting us those drinks like a waiter. Good for you being here, and good for you trying to include me in police work, letting us in on the news of the Dugghh-dales. Feeling gushy, as I always do when I drink. Wanting more to drink, Raymond not stealing any, so I could continue feeling warm and lovey instead of sad and lonely. Then Raymond said, "Guess who's here?"

"Not Joe Sanders."

"Your bud, Billy Katchaturian."

"Oh, Billy's not so bad," I said. "I'm a touch critical at times. He does his job."

"You must be drunk," Raymond said. "Trudy's talking to him. She said come say hi, she's got something to tell you."

"About the Dwyer case?"

"I don't know. Just something."

It was a wonder he knew what he was answering at all, head cocked so he could look Patricia in her pretty, dimpled face. I left Patricia in his good hands and forged my way through to the kitchen, where I could see Dollie Anderson holding a plateful of deviled eggs at a precarious angle, talking to someone in earnest. Throughout the evening, I'd see Bob or Dollie and I'd remember that they were first friends of Joe S. until a falling out. And I was selfishly sorry, because I missed Joe. I wanted him so to be there. Sometimes it seems like you can wish somebody at a place hard enough, it will really happen. But not tonight. Joe wasn't coming tonight. Not to Bob's. Bob used to work at the lab. We all used to party at his house, with its long pool, hot tub, huge patio. Now he's a private investigator, doing very well despite dozens of PIs in Orange County. Dollie works at the Orange County Law Library—a wonderful place, she says, because it's funded by everyone, via court filing fees, and therefore more directly belongs to everyone. She could stump for it. Joe would say at least he missed *her*. He never told me what the problem was, but I heard from others that he suspected Bob of doing a favor for someone at a high level in the DA's office by altering evidence on a blood-alcohol test involving a fatality. A terrible breach. I wish it were impossible to be true, but I know it is not. All human beings, as Joe will tell you himself, are flawed, and some are more flawed than others. But this night I didn't know the story to be true, and I gave the Andersons the benefit of the doubt, something which Joe did with most people. He was a hard guy to understand sometimes.

I looked in the dining room. Trudy wasn't there. I pushed on into the family room. There was Billy, sipping wine and staring at a painting of blue whales on the wall.

"Hello, Billy. I hear Trude's here. Seen her?"

"I'm all you'll ever need, doll." He stood as close as he could get without me giving ground. I couldn't help but laugh.

I had to tip my head up to say it, but I did: "Billy, grow the fuck up."

"Ow."

"Well, really," I said, but I smiled.

I started away when he called me back. He said, "Trudy says Joe told her something. You want to know what?"

"I'll ask Trudy, thanks."

He sauntered over. I moved off.

I couldn't find her. I went back to where Patricia and Ray were, on the way putting down my margarita glass and pick-

ing up somebody else's half-finished wine abandoned on a side
table. My nose didn't tingle yet.

Music started playing out on the patio. I recognized the
song, a Don Henley, remembered that I liked his sexy voice.
Raymond was swinging his shoulders. I knew he was about to
ask Patricia to dance. He asked me instead. Maybe shy. Him.
"Not yet, Raymond," I said.

"Aren't you a little bit drunk yet, Smokey, my pal?"

Patricia looked at me and said, "Smokey? Where'd that
come from?"

Raymond loved this. "You mean you don't know about her?
Well, let me tell you . . . no, Smokey, you tell her. You're holding out on your friend."

"What—tell me," Patricia said.

"Oh, it's nothing. Raymond's got a weird sense of humor."
Then to Raymond I said, "Dance with her. Keep you out of
trouble."

A smile crossed his face. As they moved out onto the floor,
Ray in his red knit shirt that stretched nicely over his pecs,
the pants that fit tight over perfect buns, I thought, I really
am a lucky woman, to have friends like this, and realized I
was out of liquor.

Getting drunk's a fun thing to do. You're not supposed to say
that, not supposed to like it. I wish I didn't; I'd keep my nose
cleaner. But at Bob and Dollie's party, they had good booze
and a new CD player, and I was long overdue. After all, Raymond said I needed a party. Thing was, it took only those two
and a half drinks to souse me up good, and I wound up back
in the dark end of the patio, dancing with Billy K.

Strange how much better some people look when you're
drunk. He smelled nice and felt good. In the fast numbers he
found chances to hold me too tight and I should have known
better. On the first slow song—an old Carly Simon, her sweet,
plaintive voice singing about the boys in the trees—he pulled
me into him, and I was amazed and somehow relieved at how
good it felt, body-to-body. Held me so he read me, both of us
anticipating the next movement almost like a challenge, who
could move least and yet know. I shut my eyes and just en-

joyed the sensation of a warm and living body next to mine, he anticipating me, me anticipating him, the music disengaging us from the world. Maybe I was wrong about Billy. Give him the benefit of the doubt.

Another fast dance, and now I was smiling at Billy. Having a good time, not trying to second-guess. I saw Patricia and Raymond dancing too, Patricia looking a little awkward dancing with someone so much shorter, but happy. When I caught her eye, she made Raymond ease over.

She leaned out toward me and said, "Hi, Smokey-y-y," drawing out the name. "You were holding out on me, you stinker."

"Oh, please," I said.

Billy was taking this all in, grinning at me too. The smile he smiled then was not one I liked. But it was a party, and these were my friends and colleagues, and what the hell, who needs secrets?

I laughed and said, "Goddamn it, Raymond, you told!"

Billy pulled me close and I felt how hot his body was. He put his damp face to mine, and left his cheek there. He said, "I'd like to see how you got your name sometime."

"Hmph, forget it."

"You could show me," he said. He eased me into him, groin-to-groin like magnets, and though I pulled away I felt lightheaded. His leg was where it shouldn't be, and my arm of its own accord crept higher around his neck. I was drunk, I was tired, I wanted to be with Joe. Weak, and, yes, lonely. And I went home—goddamn me—with Billy The Fuck Katchaturian.

I was still lit when Ray and Patricia drove by Billy's at two A.M. and Raymond came up to the door and rang the bell, asking if I was all right. Billy and I hadn't even made it to the bedroom. We'd done it on the living-room floor with two giant pillows for help and his white, big-eyed cat watching from the end table. I had most of my clothes on when we fell asleep.

When Ray came to get me, I said, "Bless you, Raymond," and when I held up my hand for him to pull me up, I said, "Bless you, and as my grandma said, who was from Missouri, good on your ol' head." Then, "I'm drunk, Raymond," and I began to cry.

"I know you are, Smokey."

Then I saw Patricia. She looked like a Barbie doll. I felt very sad. I said, "Hi, Patricia. Can we go home?"

Billy tried to argue with Ray, then gave up and was saying something to me, the words like oatmeal on the airwaves. I kept telling Patricia she was *so* pretty, and how glad I was she became my friend. It was the first time I saw a worried look on her face. The first time she didn't end a sentence with a giggle.

She said, "We're taking you home, Samantha," and glared at Billy K.

CHAPTER
10

So much for Fridays. The whole weekend was mine to worry about how I was going to deal with things post—Billy Katchaturian: rumor control, Billy himself, and the coursing fear of contamination. Casual anything doesn't mean what it used to. In any case, it was an utterly stupid thing to do.

I thought about going back to bed and awaking with a new nightmare. Instead, I got in the shower and stayed long past the limit imposed by my raised awareness about water shortages. The steam made my brain feel like a pea in weak Jell-O. I turned off the water and forced my legs to work. Center tilted off for me though; the edge of a hangover dizzied me whenever I made a move, and I wondered if I'd better stay near the utilitarian ceramic. I toweled myself off and sat down on the bed for a moment. Maybe I'd just go into the office. Trudy might've left a message on my desk. What could she have wanted to tell me? If Firearms or Fibers or Prints came up with something, they'd report it to Joe first, who'd report it to Svoboda, which would mean I could call him, but I didn't think results would be in yet. Unless it's an officer-involved shooting, God forbid, the cases get in line. It can take weeks to get anything back.

I downed aspirin and microwaved coffee while I fumbled through the last two days' mail. There was the hospital bill in a piss-yellow envelope. I couldn't deal with that. There was a magazine renewal, two freebie newspapers, junk, junk, junk, and my brother's peculiar loops on a cheap envelope whose glue didn't stick. I didn't want to read his letter, but I opened it to the first fold. My brother is a nag: I don't keep in contact

75

with our parents enough. They worry. A phone call once a
month wouldn't hurt. But he's eleven years older and had a
different relationship with them than I did. We could easily
have had different parents altogether, and one day Nathan
could have just come up to my restaurant table and said, Hi,
I'm Nathan Montiel and I think for the hell of it I'll be your
brother.

For a living he does some invisible thing with play money
in Cherry Hill, New Jersey. He supports more ex-wives than
I can keep track of, along with this year's future ex, who reminds me of an unfunny Lily Tomlin. Her charm is that she
brings to the union an inherited and lucrative construction
business. You'd think with all his money he wouldn't hand-
write me letters, but I guess he assumes I'll be more likely to
read them if they are in his own inimitable hand. "Sammi,"
this one started out—no Dear—"I'll be in California December
23. We can get together." No "Would you *like* to get together?"
or "Do you have *time* to get together, and, by the way, how are
you doing?" I turned it over, telling myself I'd read it later.

I didn't really want to go into the office, but I couldn't settle
down. Get a grip, I told myself, and just then my head decided it definitely needed to be on a pillow. The pale green
one on the couch looked good. Lying there, I decided I'd
think about something else for a moment, no bad stuff. That
lasted about two seconds.

I got back up and opened the drapes and slid the glass door
open too. As I looked across the bay, I tried to remember
there's another whole world out there, one not independent
of human conflicts certainly, but at least placidly unaware,
though there are frauds and thieves among the birdlife
too—the starlings, or the brown-headed cowbird that lays its
eggs in the nests of others and forces surrogate parenting.

The sun was casting an all-over yellow light that took the
edge off objects. Already the temperature was eighty on the
small thermometer tacked to the window frame. I reached behind an easy chair for my field glasses, which rested on the
floor, then stepped out on the balcony, my big red towel still
wrapped around me.

I sat on the painted stool I keep out there, and looked over
the bay. Some days seven-foot tides cut in from the Pacific,

and in a few hours they can drop to almost nothing, exposing hundreds of acres of mud and marsh. Through the lenses, I watched the shore birds probing the glaze with their scythe-shaped bills.

Every few minutes, a gashawk noses across the blue—that's environmentalist talk for *airplane*. Because of noise-abatement requirements, pilots must lift off from the airport "high-nose," cut the engines to the minimum to stay aloft, and then make a complicated turn to cross over Back Bay so they won't wake the sleeping rich in Newport or disturb the honkers. It's a di-saster waiting to happen; but, for me at least, the eerie floating planes in that vacuum are just as pretty as birds, in a way.

I've come to know more about birds and ducks than I ever thought I would, living by the bay. Waterfowl are drawn from their flyways by the freshwater runoff from Santiago Peak and Modjeska, which form the nearly six-thousand-foot Sad-dleback Mountains. Within the mix of fresh and saltwater, sea creatures gather. Grebes and gulls. Surf scoters—also called "skunk heads" because of their black-and-white coloring; they feed off shellfish and grunt while they do it. Pintail ducks, their hind ends struck upright out of the water for as long as thirty seconds while shopping in the dregs. I've seen can-vasbacks, shovelheads, mallards, ruddies, teals, widgeons, and buffleheads all in the same inlet, and a black-and-white duck with a red eyepatch I haven't identified yet. I can tell a snowy egret from a cattle by its yellow slippers, and an adolescent gull from a grown one, I think. Well, maybe not. And there are godwits and willets and the beautiful white avocet with black-tipped wings and an upward-curving bill; and under-neath the water there are dozens of mollusks and creepy-crawlies in this wondrous living laboratory.

In the late afternoons, there's a pink-and-golden sheen on the stands of willow and mule-fat and across the bright-orange stringy parasite called dodder that laces itself in patches upon the pickleweed along the water's edge, a tiny succulent that stores the salt in its picklelike sections, then sheds them to get rid of it. There's sea fig and saltbush and tree tobacco, and, on the cliff sides, yellow bush sunflower all year round. Often, out on the gleaming mud, or in a patch of saltgrass, I'll see the great blue heron, motionless as a piece of driftwood, waiting,

waiting, for the slightest movement underfoot that would furnish a meal. Looking out from my balcony restoreth my soul.

I must have been out there a good fifteen minutes, and then, for whatever reason, the visage of Jerry Dwyer dead on the Kwik Stop back-room floor came back to me. I thought that maybe I should put on my sweats and go jog around Back Bay, or go down to Balboa Island, a couple of miles straight down Jamboree to the Pacific, and have a croissant and egg.

Maybe I'd ask Trudy Kunitz to come with me. I went rummaging in the piles of paper and envelopes along the kitchen counter under the wall phone, and found the booklet with the crime-lab personnel phone numbers. I'd never called Trudy at home before. We were friendly on the job, but not friends as such. She has a hard time looking me in the eye. I don't know if it's because she doesn't like me or she's that way with everybody. But I liked Trudy right off. A definite noncomplainer. One slow afternoon both of us reorganized the stockroom; when I suggested it, she looked at me over her round metal glasses and said, "Sure, it all pays the same." She has shapeless dark hair and pale skin afflicted with breakouts along the jawline. I've never seen her in anything but stovepipe jeans and dark colors to hide what I think might be big legs. Her job as an artist is to do the sketches of corpses when they need to be ID-ed, for release to the papers, or she refines the scene sketches of others for use in court.

There were only three other names between Katchaturian and Kunitz. I dialed her number, thinking that even if she didn't have information on the Dwyer case, maybe I could figure out if she knew already how big a fool I'd been last night, figure out how much damage was done. I wondered if Joe knew already.

"Trudy, this is Smokey."

"Hi, Smokey," she said, as if she'd been up for hours and was used to me calling her every Saturday morning. Friendlier on the phone, almost happy. "What's up? We got a hot one?"

"No, nothing really. I'm sorry to bother you at home, but I heard you had something to tell me, and I didn't get to see you last night."

"Oh, yes. I told Billy. He didn't say?"

"Just you had something." Did she know about Billy and me or didn't she? God, how embarrassing.

"Oh. It's that thing you brought into Property. I understand you're kind of hot to see that case solved."

"Yeah, I am. Did someone ID it already?"

"Well, not exactly. But sort of. Julio Hernandez says it's a collet."

I knew what a collet was, though it was one of those objects you learn the word for once and think you'll never need again. "It goes on the end of a drill, I think, for holding the bit in. Right?"

"I think that's it."

"It didn't strike me as a collet because it was too big. I've seen small ones on my father's drill, I guess. So you think we have something worthwhile here, Trudy?"

"May be. Julio, see, knows about welding. He makes these little airplanes out of sheet metal and stuff and hangs them up for mobiles, sells them even. There's one over his desk. Go take a look. He says he solders, not welds. For some reason that's an issue. But, hey, I'm impressed. Looks cool to me. That thing you brought in—it's fused, he says. I guess it got too hot or something."

"Could he hazard a guess as to what it might belong to?"

"Nope. He couldn't figure it."

"Okay. Well, thanks, Trudy. We know any welders?"

"No, but Tools found something else about it."

"Let me guess," I said. "No prints."

"That's correct. It's crosshatched, like gun grips. But that's not all."

"Then, *what*?"

"Those guys in Tools are great, you know?"

"Trude, for God's sake," I laughed, "you want me to play twenty questions?"

"Sorry. But it's fun, isn't it, like a big puzzle? That's what I like about this work. It is definitely intellectual. Definitely better than crosswords, huh? Okay," she said, "here's the deal. Another guy in Tools put his tongue on it, the collet thing? He does that a lot, he says; tastes stuff, smells stuff. He can tell all sorts of things that way. I told him he better not be sampling any cyanide capsules, and he says, no, he uses them for party favors. That's the new guy from Boston. You meet him yet?"

"What sort of things did he find out about here?"

"That your collet had been in saltwater. As in ocean."

"Okay . . ."

"So he calls around yesterday afternoon, describes the thing to somebody. They think it might be a diver's tool, goes on an underwater cutting torch. Hey, Smoke?"

"Yes?"

"Julio says the guy's got the busiest pearl-tongue he'd ever seen, and he was laughing. You know what that means?"

"I think so." I had to smile at her voice; I wondered if I should tell her. I sat down on the floor, resting my head on the wall. "It means he's good at oral sex."

There was silence on the other end.

I said, "Trudy, did Joe Sanders tell you I was particularly interested in this case?"

"He told me *he* was particularly interested in this case. He told me you may have found something important."

"He didn't act . . . funny?"

"No. Not at all. What do you mean?"

So Joe wasn't spreading it around that I was a borderline incompetent. I said, "I'm surprised he mentioned it, really. We don't know if it's even remotely connected to the crime. I found the thing way off in some grass at the edge of the drive-way, far from the taped area. Is Joe, do you know, following up with Mr. Dwyer on whether he had any workmen around, welding?"

"Well, here's the good part, Smokey." Trudy must have been pleased to have someone to talk to on a Saturday morning, the only reason I could figure she was drawing this out. Then she dropped the bomb. She said, "One of the men your friend Ray told me you saw at the jail last night? Brothers, both felons?"

"Yes?"

"One of them's a diver. A deep-sea diver up in L.A."

It took a second for it to sink in. I thought the Dugdales were dead gone. Irrelevant. Not apropos. The little one, Phillip, was a housepainter. But the other one, what was he? Did he say, in there? Did I miss it? We'd come in late. The two brothers had been detained for some time before we got there, and we were there only about half an hour. So I didn't hear how the tall good-looking one earned his money when he wasn't doing convenience-store robberies. If it's too good to be true, it isn't; and yet I wondered if Gary, because of his grudge, might take a photo lineup over to Emilio at the taco stand with the Dugdales' mugs mixed in. You take half a dozen mug shots of people who look like the described perpetrators to the witnesses, instead of them coming to the station and going through hundreds in books. The photo lineup is not very reliable, but it still seems to convince juries. Even so, but I wanted Gary or the detectives to have tried it anyway with Emilio, except that the whole process would probably have made him poop his pants, poor little guy.

"Trudy," I said. "Want to join me for breakfast? There's a nice little place on Balboa. Where do you live? My head needs coffee, my stomach needs gruel." It'd be a chance to know her better, and we could discuss the case.

Her voice dropped, and she told me that she lived in Tustin, and that she'd like to, but by the time she got down to Newport after baby-sitting her wash in her apartment-house laundry room, it'd be real late. I didn't know if she made up the details or not, but it seemed like a legitimate excuse so I let her off the hook. "Another time, then," I said, and she said, "Sure." But I wanted to *do* something. Get out of the house. Get some fresh air. If only Joe L. Sanders weren't married, I could call him up and we could go figure this new piece of information. We could go talk to Mr. Dwyer. We could see what Gary Svoboda had to say about the collet. We could even drive out to L.A. harbor, where the ships come in. Where deep-sea divers hang out.

Have a look around.

CHAPTER
11

No, I didn't go. Then. By the time I ate, gassed the car, did bills, wrote a reluctant note to my parents telling them I was fine, nothing new, I'd had time to regain my balance. Trudy doing her wash reminded me I needed to do mine. Chores help. I was folding clothes on the bed when the phone rang at two. It was Patricia. I scooched the clothes over and lay down.

"You sleep all right?" she asked me. "I was afraid to call earlier." Her tone was hesitant, as if she thought I was going to be mad at her.

I said, "I made a fool of myself last night. A total dope-ette."

She kindly said, "You weren't the only one."

"Oh, really? That naughty boy Raymond. What have I done? You and my buddy?"

"We didn't get to the stage you're thinking, but serious enough. I think he'll be calling."

"You remember—"

She said, "He's got a girlfriend, yes. He told me. They're not getting along all that well. But listen, there are two things I want to talk to you about, Samantha. One, I'm insulted."

"I'm sorry. What'd I do?"

"Why didn't you tell me you were a . . . a . . . dancer once? Did you think I'd think less of you?"

"Oh, that. It was a long time ago. It was nothing really. I was living in Nevada. It seemed an okay thing to do at the time."

"You're embarrassed about it."

"If I were embarrassed about it, would I let people call me by my stage name?"

"You're not embarrassed but you couldn't tell *me*."

"I don't mind it—I just don't announce it to people who don't already know. The people at the lab know because I let it slip out one night when I had too much too drink, okay? You can understand that, can't you? Didn't you have a wild period when you were younger? That was mine. That was it. Not very exciting. It was just a job. You want to know what I did after that? I became a grocery checker. Now, that's exciting."

I rolled onto my shoulders and pointed my toes at the ceiling, trying to stretch, as long as we were going to be here awhile. I said, "Then I met Bill and went off to the academy and got married, the whole thing. No big deal. I wasn't a *prossie*, Patricia. You didn't think that?"

"Well, no. Not that. Anyway, I couldn't figure how they'd let you be a cop if . . ." She was silent again.

I pulled my legs in then, rolled down, and did a few leg extensions, keeping my abdomen tight. "Like I said, it was a long time ago. I was seventeen. Believe it or not, I never lied on my application to the academy, and if anybody investigated, it never came back to me."

When it was just quiet on the other end, I said, "Hey, you want to come over? It needs a dark, quiet bar to tell about it. Come on over, we'll go someplace."

"I have errands to run."

"Patricia, it's *my* life. What does it have to do with you?" I didn't know how I was going to get around this. I sat up and my head hurt. "What's two, you got to tell me?" Two things she wanted to talk to me about.

"I don't know if I'm imagining it or not."

"Are you crying, Patricia?"

"I'm not crying. What do I have to cry about? It's just I hate mentioning it."

"Mention it."

"This morning I go out to get the paper—you know how my apartment has that little alcove they call a porch? Well, there's an egg sitting next to my newspaper, just like a hen laid it there."

"It's not Easter yet, is it?"

"Not that I know of. Listen, I'm not kidding. So I don't think too much of it at first. I pitch it off down the bank near the bike path, where all that brush is? Because I think maybe it's rotten. Or it's got a puncture hole in it with cyanide injected or something."

"I'm a bad influence on you, Patricia."

"There're all sorts of crazies in the world, right?"

"Right."

"Okay, then. Just a minute. I have to pee."

I waited. In the background I heard the mechanics. I didn't tell her, when she returned, that I really don't need the details of her absence.

She began again: "Later I go out to my car and find another one, another *egg*, plastered on my *windshield*!"

"Kids," I said. "Kids did it. They go down the streets popping windshields with pellet guns for the hell of it. Happens all the time, the little shits." I said this at the same time my skin fairly tightened across my chest. I get real suspicious when it comes to things happening around women. I've had a few experiences myself.

She said, "I had one hell of a time getting it off, let me tell you. It's like *glue*. I didn't see anybody else's car with eggs on it. They're all out there in the carport same as mine, and mine's the only one with egg on it. Now, how can that be? Gives me the literal fucking creeps, I mean it." Then she laughed and said, "So, what d'ya think?"

"You dating any weirdos, pal-o-mine?"

"Not that I remember," she said, and loosened up a bit with a sort of laugh and moan and sigh all at once. "Jeez, what's the world coming to, Samantha?"

I told her I was sorry it happened, but I wouldn't let it ruin my day. I said we'd get together for dinner or a movie—huh?—soon.

"By the way," she said, "I scraped the egg off with a pancake turner."

I laughed and complimented her on her ingenuity.

Something happened to Sunday; I don't know where it went. In the evening, when I was coming back from dawdling at a

CD store, I slowed near Dwyer's Kwik Stop and pulled up into the driveway.

The store was still closed. I expected any moment to see Jerry stepping up to the door with keys to open it, or the lights to go on and Jerry and Mr. Dwyer in a kind of yellow tableau at the back of the store, ringing up purchases, answering questions.

There was instead an early moon casting shadows from the eucalyptus trees onto the shingled roof, pasting the lot in front in a wide rectangle. The wind pulled at the leafy shadows, and the whole dark cutout of Dwyer's Kwik Stop rippled like a painted blanket. I put my head back and closed my eyes.

A moment later I felt as though someone were behind me, though my window was open an inch and I would've heard someone walking or driving up. I glanced in my rearview mirror, then looked left, out onto the street, and saw a four-wheel-drive vehicle with a man in it, no lights. When I'd pulled in, was it there? The man brought his hand up and drank from a can, but the misty sulfur-glare of the streetlights only furthered the shadowed gloom inside the car so that I couldn't see his features. The can glinted momentarily as he flipped it, empty, into the backseat.

I kept my face turned to him so that if he were aware of me he'd know I was aware of him. Soon the engine started, the lights pulled on, and he eased out into the lane and moved on. I looked for a bucking bronco on the spare tire barnacled to the back, but couldn't see it.

CHAPTER
12

Monday I learned that the T-wrench Joe had found in the restroom had indeed been dusted, with no results. That is, they got finger creases, but not finger*tips*, the only measure worthwhile. I asked if they printed the underside of the tape, at the closure end; a new process allows us to grab those sometimes. Yea and nay—yes they did, and no, they didn't grab anything.

My supervisor, Stu Hollings, was new to the post and a hands-off kind of guy, which could also be read that he didn't much want to get involved. He called me into his office to assign me to the paperwork on a gang-related shooting, with Bud Peterson as team leader. Wouldn't Bud love bossing me around. I was to check for proper completion of forms, coordinate the sketch and photo work, review ballistics reports, and write a summary; in general, make sure things moved along. Reporters were all over this one because the victims belonged to a brave family whose house had been a target several times after the father stood his ground against the shooters. This time a boy in the bed of a truck parked alongside the house was capped by a volley from a full automatic, and the mother was shot in the leg as she was bringing in groceries.

When I went across the street to the sheriff's station, specifically to the photo lab, Billy Katchaturian was with a deputy, looking over glossies from another crime scene. I did not want to coordinate anything with Billy, but I knew I had to get over that hurdle. When I walked in, he made no acknowledgment of me at all. I wondered if that was bad or good; decided it was good. He propped a photo up on the counter, of a woman in what used to be a white dress. She looked like she was pregnant. With her head at the angle it was and the amount of blood on her clothes I knew she was nearly decapitated. Probably by a husband. Oh, what people keep doing to each other. I looked at the rise of her belly and felt a heaviness in my chest.

Billy said to the deputy, "The hands." I looked too and saw that both were red, like curled roses on white stems. He put that picture down and pulled another one up taken from the opposite angle. The third was a blowup of the back of her right hand, on a white background. I knew this one had been taken in the morgue, after the rigor mortis had relaxed, because of the piece of butcher paper for background. The hand was spread out, as if demonstrating how to do a handprint for mama. Black blood was etched in rims around the nails, sunken into the cuticles. The nails themselves were long, perfectly shaped, fluorescent pink. "Look at the nails," Billy said. "This one's gone," he said, pointing to a bare middle finger. "You find a pink neon job laying around?"

The deputy didn't say anything for a while, writing in his small tablet. "I'll find out," he said. They could find the fake nail in a suspect's collar or a shirt pocket. They could find it in a shoe, or on top of the refrigerator.

I waved a hand and said to Billy, "I'll come back later." Down the hall, I grabbed a cup of coffee. When I returned he was alone. I'd rehearsed what I was going to say. I had with me the file folder on the gang shooting, containing Trudy's sketches of the house and the truck parked next to it. She wanted Billy's shots so she could verify angles from the street to the truck.

Billy kept smiling at me this time, dragging his eyes over me as he told me how pretty I looked. I had on a black tailored rayon dress with black opaque stockings and a lime green jacket, dressier than usual. Maybe I needed to do that to face him. He was wearing a crisp pair of navy blue pants and a burgundy shirt with a burgundy tie, something I hadn't seen him in before either. His belt buckle was a raised silver spider with a red hourglass on the back made of two rosy pieces of coral. I said, "Billy, if that's supposed to be a black widow spider, the hourglass goes on the belly."

He gave a quiet laugh and said, "You have to criticize my genuine hundred-dollar buckle? I got that off an Indian in San Francisco."

"It's gross," I said. "It reminds me of that truck with a big black spider on it, that exterminator company? Like, sure, I'm going to call a guy with a big ugly spider half the size of me on his truck."

Billy was purring. "Mmmmm," is what he said.

"Hey. I don't want it to be difficult. We have to work together. We don't have to make it difficult."

"Who's difficult? I'm giving you a compliment." He settled an arm on the counter and crossed one ankle over the other while continuing to look me up and down.

"We have to work together," I said, "but I want to keep it professional."

"No problem. No problem at all. But so what *are* we doing tonight, hmm?" He put two fingers on my forearm, which I hadn't realized until that moment was resting on the counter too.

I said, "As far as I'm concerned, nothing happened the other night."

"Wow. That's downright mean. I didn't know you could be so mean, Smokes. Right to the heart." He straightened up, a hurt look on his face. In my gut I knew that he expected this, and that his reaction was all part of the play.

"Know it. We are definitely, definitely not continuing any sort of relationship. So focus your attention on someone else, huh? Like that new one in Tox. Okay?"

"What new one?" His eyes lit up.

I couldn't help but laugh. I didn't hate him, after all. I recalled how good the man felt, dancing. Humane, you might say. Sensitive. Sensitive? Well. "I don't have time for this, Billy."

"I'm not your type is what you're saying."

"I guess that's about it. Nothing personal. I don't mean to hurt your feelings."

"You know what you'd say if the tables were turned—if I were the one dumping you after a one-night roll in the hay?

You'd say, 'Oh, those men. They only want one thing.'"

"Knock it off, Billy. I was drunk and you know it."

"You weren't drunk when we started. You were talking a blue streak in the car. You don't remember begging to see my place?"

"That is total bullshit, Billy, and you better not go repeating that to anyone else. Get this straight—" The tops of my ears were turning fiery hot. I started trembling a little I think, because I hated losing my temper, because I hardly ever do, and when I do I lose all sense; I say and do things that shake me for hours. "Don't fuck with me, Billy. You really don't want to do that."

His expression fell back into something like real human being—ness. I took a breath. "Look, I have no right to ask you to keep this to yourself. I played, I pay. I know that. But I would, of course, *prefer* you don't go announcing what happened over the speaker system like some *M*A*S*H* replay, okay?"

"Hon, would I do that to you?"

I shook my head, confused.

He said, "God, how you can kiss." He moved closer to me, until I felt there was no place to go.

And then, lamely, I said, "Leave me alone, Billy. Jesus Christ, I've got my own problems. I've got somebody *following* me, maybe, some sicko—"

"I don't blame him."

"I'm telling you, I can work with you, I can say, Okay, we had a moment there. But that's it. Let's have mutual respect. Let's do our jobs. And move on. Okay? Okay, Billy?"

"Somebody giving you a bad time besides li'l ol' me?"

"No."

He was grinning a stupid grin and looking my face over as if he never heard a word I said.

"Because if you can't handle that, we're going to have to have a serious, serious talk, you and me, and I'll guarantee you, you won't win."

I expected him to say, "Ooo, you're so cute when you're mad," or anything else to keep up the game, the palaver. I stepped back, shoved my hands in the pockets of my jacket, and just looked at him.

He said, "You know something, Smokey? You have no sense of humor."

"You could be right," I said, and moved to the counter to open the folder he handed me. I removed the two photos Trudy'd wanted, put them in my folder, and started to go.

As I headed down the hall, I could feel his eyes on me. It nearly killed me when I remembered, but I had to stop before I reached the door. I squeezed my eyes closed, then turned around and asked the question: "By the way, did you use any protection?"

Maybe good dancers have these small flotation pockets of civilization that come bobbing up when you're in a cold ocean and there's no raft in sight. He answered, "Of course, dear."

There was a fire drill in our building. Just like in the old days, just like at school. Half an hour before quitting time. So I grabbed my purse before I exited, slipped around to my spot in the parking lot, and booked out of there.

I also took a one-to-one sketch Trudy made me of two pieces of Case No. 90-3284 HW's physical evidence: the T-wrench and the collet. She said when she gave them to me, "What are you going to do with that," and I said, "Oh, just show them to my dad." Maybe I *didn't* have enough to do, like my new supe Stu Hollings intimated. Maybe I was bored with the other cases that came across my desk, even the gang shooting, I don't know. It's not like the idea formed itself clearly in my mind right away, or even when I had Trudy do the sketches. It wasn't, in fact, until I got another phone call from Patricia that night.

"Smokey, something completely weird is going on," she said, calling me Smokey, as if she always had. "I *know* I locked my door this morning. It was open when I got home tonight."

"Are you sure? I do stuff like that all the time. Especially when I've been putting in long hours. Yep, even me, with my skewed eye on the world. You putting in long hours? You extra tired, Christmas shopping, or something?"

"No, not really. It's just not like me is what I'm telling you. You think, sometimes, Smokey, I'm dippy. But I'm not."

"I don't think you're dippy!"

"That's okay. I'm not mad."

"Wow, Patricia . . . you're really upset about this, aren't you? Let's talk about this. Is your landlord peculiar or anything, like maybe he's a snooper? I had one like that once."

"No," she said. "And, it's a she."

"Could—" I started to ask the obvious: if she'd given a key to anyone else. She interrupted to tell me there was something that frightened her more than the fact that her front door was unlocked. She did a lot of hesitating as she told me the rest. She went, she said, to use the bathroom, and when she lifted the lid, there was an unflushed bowel movement in it. I pondered this, afraid for her but not wanting her to know it. It was just creepy enough, there could be something to it. Burglars often leave calling cards. Sometimes in the middle of your bed; in your kitchen sink; in your rolled-up panties. Who can measure the amount of hostility there is in this world?

"Maybe you got a plumbing problem," I offered.

"You don't get it," she said. "The color . . . the . . . no, this was not, this was not . . ."

I said, "Maybe it's the drought. Maybe we have a water-supply problem, a reservoir dried up or something."

"I don't think that's it."

"You think it's that guy you were dating? The one who was harassing you for a while?"

"No. And I don't have a plumbing problem. The toilet flushes fine. The dishwasher works. Everything works." She sounded piqued.

"Good," I said. "That's one on the plus side, then. See, life's not so bad. And you haven't seen anyone strange hanging around? I mean no strangers?" She assured me she hadn't, and I told her to be sure, extra sure, that she locked doors anytime she went out, even to empty the garbage. Then we slowly began to make jokes about the toilet business, tee-hees you'd find funny in third grade. I told her the origin of the term *crapper*. She actually knew enough about it to argue with me, to tell me it wasn't invented by John Crapper; it was invented by somebody else, but she couldn't remember the name. I heard the softness return to her voice, the disarming Melanie Griffith tone. Then we talked about planning a ski trip together at the end of February, something to break up the long dry spell between holidays. All the cute guys go skiing, she said.

And then, after I hung up, as if I'd been waiting for this moment all along and couldn't admit it to myself, I got out the phone book and looked up "Diving." As in deep-sea. I had a Los Angeles phone book as well as an Orange County. "Divers" came right after "Ditching Services." Then under "Diving" the boxed ads for several companies announced their specialties, including "Propeller Removal"; "Underwater Inspection"; "Salvage"; "Engineering Consultation." I looked back at "Ditching," and, on the same page, "Dishwashing," and I thought about all the unique and possibly exotic jobs in the world, and all the ordinary and homely. With real people going to work every day, in real and separate places, figuring out the answers to engineering problems involved in digging ditches. Figuring out the unique choreography of automatic dishwashers: the belts and gears and brakes and motors. Brainstorming on how best to cable up and remove five-hundred-pound ship propellers. I'd forgotten ships *had* propellers. I thought how nice it must be to have a job where the opponent is inanimate, will sit there waiting for you, passionless, to get the better of it. Down the long list under "Diving," I checked off three places, all in San Pedro.

The next day I asked for the afternoon off. Still a little weak, I said. I ordinarily don't lie, but I learned a long time ago that management doesn't want the truth, because *they* have to lie to someone then, and so on, upstream. Better to say you're sick.

On the passenger seat of my car was the map I'd pulled out for L.A.-Southern, showing the harbor area. I put the yellow sticky with my notes on it on top of the map and headed out the 5 to the 22, to the 405, to the 710 South, to PCH, to the 110 South, and then to Gaffey. Here was new territory. I needed a change. Patricia should be with me. She'd like the dockhands.

CHAPTER
13

Communications patched me through to Gary Svoboda. I was parked with my window down on a sloping side street in San Pedro not far off Gaffey. Over warehouse roofs in the distance, I could see loading cranes at the wharves, and beyond that, a scattering of ships and barges silhouetted on a sky the color of bleached tin. Gary was off a high from two hours ago chasing a jewel-heist suspect around the parking lot of the Westminster Mall. His voice was strong and urgent when he spoke, the adrenaline still at work.

"So what's the latest on the Dwyer case?" I asked. "Did you take photos to the Mexican guy at El Cochino's—Emilio—what's his last name? Sandoval?"

"No, I didn't."

"Well, why not, Gary? I thought you were hot after those two you thought maybe did it."

"I forgot."

"Shit, Gary."

"Hey, listen, you want to hire me some help? I got one hour sleep last night. There's more of them than there is of us."

"I don't think so, Gary."

"My ears are ringing. My stomach hurts. I'm an old man. I should retire."

"No way," I said.

"Hey, the crooks are stealing Christmas."

"I know. I'm sorry."

"We had fourteen B-and-E's last night, can you believe that, and one murder. Two creeps grabbed a girl at a motel and handcuffed her to the balcony outside, went inside the room,

and screwed a twenty-five in her boyfriend's ear. We get called
in for a canvass since we're in the area anyway. And that was
the first two hours. You want to hear the rest?"

"Ah, you love it, you old horse," I told him.

"I guess I could have somebody run a six-pack out there."
He was referring to a set of mug shots. "But I think it's a
serious waste of time."

"So's sitting on Harbor Boulevard watching whores go by,
but you guys do that."

"Look," he said, "I'm supposed to talk to the Dwyer kid's
father today. I want to talk to him a little more about the kid's
friends, like that, though I don't think we got a problem there.
Looks like the boy led a clean life. I'll bring a pack by the taco
stand, then, okay? How's that suit you?" I said great. He said,
"You know the case's pretty much been turned over to the
homicide dicks, don't you?" Yes, I knew. The detectives, their
progress, he didn't know. Harry Felton—who's that, I say; the
bald detective, he says, the one with the arms, you ever see his
arms?—Felton's knee-deep in an officer shooting happened
over the weekend. The other one, Ted Reddeker, don't do
nothin' but pick his nose.

I laughed at that, said, "That's not fair. People kill, pardon
the pun, to work Homicide. He must do something, be good
at something."

Gary said, "Where you at, anyway?" He heard my phone
cut out, go staticky. When I told him, he hit the roof. I let
him get it off his chest while I was admiring the look of San
Pedro. The sky was overcast, and the smell of the ocean
drifted in through my car window. This was an area with an
old-neighborhood look, of small stucco and clapboard houses
and women pushing strollers along cracked sidewalks.

"You have absolutely no business out there, Smokey. None.
Now, I mean that."

"I can take care of myself. Don't worry."

"First off, that's not your *job*, and second off, my chief hears
about it and tells ol' Joe, you'll be supervising recess at Madi-
son Elementary."

"Let me worry about old Joe. He's not my boss anyway.
What I hoped to find out from you, the reason I called you
in the first place, is where Roland Dugdale works. You can do

that for me? You remember the name of the company?"

"*I* am the investigator on this case, not you, damn it. What's got into you?"

"Come on, Gare. You remember—I was a sworn once. I can do this. What would it hurt? Maybe I can help. It'll take half an hour out of my day and not encroach at all on *your* busy day. We could be a step ahead."

"You could screw things up."

"I'm not going to screw things up. I be cool, man."

I could hear his brain churn, whether to continue chewing, or give me the information.

"Hannifin, I think. Hannifin Diving."

"That's on my list."

"What list? Now, listen, that's rough trade out there."

"I'm only going to go ask general questions of somebody probably hasn't seen a pile driver in thirty years, somebody in the office, okay? I'm going to ask if they know what the tools are we found at the crime scene. Remember the brass thing and the wrench?"

"God! You removed the evidence?"

"No, no, no, no. Gary, you've got to have a little trust. I've got sketches is all."

"I better come down."

"Gary, you don't need to come down. I *said* I didn't take the stuff out, I'm not *going* to take the stuff out. Just the sketches. You come down, everybody gets paranoid. I told the guy on the phone my grandfather left these tools in a chest. And he bought that."

"I think maybe Felton already made some calls. Had to. He would've talked to Hannifin by now. It's probably all in the report. I just haven't had a chance . . ."

"Gary? Take a Valium and call me in the morning, okay?"

"Christ," he said, and I could hear him softening. He said, "You got hair, I'll give you that."

"Got to learn to improvise, Svoboda. See, that's an advantage, I'm not in uniform."

"If I tried that I'd never get away with it."

"Your problem is you got too much of an honest streak in you, that's what. They'd read your little cherubic face. Better watch out, you'll make captain one of these days."

He grumbled, but I knew he liked the suggestion. "When the cows come to roost."

"Gary—ten-four, all right?"

I figured somebody must have checked on Roland Gene's alibi; otherwise, they wouldn't have let Roland and his brother Phillip walk out of detention Friday night. But if they hadn't, if someone slipped up, got busy on the weekend; if Reddeker really was a fuckup or friend Gary himself wasn't leaning on this as much as he could. . . . Then again, they couldn't really press the Dugdales too hard unless they arrested them on suspicion, and, like it or not, I guess they didn't have enough to do that.

I called Gary back.

"Gare," I said. "It's Smokey."

"In trouble already?"

"You're holding out on me. You've got other suspects, don't you?"

Silence for a moment on the other end. Poor honest dear. As mad as he was about the Dugdales, I could not picture him giving in so easily. He had to have other suspects.

"You get back, we'll have a drink, okay?" he said.

Okay. That was enough. When I hung up, I thought, I could call Harry Felton myself. But then there'd be two people pissed off at me and more chance of that getting back to my boss as well. Also, it was two o'clock. My appointment was for two-thirty. I had to find the place yet.

I squeezed out behind a slow-moving truck with lapping branches hanging off both sides and sticking through the slats at back. Not being able to read the street sign with the truck ahead of me, I missed my first turn. Then, doing a U, I saw a green pickup approaching at a high rate of speed. It startled me. I remembered Emilio, the boy at El Cochino, talking about a big focking green pickup. My first reaction was to do another quick U, chase that sucker down. But this one was a new model, and I figured, boy, I'm getting jumpy.

Passing dozens of holding tanks, I drove onto one of the land spits that separates the channels. Railroad tracks ran the length of the spit. I drove slowly, fifteen miles an hour, looking up at the huge white tanks looming all around me. Through spaces between buildings I could see the gray-green water in the channel, and, on the other side of the channel, a few buildings associated with the Federal Correctional Institution at Terminal Island.

Straight ahead, perched on top of a building, was a small tank resembling the Tin Man, arms and all, looking as if he'd query all who passed. Individual red railroad cars nosed into warehouse doors like huge battery packs plugged into mammoth outlets. Men on the platforms waved arms and lifted things, barely taking notice of a small white car creeping by.

Mr. Davis was a little man. He wore brown pants and a green-and-blue-plaid shirt buttoned to the neck and anchored with a bolo tie, the fastener a miniature diving helmet in dead-dipped brass to give it a "been around" look. Facing outward like a pig snout was a green glass representing the diver's sighthole. It looked eerily like a tiny camera, or a window into parts of Mr. Davis I didn't want to see. But Mr. Davis was nice as he could be, and he shook my hand with strength and liking. It made me feel not so good, to be here under pretenses. I never wanted to be a private investigator—wouldn't like the lying you just have to do.

"Well, you can come right in here, little lady," he said, ushering me up the long wooden ramp from the driveway into the cavernous shop storage area, which was located in a corner of a warehouse. "This used to be Davis-Hannifin till I sold out a year ago. This here"—he was indicating a small vehicle of some sort, futuristic-looking, a clear bright blue, lying on its side—"is a motorized hull cleaner. It's got brushes on the bottom. A man rides it like a motorcycle right over the hull, scours off all the garbage. Ever seen one of them before?"

"No, sir," I said, "I sure haven't." Gear of one sort or another was hanging everywhere in the dark interior, or stacked neatly or not so neatly on metal shelves and on the floor. Cliff swallows had built jugs of mud along the crossbeams overhead. Orange rubber diving suits, headless, the arms and legs stiffed out and fat, with tears and mottled peels in them, hung on hooks drilled into the beams. Ready-wear for giants, not ordinary men.

Mr. Davis said, "We'll go into the office," and I followed him into a room that looked like a replica of a ship's quarters—or a San Diego bar trying to look like one. The small room was low and crossed with exposed beams, creosote glistening in stripes where the wood had cracked. Two dried blowfish dangled from fishline at either side of the room, one with a low-watt lightbulb in its belly. A green banker's lamp and a computer sat on the desk, behind which was draped a heavy-duty fish seine carrying colorful shells and one lone starfish. The whole thing cozy. Just give me a whiskey. I was chilly. I almost asked for one.

Mr. Davis stood in front of a chair with a leather-strap bottom. I figured this was where the divers sat; they couldn't hurt it too much. He motioned me to a chair whose seat was once red velvet, the center now bearing a woven straw cushion. "So you have some tools you want me to identify?" he said.

I looked at his lined, tanned face, his widow's peak over the deep forehead wrinkles, the eyes a calm dark brown, and thought, This is a man who's done his work, who's built a business and is happy with it. Who's sold it for enough that he can come down here on his leisure time and walk in like he'd never been away; whose ex-partner would still let him.

"Well, all I've got is sketches. My father would have a hissy if I took them out of the house. He wants to write to some magazine columnist and see if he can tell us what they are, but I figured, gee, you're right here, and you were kind enough to—"

He gave a quick wave of his hand to stop me. I pulled the folded piece of grid paper Trudy had given me from my pocket and leaned out toward him. "This," I said, pointing to the collet. A smile crossed his face.

Sweet salt air blew in. The blowfish near the door slowly floated and turned, its mouth open now in front of me, its hollow eyes taking it all in.

"That's a torch collet," Mr. Davis said, leaning close enough for his shirtsleeve to touch my arm.

Just then a young blond man in a yellow tie appeared in the doorway. He glanced over at me, then squinted at the amber-on-black computer screen that was twisted halfway in his direction. Mr. Davis looked up. He said, "Come on in, Ross."

"No, I just wondered . . . did the Barranca job come in?" He talked in a soft drawl and seemed pleasant.

"Not yet," Mr. Davis said. "Ask Harry when he gets back, though. He's gone to the post office."

"I've got a bunch of calling to do yet, but I hired two more divers and one driver."

"Good goin'," Mr. Davis said, and the young man moved off. "We have trouble sometimes, rounding up men when we need 'em," he said to me. Then, his attention returning to the sketch, "That there's a torch collet, and that's a T-wrench."

"Is there some special use for this T-wrench?" I asked.

"We tighten wing nuts on the brails with it."

"I beg your pardon?"

"C'mere," he said, and got up. He led me back out into the shop. We went over near a wall and he showed me a diver's helmet, looking like a crouched octopus behind some cardboard boxes. He touched the toe of his shoe to the convex ring at the bottom of the headpiece. "This here's the brail. You fit the helmet on the suit, you tighten the nuts to the rubber so it don't leak."

"I see," I said. "This is a special wrench, then?"

"Well, no, I wouldn't say that. You could pick one up at the hardware store." My heart sank. No special nature to it, no special significance. "What about this other thing?" I said, tapping the grid paper. "Is—"

"Now that's peculiar to the trade." He walked around the boxes, and I followed him. At some chest-high bins that had small hardware pieces in them, he rummaged till he brought up a thing just like the one I found in the grass outside Dwyer's, only it was shinier.

"That's it," I said.

He held the collet up close to me and pointed to the white lumpy metal in the center that looked like the corrosion you get on your car battery cables. "See this? This happens when it arcs out."

"I'm sorry. You'll have to help me a little more here. Arcs out?"

"Your granddad has this?" He meant the white stuff.

"I . . . I think so, yes."

"This is a collet for an underwater cutting torch." He was jostling it in his palm now. "Diver sticks a tender in here in the center and heats it to the temp of brimstone. Then he fixes a bridge or cuts a ship apart. Sometimes in so doing it arcs and fuses the tender." He was poking his long finger into the center to demonstrate, so I could figure out what a tender was. "Melds the tender to the collet. So now he's got to get a new one. A diver carries around six, seven of these things in his pockets. We can't keep them in stock hardly."

The Dugdales *had* to be there at the Kwik Stop. How many divers loaded down with collets could there be in Orange County? I couldn't wait to tell Svoboda; yah, yah, look what I found.

I asked other questions, as if I had a general interest in diving. I asked if divers were unionized, and if they were paid well, getting a yes and a yes. I asked where the divers mostly came from—the navy?—and Mr. Davis said no, most all from the oil industry out of the South: Louisiana, Texas, Arkansas. And yes, I asked if he knew Roland Dugdale. If Roland worked there.

Mr. Davis turned full-face to me and narrowed his eyes. The light from the shop's open doorway caught the snout of his bolo-tie diving helmet, turning the green glass blank. Mr. Davis said, "Now, you should've told me, honey, who you really are."

CHAPTER
14

I saw Joe Sanders in the grocery store in Newport Beach, which is a long way from Tustin. I'd just arrived at Farmer's Market in Fashion Island, a spoke-wheeled complex of expensive stores, the whole "island" rimmed by towering white office buildings.

Outside, Christmas music piped from palm trees strung with tiny white lights. A gigantic, decorated spruce, cut for the occasion, dominated the plaza. I was coming down the escalator, intending to get something quick to eat in the food park, and there he was, in one of the grocery aisles off to the side, choosing milk.

If I went over and said hello I'd wind up telling him I'd been to San Pedro, and I wasn't ready yet. When I reached the bottom of the escalator, I wheeled around the far side and went back up. I ate at Wienerschnitzel on Jamboree, wondering about Joe. Something was going on, that he'd be this far from Tustin. Then again, maybe he had relatives here.

The next time I saw Joe, he was stabbing fat. All day Wednesday he'd been in meetings, and I was busy. That morning I'd phoned Detective Felton. The bald one with, as Gary said, the arms. I told him who I was and that I did something a bit out of my work scope but hoped he wouldn't mind. He listened politely. I remembered his demeanor while questioning Phillip Dugdale in the interrogation room: listening for a long time, then quietly asking him questions as if he needed that long time to dream them up. Asking Phillip about painting, and did he win the Lotto. And then saying, You're pissing on my leg, Phillip. An ace.

Talking to Felton, I was hesitating and repeating myself. At the end I got control. "The important thing here is that Roland Dugdale's a diver and a piece of diver's gear was found at a murder scene."

He said, "All such information comes to me. First." He seemed provoked, but not irate. He asked me a few questions about how I knew to go to that particular place, Hannifin, and how I got there. Dry; no emotion, as if taking notes.

What I didn't tell him was that I practically got escorted out of town, Mr. Davis following me in his brown Lincoln all the way back to the main road, though I thought at the time maybe he was just on an errand. Mr. Davis lost it with me but not too much, just turning grim-faced and shutting down and telling me, "You know the way out." When I'd gotten back in my car and looked up through the windshield, I saw him standing there framed in the large black square of the warehouse door, though he was down at the bottom of the ramp on the asphalt, his blue plaid elbows arrowed out, his hands jammed solid on his hips. I'd put my sunglasses on because of the white glare from the sun trying to break through the overcast, and maybe because the shades feel like a mask. And then the next time I looked in my rearview mirror, about to make a turn, I saw Mr. Davis in his brown Lincoln.

So I didn't tell Detective Felton that, and I didn't tell him I knew that Detective Reddeker, the one in the pink shirt, had called Hannifin Diving Service regarding Roland Dugdale's employment record, that Reddeker had made Mr. Davis's ex-partner look up Roland's time sheets and then call Reddeker back. Roland had worked the day of the murder. He even accrued premium pay for overtime. I didn't tell Felton because Reddeker would or had, and because I wanted to keep the heat on in a case that could quickly get doused with hundreds of other homicides we have in a year.

I asked if he'd had a chance to interview any of Jerry Dwyer's friends yet. Once again he was polite.

"We have. That's all taken care of, nothing out of the ordinary. The boy's friends are confounded," and I thought that

was an unusual word to use but a good one, and wondered
what kind of man this was.

"A robbery gone wrong," I said.

"That's what it looks like."

"What you're saying is we're going to have to wait till a suspect is developed. Is that right?" I could hear another phone
ringing near him, and hoped he wouldn't say he had to answer it.

He said, "That's about it."

"Thanks anyway. You're a good man, Felton." And as soon
as I said it I wished I hadn't. He could think I was being con-
descending. People do. Me being two ticks above thirty and
he maybe fifty.

He said, "You cleared up on everything now?"

"Thank you very much for your time, Detective Felton." I
said good-bye and hung up.

Late afternoon, I asked around if anybody'd seen Joe, until
I found a serologist who was putting away blood samples in
one of the household refrigerators that stand in the middle of
the room, back-to-back, with alarm wires attached to them. A
little overkill, I'd say, but otherwise people would be tempted
to put their lunches in there. "He's in the back killing roast."
The technician clicked the combination lock back on the door
then and thumbed the sign that read EVIDENCE—DO NOT FON-
DLE, as if the tape were coming loose.

I said, "I beg your pardon?"

"Back there," he said, nodding toward a room we had used
for the freeway killer's investigation, eight desks in there then,
nearly empty now. "Stabbing meat."

And he was. He was in a lab coat, standing near a slab of
roast on butcher paper, the paper covering a desk. I knew
what he was doing. It just took a second for it to sink in. I
knew he had to skewer pork fat onto the roast too, because
meat comes trimmed nowadays and the human body's muscle-
to-fat ratios have to be matched. But human fat is different,
spongier, and yellow. Oh, well. I hadn't seen anybody do it,
but I'd heard about it.

I came up from behind. "I think it's tender now."

"Hi, Smokey," he said, almost relieved. He glanced at me,
then back to the roast.

"Are we having a cookout?"

"What we're having here is Sanders's unsuccessful attempt to learn what kind of hole a kitchen knife makes. As opposed to, say, a jackknife."

"Seems pretty straightforward to me."

"Not this one. This one happened when you were off."

I moved in closer to see what damage Joe had performed on the roast. Behind him on the counter was his notepad, and I guessed that every time he made a few furious strikes he'd pause and write something down. Next to the notes was a magnifying glass. He said, "We have the knife, with the victim's blood on it. So we *know* that's the goddamn murder weapon. But the wound doesn't match the characteristics of the knife." He shook his head.

"Who was the victim?"

"A woman. He was a biter, too."

At one time I wanted to know everything. On a street in Oakland, in what was, shall we say, the less glamorous part of town, I was watching some undercover policewomen tricking tricks. Down the sidewalk came a man with white sideburns crawling to his chin and the deep chalky-gray skin of African heritage. He wore a tailored gray suit nipped in at the waist, double-breasted. He could have been a retired "supervisor" himself, stopping every once in a while to talk to the women on the streets. When he came up to one of us bad/good guys in a miniskirt and mike, he said this, his voice a polite but steady baritone: "For in much wisdom is much grief, and he that increaseth knowledge increaseth sorrow." He'd go on down the street, talking to the regular girls, talking to one of us, those words about wisdom and sorrow. The girls would say, "Say *what*?" or "Get lost, old man," or something of the like, and he would stroll on. But the oddity of it stayed with me and came back to me time and time again, the first occasion after examining belt and burn marks on the corpse of a six-year-old boy from the ritzy part of Oakland near Berkeley Hills, his mother a lady who served on the board of a hospital, and his father a scientist out of Lawrence Livermore. Today I know the quest for some kinds of knowledge comes at high price. Joe says all change is loss, and all loss must be mourned. *Sí*, and so must some varieties of gain.

"Maybe I'm slipping. I can't figure this one out," Joe said. He whaled at the piece of meat again.

I said, "The wound gets wider when there's a struggle."

"Yes, I know that." He stood away from the table and turned to point at his notepad with the knife, pushing up the page and flipping it over to reveal a drawing meant to depict the vertical wound. At the top of the cut, a short horizontal line jagged off to the right. "That," he said, the sticky tip of the knife touching the line, "I can't figure out. This peculiar little edge here, this quirk. Why is it there?"

"Is it important?" He looked at me with a quick raised eyebrow, saying, Whatsa-matta-you? I leaned in to look at the drawing again, and said, "I only meant, if they've got the knife and they've got the dead person, what difference does it make?"

"Evidence has to be interpreted, Ms. Brandon. For shame."

"Maybe you should use flank steak," I said. "It's tougher. How old was this lady?"

He probably didn't like me criticizing. After all, he was the one who taught *me*, directly or indirectly, as I watched him in the department over the years. He said, without looking up, "Sixty."

"Hmmpf. The only sex old women get is from fifteen-year-old rapists, right?"

"Is that supposed to be funny?"

"Sorry. You're a little out of sorts, aren't you?" Joe knew my humor; he usually laughed.

He said, "We do have a suspect in custody. I sent an odontologist over a minute ago with a warrant to get bite impressions from him. We think a neighbor did it, a guy she played cards with. And he happens to be fifty-nine."

"Jesus," I said. "Does it ever end?"

"For this one it does," Joe said, and he was looking at the beef as if it were the victim, as if he placed the X-Y coordinates on the screen, pressed the "Build" button, and the human form imposed itself over the slab.

While we were speaking of suspects, I asked him if we had any more information on the Dwyer case, or any other suspects. Gary hinted he might have some other suspects. He was being coy, Joe. Give me the dope. What do you know?

He put the knife down on the desk behind us, checked the front of his lab coat for goo, then perched a hip up on the desk. "What I hear is they did a sort on stop-and-robs, as you suggested. They developed another candidate list. A couple fit the El Cochino witness description."

"Yay!"

"Don't get too excited. He's all we got, but it's all circumstantial. Emilio didn't *see* them commit a crime." This was true. "A couple names on the list do small-store robberies—shoes, yogurt—places off the side of a string of shops, where getaway is easy. They're just doing look-ups at this point. Two tall men they're interested in . . ."

I was shaking my head. He asked me what was the problem. I said I didn't know. Then: "Emilio's talking tall guys, about nineteen, right?"

"Right."

"How do we know Emilio can judge ages? Emilio says they were about nineteen. You get a look at Emilio's face? I would've bet a dollar Emilio was thirty-five if he was a day. He says *he's* nineteen. Now, those Mexican summers might melt rubber, but if he's nineteen, I'm ten. Maybe he doesn't know the English for any other number but nineteen. I say we scratch the ages."

Joe said, "You told me the Dugdales were one tall, one short. One has brown hair, one black, right?"

I nodded.

"That is definitely not two tall, no matter if they're nineteen or forty, and he said they were tall. What you got there, my dear, is real skimpy."

"They do convenience stores, Joe. How right-on could you get? I mean, that's a specialty to be proud of. These two are *in* the area, and they're creeps on wheels. Okay, look . . . the dark-haired one, Phillip George. Maybe his hair's not black naturally. Maybe it's dyed."

"Maybe he took the lifts out of his shoes, too?" He was sliding his roast now into a big plastic sack he pulled up from the floor.

"They're buttwipes, Joe."

"That doesn't convict a man."

"Gary's going to show their pictures to Emilio. I want to talk to Mr. Dwyer. In fact, I'm *going* to talk to Mr. Dwyer. You want to come along?"

He stopped fidgeting and looked at me. "You don't do anything without clearing it with the investigating team. You are not an investigator."

"Why can't I—we—talk to him? That's not interfering. How's it interfering?"

He was removing his lab coat. With the motion came a scent, the sweet smell of something men's wives buy for them in a department store, and I felt lonely and confused and both wanted his approval and wanted to get away. A quick way to end this conversation was to tell him I'd spent yesterday afternoon in San Pedro, at Roland Dugdale's place of employment.

He blew up. He never used to lose his cool like that. I don't mind saying it humbled me—no. Not that. It scared me; I had a lot more to learn before I'd say humbled. I told him I'd talked to Felton in Homicide, but he turned and actually grabbed my arm, pulling me into a chair, and said, "You're going on suspension, young lady, as of right now."

"You can't put me on suspension. I don't work for you. Check with Stu Hollings, you want me suspended. And quit treating me this way."

"What way? You mean like an adult?"

"I have *been* an officer, Joe. I know what I'm doing, I know how to handle myself. And where do you get off manhandling me like that?"

I stood back up out of the chair and stepped away from him. The slippery soles of the new shoes I was wearing nearly took me farther than I wanted to go. I said, "I didn't compromise any investigation. I didn't do anything wrong, unless you're talking about a violation of some policies and procedures handbook that some contractor took two years to write and doesn't signify two *minutes* after it's done. What I did was *add* to the case. Detective Felton never batted an eye. He appreciated it."

Joe was quiet. He'd moved to the side of a desk, to put more distance between us. He said, calmer, "What's got into you? You bored with your desk job? You want some excitement? That it? You want to go be a cop again?"

"No, that's not *it*. I want to see Jerry Dwyer's killers caught is all. Is that so wrong? I'm afraid the case will get buried. You know what happens."

"This case is not any different from any other case. You think this woman's"—gesturing toward where the roast was balled up in a bag—"this woman's relatives, her kids, think Jerry Dwyer's case should come first? You think they're not hurting? What about the four-year-old with the bullet in his eye, huh, from a carload of fucking creeps? Everybody wants to come first. Everybody comes first. Everybody." He glanced away for just a second, then said, "That case is not going to get buried."

I looked at him, not giving an inch but saying quietly, "How do you know?" I didn't want to upset him. I knew he was the best there was, I knew it the day I met him, heard him speaking at one of those annual conventions we forensics people go to. And after a year of finagling, I got to work in his department, and never did know precisely just when it was I fell in love.

"Because," he said, "I'm not going to let it get buried."

"Okay, I'll get out of your face."

"There was a call for you here this afternoon. From Mrs. Dwyer."

Of course. There was a Mrs. Dwyer. Somewhere in the Midwest.

"Mrs. Dwyer?"

"She wanted to talk to you because you're with the police, she said. You knew her son."

"You told her I wasn't with the police."

"I did."

"But you said I'd talk to her."

He nodded. "The number's here," he said, drawing out from his pocket a crumpled piece of notepaper. "She's staying at the Cozy Inn off Newport."

He came close to hand me the note, and why then, at that very moment, and at that very time and place, people not all gone from the office yet, he stood not six inches away, me smelling his smell and him breathing hard, not touching but looking down at me, at my mouth, and then kissing me—hard—I'll never know. But he did.

And then he turned and walked away. Out the door. Bippo.

I yelled after him: "You can't do that, Joe! Dammit!"

A man I didn't know walked through the room from the other side, and gave me a look that said here's one he wouldn't want to work with.

Joe's kiss upset me for fourteen reasons, though part of me fired from the thought of it. I went home that night and watched an episode of *Roseanne* I'd seen before. I laughed all over again. She's got A, as the kids say, for Attitude. Read between the lines; you hear some smart stuff. I thought John Goodman would be fun to cuddle if he'd just pull his pants up in back. I tried not to think of Joe.

Even though it was ten o'clock before I dialed Mrs. Dwyer, there was no answer in her room. Maybe I waited that long because I didn't know what the call was going to be like, didn't want it to be some long teary thing with me having nothing to say that would heal a broken heart. No, that wasn't it. I knew what it was. I'd have to, if I talked with Mrs. Dwyer, be listening to her and living old pain for my lost Bill in the other part of my brain. I'd have to remember how much it hurt, and which days after his death were most keen. I'd have to remember how for days and days I couldn't stop saying his name, trying to call him back.

So I dusted my apartment while I listened to K. T. Oslin's lusty voice on her "Hey Bobby" cut, her raunchy "Do ya wanta, huh? Do ya wanta huh, huh?" and felt good, even danced a little, dropping the duster and watching myself in the dark glass of the slider, then stopping, seeing I was looking smaller in the chest some ways and wondering what the heck was happening already—did it have something to do with my op? Maybe I needed a new bra. I didn't finish dusting; instead, I watched TV until I couldn't avoid making the call any longer, relieved when Mrs. Dwyer didn't answer. I plopped on the couch and read the latest *BirdWatcher's Digest*.

Patricia rang my doorbell as I was getting ready for bed. Under one arm was a bunch of roses and ferns. Her dimples twisted full force through the happy smile. I knew those roses weren't for me.

"Smokey," she said. I was Smokey now for the rest of my life. I didn't mind, but it seems funny, how one tiny episode in your life hangs on. "You are definitely," she said, "not going to believe this."

"You got proposed to by Donald Bren," I said, closing the door.

"Who?" She came in and walked over to my dining table and put the roses down, pointing the bottoms of the stems off the edge so they wouldn't wet the wood. Good girl.

I said, "God, Patricia. Only the richest developer in Orange County. Probably the world. Try billionaire. He owns . . . Irvine Company, I think. Yeah. Irvine Company. He's single, and he's handsome. I saw his picture in the paper. He just bought a lot on Harbor Island for fifteen million, can you dig it? He doesn't wear suits, you could meet him in the post office, find some reason to go to Newport Beach to mail a letter."

"Got it all scoped out, huh? Doing a little scouting yourself down at the local PO? Gooood. Good for you." She seemed positively jubilant. I offered her a drink even though it was almost midnight.

As I crossed to the kitchen, I caught my reflection in the slider again. Patricia made me smile without me even knowing it. She's good for me, that's what she is, I thought. She and Roseanne Barr, who'da thunk?

"No, listen, I got to run. Work tomorrow, you know. But what I wanted to tell you is something you are not going to believe. And I don't want you to be mad."

"Why would I be mad?"

"Well, mmm, because."

"Because what? Come on. Lay it on me." I had something I wanted to tell *her*. About Joe. Him kissing me. We could figure it out. She didn't know how I felt about Joe. I suppose I talked about him quite a bit, but I never came right out and said how I felt, because I was ashamed. It's not a thing you do to a marriage, fool with that. You leave that stuff a-*lone*.

I waited. She was having trouble finding the words, starting out, "See . . ." and then, "Well . . ." and then, "How do I explain. . . ?" By this time I was fixing myself a drink. Wine I'd opened weeks ago and stuck in the refrigerator. Uncouth, I took a taste from the bottle. It was still good.

"You sure?" I said, waving the bottle in her direction.

"Wait. I have to tell you this first."

I laughed. "Who is this hunk of irresistible manhood?"

She waltzed over to the counter that separated the living room from the kitchen, looked beneficently down at me, and said, "You sure you're ready? I don't want you to be mad. It's someone who just moved into my apartment complex. *Totally* by coincidence."

"Patricia."

"Okay," she said, and sat at one of the bar stools, resting both folded arms on the counter. "Here it is. I went out with Roland Dugdale."

I wasn't sure I heard her right.

She said it again. "Roland Dugdale." Big green eyes looking at me like she'd just learned about Christmas. "Yoo-hoo," she said, waving a hand. "You there?"

CHAPTER
15

"Fucking *culo*."

"I'm with you there," I said, "whatever that means."

"Why is it women think criminals are glamorous?" Ray and I were sitting in Baxter's Restaurant. He'd ordered a grapefruit and oatmeal and I had toast, that's all, because neither of us are really that interested in breakfast.

"Because a certain percentage of them have charisma."

"Charisma my ass." I made a movement with my head as though that could be considered. He grinned and said, "She's nuts," beaching his arm on the table. He slid his scoured grapefruit ahead of him and gazed at me with hurt eyes. "Women are nuts."

"Thank you," I said as I smeared more strawberry jam on my toast.

"I don't mean you."

"*People* are nuts," I said, and continued eating.

"You know what Yolanda tells me? She says she wants to be married to a rodeo rider—she's watching that yippy-ki-yo stuff on TV. I tell her fine: Happy trails to you. Jeez, I wish I could get some hot coffee around here." He twisted around, hunting for the waitress.

"I'll call Patricia tonight, Raymond. I'll get her talked down. Last night wasn't the night."

"You better. Those guys, even if they're not responsible for that murder, they're responsible. Get my drift?"

"Just by being in the world, you mean."

"You got it."

I said, "She's got a playful streak is all. Flirty, like me, only I know who to flirt with."

He looked at me awhile, then said: "Something's bothering you though, big time."

"Is it too weird, or what, Roland Dugdale checking out a new apartment in the very apartment complex Patricia lives in? Freak of time, as Joe says, or no. Give me a break."

"I'll bust his *cojónes* if you want me to."

I waved a hand to dismiss him, but I said, "She told me a few days ago that strange stuff has been going on at her apartment, like maybe somebody's been in there."

"Shit."

"My sentiments exactly. In fact, that was one of the particular substances involved. One day there's an egg smashed on her windshield, another day there's a turd in her toilet she says is gratuitous, and her door is unlocked. I don't know, Ray—there are a lot of fuckin' creeps in the world who do things like that for their jollies." He shook his head, leaned back, and looked out the window, as if to say such things are simply incomprehensible. "Guys can get your number easy. It's spooky. When I was a grocery-store checker, this man I see in the store every day shows up at my house one night at midnight. Don't ask me how he knew where I lived."

"He do anything?"

"He was drunk, wanted to come in. I said I had a gun when I didn't have a gun. Begged me anyway. Cried a little."

"You let him in?"

"You ask a lot of questions, you ever notice that, Raymond?"

He flagged down Tamara for coffee, looked at me in that knowing, brotherly way, and then said, "What's this character look like anyway? This Roland asshole."

"Actually, he's good-looking."

"Oh, great." He rolled his head.

"I mean, hard features, tight. Not as good-looking as—I don't know—who's popular now?" I said, and couldn't think of anyone. The actors I like nobody ever heard of. "You're handsome too, Raymond," I crooned, then ate my toast.

"It could be coincidence."

"You know what bothers me, Raymond, besides all that? When she knows me, when she knows what I do all day, how could she be so bare-ass stupid as to date a convicted felon? That's pretty self-centered, huh, of me?" He cocked an eyebrow in assent. "I can't help it. If she were really my friend she wouldn't do something like that."

"You said he had charisma. Hey," he said, shrugging.

"The guy's kind of like a good ol' boy," I said. "A Texan."

"A rodeo rider, I suppose." He looked at me out of the corner of his eye, and we both laughed.

"Brownish hair, blond at the sideburns. Real green eyes. Medium build. Kind of like yours but not as nice. Tan—which is funny, 'cause he's a diver. Where do you think he gets a tan?"

"All over his body."

"I mean *where*. What does he do for recreation, for fun? Where could we go spy on him?"

"Maybe he sits on the beach for his breaks." He tipped his head back, winged out his arms, and said, "Shoot me some rays, dude."

"You're right. I got thrown by the overtime, thinking he's underwater all that time, morning to night. Maybe he gets whole chunks of time off in between."

"How old is he?"

"Thirty-one I think his sheet said, didn't it? You're the one read it off your MDT."

He nodded, lifted my last triangle of toast off my plate, the one I was poking at with my knife, and took a big munch out of it. An arm went up on the booth back near me, Ray's Highway Patrol shoulder patch taking a beam of sun, the grizzly bear by the goddess Minerva's knees, looking for all the world like a pet dog sniffing the bushes to see who'd stopped by lately. The leaves were supposed to be grape leaves, not bushes, a nod toward California's agriculture. Minerva had something to do with arts, science, peace, and war.

"Not to change the subject or anything, but I'm thinking about going through LAPD academy."

"That's wonderful, Raymond. But why?"

"I get tired of being the Rodney Dangerfield of the freeways. I got a pal in L.A. could put a word in for me."

"You wouldn't need anyone to put a word in for you, Raymond. You're good enough."

"You know how long it would take me to get anywhere, me being a Moe?" He was using a code word for *Mexican*, the nonthreatening kind, as in, We got several Moes on that four-fifteen—meaning several bystander Hispanics on a disturbance call. Cops use racial code words, not always respectful but not always disrespectful either—more in the way of club talk, inner-circle stuff, evolving for any number of reasons, clever, not-so-clever, but a lexicon that has behind it different impulses at different times. Some cops do it for fun, tough talk for tough trade; yet I've heard racial epithets from people who were the first to defend minority rights and human dignity. All is not what you see on the surface, or, in this case, hear. When it's women being referenced, sure, I feel the sting, but I try to consider not only the source but the context. A cop last month stood outside with me by a hot dog vendor, telling me about two splibs, blacks, who put a hole in the thigh of his partner, and now he's got to put up with a gash—meaning female—partnered to him. Looking this Smokey Brandon female right in the eye as he was saying it, so that I stood there trying to figure out if this was one more test, and just who the hostility was directed toward—me, the partner, or the culprits—deciding it was a little bit of all three, and winding up thinking, You're never going to change the world, Smokes, just your tiny piece of it—maybe.

Ray himself saying, "Because I'm a, quote, Hispanic? A born-and-bred East L.A. Moe?" And me feeling one with him then, and yet apart, because I can't quite feel his difference, nor he mine.

I said, "Captain Riley in the sheriff's is black."

"Jewish too I suppose."

"Could be, Raymond. Listen, I hear LAPD's over half minorities now. The whites are hollering. That's good, huh?" I said, probing for what was really bothering him, not sure yet I had it right. He changed the subject then, back to the Dwyer case, and it took me by surprise. "Any more suspects developed in that case of yours besides this *minga* and his shithead brother?"

There it was. Cute Patricia and her selection. I said, "Hey, if you're going to start talking Mexican, you better start teaching me."

"You want to learn Spanish?"

"Just the dirty words."

That smile of his, the even white teeth showing, creasing across his face, and then, "Oh, just the dirty words. Nice *señorita linda* like you? Nah, you don't want to do that. You want to take a course in college, eh?"

"Fuck you *and* your burro, Raymond. They're not gonna teach me street language in junior college. What's a *minga*? Tell me."

"You get it from the context."

I gave him a disgusted look, and then he told me: the single most significant part of the male anatomy, if you had a male anatomy. "A prick," I said, and then instinctively turned to see if the waitress was approaching with a refill or something—wouldn't want to offend the citizenry. "A prick by any other name is still a prick. By the way, I did see a report on the round recovered from Jerry Dwyer." I'd forgotten to tell Joe that. I'd forgotten it myself—that was Tuesday, the day I went to San Pedro. "They were using Glasers. Who has Glasers except law enforcement?"

"I didn't shoot him." He looked like a little boy then, and I had to laugh.

"Think with me," I said. "Who would have Glaser ammo?"

"Your boys into guns? The *Dug*dales?"

"I don't know. Svoboda said one of them used a knife to threaten a storekeeper once. Gun freaks don't usually dig knives. I've seen Glasers demo-ed, but I haven't fired any myself—they came out after I left the force. Those and a thing called Thunderzap, twice the speed of sound. They shatter, it's like a frag-bomb."

He smiled. Pretty, brief, and troubled.

"That's what killed Jerry Dwyer," I said, the picture of Jerry, not the one in Billy's photographs but the one in my full-color memory, flashing into my vision and out again as fast as I could make it.

Raymond said, "It's like Gucci handbags and what do you call those watches?"

"Rolex?"

He nodded. "Everybody's gotta have one, even if they have

to rip it off your G-D wrist. Rich guys are wearing cheapies now so they don't get robbed, can you beat it?"

"Breaks *my* heart."

He finished off the last crumb on my toast plate with a finger swipe, then scraped his grapefruit shell one more time. I asked him, Raymond, do you want to order something else? But he said no, he was on a diet. I said, "Think of this a minute, Ray. This is what's mysterious to me—back to the Dwyer case. If the witness—let's call it semiwitness—next door at the taco stand says the bad guys were hanging around awhile, why? You rob somebody, you do it quick, right?"

"Could be an argument over something. His friends come in to see him. He says, 'Hey, jerkoff, I saw you out with my girl last night.' His friend gets mad, draws the—what'd you say it was? A twenty-two? Draws the twenty-two out from under his shirt where he keeps it to be cool, but it goes off. Didn't mean to shoot his buddy there, just meant to lay into him. Buddy Number Two panics. They're in deep-shit doo-doo now, going to prison till the end of *Star Trek* reruns. They say, 'Hey, grab the cash, make it look like a robbery.'"

I sighed. "It could be anything. But not that. His friends wouldn't shoot him *again*, if it was an accident. He was just a big goony kid and all his friends are big goony kids. I know. I've met some of them. They'd come by the store Saturdays. I even partied with them one time by accident, in Bobby McGee's. I was supposed to meet a date there, but I got stood up."

Raymond was looking at me with amazement, grinning, starting to ask me something.

"So?" I said. "It happens. I ran into Jerry, he introduced me to a bunch of his friends, we danced a little. They even invited this old lady to a party afterwards, but I didn't go. This was not a kid who ran with punks."

"Everybody's got enemies."

"No," I said.

"Okay. Then these are pros. Sort of. They been checking out the place for an hour. They been watching how he does things, how much money he salts away."

I was shaking my head, because robbers don't want to hang

around. "In and out, in and out, that's what a robbery's all about."

This conversation was not going anywhere. I wanted to go follow Mr. Roland around, *do* something. I glanced at my watch: fifteen minutes before I'd have to go.

"Raymond?"

"What?"

"We gotta go."

"What's the matter," Ray said.

"Oh, nothing, something I just have to do today, make sure of today."

And then, as if he could read my mind, "Nothing back from Prints yet?"

I said, "Nothing substantive." But what had hit me was, did anybody get the magazines? "I wonder, Ray—if the killers were in there awhile, wouldn't they be thumbing through the magazines, maybe, checking out the bubble-breasted women in bikinis and the jazzy Mack trucks?"

He nodded as to the possibility.

"We can laser them."

"How does that work, anyway?"

"Vitamins and other natural substances found in perspiration glow under the light. Normally, with paper, you lose the ridge detail, especially if it's humid, but it wasn't humid that day."

Ray was looking at a different waitress across the room serving other people, her short skirt tipping up high in back. He said, "How could she go out with that guy?"

I thought he meant the waitress at first, and I looked. Down the back of the woman's right thigh were four small, round, greenish bruises. I wondered if they were finger marks, somebody eager last night.

He said, "I just don't understand it."

CHAPTER
16

I called Patricia at her work that afternoon and talked to her for about ten minutes. She kept telling me that she wasn't losing her head, she'd go slowly; that I—and Raymond, whose business it wasn't anyway—were overreacting. Give the guy a break, she said; not everyone makes all the right choices at first. She's telling *me* this, after she saw me with Billy K.

"He makes me laugh. He's sexy."

"Oh, puh-leeze."

"Remember Jerry Reed?" she said. "Used to play in those pictures with what's-his-name, the guy in, oh, you know ... they played in those movies where they smash up all those police cars? I know—that guy in the wet suit in *Deliverance?*"

"Burt Reynolds."

"Yeah, well, he reminds me of him. You know, a fun guy, little ornery around the edges?"

So now Roland was either Jerry Reed or The Rifleman. I said, "Oh, he's fun all right."

"I've dated someone with a record before," she said, or rather whispered, because she was at work.

That took me by surprise. In fact, I was shocked. "You never told me that."

"Well, you never told me you were a stripper before, now, did you?"

I shut my eyes, didn't say anything.

"Roland let me know his whole history. He even told me he'd been picked up and questioned last week. Now, *that* is honest. God, can you believe?"

"The coincidence of him moving in practically next door?"

"Yes. That you and I were right there, right looking at him through that mirror, and six days later . . ."

Yes, I could believe the coincidence. Coincidence kills. That's what it's all about. You, here, in your parents' house when they're on vacation and a plane drops out of the sky on *their* house and no other; you, there, when one mad Iranian decides to drive his truck into a barracks, and you supposed to leave yesterday. Or even simple things, like you in a strange part of town, crossing the street, seeing your boyfriend eating corn dogs with a girl who makes it clear she knows how to use her lips, him practically falling down her blouse. Or you asking for a job at the very same moment one comes available. Coincidence. It's not all bad. I could believe it. Most of the time. But I also couldn't help wondering whether the Dugdales had seen Patricia's license-plate number down at the station, sure that this whole mess was somehow my fault.

"I told him all about you. He wants to meet you. See, he's trying. Give him the benefit."

"You told him what about me?"

"That you do police stuff. I didn't tell him about the other, the stripper business, 'cause I figured—"

"Patricia?"

"What?"

"Enough, okay? I've got to go."

When she said good-bye, she sounded hurt, but I couldn't help that.

I felt a knot in my stomach that a trip to the water cooler couldn't settle. Back at my desk, I dialed the Cozy Inn. I could listen to Rowena Dwyer, and maybe that would be a good thing, not a sufficient thing, but a good thing, to do.

It was three o'clock. Mrs. Dwyer answered. I told her who I was and that I'd gotten her message—and that I was very, very sorry about her son. The voice I heard was not what I expected. The only piece of information I'd had about her was that Jerry had said his mother was a good businessperson. Maybe I expected some corporate heavy, though in the Midwest, where? Chicago, but he didn't say Chicago, and I didn't think it was. The voice was so soft I thought I'd awakened her. She said yes, she wanted to talk to me because her husband—her husband, not her ex-husband, she said—mentioned me. "You're not on the police force, but you're somehow. . . ?"

"I'm a forensics specialist," I said. "Do you know what that is?"

"Not exactly."

"I collect evidence from a crime scene. We process it at the crime lab and try to figure out what happened."

She thought immediately only of fingerprints. I told her we didn't have much. What I didn't tell her was that even if we collected latents—the fingerprints not in blood, but the hidden ones, like off the magazines—matching up is not a certainty; neither is the process fast. If a print isn't nice and neat, as on a fingerprint card, with each little pinky rolled by a cop and pressed in a square so you know where the top is and where the bottom is, matching them up is hell on wheels. After working six months in Prints, you need glasses, even with the aid of a computer, though the computer is such an improvement it's hard to complain. I'd tried reaching Betty Brankoff in Prints earlier, but she wasn't there and whoever answered her phone sounded like he'd been on codeine too long. I left a message.

Throughout our talk, Mrs. Dwyer would stop, gather herself, and press on, but I got the idea that she was a strong person from what she said soon after our conversation began: "Jerry died seven days ago," she said. She didn't say, "It happened seven days ago," or talk about a better place, or ask why it happened to him. She said, "Jerry died seven days ago. That's seven days his killers have been alive that Jerry hasn't."

I asked her what it was she thought I could do for her, why she wanted to talk to me. She said, "I'm not sure what at the moment. But I want you to know I'm here and I'm going to be here for a while. I may need to get in touch with someone."

I said that I understood, but that if she wanted a counselor, I could refer her to the Social Services Department. It sounded cold to me even then.

She said, rather brittlely, "That's not what I meant. If I find out anything, I'd like to talk it over with someone close to the case."

"I'm not really the one—" I began, but she interrupted me

with this: "Could we meet, Miss Brandon? I'd really like to talk to another woman."

"I'm sorry," I said. "I'd like to, but you really should be talking to sheriff's investigators. Have you met Sergeant Gary Svoboda or talked to a Detective Felton?"

"I met Detective Felton. I expect to meet Sergeant Svoboda tomorrow. Tomorrow's the memorial service. In the afternoon I talk to your sergeant." Tough cookie, she'd talk to the sergeant the afternoon of a morning funeral for her *son*. Once more I said I was sorry; that Jerry was a wonderful boy. I started to say: Because I really do understand. But why bring in someone else's grief? "Sorry" is what people said to me when I lost Bill. Other cops, their white dress gloves covering my hands, their eyes red with the emotion they couldn't bring to their lips but for that one inadequate word, said it. Their wives, hugging me with terror in their eyes, said it. You have to go through it in your own way, your own time.

I said, "I could maybe meet with you next week." I'd give her time to get the service over with.

She said, "I'd like to do it tonight, if possible."

It was a peculiar place to meet, Gianni's in Crystal Court, beneath the escalator. I never liked the idea of the place. You're dining at formal tables, served by waiters in tuxlike uniforms, while shoppers glide up and down the escalators next to you with their bags from fancy Italian dress shops, observing, if they wish, which fork you choose. Crystal Court's on the *fahncy* side of South Coast Plaza. Mannequins wear world globes for heads and sequined swimsuits with sequined beach capes. Women with red-red lipstick and white-white skin take their time strolling between shops, and men with silk hankies peeking out of their breast pockets glide by with them. The floors are pink marble, the elevators gleaming brass. On weekends someone's playing classical music on a black baby grand at the throat of the escalators, and now that Christmas was nearing, carols were being played. A gigantic fir tree with toy trains humming around it stood in the center.

We were to meet at five-thirty, and I told Mrs. Dwyer I'd be wearing a tan safari shirt, a black skirt, and black stockings.

It still hadn't rained, and the temperature had shot up to the eighties, so I was without a jacket. She said she had blonde hair and would be wearing a turquoise dress.

I sat dragging my fork over the white tablecloth at one of the little tables, making corn-row patterns. The waiter had brought me coffee and now wine, but he was still glaring though there was hardly anyone in the place. Six-ten, and no Mrs. Dwyer. When she was forty minutes late, I decided to leave. Maybe she'd changed her mind. I couldn't see the waiter, of course. A couple of women who came in after I did were looking around too, so I dug in my purse for money, preparing to leave, when I heard an "Excuse me." A slender blonde woman stood over me. "I'm so sorry," she said. "I just didn't understand the traffic." She extended her hand and said, "Rowena Dwyer."

She was younger than I'd expected. Under her eyes was shiny white stuff to hide circles. Her face was square, pretty. She wore a necklace of tiny white ceramic roses.

As if on cue, the waiter came out. We ordered salads and more wine and wound up mostly not eating them, me getting afraid that one of us, after the wine hit bottom, would get sloppy. I suggested bread, and called the waiter over again. Okay, a side of pasta too.

What Mrs. Dwyer wanted was something I couldn't give: assurance that the hideous thing that happened to her would not happen to some other mother's son. Verification that people did indeed spend the rest of their lives in jail for crimes like these. I couldn't tell her that, either. Sixty percent of all violent crimes are committed by 10 percent of the people that get put in prison, so what does that tell you? It tells you the creeps get out to do more crime, and, in fact, a fifteen-year sentence for murder one is usually completed in seven.

"I left Jerry with his father when he was fifteen," Mrs. Dwyer said. "You can see his father is a lot older than I am. I needed to get my head straight, and he was a good father, so why not?" She was blaming herself for not having had more time with her son. She asked me if she could smoke in here, and though I didn't think so and didn't care for it myself, I nodded. As she lit up, she tossed her shoulder-length hair back. I could imagine what she'd look like at a bar, this single lady, making no-nonsense talk with someone eager to take her home.

"What do you do in Wichita, Mrs. Dwyer?"

"Call me Rowena." I thought she'd be about forty, forty-two. "I'm a creative facilitator," she said, and smiled for the first time.

"What's that? Art shows or something?"

"No. I put inventors and buyers together. A matchmaker. Only it's business, not love."

"That sounds very interesting."

"It can be."

"Mrs. Dwyer, what kind of friends do you think your son hung out with here?"

"I've talked to my son's friends. That's all I did the first two days. Police talked to them too."

"You're pretty sure, then, that nothing funny was going on? I mean, even peripherally, with Jerry an innocent bystander?"

She looked at me dead-on. "Kids don't bullshit me." She took a deep drag on her cigarette and then said rapidly, "Jerry was a handful, yes, when he was younger. But it was because he was big as much as anything, didn't know what to do with all that motor energy. But he never lied to me. He'd come right out and tell me what he did if I asked him. I know the kind of boys he hangs out with. They're all right. I don't think there were drugs. I don't think there was that kind of trouble. But, then, no mother wants to think her kid was into drugs, do they?" She looked at me with an expression of instantaneous doubt and disgust, that maybe she'd been taken in, like thousands, maybe millions, of other mothers.

I said, "I just wanted your opinion. I've met some of his friends too, and they seemed all right."

"It was a robbery, pure and simple," she said. "They brought in that one set of suspects, didn't they, people who do this sort of thing? Then they let them go. I'd like to know why. Nobody will tell me anything."

I told her the Dugdales weren't suspects—officially.

"So they have no leads is what you're saying."

"The police don't tell us lab people everything either."

"So they have nothing."

I couldn't say they did. But what I could give her were the

histories and personalities of people I worked with, their dedication, their cleverness. I told her what I'd said before, what I'd heard others say along the way, in the academy, on the force, and here now, in the lab. That murder is unacceptable. That homicide cases stand open until they're solved. "This one won't get lost," I said, echoing Joe Sanders. "It may not be today, it may not be next week, but it'll get solved."

"That's not good enough," she said.

I said nothing. Waited for her to make the next move.

"Listen," she said, removing the motel's card from her handbag and writing "Rowena Dwyer—Jan. 2" on it. "I'm staying here a few weeks. Other times I'll be at George's." She said she tried staying with her ex-husband when she got out here. They'd hold each other and cry. It got too much for her. She had to leave, and took the motel room then.

"I don't mean to be impertinent, Mrs. Dwyer . . ."

"You're not. Say it. What?"

"Why are you staying?"

She took a sudden drag on her cigarette, blew it out, and said, "I don't know. Let's say it's to keep on somebody's ass. You can understand that, can't you?"

Climbing the stairs when I got home, I felt jittery, maybe from too much coffee, and when I saw my screen door propped open with something, a wash of dread coursed over me, and almost satisfaction, as if I'd been expecting something to be amiss, and now it was. In the door was a rolled, throwaway newspaper; that's all. But mine had come already this morning, and I had tossed it in as I was leaving for work. The paper was tilted up on its end in definite purpose. I picked it up and went in, and when I threw it on the counter above the garbage can, I noticed a long weed fall from it; and when I went to pick them both up to chuck them, I had a strange feeling, and unrolled the paper, and saw a handful of buckwheat, its clusters of pink flowers mashed, and a torn branch of lemonade berry, the red berries from it bled onto the newsprint. Fuck this! Was this funny? Somebody's idea of a gift? I wondered if some new cowboy had moved in downstairs—I recognized the flowers from the marsh below the bluff west of my house.

The next morning I tried to see Joe. "Gone on a trip," somebody said. Gone. I should have made a point to see him more during the week, learn what the progress was on the case. The kiss threw me off. As much as I cared for him, that strange kiss made me wonder if I'd estimated him correctly. I'd tried hard not to give the incident more than fleeting moments of thought, and didn't drop by as often as I might have had it not happened. It was just too overwhelming, trying to figure what a sudden, aggressive, even desperate kiss meant. I didn't have *time* to think of what I was going to do about it, or frame whatever it was I should say when the subject came up. Maybe, I thought, it would never come up. We'd just go on like nothing happened, two people who enjoyed working together. But it had also occurred to me that he was from the old school, a generation away from mine, in which if a woman fell victim to her own bad judgment and to unforgiving office gossip, she became, in some people's minds, open prey. After all, I'd misjudged Patricia. Why not Joe?

I went to talk to Trudy. "Who's in charge of the Dwyer case while Joe S. is gone?" I asked her. She shrugged her shoulders and looked at me blankly, a pencil still in her hand.

"Talk to Stu, I guess." The distance seemed to be there again. She returned to her drawing. Under Trudy's wrist a woman's face was taking shape.

"A Doe?" I asked. She said yes.

In the course of a year, the coroner's office would see approximately 2,500 bodies, maybe 150 of them murder victims. Of those 2,500, maybe 100 will have no ID for a while. Then the coroner's people go to work trying to identify them, bringing in specialists who reconstruct faces—by sticking match sticks in the bones at certain heights and then blanketing over the whole thing with clay—and running restored fingerprints through the sheriff's computer system, and then the state's, and the FBI's. People want to *know* when their loved ones die.

I told Trudy about my concern, the magazines. She didn't know. I went back to my desk and phoned Gary, left a message, then called Bud Peterson. He told me the magazines had been sprayed with ninhydrin to bring up the latents.

Joe Sanders came through the doorway of my office and stopped as soon as he saw me on the phone, turning as if to go back out, but waiting. So he *was* here. He hadn't left.

Maybe he'd thought it through and decided I deserved an apology. I held his look but had to talk to Peterson.

"All of them?" I said.

"We can't do every magazine, every page."

"Well, then, you *didn't* dust them."

"I said we did."

Joe waved a hand at me and left.

Peterson was going on: "We do our job in a conscientious manner. Just like you. We got lifts off plenty other places."

"But none turned out a positive."

"Yet," he said.

I was getting nowhere. I had a lot of work to do. After I hung up, I started in on just getting paper off my desk again. It piles up like you wouldn't believe. Somebody wanted to start a softball team—the first and the third sheets in my "In" bin. A missive misdirected to me: a report on an infant SID case that turned out to be botulism. Then a reminder from Joe, in memo form, that we shouldn't use the term *perimortem* to convey the approximate time of death; it won't hold up in court.

I got a call from Joe one minute before lunch. Still here. "Smokey, I have to tell you: I'm sorry."

It took me by surprise he'd bring it up first. "What's going on, Joe? You've been different lately."

"Smokey, I can't talk now. I just want to apologize and tell you it won't happen again."

What came out was, "That's cool." Put some distance between us, even generational. It brought silence on the other end, and then I felt pity. He really shouldn't be in such a spot.

"We'll talk, Smokey."

"It's okay, Joe—I *said*. Really."

"No. We'll talk."

"Wait, Joe. I'm a little bugged right now. I found something on my doorstep that kind of unnerved me. Just flowers rolled up in a newspaper, but it kind of bothers me."

"You've got an admirer."

"They were crushed. Wrung, is a better word for it."

"I've really got to run, Smoke."

"Have a good trip."

I put the phone down, realized I was tired. No, I was hungry, the smell of popcorn wafting my way from the direction of the microwave. Trudy Kunitz came walking down the hallway with a paper bag of popcorn. "Trudy," I called. "Spare some of that?"

"Sure."

As she marched in, I opened my drawer and took out a folded paper towel from the ladies' room. She spilled out about two handfuls onto it. "You're a lifesaver," I said.

"The old stomach complaining, huh?"

"Say, you want to go to lunch?"

"I've got a big backlog. The DA's office is on my back for some stuff too. That biker case? The third victim in the biker case died this morning, so we got a triple." She was referring to two, now three, execution-type murders that occurred in Anaheim, the place where kiddie kitsch meets violent crime.

She said, "Do you know there's a word for stomach rumbling?" She was going to tell me. *"Borborygmus,"* she said.

"It's that obvious?"

"I could hear you out in the *hall.*" She was being positively friendly. She looked me directly in the eye and leaned one haunch against the end of the desk while she munched her popcorn. Maybe all she needs is a prop like popcorn.

I said, "I like your blouse."

"Oh, yeah, I bought it off my brother." It was black and had lightning strikes across it in rainbow colors. "My brother's eleven. I can wear his clothes. The shirts, anyway."

"Whatever works," I said, smiling at her.

"Hey," she said casually, shoving three fingers' worth of popcorn in her mouth, "you hear Sanders left his wife?"

CHAPTER
17

So Joe L. Sanders left his wife, huh? That really pissed me off. How could he leave Jennifer and move, apparently, to my neck of the woods, and not tell me? Feel so sorry for himself he grabs me as if I'm his property and plants one on me that even hurt my lip? At the same time I wanted to tell him I'm sorry, that I know it hurts to lose someone, even when it's long overdue. I'd loved before and I'd love again, and one thing I know is that love don't come without price, pardon the lack of grammar. And then I'd tell him not to come within fifty feet of me till he gets over his divorce-dotty-blues, wherein everybody's nuts for at least a year and a half.

Friday afternoon I got in touch with the woman in CAL-ID about the magazines. She said on magazines in store racks there could be billions of fingerprints. Billions and billions. And then she said she never saw any magazines from the Dwyer case.

I called Gary's number. A deputy I didn't know answered and took my message asking about the photo array.

An hour and a half later I stepped away from my desk for five minutes, and, wouldn't you know, Gary called back. Kathleen answered it at the front desk. She left a pink slip that said, "Gary Boda. No luck on mugs," and then "K.K.," her initials, and the eyes and mouth of a happy face. She was lousy about taking messages; I was glad she got that much. But she was definitely cheery. The lab director liked cheery.

The "No luck on mugs" disheartened me. Gary wasn't supposed to take the six-pack to Emilio until tomorrow, but he must've squeezed out an hour.

That night I got home and walked my old-lady neighbor's dog, even though it was really too dark to take him safely down to the bay. Mrs. Lambert gets along fine most of the time, but sometimes arthritis prevents her from letting that beautiful thing out, and I feel sorry for him. She named the setter after the redheaded boyfriend who gave the pup to her for her sixty-third birthday. The dog stayed longer than the man. Farmer whimpers and slobbers when he sees me, knowing what I'm there for. Down on the path, he strains to investigate. If I think a park ranger isn't bound to come by, I let him off leash and he plays games with whatever croaks or whistles under the brush, then comes running back, tongue dangling out one side and a smile on his face. He gets locked in the mud sometimes, comes clogging out with black rubber balls glued to his feet. More than once I've nearly landed on my fanny in that mud-and-plankton biomass. Back at the condo, out on the front lawn, I have to hose him off. I keep a small bottle of dishwashing detergent in the bushes near the faucet. He whimpers, but he loves it, I know he does.

This evening it was colder than I liked, a wind cutting in off the farther waters, though it had been hot all day. My ears began to ache soon after we went out. I wouldn't let Farmer go far. I felt grouchy, and sorry I took him out in the first place, and, after about fifteen minutes, took him home. Climbing the stairs, I thought about the silence in my apartment, and that there was nothing on TV Friday nights anymore since *Miami Vice* went off. My favorite had been *Crime Story*, its endings bitter or unresolved as in real life. They moved *America's Most Wanted* to this night, but I got tired of watching it and always felt a little prurient doing so anyway, I wasn't sure why. So I went out for roasted chicken and a salad from Albertson's before I picked up my groceries.

When I got home, I wondered who might still be at the lab. Before I unloaded the groceries, I dialed. Billy answered.

"You're always there," I said. "Or somewhere."

"Everybody's gotta be somewhere. Actually, I was waiting for you to call," he said.

"Listen, Billy? Hearken back to the Kwik Stop murder in Costa Mesa. Did you see anybody collect any magazines?"

"Wouldn't Joe be able to tell you that?"

"He's on a trip somewhere."

"You call Prints?"

"Yes. I get conflicting stories."

"Check with Property."

"I'm asking you, Billy."

"I have no idea. My job is taking pictures. You figure the killers thought they were in the library?"

"I think the assailants were in that store a long time before commission, and they might've been looking at magazines, you know, to eyeball the place awhile."

"Can't help ya, doll."

"What could we have missed? Think, Billy. I know you just do photos, but brainstorm with me here."

"You make it sound like I *just* do photos. I'll have you know some people value me for other expertise."

I was silent, thinking about what other avenue I could push somebody to pursue. Billy was trying to be funny, and I wasn't cooperating.

He said, "Hey, it's Friday night."

"I know it's Friday night."

"You got a date?"

I was quiet again.

"Obviously not, or you wouldn't be on the phone to me. How about it? Let's you and me go out. Maybe to Dove Street. Been there?"

"Yes."

"Okay, maybe to . . . I know: Crackers. It's a great place. They got singers, dancers, a guy in a gorilla suit who'll dance with you better than me. Well, I take that back. But you can eat good ribs and sing along to the dirty lyrics."

"*No*, Billy."

"Why not?"

"I'm not going out with you. I told you that."

"All work and no play . . ."

"Stop wooing me with clichés. *Stop wooing me.*"

He cooed and whined a little bit, but he knew it was a losing game. I couldn't get mad at him. I finally even had to laugh when he asked me, "You don't like people of Armenian descent, do you?"

"Who was the patrol cop on that case, Billy? You remember?"

"Senior Patrol Collis Banks."

"Hm. You're good, Katch."

"That means you've changed your mind? No. Sigh. But talking to Banks won't do you any good. Why don'tcha just read the file?"

"Why won't it do me any good?"

"He's done gawn, my purty little thang."

"What do you mean, he's gone?"

"Moved on to LAPD. The Big Time. He was telling me that the day of the crime. He lateralized over there, after waiting three years."

"Oh, no. I could still call him. Maybe there's something that's not in the case file."

"You could. If his tongue's not up the chief's ass so he can make it to the phone."

"Take care, Billy."

"I always do."

When I hung up, I remembered the round cloud of cat at Billy's place, whose head turned only once in a while to check on some sound perhaps, and that part I liked.

Saturday was the funeral. Maybe I should have gone, but I felt somehow it would be an intrusion.

It had been hot for a week, and Christmas was around the corner, and the whole thing made me grouchy. At ten-thirty, about the last moment I had to make up my mind about going to the service, I walked down to the bay, and soon I was sizzling. Someone I passed there said he heard it was supposed to be 98, 99 degrees today. I continued on to my three-mile marker, almost the complete circuit of the bay, and back again, and began to feel sick to my stomach. Once I meant to duck into the shade of a mule-fat tree, not careful to look first, and just about got plowed under by a group of about twelve bicyclists in helmets and neons, the noise as they whizzed past like strong wind in a tunnel. I jumped back into some low-growing red leaves and thought what we need is a Chippie, a CHP guy, down here for the bikers. Then I thought, looking at the leaves sweeping my ankles, Oh, great: "Leaves of three, let it be," thinking poison oak or ivy.

Sunday morning I went down to the Winchells' where I knew Raymond sometimes grabbed coffee. It's true what the comics say, about cops and doughnuts. Coppers don't get those guts for nothing, though Orange County cops are pretty fit, I'd say. Ray's *mogambo* wheels were out front. I caught him coming out.

"Can you spare an old bud some time?" I said.

"Sure. Come along with me down to the substation. I've got something I need to drop off." He works South County, out of San Juan Capistrano, home of the swallows. A friend took me horseback riding at the San Juan stables one day, pointing out that our sheriff's wife is the owner. There was a stew about that once, her business somehow mixed up with his, and more stew about how the sheriff acquired the building supplies for the house he built up on the side of a hill overlooking the 405 freeway, but I never got into that sort of gossip—it's easy to accuse, hard to defend. That's why we have The System. Joe keeps reminding me of that, even as we do the lowly evidence analyzing: Don't push, don't prove something that's not there—that's not your job. Use care, common sense, good judgment, once in a while gut feel. Keep current in the profession, which was what he was off doing now, I learned—taking a seminar—and keep an open mind, but don't judge. Every one of us does, even he. But he won't say a word about the sheriff.

"Raymond," I said while we were in the car, "putting your and my feelings aside concerning a certain pair of criminal-type no-goodniks, do you think I'm obsessing?"

His intelligent face showed a little tautness at the jaw, but he said, "All you got is a collet and an opinion, babe. Am I right? Could be a collet like that is used in a bunch of different trades."

"I told you. The man in San Pedro said they don't fuse like that in any other profession. Usually."

"That could be something, that *usually*. When you let your mind run away with you, you *can* start to see things in the shadows, friend." He tilted an eyebrow at me.

"God, it's hot," I said. "How hot do you think it is today?"

"Upper eighties."

"Shit, don't they know it's December around here? Why do we live here, Raymond?"

We drove for a while, me frowning a lot, I guess, because he said then, "I don't like it either, Smokey, Roland Dugdale up next to your friend so convenient like that. The Kwik Stop thing and everything. But it's so bizarre, how could it be anything but coincidence? I mean, can you feature the guy committing a crime and then hanging out near anyone who has anything to do with the Po-lice?"

"He does have a record of these things, stop-and-robs."

"I know."

"So what can I do?"

"Nothing that I know of."

"*Fuck* this, Raymond."

He drove a long time without saying anything, throwing on his yellows just to get people out of the way. I felt bad that I was so grumpy, so I rode the rest of the way with my mouth shut.

Monday came, and Tuesday slipped by, because I got involved in matching duct tape found in some bushes and on the mouth of a floater in a bad state of decomp, discovered in the Peters Canyon Reservoir.

It wasn't that I forgot about Jerry. It's just that there're only so many hours in a day—exactly what I was worried would happen. His face was getting dimmer and dimmer to me.

And then on Thursday a lot of us were out in the scrub brush near Rattlesnake Reservoir and Hicks Canyon in the eastern part of the county, searching for body parts.

CHAPTER
18

I found a foot, and bagged it. It was a man's. I found a torso under a sheet of drywall, and was able to heave the wall over because I was standing on a coffee table. Even with the stomach down and the head gone and the legs under the L of an upside-down couch, I knew it was a woman's because of the crease of bra strap across the back, under the navy blue knit shirt.

We were fifteen miles out in the Loma Ridge area near the edge of a new housing development. The pattern of houses funneled out through sparse stands of black oak, chaparral, and coastal sage scrub. We were there probing one small pocket of red-roofed stucco houses that should've been impervious to any disaster save a random coyote snatching small white dogs in the misty A.M. But early *this* morning, at the right-most end of the funnel's triangle, it was as if a bored, bony witch decided to poke a knobby hand down on a map one day and say, "Here, right . . . here," and a four-seater Cessna took a plunge. Now a bunch of normal-looking people were deep in the wild purple artichokes and dried deer grass, matching parts. The torso I found was the third so far dead on the ground.

I looked around for help and saw the rookie Simmons near one of the refrigerated moving vans we'd had to rent to supplement our own Coroner's Disaster Team vehicles. He wasn't just standing around messing up dust this time. He'd been working with the forensic anthropologist we rely on so much in cases like this, helping her bag and filling out tags as she reeled off the info. Now he was drinking from a cup out of

one of the big insulated water jugs we use for remote loca-
tions. I couldn't recall the rookie's first name, so I waved him
over by calling his last, asking could he bring a stretcher and
a few more brown plastic bags. He yelled, "Right," and slipped
his mask back on, while I peeled off my gloves and dug for
another pair in my hip pocket; the rubber had sheared off
somehow on the little finger of one of the ones I threw down.
The anthropologist was off to the right and up ahead of him,
unspringing a wide-brimmed hat I'd seen her wear before—a
funny pink, purple, and yellow Southern-belle thing with a
chin strap and bead to pinch it in place; with a flick of her
hand, she would twist it into a figure eight to fit into a front
pocket of her army-type vest. All morning the sky had been
bright white with overcast, and now there was a disconcerting
yellow cast caused by the earth's present tilt on its axis, a winter light that always depressed me more than a cloudy day.
The anthropologist slipped sunglasses on, the kind with an
iridescent patina on the lenses, saying "beach scene" more
than "crash site." She'd had to have a little skin cancer removed from her nose. Normally she would've had the hat on
before this.

This woman does most of our reconstruction work, building
clay faces out of skulls, identifying and dating bones. Her
name is Jeri Landsforth, a Ph.D. and a real soul. I thought if
I ever got tired of working for Joe—or around Joe—maybe
I'd quit and go see what I could do for her. Simmons was at
my side when I heard Jeri's hollow voice sound out, "Aw, no."

We stepped over the debris to where she stood, her hands
hanging down by her sides, eyes fixed on a pink puff of something. Coming closer, we saw it was a little brown baby in a
pink bunting suit—just there, eyes closed, fist to its tiny pug
nose, no visible damage, as if it had dropped off a stork's
wing. But not breathing.

I heard myself say an "Oh, no" too, and Simmons utter a
quiet "Shit" inside his mask. He poked a finger up inside his
glasses and touched the bridge of his nose.

Jeri reached down with both hands and plucked the little
thing up, turned, and headed back toward the van, a gasp of
wind flipping up the front brim of her hat and pasting it
there, forehead bald to the sun.

Simmons and I walked back to the spot I'd left. I told him we were looking for a woman's head, and a right arm.

On block-wall fences and the unfinished hills beyond the housing tract were people, not many, watching, figuring out what happened and whose house it would've hit had it been a little to the east or a tad to the west.

We worked all night, the fire trucks bringing in special illumination setups. We had to, to secure the area from all sorts of raiders, furry, feathery, or otherwise. Once or twice I looked up to see a string of colored Christmas lights along the eaves of a house, and I wondered if the people inside felt terror, or gratitude, or sadness, or calm, and pondered what part religion played in most of their lives, and if any of them could adequately explain away this.

My new boss, Stu Hollings, was there the whole time, I'll give him that. He works. What he lacks in personnel skills, he makes up for in dedication. He said, when we were all gathered at the Irvine P.D. Communications Vehicle on the second afternoon, "You've done a good job here, people." I was pleased to hear it from him, for a lot of people who don't often work overtime worked for this one when they could have been out crawling malls for Christmas. "I want you to go home and relax, try to do some things that'll clear your minds. Go see a movie, or . . ."

And someone interrupted and said, "They're more bloody than this," and everybody laughed.

The night before the air disaster, I'd called Patricia after work and got her answering machine. Three days later, on a Saturday, she called me. I was lying on the couch with my binos, looking at a pair of ruby-throated hummingbirds that regularly come to feed on the four-feet-high purple Ladies of the Nile in three pots on the patio, and on the tubular pink blossoms of my hanging Christmas cactus. "He's been in here again," she said.

I sat up. My arms felt heavy.

She said, "Someone's been in my apartment. You know how your milk carton tents in when you close it?"

"Yes."

"Well, mine was tented out. Out, instead of in."

I could picture it, but I said, "That's all?" The humming-birds zinged over in front of my picture window and hovered there, staring, as if to ask, Who is that on the phone, and, Can we come in?

Patricia said, "Like somebody drank from it, is what I mean." She sounded annoyed with me. "You know how boys drink from a carton and put it back in? That's what it looked like. My brother used to do it all the time. Someone drank from my milk and put it back like that." Patricia had lost her brother to cocaine long before it was the drug of America's choice, way back in the mid-seventies, when she was fourteen. She sounded pitiful, really. I said, "Are you missing anything? Jewelry. . . ?"

"No. Well—my blue leather belt. But that's been missing awhile." She let up a little then, and laughed and said, "You steal my blue leather belt, Samantha?" That was the first time she'd called me Samantha in a while. I took it as a sort of apology, for making too much of my youthful past. "I know what you're thinking," she said. "But you just *know*, you just somehow *know*, when somebody's been in your house. Like what I told you about before, in the toilet. And before you say anything, let me say there was something else, too. My curtains in front? They were pulled off to the left about three inches, like someone was standing there to look out."

"Patricia, I know you're worried, but who could go in there? Think about it. If I sweated every time I put my keys in the refrigerator, I'd be looking up shrinks' phone numbers." I said this, after Ray's little lecture to me in the car, but I felt my stomach muscles go tight, and the picture of the rolled newspaper with the lemonade berry branch squashed in it came to mind, and while we talked I thought of the several other times weird guys have done weird things to me, but I didn't mention it.

She said, "Maybe you're right. Listen—change of subject. I want you to meet Roland. In fact, I have a great idea: We're going out on the Seal Beach pier tonight, have dinner out there. Watch the sun go down. Why don't you come?"

"No, thanks, Patricia."

"You'll see Roland is only trying to get along in this world.

He's really major sweet, Samantha. His brother Phillip also. The whole family—well, the father's dead, but the mother had an addiction problem and is now drug-free and Phillip is in Alcoholics Anonymous."

"A regular all-American family," I said.

"You're not even willing to give him one ounce of a chance, are you?"

I closed my eyes and didn't say anything.

"Think it over. You might learn something," she said. "Not all people are bad. Even ones who maybe did bad things for a while. Well? You coming?"

"I don't think so."

"Coward."

Here was an opportunity to interview my main suspect. And I was passing on it? "You have such a way with words."

"We'll pick you up."

"No. I'll drive. I like my own car."

"Be that way."

"Yes, ma'am, I will."

At the restaurant, I spotted Patricia's orange Peugeot right away because the lot wasn't that crowded yet. I thought, The guy uses her car, her gas too, all the time?

She and Roland were at a back table, up against a window. The sky behind them was white and stark, and the sun's brightness pitched a solid glare off the green water whenever it broke through the clouds. They weren't going to get a good sunset after all, it looked like.

Patricia was wearing a tangerine East Indian–type dress, flowy. A pearl comb pulled her auburn hair back over one ear, and she had gotten a bit of a tan since I last saw her, so that when she smiled, she was a definite show-stopper. "Hi, c'mere and sit down," she said, all in one breath. Roland half-stood when I approached; the gesture surprised me. I took the chair beside Patricia as she said, "Roland, this is Samantha Brandon; Samantha, Roland." As he forked over a hand and shook mine, Patricia added, "She goes by Smokey." A grin crawled to one side of his mouth. I held on his eyes, the duplicate color of the ocean behind him, long enough to say, I'm ready to read you, baby, make no mistake about it. His hair was clean and, with the bleached tips, looked polished, and I wondered if he didn't do a dip with Miss Clairol himself, though that's okay if he did; lots of SoCal men do. He had on tight rock-washed jeans and a black short-sleeved shirt with a vertical light green stripe in it, a tight, strong package, and if I shut my mind off, I could see the appeal.

I'll give him this: He was direct. He said, "I hear you're a cop."

The busboy came with water, and as I sat waiting for the arms to get out of my face, I caught Roland's other look, the one behind the innocent statement.

"I work in the evidence lab, is all."

"I thought about being a officer of the law once myself."

"No kidding."

Patricia said, "Will wonders never cease?"

"It was that or the navy, long as it's blue. But Okie boys don't always make the best choices for theirselves." And then he drilled a long look at my friend and added, "'Cept starting right now. Ain't that right, Snookums?"

"Give me a *break*," she said, but she liked it. "You call me that one more time, and I'll give *you* a break."

He asked me, "Y'all were down at the station, when me and my brother were conductin' business there, huh? That's what Snookums tells me." Patricia's leg jumped and Roland's moved and bumped into mine and held there four seconds until I moved mine. "She's got a nasty boot," he said.

"It's a small world, I guess."

"I think she's got a boyfriend locked down she don't want to tell me about." He reached his right hand over and swept his forefinger across the back of her hand like a windshield wiper. Then he slowly cranked his head to me, and winked.

I said, "I thought I saw you in the parking lot."

"Now, if I'da seen two pretty little dollies like you, I'd sure remember it. No, Phil and me picked up our fishin' license and then we did split."

"Fishing license?" Patricia said.

"You don't get them there," I told her. I smiled at Roland then. We're all just good buddies here.

He nodded to me and half-winked. "You could put one over on her, couldn't ya?" Drawing Patricia's hand to his lips and kissing her knuckles, he said, "I saw this one climbing in that orange Frog car, and I just said to myself, Now, that's a pretty good-lookin' long tall drink o' water."

A waiter with dark hair dangling in his face came and took drink orders. I said I wouldn't be eating. Patricia gave me a look without expression, but I knew she was critical. I'd hear about it.

I said, "What kind of work do you do, Roland?"

"Whatever pays best."

"He's going to start studying computers." Patricia smiled.

Roland clinked the tines of his fork on the empty wineglass, to the tap of "Shave-and-a-Haircut, Four-Bits." He said, "I've been doing some ocean work, underwater repair, like on them offshore oil rigs?"

I nodded. Tell it all, Dork Man.

"My job's going to finish up here next week. I might go to Hawaii. Anybody want to come along?" He smiled at Patricia and pulled her fingertips to meet his so that the two of them sat there making spiders, and then gave me a look that said we could make it a threesome if I want.

The drinks came. I swallowed an old-fashioned in three mouthfuls and chawed the fruit while Patricia talked about making money in real estate and Roland's eyes turned greener. His knee wandered into mine.

I said I had to go. Roland said, "Hey, Mothers Against Drunk Drivers'll getcha. You chucked that shooter right down."

"Mind your own business, Roland," said Patricia. "Smokey can take care of herself."

"I'll bet she can. But you know what? I get the feeling Smokey—say, that's a great name, you know it?"

"See you. Take it easy." I stood up and put a fiver on the table.

Roland dragged on, his voice, I'll admit, grabbing me by the throat because I like them that way. He said, "I get the feeling Smokey here don't like me a bit. Now, how can that be, a nice guy like me?"

Patricia's face cleared and then charged with alertness, as if I might say something wrong.

I said, still standing, "I might as well come out with it, Roland. I don't particularly like the fact that you just happened

to show up in her apartment complex after seeing us that
night. That clear enough for you?"

"Oh-h, now I see it. You tell her about me, Patricia, my little
brushes with the law *a long time ago*?" He asked her, but he
was looking at me. "I thought a person got a second chance
in this country. What'd I go to Nam for if that ain't so?"

I shook my head and laughed and said, "Don't give me that
Nam bullshit, Roland, and just watch your step, okay?, with
my friend."

Patricia directed the remark to me: "Stop it—" and I half-
assed saluted and said, "Talk to you later."

Roland said, "See ya around, Sunshine."

A few days passed, and I hadn't heard from Patricia. Nothing
new turned up on the Dwyer case, and Christmas was closing
in and I hadn't bought a thing. I stopped by Patricia's apartment once to see if she wanted to go shopping, but she was
not at home; called once, but hung up before the answering
machine would click on. The idea of Patricia with Roland dis-
tressed me, but I know one thing: You can't make a person
see the truth unless they're ready. "A man convinced against
his will is of the same opinion still"—I memorized that once
when I was a kid.

And then one day I got a call on *my* answering machine
from Patricia's apartment manager. Patricia was ten days overdue on the rent, she said, and Patricia had put my name down
on her rental application as a reference.

CHAPTER
19

Hawaii must've sounded pretty good to Patricia. I called back the Fairdale Apartments and asked if Patricia hadn't given some relatives for references. The landlady said, "I been calling for three days, and zilch. She gives an aunt here too, in Moline, Illinois. I call, she hasn't been at that number for over a year."

"What about Patricia's employer?"

"I go to them first off," she said. "She's on vacation. I say, 'When's she coming back?' He says, 'One week Tuesday,' but my creditors don't wait one week Tuesday."

Five needles attacked the lower right side of the back of my head. I hunched up my shoulder. Jesus, what was this now? A psychosomatic something. I was falling apart. The problem was, if Patricia went to Hawaii, would she have been mad enough at me not to tell me? She told me everything.

I told the landlady I'd bring the money over for the rent. She said, "You better do it before seven o'clock tomorrow morning, or I'm hauling her stuff down to storage."

"Don't do that," I said, "please."

"I don't want to pack it up neither. That's no fun and I got plenty to do here. Can you be here by seven A.M.?"

"Yes. I'll be there."

"Then everything'll be all right."

I thanked her. She said, "Sometimes these young ones go off. They're havin' a good time, they forget. I know how it is, I was young once. But you got to pay the piper."

"Patricia wouldn't have gone off without paying her rent, ordinarily. I know her. There must've been an emergency."

Of course I didn't know her, as the last few weeks' events had revealed.

I thought I heard a sigh at the other end. "Could you bring cash?" the landlady said. I said, Yes, and thanks again, and started to hang up. "Better bring maybe three dollars more to pay for Moline."

I sat near a window in the law library where I could look out on the concrete courtyard and see all the people threading their way between a hot dog vendor and the Federal Building, and looked up Mr. and Mrs. Harris's neighbors in Greensboro, North Carolina, in a reverse directory. When I got names of people residing on either side of the Harrises', I went back to my office and called an A. B. Winters first.

A soft Southern voice came on the line: "Hello?" I could hear kids in the background, and shrieks and water splashing. "Oh," the voice said, "just a moment, please." The receiver was being laid down, *ka-clunk.*

"Children," the voice called, "quieten down now, all right? Mam-maw's talkin' on the phone. Yes, William, I see, that's good. You all quieten down for just a minute, hm?" It seemed a long time until she came back. I imagined her heavy side-to-side gait across a braided carpet on a hardwood floor. I imagined a pie in the oven, and Mrs. Winters brushing back a strand of flyaway gray hair as she retrieved the phone. "Now, what can I do for you?"

As if on cue, Joe L. Sanders appeared at my door. He looked a little put out because I was on the phone. He walked in and took a pen and a piece of note paper off my desk and began to write something.

"Ms. Winters? I'm calling from California—"

Joe looked up, raising an eyebrow. No doubt he'd ask me what the long-distance call was for later, as if it were out of his own budget. Stu Hollings was a bean counter too, but not as bad as Joe.

"You don't know me, but . . ." I said, and asked her if she was a neighbor of Patricia Harris's parents, only I didn't say Patricia Harris's parents with Joe standing there; I said Mr. and Mrs. Herman J. Harris.

He slid the paper toward me, glanced at me, and left. The note said, "See me before you go home. Please." I wanted to say yes to him or nod or something, but he never looked back.

As I spoke to the Harrises' neighbor, I tried not to alarm her, and I think I was successful in that. She said the Harrises had been on a cruise to Spain and the Greek islands for two weeks. They had one more to go. The first they'd ever been on, and they were very excited.

"Was their daughter Patricia with them?"

"No, I don't believe I heard them mention that. Can I do anything to help?" I told her no, I'd call back. She said, "I think they said the Greek islands," then paused. "Are there Greek islands?" And then answered herself: "Yes, I think so." She laughed and said, "I've never been."

At the front driveway to the Fairdale Apartments, a free-standing directory holding the names of the residents was enclosed in a wood-framed glass box. I looked through the strips of blue-and-black labeling tape for "Dugdale." Found it. Whoever punched the label hit the ampersand instead of the pound sign: &210. The manager's was #100.

Driving through passageways narrow as alleys, I intended to spot number 210 first, lock its location in my mind, and come back to it later, after handing over seven hundred of my hard-earned dollars.

The apartments were grouped in circular segments and painted deep gray with white trim. Clouds of lavender impatiens and pink vinca poofed out along patches of too-green lawn by each apartment, the sod newly installed in visible blocks. Palms, their fronds still tied up at the top to prevent transplant shock, lined the roadways. Rustlers can get five thousand dollars for the tall ones, complete with nesting rats, but these palms were only about ten feet high and probably worth no more than five hundred, so they just might survive awhile. Nailed high into the stucco of some of the end apartments was an occasional brass unit letter out of sequence. This is a test: You can't live here unless you can figure out the system.

Halfway down one of the asphalt passageways I saw a Bronco parked under an open carport with maybe thirty empty spaces around it; black, looking like one of our police vehicles without the six-pointed star on the side. Ours are full of wooden drawers holding flares, lanterns, first-aid stuff, yellow tarps. But this one, if it was a Dugdale's, full of what? Diving gear? B-and-E goodies? I stopped behind it. The license plate bore an unremarkable seven-character tag, but it was the plate frame that interested me, and I memorized the license plate anyway: two-Mike-Hotel-Xray-six-fourteen. The frame was from a dealership in Victorville, a high-desert town a solid hour and a half northeast of Los Angeles, full of coarse sand, strong wind, and spiky Joshua trees. The city used to be little more than a highway gas stop; a drunken man could walk home hoisting his brown sack in happiness and baying at the moon until about ten years ago. Nearby, Roy Rogers, Dale Evans, and their stuffed horse, Trigger, could listen to the wind whooing out over the far hills that cradle dude ranches and spas deep in their shadows. Now there were Kmarts and apartment houses within rock-throwing distance of the freeway. But restaurants still served country breakfasts with white gravy, and women with rolls of flesh around their middles laughed hard, talked with cigarettes in their mouths, and didn't give a damn. The thing was, it was still a desert town, with a desert mentality, and somebody like Roland Dugdale would be from Victorville—or Texas or Oklahoma—the point being, someplace with large landscapes just a little left-side of the law. I almost pulled into the spot next to the Bronco. But I went on. Find the lady. Pay the lady. Come back. Go knock on Roland's door and ask what the fuck he thought he was doing.

I found her, I paid her. She gave me a receipt I was prepared to ask for, then said, "I guess you know if she doesn't show up, I'm entitled to store her stuff and let the apartment out to somebody else." She was wearing an all-over bright-pink polyester pant outfit, and her hair was orange and thin on top so you could see the very pale scalp. She said this to her desk while she was putting away my cash, and when I didn't respond, she looked up at me.

Fastening the latch on my purse, I said, "No, I didn't know that." I smiled and said, "But I'll sure look up the code," and left out the screen door.

I must have driven at least twice past the spot where I

thought the Bronco was because of the damned layout—and because I couldn't believe it was gone. Not that soon. But it was.

I wheeled into a slot and got out, seeking number 210. When I found it, my heart was beating hard enough for me to hear it in my ears. I took a breath and knocked. Waited. Saw a bell nearly obscured by bushes, and rang.

No answer. As I started off to walk the opposite direction around the hexagonal path, I slowed and looked in a window of apartment 210. A red sweater was draped across the back of a couch near the window. On the floor at the other end was a mound of clothes near an empty laundry basket, and across from the couch a guitar case leaned upright on a cantaloupe-colored loveseat. The furniture was whitewashed pine and the colors were fashionably soft—so far, not a place, it seemed, that a country boy or a deep-sea diver would rent. Doubt swept over me. Did I even have the apartment number right from the registry? I was confused and felt foolish lingering at someone's picture window like a snoop. I stepped away but glanced back and could see the corner of the dining-room table. Outlined there were two wine bottles and several beer cans. Now, if I could just see a diver's suit, a helmet with brails. How about a gun, a pistol, say, with big focking rounds lined up ready to be loaded. How about something *concrete*, I told myself. And walked away, disappointed, disgruntled, and disgusted.

CHAPTER
20

All week it wore on me, where Patricia could be, and how this thing happened with Dugdale. Saturday I worked, and Sunday I did the usual maintenance stuff: grocery-getting, laundry, gasoline. Then, back from my last foray out, my key still in the front door and the door open a crack, I heard a familiar engine, and looked down. From the second-story walkway that leads to my unit, I saw Patricia's Peugeot pulling around the circular red-brick courtyard, seeking one of the few parking places available to visitors. There's a stone fountain in the center of the courtyard, with small yellow and blue flowers popcorning around it, and the sun turned the cascading water into a cellophane umbrella.

Both front doors opened. As Patricia folded out of her side, Roland Dugdale ducked out of his, wearing a lime-green shirt, an open brown leather jacket over that, sand-colored shorts, and beach thongs. Then the rear door opened, and the top of someone's head, a woman's, emerged, the hair shiny and dark, chin-length. Patricia said something to the woman, and then they were all of them coming toward the stairs below where I stood on the balcony, Patricia looking up, spotting me. She called out, "Smokey, here! We've come to say hello."

I just stared and let them come up, pulling my door shut, and moved to the top of the stairs—Roland Dugdale wasn't coming into my apartment.

A long box of sun lit up the pebble-surfaced stairway and fired Patricia's hair as she ascended.

Roland looked up once, his green eyes splintering into mine. Between Patricia and Roland, the other one, the girl, about my height but more delicate, and pale. As she squinted into the glare of sun, I saw that she was young, younger than Patricia and I.

"Smokey . . . what's the matter?" Patricia said, coming toward me. "Listen, you shouldn't have. You didn't need to do that. I mean, thank you and all, but really, you didn't need to pay my *rent.*" She laughed her nervous laugh, with only one of the two dimples forming. "I brought money to pay you back." She began ferreting in the black patterned purse that hung from her shoulder and across the Australian outfit I knew she got from Olivia Newton-John's billabong shop or whatever she calls it, at Mainplace. "Here, meet my friend," she said, extracting a wad of bills from her purse and waving it toward the pale girl. I saw the perennial sweetness of Patricia's face, and in her eyes the readiness to accept all things, and thought for a moment, She's better than I, kinder, more tolerant, open. Innocent; and that man too, and this new girl, this Southern California Saks Fifth Avenue–decorated girl standing behind Roland; in this country, *innocent* until *established* guilty by means I was privileged to have at my disposal, not by bias, not by reaction, not by emotion. Innocent. Look Roland in the face and acknowledge innocence. Look.

"This is Annabel Diehl, she works with me, and, of course, you know—"

I didn't even look at Annabel. My attention was focused on Patricia, the way she looked at Roland then as if he were a football star, only with a dash of reserve, maybe fear, as if at any moment, at the wrong word, he'd turn on his heels and leave three women standing there alone.

"I think we better talk."

Roland opened his jacket and pulled from it three stems of blue lantana he must have grabbed by the fountain. "A pretty gal like you should get flowers every night." He thrust them forward at me, and I looked at Patricia.

"Roland!" Patricia said. "Where's mine?" When she saw I wasn't taking them, she did. And then Roland turned, taking Annabel with him, to lean over the balcony and watch, I guess, the fountain. The son of a bitch. It had to be him, with the paper and the lemonade berry.

"What is going on here, Patricia?"

Roland and Annabel stayed put, Roland cocking an arm out to rest on the balcony railing, but definitely around Annabel. As I would peer out around Patricia in the next few minutes, I'd see Annabel's face turned up to him, smiling, and then it would reflect uncertainty and in another instant reverse itself to become self-conscious, aloof, a photographer's model trying to look alone and worldly as she stood on a balcony with wind blowing her hair and skirt, hands jammed tight in the pockets. She wore a doe-skin jacket, cream-colored skirt, cream stockings with little knobs all over them like I never had the nerve to wear, cream high heels.

I took Patricia by an elbow and pulled her even farther away from the two. I laid into her, asking what the *hell* did she think she was doing, where the *hell* had she been, and what *frigging* idea had planted itself in her brain that she thought she could come breezing in here, my place, with a man suspected of murder.

She said, "God, what happened to you? You met him. He's fine, just fine."

And when I held my rigid glare too long, she turned around to Roland and her friend and said, "I think we made a mistake."

Roland shrugged. "You got it. Guess we better be movin' along," but he didn't look like he wanted to be movin' along.

A sharp breeze cut in through the balcony and under my unzipped jacket, and I could smell the gasoline still on my hands from the last errand. At our head level just outside the walkway a white gull flew by.

Patricia had her hand all this time in the yaw of her purse. She'd put the wad of money back in, and now she pulled it out again. "You shouldn't worry about me," she said as she handed it to me. "I'm twenty-nine years old. I can take care of myself."

"It looks like it. What's with Miss Nordstrom over there? She taking care of herself too? I don't appreciate it you go away and nobody knows where you are. I'm sure your boss doesn't appreciate it either. You're hanging out with a criminal. You think of that? Are you in love or just shootin' in both arms?" I stepped out so I could see Roland, what he was doing, and to break the moment. He caught my eye and moved

toward Annabel and put his hand on her upper arm, said
something to her. I couldn't hear him, but I knew whatever
he was saying to her was for my benefit, for me to watch and
wonder about.

"You don't know it all," Patricia said, low, dark. "You're
smarter than me, I know that. But you don't know it all. I'm
just sorry. I thought we were friends."

I never knew she thought I was smarter than she was. I
said, maybe softer now, "We are *friends*, Patricia. What friends
do is look after one another. Confide in one another. You
didn't confide in me. You didn't tell me you were going to
take up with him until after you already had. Because you
knew what I'd have to say. And you lacked the courage and
the respect to tell me. You're not dumber. You're just not honest." That sounded so cruel, and I could see the hurt in her
eyes. "Where were you all this time? Did you give one thought
to me, or your parents, or your job, for Christ sakes, even one
thought?"

"Nobody can talk to you." Her mouth drooped, and then
the lips parted, as if she wanted to say something else but
didn't know what.

Whispering, I said, "You knew what I felt about that murder in Dwyer's. You knew police suspected Roland and his
brother—God, you were there with me in the observation
room. And still, you took up with him anyway."

"If you were so against him, why'd you come to the pier?"

I heard an apartment door close, and felt the floor of the
walkway begin to shake with someone's steps. The clip of high
heels pocked behind me, and Patricia and I stood looking at
each other as the woman approached and headed for the
stairs.

"You think I'm a hard-ass, but I know these kind of people
better than you do. What about all the talking we've done?
What about all the stuff I've told you I've seen? Your brains
are between your legs, Patricia."

And that was all she wrote.

She started away, turned back to say, "You're hopeless."

Roland then was moving toward us, Annabel thrust ahead
like a figure on a ship's prow, his hand on her elbow. "You
girls ready? We goin' to roast wienies on the beach or what?"

He rubbed his palms together like making fire the Indian way, then settled on his feet and hooked both thumbs in his pockets, smiling his lady-killer smile first at Patricia and then at me. His eyes searched mine, and the white teeth showed themselves, See, I'm harmless. And for just one half of one second I forgot who he was, saw the intimacy between him and Patricia, and felt left out.

I looked at Annabel and said, "Hi."

"Hi. I'm supposed to be at work. I'm supposed to work overtime," she said, and laughed faintly.

"I know how that is." I was trying to figure out what it was about her that was off.

"We're playing hooky," she said.

I saw it then, behind her dark eyelashes. "You're higher than helium," I said.

One side of her mouth crept upward. She leaned back against the railing, raised her head as if to catch the sun, but there was no sun there, we were all in shadow.

A knowing and seductive expression moved into Roland's face. I'd seen it a thousand-thousand times, from men at the bar after I'd finished my set of dances and needed a drink to cool off, at the table near the door when the bar was closing, or in the parking lot. I'd seen it from my father's friends in the backyard at our barbecues when I was only thirteen, and still once in a while with new cops, cops I didn't know and who didn't know me, who I was. So it was staring/glaring time again.

I said, "Your parole officer know you're associating with a user?"

His face went slack. He said to Patricia, "What is this? What you doing to me?"

She said, "Nothing. I'm sor—"

He pitched around, taking Annabel's arm again, and said, "We're bookin', baby."

Patricia went after him, her ankle-length, blue-and-white Australian dress with the ruffles on the bottom kicking up with each step. Then she stopped and looked back and said, "Thanks a lot, Samantha, for your understanding."

I was Samantha again. This time I didn't say anything. The smart one with nothing to say.

* * *

That night I thought the wind had kicked up, sending leaves ticking against my window. I wandered into the living room, thinking how I regretted the leaves this year, mostly brown, from a summer so hot and dry. The two liquidambars in front of my condo, resembling sycamores but from the witch-hazel family, halfheartedly got to the yellow stage about a month ago. While my back was turned, a *pop* issued from the window, and I looked and saw, because of my neighbor's balcony light, a crystaled spot in the glass, and saw that the wind was not blowing, for the Christmas lights on her tree did not sway. As I slid open the door, another *pick* sounded to the left of me, and then I saw the pebble bounce onto the patio floor and out through the railing. What the *hell*, I thought, and knew it was Roland, knew it, and knew I could not prove it, would not see him as I stepped to the railing and looked down. For a moment I thought I saw something move among the black clumps of bushes fifty yards from my place, leading down the bluff, and thought, Well, I guess the guy's at least got a good arm.

I went in and closed the door and slipped my sawed-off broom handle in the channel of the slider, checked the front-door lock again, and waited two hours in the darkness to go to sleep.

In the morning when I left for work, not across from my door, but the next, was a brown female pintail lodged between the iron bars of the railing, bent to a U, butt out, legs and neck in. I went back in and got a plastic trash bag and a trail of paper towels and stuck it in. Tell me it flew through the railing and bucked back out.

CHAPTER
21

Stu Hollings decided to send me to Westminster first thing Monday. Little Saigon. A very fast station there, as cops say, lots of new violence among the immigrants. So many criminals, so little time. Same as in Long Beach, in L.A. County. In both those cities the contrasts are newer, the abrasions fresher. In Westminster, though the street signs are still lettered in Olde English, the town now plays host to fourteen-year-old Asian thugs with mag pistols and assault rifles. They burst into homes and murder praying women or anyone else who won't satisfy demands for hidden stash; and these crimes often go unreported because the populace is afraid. Watch the news; study history—it's the young. They refuse heart.

My boss and I were walking up the front steps of the lab, fresh asphalt in the back requiring us to park across the street, when he told me about the shooting in Westminster. Stu had come from getting doughnuts, a white box in his hands, which meant he'd already been at the lab and went out again. Like the little piggy who gets up earlier and earlier to beat the big bad wolf, you can't arrive before Stu Hollings. Joe used to be like that, first in, last out, before his heart attack, and I used to try to beat him. No more. Not only does Joe not arrive early, it just isn't fun anymore.

He held the door for me. "This is a homicide, a forty-year-old owner of a doughnut store." For one flash of a second, I thought, Surely he didn't get the doughnuts he's holding *there*.

We stepped in and paused in front of Kathleen Kennedy's reception area. She'd put a small Christmas tree on the counter near the wall, no decorations yet; and no Kathleen, until she whisked around the corner carrying a stuffed elf in a sleigh with a Santa cap on. She smiled when she saw us, asking, "Isn't he cute?" and turning Santa-elf this way and that.

I nodded and proceeded down the hall, Stu behind me. When he caught up to me he said, "She's nice, isn't she?" waiting for my confirmation with a special light in his eye. Sometimes I think I'm not a woman—neither a woman nor a man. I look at Kathleen Kennedy, I look at the director's secretary, who bounces and twitches and makes guys happy with her high tinkly laugh, at others I could name, and I think, I am not like them. So who am I? I'm fond of men; more than I should be. But I don't want to be one. The Kathleens of the world are a mystery to me, and I don't know why exactly. Even Janetta, in the coroner's office. The saving grace for me is people like Jeri Landsforth, the anthropologist; and Dr. Schafer-White, the pathologist, a mommy who probably dresses her little girl in velvet dresses the same day she'll be stabbing livers with a scalpel, just below the rib cage, and slipping in a thermometer to read the time of death. When I think of those two, I think, Okay, I'm not alone; and besides, Raymond likes me, and Joe.

"Killed her with one shot," Stu said, bringing his right thumb up exactly between his eyebrows. "Westminster requested our involvement. They want someone knows what he's doing. You're him. Joe Sanders is actually the one who called back and would like to have you out there."

We'd reached his office, and went in.

I said, "If it's all right with you, I'd like to talk to you in the future about my next step here. I mean, I've done just about everything except DNA, and Johnson's hogging that all right now. I'd really like to do something else; you know, take some training. Carnivorous insects, for instance. There's a course at Fullerton—"

He'd set the box of doughnuts on the desk and was hanging his jacket on the back of the door, glancing out the doorway as he came around, as if to see who else was or wasn't at their desks. "You have a problem, Smokey? Working scenes since you've been back?"

Stu was about the same age as Joe. Transferred in from

Indianapolis a year ago. He was a big, plain-looking man who looked like he'd sell tires or teach history or be the guy who tries to sell you refrigerators as you get off the escalator at Sears. Egg-shaped face with a shiny forehead, round bifocals. He was okay but I couldn't get a fix on him, couldn't figure out who he was yet besides being good at following procedure. Definitely a company man, which I both liked and didn't like; I like them honest enough to go by the rules yet imaginative enough to break them, so there you go, hard to please.

"If you mean am I queasy, no. Nothing like that."

"You have a problem with any personnel?"

"No."

As he was asking me these questions, his eyes shivered in that weird paroxysm some people's do when concentrating, as if reading a page right-to-left and not ever catching up. He moved over behind his desk and said, "That case from Mission Viejo, the one with the boy in the hills? The cop dries the shirt in the *sun*," Stu shaking his head. "Can you believe it? On a tree branch, out in the sun." He unlocked his desk, fidgeted around with the stuff on top, and tore off yesterday's calendar page. "Then the idiot folds the shirt right over the wound holes. Who trains these guys anyway?" looking at me for an answer.

"As a matter of fact, the lab gives tr—"

"We have plenty of technicians on bench work. The spec is well covered. Blood alcohol's getting busy, but that's not where I need you."

"With all due respect, Stu, I can't be everywhere."

He looked at me with a new evaluation. "Have I forgotten a case you're on?"

"I'm helping out wherever. And that's fine. I like the variety."

Still standing, he was reading a paper on his desk. Then raising his head, he said, "I thought everybody liked field work best."

"I like field work."

"Don't like the hours? More predictable hours here? Your boyfriend. . . ?"

"Stu, I said I like field work." What I hated was somebody insinuating that personal interests interfere with professional

ones, or that because I'm a woman I don't have the level of
interest a man would. This conversation was pinning me to
the wall, though. The fact of the matter was that my resistance
was up to going to Westminster *precisely* because I was a
woman and Joe-baby a man, and that galled me more than I
wanted to think, for without that tension, I wouldn't be having
this inane conversation with Stu Hollings in his office. I said,
"This time of morning I should make it in what? Thirty
minutes?"

"Good," Stu said, cutting open the tape on the doughnut
box with his fingernail and lifting the lid. "Want one?"

"No, thanks."

"Got to watch calories, huh?" He smiled at me, returning
his gaze to the pink-and-chocolate mounds. His shirt pulled
tightly across his stomach, his sleeves rolled because his wrists
were so thick.

I said, "I'll present more information regarding that course
in carnivorous insects I mentioned later, okay? We can talk
about it then?"

"You do that," he said, neatly laying out a folded paper
towel for his doughnut to rest on.

At my desk, I grabbed my kit containing the things needed
for collecting and preserving samples, and put it on top, flipping the latch open so I could check my supplies. Joe would've
already done most of the work. The blood would've clotted
and unclotted by now, he could get good samples, and he
knew what he was doing. I couldn't see why he needed me. I
checked my supply of filter paper. I needed more gloves. The
elasticized strap on my eye protection was getting unelasti-
cized; I'd have to replace it sometime. Swabs, syringes, Luminal. Razor blades. Tweezers. Saline solution. Mason jar. Small
tubes. Joe would have dry ice. Thermometer/barometer. Evidence envelopes—plenty of those. Tape for lifting prints.

Billy K. would be there, probably, but I thought I'd better
bring film for my own camera, the one I kept in the trunk
and hoped all summer wouldn't fry. I rummaged in the back
of my top drawer, didn't find any. Then opened the same big
left-hand drawer where I'd temporarily stored the brass collet
from the Dwyer case before I had the good sense to take it to
Property, and maybe not the good sense, since I hadn't han-

dled it correctly in the first place and it seemed to mean nothing to anyone after all, and looked in there. Thinking how much time had already passed on the Dwyer case. Thinking of the Dugdales, and what was happening to my frilly friend Patricia, losing her bearings. Mad at myself that I'd been dwelling too much on my own puny emotional problems with one Joe-London-Cutie-Pie-Sanders while all this was going on.

CHAPTER
22

"It's fly specks, I'm telling you."

"It's paint."

"No."

"Why not?"

I said, "What's it painting here? What's it depicting? Not holly berries." Using the eraser end of a pencil in the corner where the window met the frame, I shoved open the metal door that led from the kitchen into the customer area of the shop. We'd been checking stain on the door's window.

"It's flies," I said.

"What makes you think so?" Joe said.

"*Because,* the way they're grouped."

"We don't have flies in December."

I stopped, saw he was sort of smiling. He used to do that to me when I was a lab rook—test me, see how much I believed my guesses.

I said, "I don't care what time of year it is, certain conditions, you get flies. Here . . ." I started back. He wasn't following. I said, "The edges. Come back and look."

He didn't move. He did raise his eyebrows and thrust both hands on his hips. *Now* what did I say?

Finally he came over. Looking back into the kitchen through the door's window, I saw the Westminster cop, whose shoulders blocked most of the view farther in. A woman's legs and feet extended on the floor ahead of him, like tiny alien legs emitting from his shoulder. She wore black moccasins and no socks or stockings. The legs had broad stain on them, almost as if they'd been wiped.

I said, "We should do prints on the legs." The puffy ankles meant the skin would be firm. Many times investigators don't dust certain surfaces because they think they can't get prints, or they don't know what we barn boys can do with our technology. Once we found a perfect, clean set of four on each of the undersides of a victim's arms who'd been raped and murdered right after toweling off from a bath. The girl was thirteen; the killer was her neighbor. That was the first of many times I would've liked to have seen Star Chamber justice—the personal, uncomplicated meting out of penalty I would sooner call repair.

The Westminster cop turned around, a question in his eyes, when I tapped on the glass with the pencil, showing Joe the edge of the red concentration. I shook my head no, and spoke to Joe again.

"Little parentheses. Foreleg, middle leg, rear leg. Foreleg, middle leg, rear leg." Fly footpads had left the pattern. Find six red specks away from the main mass, and you could see it clearly. I said, "Flies."

"Hm. Not bad."

"Who needs a course in insects?" I said.

"You taking a course in insects?"

"Maybe. I'm bored."

"Why are you so edgy today?"

"I'm not edgy."

I went back toward the front of the shop, Joe somewhere behind me. I passed the white plastic table with broad splats of blood across it. "Let's see what else is around," I said. Joe had taken smears, using Q-Tips and slides, of the blood on the table and on a chair leg. It's not unusual to gather fifty, seventy-five blood samples from a scene. Joe had already syringed the larger pools in the back near the victim.

At the front windows, he stood to my right, both of us inspecting the poster paint applied to the glass, he at a cluster of poinsettia, I at a camel with a belt of jingle bells scooping around the hump. I said, "Hey, Joe."

"Hm?"

"You know if you wear a bell on your backpack in the mountains, you scare a grizzly away?" He looked at me with his features pulled back, the expression lightened. I nodded toward the camel. "I mean really—you think there's grizzlies in the desert, that's why the camels wear them?"

"I hadn't given it much thought."

"It's fucking Christmas and I haven't shopped yet."

"I thought all women shopped."

"Think again."

"You had all that time off."

"Right."

He moved closer to the front door, away from me. I saw the patrol cars out in the lot, the curious people standing off behind them, the yellow crime-scene tape swinging like a jump rope in slow motion from the wind.

Flyaway blood had lodged along the door frame. More on the east wall. Joe's kit was set up on the field table. He went to it, bringing back with him a cotton swab he had dipped in saline and a slide. As he swabbed, I asked, "Somebody do a panorama in here?" referring to a method of stepping in, standing in one spot, *click, click, click, click* with the camera, and delivering up if not a 360- then at least a 180-degree representation of the scene.

Joe said, "Billy Katchaturian did."

I checked the sill, where two flies were exploring in opposite directions.

It was a peculiar moment to bring up the subject, but I said, "You're right. I *am* cranky. There's a reason."

Joe stopped his repeat examination of the glass to look at me.

"Maybe this isn't the time or place, but I want to know something. Since you asked." I stood facing him; I guess I expected him to read my mind.

"Well?" he said. I liked the look of him, the caution, the kindness. "What?"

"I want to know why you didn't tell me you left your wife." Now I thought I saw regret and surprise, and then a disturbance I couldn't name. I continued, "Not that you *needed* to tell me. I have no claims on your privacy, God knows. It just would have been something, you know what I mean? It would have meant something to me."

He looked out the window, into the world out there: a woman in shorts getting something out of her trunk near

Builder's Emporium, looking over at the yellow scene tape, and frowning, a Vietnamese man glancing our way too, then tugging at his son's hand, who trailed behind him, the boy's small, triangular face turned our way. Joe said, "Can we talk about this someplace else?"

I moved off to the other side, where there were red "Merry Christmas" letters and something printed in blue I assumed was Vietnamese. Several red-black drops had splattered on the wainscoting near the floor. I swabbed it and transferred it to a round of filter paper, wrote a label, and set it near the others to dry in the tray.

Then, down the right lower corner of the window, behind a starved philodendron with leggy yellow stems, I saw a white terry-cloth towel on the floor. I said, "Something here," and Joe came over. We moved the plant.

Joe took a dowel and lifted the stained cloth overhead like a torch. On the glass above the plant was more red stain, where I guessed the camels were heading, toward the snow—what do the Vietnamese know about deserts?—they can paint camels in snow if they want to. The towel had hit the window there and slid behind the philodendron, I supposed.

"He'd go out the front?" I said. "Why go out the front if he capped the woman back there, where there's a perfectly good back door? That doesn't make sense."

"It will. Guy's probably a proofreader in an M&M factory."

We went back to the kitchen, where the victim sat upright against a cabinet. Her head was hooded with a towel, the edges of bright stain in the front fanning to pink at the crown. The towel must have been wet when the killer put it there, avoiding having to look in the woman's eyes as he closed this life down forever. I said, "Killers cover the faces of victims they know. Isn't that right? They can't look in their faces?"

"That's a good bet, especially since the round is *through* the towel." By the sink, he took up a long fork from the drainboard and scratched around in the gray water for anything on the bottom—a knife, a gun—because the tools of destruction are often left nearby, almost as a dare, but sometimes because, as Joe says, criminals are stupid.

Billy Katchaturian stood outside the back door with his camera, shooting more pictures from that angle. The Westminster cop was behind him, a young man with taut skin over high cheekbones and an alternately frightened and intense look on his face. Billy hadn't even said hi, maybe because Joe was there. I didn't want to think about it.

"I think we have two victims here," Joe said, indicating the front of the shop.

I said, "I think we do too. The woman wasn't going anywhere," referring to not out the front door, and not to the table to splatter fluid after she was shot. Bullets in the brain don't let you do that too well. "So where's the other blood coming from?"

Joe shrugged. "Could be there was someone else here, someone kidnapped. The patrolman told me his partner interviewed both sides of the store and across the street. There's detectives at Alpha Beta now. Looks like nobody saw anything. Just like the Dwyer case." His voice dropped before he said "the Dwyer case." No, I thought, not just like the Dwyer case. He added, "The woman definitely had a husband. He could be the one. Victim number two, or murderer number one."

"I've got to talk to you about the Dwyer case. I mean later."

Joe took out his notebook and wrote something. He said, "Okay. Let's stop on the way back to the lab, have coffee somewhere."

I said, "Could somebody call the officers who are at the husband's? We should Luminal the sinks." Luminal is a peroxidase solution we spray to find traces of blood where people have cleaned up, or forgotten to clean up, say, under faucet handles or around the top of the sink where the water would have risen. Spray, swab, throw a blacklight on it; get Billy K. to photograph it as the fluorescence blooms. "But that still doesn't explain the spill on the table, right?"

"Right."

"Of course, as you say, if there's a *second* victim, he could have been hustled out, punched or something. Blood flies onto the window. Killer makes him go home to dig out any valuables—shit, take the whole thing, the TV, the garden tools, the Hyundai."

Joe listened, rubbing his cheeks as though checking the stubble. He turned to look at me, nodded, said, "Not bad."

* * *

Already we were arguing. We were walking toward the Westminster Municipal Court. Joe decided we could get a cup of coffee near the courthouse, after he'd taken care of some business. I didn't ask what it was, just followed in my car.

We'd started the argument in the parking lot. He was saying the doughnut shop was similar to Dwyer's, and I was saying fucking no way. When we got into the broad expanse of sidewalk and grass near the buildings, I really zapped him, unfairly, I suppose, saying his judgment was screwed because he was getting a divorce. Wanting to mention the divorce again so I could get some things straightened out here. I said, "Your mind's on how much alimony you're going to have to be paying for the rest of your life." Only kidding, boss.

We'd paused not far away from a big tree whose bare branches fingered up symmetrically like a menorah, and under the tree with no leaves I could see a bird, bigger than a jay but smaller than a hawk, tearing at a lump. I studied the bird, trying to identify it and thinking of the pintail on my balcony.

Joe said, "This has been coming on for a long time, Smokey. Jennifer takes care of herself. She's not expecting anything from me. As a matter of fact, we've been separated a long time now."

"Oh? How long?"

"Three months."

"You dog, you!"

"What? What's the problem?"

I started walking again. The sun was out, burning off remnants of a fog, and I couldn't decide if I was cold or not.

"You didn't come visit me in the hospital and you could've."

He said he could have anyway, even if he was still with Jennifer. In fact, she would've come along. "I thought you didn't want any visitors."

"You were right. Thank you. Thank you for not visiting me. It was the noble thing to do. I looked like hell. I saw myself in the mirror the next morning and wanted to call the police."

He laughed, and we started closing the distance to the entrance of the courthouse. I saw a bench and sat on it, surprised at how cold the bench was through my jeans. "I'll wait here," I said.

He stood above me. "I figured you'd be upset—the kind of operation it was. I'm sorry."

"Not all women regret losing those things."

"How was I supposed to know that?"

"Why'd you kiss me last week?" Lay it on him. No more beating around the bush. The cad. I waited.

"Because I'm nuts, I guess," he said. A deep sigh sank him down to the bench beside me.

"All divorced men are nuts. I don't date them."

"That's wise."

"Neither do my friends."

"That's good," he said, slowly nodding his head. Then: "Smokey, I apologize about what happened in the office. That's bottom line here, isn't it? I apologize. I was screwy. I had a hell of a week and a worse one after that. Not that I'm making excuses—well, I guess I am. I'm sorry, is what I'm saying."

A moment passed before I said, "There are ways to approach a woman, you know."

"Are you going to let me apologize or not?"

The bird I'd seen under the tree was visible now in my dead-on view. Almost as soon as I focused on it, it flew up to a branch, calling, *killy, killy, killy*. Blue wings, rust body. "That's a kestrel," I said.

"What?"

"That bird over there. See? On the branch. A small falcon, sort of. American kestrel, it's called. I was trying to figure out what it was when we came in. You can tell by the blue wings. See the blue wings?"

"How do you know that?"

I shrugged. I wanted to tell him about the pintail.

He said, "Are you going to let me apologize, Ms. Brandon?"

"All right," I said.

"Thank you."

Out of the corner of my eye I saw his pretty silver hair, and all of a sudden I felt, for no reason I can explain, a wave of profound sorrow and deep weakening. My hormones were probably out of whack.

"Can we be friends again?" Joe said, curling three fingers into my palm.

I said, "I want to talk about the Dwyer case now."

He shook his head and smiled, and so we did, holding hands for a long time, and wound up arguing again. I accused him of letting the Dwyer case get buried, and he said he hadn't, that there were two very hot suspects, one named Lee Yardley who looked very good, operates with a hood named Burns on small-time stuff. Another named Forrest Sinclair. This I did not want to hear.

He said, "Sinclair's been snitched off by a yellow wanting a court favor." Yellows are minimum-security inmates, but not as minimum as whites. Whites are there for infractions—drunks, disturbers of the peace—but because there's no room at the inn, they're out as soon as they're sober. A yellow's a misdemeanor customer, usually a repeat who couldn't bond out. Jail colors change now and then, but right now the maxies wear orange jumpsuits unmistakable in the general population. Blues are camp inmates, real low on the security scale for Orange County customers, but higher power in L.A.—it could get confusing, an O.C. cop and an L.A. cop together, talking colors.

Joe said, "The yellow burned Sinclair. Says he read about the Dwyer murder and knows who did it, could they make a deal? Detective Felton checked it out. Turns out Sinclair's got: one—no alibi; two—he's on the pipe, which would give him motive; three—and most significant—he's an ex-cop, accounting for the Glasers."

"Oh, shit," I said, sorry to hear it, sorry someone who was sworn would get his head so unscrewed. We used to talk about those kinds of cops, in bars, at buddy get-togethers. But we'd talk about them with the word *pukes* on our lips. With meth, coke, crack, crank, and every vein of mother-lode dope you can imagine attracting truckloads of both real and fake green, it's just too much for some badges, and they cave.

I took in what Joe was saying about the possibility of this ex-cop Forrest Sinclair performing nasty business, but the old cerebrum said Forrest Sinclair did not do Jerry Dwyer. "There were *two* in that case, Joe. How tall's this guy?"

"Smokey, it's being taken care of."

In the bay behind my house, along with the littleneck clams, are gaper clams. Those things are *ugly*, but they're survivors. The shell gapes open at the side, like a sneer, permitting the feeder tube—which has grown thick as a man's penis—to ease up as far as two feet out of the mud. There it stands, minding its own business, waiting for dinner to come by, its flowered siphon making cute in the currents. Instead, along comes Jones, in the person of the yellow-fish croaker. That guy chomps off the tip of the siphon tube. Yum, dinner for him. The clam survives, grows another tip, something the males of our species would be happy to do, I'm told. It was that picture of the dumb tube waving in the currents, and the yellow croaker nibbling away another live thing's possibility, that passed over me. I said, "So what you're saying is, as far as you know, everybody's happy. Fat, dumb, and happy."

He frowned and said, "If you want to call it that."

I don't know when it was we stopped holding hands. I only noticed it when Joe put his hand out on the bench again as if to touch mine. "Sinclair is not our guy," I said, standing, because now there was no doubt about it: I was definitely chilled, and glad for it, really, November having been cruelly hot and December so far emulating.

Joe said, rising, "You're upset because of your friend Patricia."

"Wouldn't you be? Anyway, how do you know that?" And then, of course, I knew it was Raymond, communications conduit in place. "Ray Vega come to you with every little thing I do?" What I was worried about, of course, was Ray telling Joe I'd recently demonstrated a colossal lack of judgment in the domicile of one Armenian, namely B. K. Katchaturian.

"Ray Vega is your friend. He's worried about you. He's a talker. He likes to get on the horn and talk." That sounded like Ray all right, bless his evil heart.

"Is nobody looking at this thing the way it appeared the first day?"

"Smokey. You know eye-witness testimony isn't worth a hill of beans. Emilio's the only one—"

Don't lecture me is what I said. Nobody seems to give a rat's ass, probably because of overwork, but just as likely because it was nobody's important son, no rich developer's boy, no cop's brother. . . . I was ranting, I know.

Joe said, "Speaking of overwork, time to roll, don't you think? Got two of Orange County's finest sitting on their duffs here." He noticed me shiver once or twice. "Come on in and wait, this won't take long. I've got to go see if I can get out of jury duty."

"Joe! Shame on you! Besides, why didn't you try when it was just a matter of sending off paper?"

He said, "They're tougher these days."

I said, "Go through with it. It'll make you a better person. See justice in action."

He moved to one side, facing the building, as if having to gird up to go in, then put a sideways arm around me and gave me a tight but respectable hug. He said, "You're a bright light in my life, Smokey. I shouldn't tell you that."

I let myself ease into him, then turned, thinking, Yes, it would be all right to kiss him now. But I didn't. I smiled, though, and said, "Well, maybe we'd better skip the coffee, huh? Do it some other time?"

"Right," he said.

We stood just a second, looking at each other, and then we went off, he to his and me to mine, as if some bridge had been crossed and we'd meet again at the apron of another one soon and have to make a decision again. And I felt better than I had in a long time, and scared, all at once.

I climbed back onto the freeway in the wrong direction to my state of mind at the moment. That is, I headed back to the lab. I *felt* like heading out to San Pedro. But how would I extract a different story from Roland's bosses anyway, one that said, Oops, we made a mistake, Roland *didn't* work the day J. Dwyer was killed? No, the thing to do would be to go see Patricia when Roland was with her. Feel the jerk out, swallow my bile and get friendly. Sure, you were right, Patricia. Like, I was wrong.

CHAPTER
23

"Hi, Gare. It's me, Smokey. Can you talk?"

"Sure thing. I'm just doing reports. What's up?"

"I hear we've got a Forrest Sinclair in the population somebody rolled over on. Is that right?"

"He's in the population all right, and I gotta tell you, Forrest Sinclair could do whatever scuzzy thing you put on him, but it would be a personal thing, not this. He's got a temper. Give you an idea, he broke into his ex-wife's house and wrote nasty stuff on her mirrors. She lives in Orange, up there by that lumberyard that does the woodcarving classes? I forget the name. Great big one."

"I don't know, Gary."

"He's a real beaut. Once he beat up a guy behind a disco for getting in his face. Guy spent two months in the hospital and never turned him in."

"For an old man hangs around the house a lot, you're sure a window to the world."

I could hear paper crinkling in the background, like cellophane. He said, "He's a zip. I worked with him a little as a junior. He likes to think he knows it all, you know what I mean?"

I grunted a reply so he'd continue.

"Used to like burgs nobody else could figure out. He's smart, I'll give you that. Too smart to do a stop-and-rob with a murder in his hind pocket."

"What's he in for?"

"Well, his first turn was for B-and-E's. Thought he knew everything because he'd been a cop. He'd break in a place, drink the good wine, spread out the paper like he took a long time readin' it. Then pocket some jewelry or a few syringes, and go out the front door. Joe Citizen'd replace the locks, the doors, the whole bit. Two weeks later, Forrest Sinclair would be in there again. He did it for laughs, that's what he told his public defense who told it to me on the sly—he's a member of my church. Oh, he *could've* graduated to person crimes, but I don't think so, not that one. Most burglars are cowards. They don't wanta get hurt. Take a gun into a store, you might get hurt. Besides, I got another reason for thinking so."

"And you're going to keep it to yourself," I said.

"No. Don't be so impatient. I'm eatin' some peanut brickle here." He called it *brickle*. "The granddaughter brought it over last night, couldn't sell it all. You want a couple boxes of not-so-bad peanut brickle?"

"I'll send the money. You can keep the candy."

"Okay, if that's the way you want to be."

"Gary, why would the inmate try to burn him?"

"Favors. A turn out of the barrel, who knows. Let me tell you what Sinclair's in for now. It's a real hoot. A drug pinch was going down in Magic Kingdom territory—"

"Off Harbor?"

"Right. Small stuff, not a big bust or anything like that—you know, they cleaned up the hooker trade so good they can load Narc Detail. So anyway, they're waiting for the bust signal, they got a wired guy inside the room. Car pulls up. Hey, who's this? This john's gonna screw up the deal. Plainclothes on a bicycle moves in, tries to get what turns out to be Sinclair off to the side. Sinclair starts acting real funny, and the girl in the car gets out, takes off the other direction. Which makes Mr. Sinclair commence to give mouth to the officer, 'cause he just lost his date."

Gary was thoroughly enjoying the moment of telephone break so he could eat his peanut brittle. It sounded wet in my ear, all the smacking. "The wired copper," he said, "*inside* the motel, he's doing his thing, playing it to the hilt, like, 'Yo, you mf-ers, you brought the heat in, you clumsy mf-ers,' and like that. The bust by now is completely watered. So the rest of the detail goes to hassle the bejesus out of this jerk in the white windbreaker who dumped it for them, who they don't know yet is Sinclair, "and guess what? His registration's not current and they think they smell marijuana. They search the car, think they see flake in the seats. Buddy, we got a fatal error here. Your system has done crashed. They ask Sinclair can they see in the motel room he was going into, the one, it turns out, is next to the setup. 'No,' he says. Puts up a lot of bull. By now they know who he is, so they are major pissed. They get a telephone warrant and search the room, find some good old Hawaiian sunshine inside and a kilo o' Henry ain't even been stepped on yet. Sinclair's cussin' like a sumabitch. That boy is going to camp for a long while and it won't need the Kwik Stop murder case to do it."

"He sounds like a genuine multitalent to me.

"Personally, I can't see the guy dipping petty cash at a convenience store when he's got a kilo Henry, can you? You know what that's worth these days, coke in recession?"

"No. What?"

"Try three mil."

"Yow."

"You said it.

"Hey, Gare."

"What?"

"Why are we so honest and so dumb?"

"Aw, hell, I don't know. Dumb parents, I guess."

"So why does anybody want him for the Dwyer?"

"I don't want him for the Dwyer."

"I know. Who does?"

He said, "Tired cops who see a lot of dealers walk, okay? Cops who're mad they're dumb like you and me."

"Can I see Forrest Sinclair?"

"I can give you all the stats on him, that's what you want. But I really don't see why you don't let us do our business, and you keep doin' the fine job you're doin'."

"Gary, I knew the Dwyer kid."

"So? Open up some evidence for us. That's your job."

"Thanks a big one, Gare."

"I'm busy, what can I say? He's not your man."

"I heard there are a couple other suspects."

"Nah. Wishful thinking. Give the DA a menu to choose from is all."

I was coming to the final question with Gary, wondering how I'd say it since it wasn't clear to me if I disliked Roland Dugdale because he was Roland Dugdale, because he was someone with a record and was taking my friend away, or did I just not like Roland because of something working I couldn't put my finger on, something you see in your peripheral vision but not when you turn around? I said, "What do you think of the Dugdales now that the channel's changed?"

There was a pause, not long, and then, "I hate to say it, but it looks like we can trash that file."

"Ah, Gary."

"You wanted it to be those two, didn't you?"

"I guess so. Probably just because they were the ones I actually saw. All your fault for letting us come down."

"Yep. That's a danger."

I asked him about the photo lineup, had he taken a photo lineup to Emilio.

"Emilio don't work at El Cochino no more."

"Oh, shit. We scared him."

He was silent a moment, and I was wondering if he thought that was a criticism, or if he was intent on peanut brickle again, though I didn't hear anything crinkling.

Behind me, one of the new specialists was sliding drawers in and out of her desk. I swiveled to see her, and could hear a lone pencil rolling back and forth, back and forth in the top drawer as she opened it, bent over to peer in, closed it, opened it. She was a round-faced thing with whitewashed skin, and I'm sorry to say I didn't like her the minute I took her damp, limp hand. Her eyes met mine, and she smiled, said quietly, "The lock doesn't work."

Gary was talking again, saying, "I showed the shots to the family. Nothing. I even showed them to the Iranian, the guy who came in after? And the lady with the stroller. I showed them to the father. No luck."

"Did Ray Vega tell you about my friend Patricia?"

"He did. Ray was sittin' on tacks."

"Is that whole thing a coincidence too spooky to believe?" I was hoping, of course, he'd say yes, and be alarmed and suspicious and angry and motivated.

What he said was, "Hey, I met my fourth-grade teacher

from Moundsville, West Virginia, in Crown Books at Mainplace Mall last week. It's a small world after all."

"No kidding."

"You know what she was buying? An Orange County Firemen's calendar, you know, with all them twenty-year-olds in red bikinis showin' ass? Excuse me, pardon my French."

Stu Hollings had a meeting that took clear up till noon, talking about who's going to get to work in the DNA building, and who's going to be up next for training. It's quite a coup that we have a DNA lab, to the director's credit. There are only a few DNA labs in the country, mostly private, and police have to send stuff out to them, and wait, and wait. An expert was up front talking about the sieving properties of electrophoretic gel and the use of restriction endonuclease, and about that time my eyes glazed over and I caught myself wishing a bird would hop on a bush in the window behind Stu for me to analyze.

When I came out, Kathleen told me Rowena Dwyer was waiting in the lobby. She was wearing a tan suit jacket with narrow black stripes, over a black skirt. Her hair seemed blonder, too blonde I think, so that she just looked tired and older. She said she'd been getting the runaround. "I feel like no one at the police department is doing anything at all on this case." She was agitated, of course, but at the same time wanting to show me all the newspaper clippings she had in her folio from both L.A. and Orange Counties, stories having to do with armed robberies and some homicides. Some of them, I could see as she flipped through, were library microfilm copies. I pictured this lady in a branch library sitting in front of one of the big white screens turning dials, asking the librarian how do you do this and how do you find that.

I asked her if she'd like to go talk somewhere private, and I went back to my desk and wrote a note to Stu telling him I was going to the doctor's again, placing it on his desk while he was out—he wouldn't want to know the truth. I was back in an hour and took my note off his desk and he didn't even know I was gone. Mrs. Dwyer and I walked to the gazebo by the public library and, with the day warmed up now, sat just outside the gazebo in the sun. The sky was clear blue, and stacks of white clouds, a rarity in this country, moved in two columns over the tops of the buildings. Black birds with yellow eyes fluttered down from trees that were set into rounds in the concrete, and landed near us as if expecting handouts. A man in his forties, handsome behind his raggedy beard, sat not too far off from us, studying a bus schedule.

Her ex-husband was selling the business, coming back to the Midwest with her, Rowena said. He'd suffered a mild heart attack since the murder. "I just don't want us to go back there and we're out of sight and out of mind."

I let her show me every single piece she had in the folder, and told her again that we'd do our very best to find her son's killers, that I had a lot of faith in our law-enforcement personnel. She shook hands with me when she left. No tears, not even wet eyes, but a droop cutting sharply on either side of her lips, almost down to the chin.

After work I drove to Patricia's. She wasn't there. I passed Roland's number 210. No lights. I did this three evenings in a row, after calling her machine throughout the day. On the weekend I tried I don't know how many times to reach her by phone, and drove by twice.

My brother, Nathan, called. He said, "If you want to visit the folks Christmas, I'll pay your way out." I told him I hate Florida.

"You're being petulant," he said.

"I'm busy, Nathan."

"One of these days they're going to be gone and how then will you feel?"

"Guess I'll deal with that later."

"You're heartless, Samantha. A regular stone."

"Nathan, I have nothing in common with them."

"How about they wiped your little fanny when you were a baby? They fed you, didn't they?"

"Let me work this out my own way, okay, Nathan? They know I love them."

"In an abstract way."

"Yes, in an abstract way. I love the *thought* of them, happy in their Stratoloungers. Going clubbing, making pot roasts, whatever it is they do. Who are you to tell me how to feel about them? I'll see them in my own time, don't worry."

He doesn't understand because he's a miniature of them. It's funny how it happened in our family. My parents were straight arrows when Nathan was growing up. Then, in the mid-sixties to the mid-seventies, they got weird with minor drugs and did sneaky shit on each other, and I guess I wasn't old enough to handle it. I went a bit tweako myself. Straightened up before they did, but by the time they came around, they were religious, I was in Vegas, and, I'm sorry, I just don't want to hear it.

For one second while talking to him, though, I recalled Rowena Dwyer's face and wondered if those puzzled, distant expressions ever crossed my parents' countenances. And if so, I was sorry. Crum, maybe I'd have to go Christmas shopping anyway.

"You can come Christmas shopping with me, Joe," I said when he asked me out. We were standing by my car at the lab when he said he wanted to take me to dinner.

We did eat, we did shop, we did fight. We argued when I said I wanted to mix it up with Roland Dugdale because I couldn't get in touch with Patricia. Joe said I should mind my own business. Oo, the *wrong* thing to say to a Smokey-girl.

Before that, though, in the darkness of the fanciest restaurant I'd been in in a long time, Joe kissed me several times and I thought I was going to slide off the cushions onto the floor. He was wearing some sweet-smelling thing on his face, and though I can't stand being blasted by a woman's perfume, her coming at me down an office aisle or ahead of me in a store, it's a fact that men's colognes do all the right, or possibly wrong, things to me.

Joe had a smidgen too many bourbon-and-waters, and I'll say I loved the white zin. So when the back of my hand slid down to the well-earned round of Joe's belly and Joe said he was losing his girlish figger, I looked at him leeringly and said a thing I shouldn't have, smiling: "More cushion for the pushin', darlin'."

"Why, Smokey, you do have a mouth," he said, and I swear he was going to attack me right there on the leather bench.

"There was this famous actress in the forties—oh, I can't remember her name."

"Yes?" he said, drawing a finger down the side of my face and across my lower lip as I talked.

"I don't know, I wish I could remember. She was real famous, real wholesome-looking. She had very round cheeks and robust lips, shall we say. Not someone you'd think a reporter would catch with his camera under a restaurant tablecloth performing fellatio on her date."

Joe looked across the room, grinning while he thought about that. "Think there're any reporters here?" He lifted the tablecloth and peered underneath. He was about to say something very serious and lecherous to me, and I probably would've responded with the same, but the mussels and lobster were delivered thereafter, and that precipitated slight musings about where, exactly, various sea creatures come from, where they are farmed, in what waters, and I started talking about diving and what divers do, and one thing led to another.

I said, "Remember, Joe, you're the one said criminals are stupid. So, stupid Roland Gene Dugdale brings a goddamned diver's collet to a crime and leaves it there. Nice of him, I'd say. I'm going out there. Saturday. I am." Ruined a dinner.

We'd driven in separate cars. We stood in front of mine, both of us rigid enough to know the night was over.

He said, "What are we going to do, Smokey?"

"What do you think we should do, Joe?"

As if I'd provided an answer instead of a question, and nodding slowly, he said, "Turn down the heat for a while."

"You know best," I said, worker to boss, student to teacher, but it probably didn't sound that way, and it sure didn't feel that way: *I* was writing this scene; *I* knew we needed to back off awhile. Coming closer, I kissed him once again, this time tenderly, sadly, saying, "I'm sorry."

He answered, "Me too."

CHAPTER
24

Sunday and no Patricia.

Two days before Christmas I shop, bring home presents. One was a telephone shaped like a black Mustang for pal Raymond. I took it out of The Sharper Image bag and put it on the coffee table. *Zoom. Zoom.* The thing had wheels. I raised the antenna.

The rest—a fancy pin for Patricia and junk I know my parents don't need—stayed in the one big department-store bag. I'd already forgotten what I bought my dad, and my head hurt. Nothing, of course, for Joe.

On the way home from shopping, I'd stopped at a fast-food place for a chicken sandwich. I knew what I was going to wear to work the next day, the house was clean, so what would I do all night? I didn't feel like hearing a red-faced army general talk about new developments in tank warfare on *60 Minutes*, or how yet another talented and underpaid teacher was handling problems at inner-city schools. So I took an early shower, crawled into the long ruby-colored cotton T-shirt I like best to sleep in, and combed back my wet hair. It had been two months since my haircut, and I was looking not quite so scalped; maybe not quite so Sheena Easton either, if I could even dream, but if I were a tad or two prettier, maybe I could be a Theresa Russell with a murderin' little black-leather skirt. Rebecca De Mornay—now there's somebody. Her dirty broken fingernails in that film on the train with Jon Voight . . . the girl's got guts. I could still picture her in *Risky Business*, her sleekness spinning Tom Cruise's wheels, the boy in the priceless BVDs and white socks now all grown up and just as

177

stupid. Long ago, though, I figured out it's best to be average. Keep a low profile, then surprise people on special occasions puttin' on the ritz. I used to be pretty, wasn't I? It's hard to tell anymore what's pretty. Or what matters. Because once dead, none of it, none of it, does, and you think, Why in the world does anyone care what anyone looks like, anyway?

I raked wispy bangs down onto my forehead and scrunched curls at the sides, the hair there grown too long to comb back anymore like Sheena. Maybe I'd go a real deep brown with red highlights, be cutesy-pie again. Were those creases at the eyes? Yep. Did I care? You bet.

No one was coming over, but I pulled out the drawer where I keep my makeup and brushed on color anyway. Two long swipes on the Cherokee cheeks—thank you, Oklahoma—so I wouldn't look so ghostie to myself. Stood there some more, staring at myself, no expression in the pigeon-gray eyes, which were, at the moment, a touch red, to match the shirt, from herbal shampoo. "Knock-knock, who's there?" I said. "Smokey." "Smokey who? "Smokey the Bare." I thought, Smokey the B-a-r-e, making those know-it, done-it, will-do-it-again eyes, sliding one shoulder out of the wide neck of my shirt, Oh, you hot thing. Then crying, or starting to. I said, "Ah, shit," and went to the kitchen, reached up over the oven where I keep two bottles of booze, one fancy, one general-purpose.

In the dining room, I put on some old Peggy Lee: "Is That All There Is?"—not the rip-off by Christine Somebody, but the real thing by the real laid-back lady. I always figured Peggy Lee had a secret she'd only tell in the sack, next to the man who'd been doctor-lawyer-actor–Indian chief and owned a quiet hideaway in the mountains of both Idaho and Peru. I stole the Peggy Lee album from my mom when I left home, but Etta James and B. B. King I bought on my own. The blues side of town. Tell it like it i-is.

I sat down on the sofa, put my head back for a moment, and thought how utterly lonely I was. Southern Comfort is what I was drinking, and oh, you shouldn't mix whiskey and lonely in a low-light apartment when you're alone.

Trying to stop sniveling, I got up and emptied the contents of the plastic department-store sack, where the gifts were stashed in gold foil boxes and wrapped with gold sparkly ribbons: a non-do-it-yourself job that set me back fourteen dollars and left me choking.

I didn't have a tree, but if I sat on the end of the couch by the window and looked west, I could see the one on my neighbor's balcony. She was a woman about my age but from another generation, if you know what I mean. Redwood slats formed the container for the tree that always sat there on my neighbor's balcony; an evergreen, ever green. Twice a year it grew nubby pale fingers, as if it were stretching to reach the balcony edge and hoist itself over, and I'd see my neighbor out there nipping them off, and for some reason that made me sad. A week ago she had decorated it with tiny blinking lights.

I set the gifts against the window under, if you will, her tree. There. Christmas. Poured just a teeny bit more Comfort and sat back on the couch. The presents looked big there. "Maybe intent makes up for crimes, Smokey-girl," I said aloud and took another sip of whiskey.

As I leaned back, the ceiling became a movie screen where I saw the rolling hills above the reservoir, arroyo willows sticking up in the gullies like green broom heads, and *then* the little black baby in the pink bunting sleeping forever by the coyote bush and scrub where the Cessna made cornmeal of new tract homes.

In this work you learn to force the pictures away because they're worse in memory than in real life, some of them anyway. A puzzle to me, why that happens. The first time I saw a body, a traffic-accident victim with mortal head wounds, I told my partner, who was my own dear Bill at the time, that I thought it would've bothered me more. He said, "Just wait." Bill knew something then that I didn't: The pictures don't just come back to you—they become a *part* of you. You understand why man developed impersonal speech for it: the deceased, the corpse, cadaver, remains; the stiff, the floater; fish-food, decomps, burn-ups, swingers, jumpers, blues. Sometimes I think we who do this type of work must be some kind of strange. Wouldn't it be nice to have a job where you go to work and your biggest problem of the day is placating some poor homeowner who wants his escrow speeded up, or figuring how you'll get the new-parts shipment inventoried and stacked before you lose your strong kid back to college?

I was into self-pity that night, boozy and thinking maybe I could go learn computers, like Roland was going to. Then Peggy Lee started on "Me and My Shadow," and I thought then of Patricia, how she followed me that night at the station, Mutt and Jeff, me little and she big, right on my heels or clinging to the walls when she could. Of how she looked that night in Chi-Chi's with the men ogling her in her hot pink and purple and the sparkly earrings. Smiling, teasing me. Then, with Roland and Annabel Diehl on the balcony outside my door, Patricia whispering and me whispering hard right back. Patricia again, digging in her purse for money to give the bag lady. Her voice on the phone telling me, Well, I've gone out with a felon before. And then I remembered, as though I'd never seen it before, the butterfly tattooed on her ankle, spotting it that first time when I met her dancing around on the beach with a bloody foot, and forgetting about it till now. Wondering what boyfriend got her drunk enough to do that; smiling, even through my sadness, to think I'd probably have one today too had I been with her. Guessing where else she might have a tiny inked picture. I got back up and put on some Sinead O'Connor, let her lull me into doze.

When the phone rang, Ray's Mustang was still on my lap. Like magic, it could ring and it wasn't hooked up to anything. I came to my senses and crossed the room to the side table where I kept the phone. There was no voice at first, just background noise. Party noise. Then: "Smokey." It took a second for me to understand it was Patricia.

Someone else, a man, said: "Judy—a Heineken, two Becks, please."

"Where are you?" I said, leaning into the earpiece.

"It's hard to talk." I heard what sounded like a door creaking loudly, and a male voice saying, Give it a rest, buddy, will ya?, and another voice saying, Says who?, and then the sound of it moving away, so that I could say, "Yes? Yes? I can hear you okay, Patricia."

"I have to ask you . . ." she said. Her voice was muted, quiet,

as if she were cupping the mouthpiece with her hand. With
her little-girl voice it really wasn't working that well, trying to
be heard and yet not heard. I strained to hear. The voices
behind her were growing louder and all mixed up. I heard
laughter, and then: "Jubey, make that a schooner tap, okay?"
Another voice saying, "Piss in a glass, Jubey, he'll drink anything," and more laughter, and Patricia trying to say something.

"It's . . . it's Phillip," she said. "Roland's brother?"

"Yes, yes, I know, Patricia."

She paused another moment. "He's done something."

"What? What's wrong?"

"I can't talk—"

"Where are you?"

"Samantha, it's a girl. He brought her, and—"

"The one I saw you with?"

She didn't answer.

"Patricia?" I couldn't hear anything extraordinary now, but
I knew she still had to be on the line. "Annabel, Patricia? Is
she the one? What's wrong?"

I barely heard her say no.

"Is someone there? Is that why you can't talk?"

"No. That's not it. I just don't have very long."

"Tell me where you are."

"You can't come," she said forcefully but still in a whisper.
"I just want to tell you, there was this girl. Roland didn't like
her. They—"

I didn't want to interrupt, but she kept pausing, and I was
afraid for her. "Listen to me. I have to know if you're all right.
Tell me."

"I'm all right."

"You don't sound all right."

"I *am*. Listen, I'll call you later. You're going to be home?"

"Yes." I was confused. Now she didn't seem strained.

"I'll call you soon. Not tonight. Later."

"Patricia, are you afraid of something? Tell me where you
are." Silence on the other end. "Are you saying someone has
been hurt?"

"I can't," she said. "I'll talk to you later."

And that was it. *Click.*

At first I panicked. I thought, Holy shit. What the heck is going on? What'd she mean, she'd call me soon? Five minutes? Thirty? I waited from eleven till midnight, thinking she might phone anyway, and then tried calling Raymond, though I didn't think he worked second shift Saturday nights. If I could just repeat the conversation with Patricia to someone, maybe it wouldn't sound so bad. I dialed his unit, and there was nothing. I dialed the watch commander. Correct: Ray was off. Taking a chance on bringing the wrath of Yolanda down—you could make a movie title out of it: *The Wrath of Yolanda*—I dialed Raymond at home. Before I punched the last number, my finger hovering above the nine, I put the receiver back on the hook. I told myself, "You can't control everything, Smokey. Like the man said, Give it a rest."

But, of course, that is not my nature. It's not always good living alone. There's no one to bounce your late-night ideas off of. I went into the bedroom and slid into clothes. Be ready, I thought, breathing shallowly, waiting for the phone to ring. But it didn't, and it didn't. As they say, if the phone don't ring, I'll know it's you.

For the next hour, I fidgeted, trying to read, flipping the television on and off, arranging my sock drawer. Finally I went to the kitchen and fixed myself a cup of instant coffee, reached over the oven to that special cupboard, and dolloped a shot of brandy into it. I went back to the living room, curled on the couch as if I were casually calling a friend to chat, and dialed Joe's number. I could hear my heart in my ears, and on the third ring, just as I was about to hang up, Joe's voice came on.

"Let me come over," I said.

"Smokey?"

"How many of these calls do you get a night?"

Long silence on the other end, and then: "You sure this is what you want to do?"

"Yes."

Another pause. "What if *I* don't?"

I said—no bullshit—"You do."

CHAPTER
25

The fog had come in, slicking everything, forming strips of bubbles on the newly painted black wrought-iron balcony railing outside my door. The car roofs were coated with silvery wetness, the red pavers around the fountain shining as if hosed down by a movie crew for effect.

By the time I reached Pacific Coast Highway, I felt stuck in a cotton ball. If it weren't for the four gauzed green lights at Jamboree, I might've kept going and run smack into the Newport channel.

Not here, but nearly up the whole length of the state, the highway trims the coast so that off your left shoulder if you're traveling north and your right if you're traveling south you see the Pacific winking harmlessly, cut away from the blank horizon by the sun's rays, or at night by the moon's cool diffusion. Then, sometime in December when you're not thinking about it, the ocean heaves one long, secret briny exhalation toward shore, where people are out doing their holiday scramble over pitch-black stretches of curving roads, four drinks too many, and mortality stats begin to climb: a head-on here, a flip-over there.

It was on a night like this two years ago I met Raymond Vega, six miles down the coast near Laguna. The fog was sliding up the cliffs, climbing the bougainvillea stretched onto the peach-colored stucco walls of homes and businesses. It drifted across the highway in a sheet, silent, quick, remorseless. I was on my way to a bookstore when I saw the lights and stopped to see if I could help. Ray had made a Häagen-Dazs run on a slow night, the weather perfectly clear inland at his substation in San Juan. On Pacific Coast Highway, he rolls into a wall of fog and thinks, Here comes trouble. Not a minute later he comes upon a car that rode up the guy wire of a telephone pole, then folded over on itself. The old man and his eighty-year-old bride were headed back to Leisure World after a celebration at the romantic, cliff-perched Ritz-Carlton, where tea alone sets you back six bucks. The son, the only survivor, sitting on the hillside, saying to Raymond, "That man *al*ways was stubborn, never let me drive his car, ever," this fifty-year-old man with his pants wet and vomit down his shirt, *hooing*, Raymond said, while he told him this. And I, hearing Raymond tell the story while he's standing by his unit, the ambulance ready to move off, me sizing up the CHP officer with the pretty teeth and the cast-iron heart, thinking, Well, now, this is another guy impressed with himself; until he said it again, how the man was sitting on the ice plant and *hooing*—long, deep sobs—then how he turned to Raymond and said, "The turkey-ass old fart, why didn't he let me drive?"

Passing over the Dover Bridge at the mouth of Newport Bay, I could see the faint runners of lights and the pale blue prow of the make-believe Mississippi paddlewheel boat that serves as a restaurant called the Reuben E. Lee. It looked like a ghost ship, and I would not have been surprised to see a skeleton on the bridge, hollow-eyed and asking, You alone?

Joe had said, Let me come and get you.

I said, What's the address?

He said, It's late.

I said, Goddamn it, Joe, I know it's late.

Now I was into the stretch of marine-supply stores and yacht brokers' establishments where I knew there'd be parking-lot lights to aid my search for the correct turnoff. I found it, and then Hospital Street, named for Hoag Hospital. Such a name: A Texan could get confused—"You took 'er *where*?"

There was a guard gate at the complex. Jesus Christ. This is the edge of Costa Mesa, I thought, not a Lemon Heights place like where Joe and his future ex-wife lived, and here we have a manned gate, with a guard who looked like Ehrlichman, from Nixon's crew, or an aged Bart Simpson. He checked for my name on the clipboard that lay on the shelf in front of him, the name he probably wrote there just minutes ago, Joe having called ahead. The light outside the shack transformed his hair into white wheat as he peered into my backseat to see if I had a burglar hidden there. Then he stepped inside the shack, and I waited for the wooden gate arm to raise, but it didn't. I looked back. Only then did he say, his hand moving toward the button inside, and a knowing look on his face, "Okay, go on in," a grin on one side of his face only, un-hnn, and him checking his watch.

Reflective numbers that stuck up out of the shrubs fronting each section, guided me, eventually, to Joe's unit. Two hundred, like 210: Roland's, only not Roland's. A tightness formed in my stomach. I said to myself, Don't think. This is Joe you're going to. Joe-baby. Joe.

I parked facing a hedge and left the ignition on so I could use the car phone. I dialed. It rang once. Joe's voice came on the line, a low hello.

"Come down," I said. "Please."

I didn't want to be coming to him, though I was coming to him. I didn't want to go stand outside the locked glass doors that I could see in my rearview mirror and talk through an intercom, to be buzzed in like the help.

The double doors to the apartments opened, and I could see him in my mirror, standing on the step in his blue windbreaker, jeans, and pink shirt. He slid a doorstop beneath the door. I got out of the car and bridged the narrow parking lot, fog running a cold hand down my neck and pasting itself to my thighs through my jeans. I stubbed my toe on the asphalt though there was nothing there.

Then he was close, and I looked at him a moment, checking the face, the kind cut of the eyes and the chiseled, slight hook to his nose. He wrapped his arms around me, and I put my face in his chest like an apology, and shivered.

"You're chilled," he said.

The elevator was only a few steps from the entry. As we began the rise, he held me and kissed me till we heard the doors open. His lips were soft, perfect, and I felt I was decoagulating, deliquescing, my knees giving in, my cheeks and the tips of my ears burning, as if I were coming down with a cold.

"You okay?" he said as we started out down the hallway, perfectly relaxed. Like a husband: I'm coming home after a hard day's work. He's there, loving me, waiting for me, just finished building a doodad in the garage he wants to show off; or just finished polishing the Paughco pipes on his killer-fine Harley; or reading something from *Law Enforcement News* he thinks is a crock. Except this is Joe, somebody else's husband for twenty-five years until three months ago. How did I know who he was, really?

We entered his apartment, and I saw a liquor decanter and two glasses on a glass table in front of a white leather couch. Soft music was playing and the light was dim, so that I thought, Why, that bugger, he's done this before. But, then, why wouldn't he? Big boy, been around. Single. Attractive white male seeks fun & companionship by surf and sand. Well-off, nonsmoker, mature. Likes . . .

He took my jacket, opening a door to a closet behind me, hung mine up, then removed his own. I stood looking around, aware of myself, how I looked, knowing I was okay in my blue-gray silk blouse, my real diamond earrings, but interested too in the place where Joe would live. The carpet, ivory; the walls, white, with one giant pink and peach paper-molded art piece in a white frame above the couch, of seashells, I think. Set around on the side tables were pearlescent glass balls and other such things. Near the white stone fireplace, dried silver dollar eucalyptus spewed out of a tall vase shaped like a woman with long flowing hair. Nice, but the whole thing colder, more nonrevealing, than I would've expected. Joe'd be cozy wools and musky leathers, like gentlemen economists from New England, though no clutter, not Joe: Every . . . thing . . . in . . . its . . . place.

I felt his hands on my shoulders behind me. He moved close, so I could feel the whole length of him, and then he was sliding his hands down my arms. Kissing my neck, the side of my face, then turning me around, moving me back toward the wall. I started to kiss him back.

He said no, eating my neck again, my collarbone.

"Be still," he said, then took my hand and led me to the door of the bedroom, which wasn't far off from the living room. The bedroom. So soon? I thought. What about the wine? Smokey!

He leaned me against the doorway. I started again to kiss him back, my lips getting as far as the side of his mouth, until he said, once again, "No. No," his lips nibbling my diamond earring. That's what he is, a gem thief.

When his fingers started at the buttons of my blouse, my breasts turned into little radiant heaters. Could he feel the heat pulses, know how much I wanted his hand to cup them, make sure they were still part of me and not rotated off at greater and greater speed till they were out coursing the room like bright, buzzing, omniscient UFOs? My breath reached the front of his shirt and U-turned back to me. "I want—" I said, and didn't get to finish.

"Shhh. Close your eyes." He kissed me on the forehead and at the corner of my eye while holding my arms. "Be still now. Quiet," and words like that I don't remember, barely heard *then*, my ears ringing, his voice low, soft, his smell clouding me. It is never—gossips, note this—it is never the one a woman hugs, never the one she flirts outrageously with, spends all her time with, in the office. Watch instead for the one she *doesn't*. Watch for the one she avoids, walking down one hallway after she spots him walking down the other. It'll drive you crazy; who's she diddlin'? You'll never know. You will not know. Not about Smokey, anyway.

I said, "You don't make love like a married man."

"Now, that's a statement you could speculate on." He grinned, and kissed me, his mouth hot and yet withholding. In the other room, I heard the familiar chords of something on the stereo. What was it? He began kissing me again, and I recognized the song, came up for air, and said, "How did you know?"

"I know," was all he said, his lips down the side of my face, covering my neck, and the voice of the singer blues-ing out the words behind us, *Tell it like it i-is.* . . . Recalling the song's lyrics, about life being here and gone tomorrow, so baby live. Go on and live.

I felt his fingers sweep my shoulders, and my blouse fall away. Where did it go? Where did my coat go? Am I going to sleep? Not thinking, but feeling, *being*.

In my mind, free-form pictures were taking place: not the bad pictures, but good ones, of shimmering pampas-grass fans; a sand-colored mourning dove I saw once on a leafless tree, the sun striking the pale branches and the bleached autumn grasses beneath it, and the dove lifting its wings like cymbals, holding them there, airing out its little armpits, ahhh.

There was pressure on the metal fastener of my jeans. *Zip.* Quick. Joe kissing my face. Not kissing my lips. Joe whispering, "Don't do anything. Just hold very, very still. You don't have to do . . . anything."

In my mind, the picture of Joe and Jennifer dancing together at one of our parties, the grace of them together, her brown hair catching the light and her dress swinging out. Remembering that picture then, feeling dismayed, and automatically placing a hand on top of Joe's as he began to slide the jeans over my hipbones.

"What?" he said.

"Nothing."

His hands slipped around me, melting the landscape between my legs. Then kissing the top of my breast, and the edge of lace at the curve of my bra. Pulling the straps down. Just the straps, ma'am. Saving the rest. I started to help.

No.

Taking orders.

His hips pinning me to the wall. My whole body could be a mouth. Gimme. Gimme. Yum, and yum.

His lips went to the lace, over the lace, his hot mouth down then to my nipple; his tongue licking the lace off, and me bare to the world, which Joe *was* then at that moment, the whole world and nothing else.

I felt the bed under me then, the soft comforter and the real down pillows puffing out at each side of my head, and from them a scent making me intensely restless.

From my throat, a sound.

I heard the crinkle of foil, and he started to fumble, so I whispered, "Let me do that for you," then met his eyes and smiled and said, "I know: Be quiet." But I rose partway up, his dark shape standing near me against the lighter darkness of the room, and took the foil from his fingers.

When I was ready, the round braced between my lips, I leaned over and rolled it into place, as I'd heard it could be done. His hands clutched my shoulders, and now it was he who made a sound, and I lay back and closed my eyes and felt his weight shifting the bed and the heat of his body descending.

My lips against his dear face.

His husky, sweet, and hungry voice: "Smokey, Smokey."

CHAPTER
26

Our lives are not linear. Neither our actions. You'd like to think you get from A to C via B, but sometimes you jump all the way to M, then bounce back like a flea to B—actually, like a fly: A fly figures you're going to think linearly. "Little bugger'll head east, 14.66 feet per second; no problem, I'll hit him on takeoff." But no. A fly on takeoff jumps backward. Aha.

This is how I explain going to Joe's apartment before plunging in to search for Patricia. I could take care of one piece of business, cold as that may seem, and then have room for anger and hard intent.

At work Christmas Eve morning, people were getting ready to take the afternoon off. I was determined to push through my jobs, not let people come around and jaw at me, telling me what they bought for their kids and where they were going skiing this year without them. Usually I listen for a while, take up papers in my hands, smile, and say, "Isn't that great?" and then, "I have to go copy these." While I'm gone I get a cup of coffee or visit the ladies', and I'm back at my desk before they're done with the next person. Today I told Herb, an odontologist, or dentist-for-the-dead as he calls it, that I had—groan!—a special tally to do for Stu and I had to get going. Betty Brankoff from ID was with him. I didn't like fibbing to Betty, because I like her, but Herb's cabin at Big Bear just doesn't interest me that much.

Billy Katchaturian was around, going from one person to the other telling them something, but before he got to me, I grabbed a folder and waved at him, saying: "Catch you later, Billy. I'm late for a meeting," went downstairs to the library, and called Patricia at work. Or tried. They said she was sick. Sick, huh? I dialed my own answering machine to retrieve messages, thinking maybe she'd tried to call between the time I left the house and drove up again to Huntington Beach to the Fairdale Apartments, the fog having lifted and me not caring if I was late this morning. I knocked on her door and slid a note under: "Call me." This after driving by Roland's unit and seeing nothing; then knocking on the redheaded landlady's door at seven A.M., she answering with a cockatiel named Willie Nelson on her arm. Telling me no, Patricia's paid up, but apartment 210's empty now, did I want to rent it? When she said that, my mood brightened, thinking first: He's gone, out of our faces; and then: and took Patricia with him.

I was about to ask another question when the woman started talking again. The tenant in 210 moved out in the middle of the night. No notice, just like that. "Leastways I won't have to refund him the cleaning," she said. Her loose floral housedress was scooped at the neck, revealing a pasty yellow scar in the middle of her throat. With her terry-cloth slippers on, she stood no higher than my chin, maybe four-nine. I wondered if she were short enough to qualify officially for the Little People organization. A wave of pity passed over me, but I couldn't know why—she was a mean little rooster.

"What about the last month's rent?" I asked, stupidly hoping to get an address. "You going to send it anywhere?"

"No, ma'am," she said, shaking her head and combing down Willie Nelson's green crown feathers. Though the morning air was chilly, she'd opened the door wide, and I could smell the strong odor of bacon within. "He'll have to take me to court to get it. That's his punishment for movin' without a scrap of notice. Those types, they don't pay attention to money anyhow." She said it like gossip, lowering her voice.

"Those types?"

"You know. Those ones with the tattoos. Those ones allays lookin' over one shoulder, mean like. I see 'em. I shoulda ast for two months in advance, see what I'd get," she said, laughing tee-hee at such a good trick. "It's the rich guys want to hold out for every little penny. There's a renter down the corner in a Porsche puts a bill in my mailbox every time the dryer

eats one of his nickels. That's how they are. If I owned this
place, I wouldn't let the rich ones in. I'd take the other ones
first, like the one vacated 210. You sure you don't know somebody wants a nice place?"

Now, from the library, I heard the beep that told me I had
no messages and then took five minutes more and called Raymond and Gary, asking if they'd call around Huntington
Beach and San Pedro, see if there's a bartender named Judy
or maybe even Jubey, if I heard it right.

Late morning, about the time the effects of one hour's sleep
were hitting me, Raymond called. Raymond, bless his auto-
club heart, snagged a bartender for me, a woman who worked
at the Fore 'n' Aft, Huntington Beach, days. I forgot to tell
him night bartenders, was irritated with myself, until I
thought it wouldn't matter, because people switch shifts. No
dice, he said. This one's been out with the same operation you
had, just back to work and not doing nights yet.

"How'd you get all that out of her?" I said.

"Charm, what else? I'll keep at it, if you want, but it's getting pretty busy out here."

"That's okay, doll."

"Don't you worry," he said, his voice a warm wave of honey.
I missed him then, missed looking in his deep brown eyes
while he exercised his male right to practice his moves, the
solid jaw coming around as he'd look at you, like, Sweetie, I
got moves I ain't even *thought* of yet. One time I told him,
Raymond, you've been seeing too many Emilio Estevez movies, and he said, all innocentlike, "Who's he?" Okay, then, I
said, his brother, the one in *Wall Street.* "Who?" he says.
"Sheen. Charlie. You know, and you have that same grin he
does." Raymond, not one to give up easily, looked away then,
smiling, and said, "So that's my competition, huh?"

Now he was saying, "Somebody's going to be sending those
righteous Adam Henrys your way, Smokes. Just be patient.
Hang in there." Adam Henrys were assholes; code talk, even
though Ray was on his cellular, not using the airwaves, where
the FCC could be listening in.

"Thanks, Raymond, for whatever time you gave it."

"Sure thing."

"Stay out of trouble out there."

"Dig. Hey, Smokey?"

"What?"

"We found a Moe on the tracks today." He was referring to the hundreds, no, thousands, of illegals who make it up from the border, crossing at a fearful price paid to people who profit from human adversity, the ones who rape, steal, beat, and kill with virtual impunity. Still these *pollos*, chickens, come, spewing into the canyons until they reach by hook or crook northern cities such as Anaheim and Santa Ana, to pack a dozen to a room in cheap apartments where the landlord looks the other way; and in the chilly mornings go stand in empty lots next to fast-food places, hoping a slow-moving truck will stop and the man inside will lean out and say, "Three *manos* today," pick and shovel or hammer and broom, or until some citizens' group drives them away.

The boy on the tracks was probably just trying to catch a fast ride. The morgue is loaded with Does of Hispanic descent.

"Jeez, Ray."

There was a pause, and then he said, "I got overlap *and* graveyard tonight."

"Oh, no, Ray. Christmas Eve? That's awful. And still you took time to do my calling for me."

"The glamorous life of a traffic officer."

"Well, hey, Raymond. Kick ass and take names tonight, okay?"

He said, "Some poor slob of a motorist is going to wish he'd stayed at the office and worked all night."

"Attaboy, Ray. Show no mercy. Love ya, pal."

"That makes two of us."

I laughed, and then heard him sign off with, "Love ya too, Smoke."

CHAPTER
27

People started to drift away from their desks and their little coffee klatches to fuss with foods they'd brought in. I made one more phone call.

"Gary—"

"Twenty-one pitches, no hits. Sorry, sister, no bartenders by that name."

"I appreciate you trying anyway, Gary. I know a lot of bars aren't even open yet, so you probably came up with a lot of duds. What say I buy you lunch?"

"You don't have parties to go to?"

"There's food all over the place."

"And you still want lunch with an old man?"

"No, I don't. Don't invite him. Just you."

Feeding time, not with Gary, but at eleven-thirty, in the lab. Guacamole and chips. Rugalach. Falafel, and brownies, and chocolate chip cookies giving Mrs. Fields a run for her money. Salads. Meatballs bobbing in barbecue sauce. Too much.

Kathleen Kennedy and the personnel director had dressed up the long tables with paper tablecloths and a centerpiece of pine branches and candy canes.

Billy K. and Chris Cummins, the specialist in charge of the CAR, the Coroner's Analytic Robot, shared dubious honors for Good Glop in a Crock-Pot. When Chris came into the room dressed in his lab coat and a chef's hat, Billy K. followed with several bricks of cream cheese clutched in each hand. For the longest time they fussed at the table, Billy's dark head down, Chris's sandy hair bunched out like mini-muffins. As I'd pass by on my way to go do this or that, Chris'd look up from his stirring with a mad scientist's grin on his face and inhale the aroma.

"You getting high on that stuff, Chris?" I asked him.

He let go the wooden spoon, rolled his eyes heavenward, and fluttered his hands.

Chris monitors the robot, meant to take the tedium out of analyzing the whole splendid array of toxins both legal and otherwise that people use to alter their bored and pitiful states. The robot releases such solvents as chloroform into the samples, caps the tubes, shakes them, and moves them to a centrifuge where they're spun at tremendous force, causing the solvent to separate. He readjusts the pH, identifies acidic drugs, such as codeine and Tylenol, then sticks the sample back in the CAR to repeat the whole routine, this time testing for antidepressants; for anesthetics, such as cocaine and nitrous oxide; for anorexics—those compounds that suppress appetite—such as meth, the magic vitamin, and China White, a designer drug with 18,000 times the toxicity of heroin. And with each run of thirty samples, he includes seven or eight other compounds for a linearity check, a "standard," for control, so no whiner on a witness stand gets to cry "Foul."

When the time came to pluck up paper plates and feast, we gathered around Chris like hesitant school kids while he lifted the glass lid of the pot and began to spoon. The mixture was a sort of cantaloupe color.

"Smells like chili. But it don't walk like chili," someone said.

"Looks like something erupted from a very sick dog," I said, and everyone groaned and said, Thank you, Smokey, thank you very much.

"I'll have you know this product was developed in the Robert," the Robert being Chris's name for the CAR. "I call it Chris Cummins's Crimeval Chili."

My boss was hanging back, waiting near two file cabinets just outside the door, with a clear view of the action. Supervisors always wait till the last in food lines, just as lieutenants always sacrifice themselves in the front lines of a war. He asked Chris, "Is that spelled as in *primeval* or *crime* and *evil*?"

"Take your pick," Chris said, beaming, plopping a blob on

the next person's plate. Billy gave us the go-ahead, saying, If you closed your eyes, you *could* eat it—and everybody did, even me, with me meeting Gary Svoboda for lunch in barely an hour.

"Where's Joe Sanders?" The question came from a Colombian Joe had recommended for a job about six months ago.

Kathleen looked around the room, chin bobbing as she counted bodies, and said, "Yeah, we have a few people missing, don't we?" She wore a red dress with a beaded snowflake on the shoulder, and next to her, one haunch on a desk, the supply clerk was casting appreciative glances.

Luther Furijawa said he saw Joe at the morgue earlier. "We had a vegetable-oil case over there." A bony man with a streak of clean gray above the right temple, he was a man people liked and respected.

Stu Hollings, from the doorway, said, "I thought Freon was outlawed," referring to the fluorocarbon propellant base used in the cans. Fluorocarbons are cardio-toxic. With some people it doesn't take many uses to become sensitized; the heart responds by fibrillating.

"Yeah, Kathleen can't even sniff correction fluid anymore," the supply clerk said. "What's the world coming to?"

Luther Furijawa said, "That's right. Trichloroethane, the drying agent in correction fluid, has been replaced with a non-intoxicating, ozone-safe solvent." He shook his head and said, "This young man was fifteen years old, an A student, too. So sad. Dr. Watanabe thought it was a case of simple asphyxiation—suicide, or perhaps death at the hands of another—because the boy had a plastic sack over his head. But I was afraid it could be an inhalant and thereby volatile, so we examined the lungs underwater." When Luther said this, it wasn't self-congratulatory, because that is not the way Luther is. He added that the boy had been with two of his friends, hanging out, doing homework, listening to music, eating cookies the boy had baked himself. He excused himself to go to the bathroom, and never came out.

We were all silent for a moment, until I heard Trudy's deep voice: "Isn't that too bad?" she said. "Why do kids do that to themselves?" That was the most I'd ever heard Trudy say out loud in a group like that. She seemed relaxed today, smiling more, and when she finished saying what she did, her gaze settled on me from across the room with a pleasant look on her face. Standing next to her was Billy K., both of them against the wall by the window as they ate, their coffee cups on the sill. The line of Trudy's glasses came up to about the height of Billy's elbow. Her hair seemed longer, and she was wearing colors, green slacks and a red blouse, and red Christmas-light earrings that blinked off and on, off and on, reflecting on her cheeks. I wondered if Trudy could consider Billy K. a possible match. My eyes flicked over to meet his then, and I thought, Uh-oh, and looked away.

Herb, his gaze fixed somewhere in the middle of the floor, said, "The beat goes on."

We stood there with our Christmas-party plates piled with food, the bright poinsettia patterns spearing through beans and guacamole, lemon squares and brownies.

I said my Merry Christmases to everyone, hugged the men as well as the women—bless 'em, bless 'em all—and decided to leave my car in the lot and walk over to meet Gary.

Waiting for the traffic light, I thought about what I'd be doing for Christmas Day, tomorrow. I didn't expect to spend Christmas with Joe. But when he told me last night he was sort of obligated to see Jennifer and their son, David, home from college, on Christmas, I already felt lonely. He said if he got away early, he could come by later. Just like dating a married man. Wow, I didn't come anywhere close to waiting a year and a half for Joe to clear the doorsill. Patricia asked me one time how you know when you're in love. I said it was when you say his name over and over again and you're not even moving your lips.

CHAPTER
28

It was warm outside, maybe seventy-two, but cold in the café. Gary got there two minutes after me and found me sitting on my hands. He sat across from me in a booth, facing the light, the sun bouncing off the white metal tables outside, constricting his pupils to almost nothing. Our surroundings of used brick, bleached oak, and shiny brass rails were a soothing contrast to the beige bleakness of the lab, but it *was* chilly. "This could be a satellite to the morgue," I said.

"Marvellen's always cold," he said. "I tell her on trips if she'd just put her feet on top of the bologna we wouldn't need the ice pack."

I laughed because he said it with such roundness to his eyes.

I said, "At work I get coffee just to warm my hands—snake blood I guess." A waiter came up with menus. "Could I have some ho*t* tea, please?" emphasizing the *t* because in California when people hear *tea* they always think cold, don't ask me why.

Gary said, "I'm going to have the meat loaf. You?" His stubby finger mashed the menu as he looked up at me, the walrus mustache glinting golden-orange in the light.

"I don't think so," I said. "Hey, Gare, you notice I gave you the crow's nest?"

"Huh?"

"The best seat. In Oakland you watch your back."

"I watch my back, front, sides, and feet," he said. The waiter came back with my tea and Gary's diet soda, and took the rest of our order. Then Gary laid one big arm on the table toward me, grinned, and said, "Phillip Dugdale's got himself shoveling monkey caca morning to night in the Santa Ana Zoo."

"What? Gary. What'd he do?"

"You know, the Mexes you can kind of understand, they don't have all the advantages. But these here are white boys. Our pal Phillip had the bad sense to commit a drunk-and-disorderly in the city of Garden Grove, to which my friend Frank Ellis is assigned. Except for the fact he came up in front of Judge Rickenbacker, he'd be doing a sixteen-monther on assault."

"What happened? Tell me."

"Dugdale tells her this stuff with AA, how he's been trying real hard to get straight, got a good job washing dishes seven days a week if he wants it, and when he's not doing that he's down at the Cultural Arts Center, learning how to work out his frustrations in clay. Doesn't that just get ya?"

"Crooks we shall always have with us."

"Con men we shall always have with us. That guy . . ." Gary rubbed the back of his neck.

I was hopeful. "Why do those two bother you so much?"

"I told you. They're bad news."

"What'd he do to get your friend's attention?"

"You're not eating hardly a thing. You want some of my potatoes here? This is good stuff. How's the salad? Okay. Frank gets a call from a motel owner. The guy has to take a slug of booze just to calm down. He points out back, and there's Phillip sitting on the swimming-pool slide, up at the top, yelling all over the place. Frank asks him how long he's been drinking, and he says, 'I just wanted to go for a swim. Look, I'll pee in a bottle for you,' and starts unzipping. Turns out there was an argument over a broken shower rod and Phillip grabbed up a fistful of motel manager shirt and offered to rip him a new A-hole. Well, Frank gives him the Breathalyzer and he blows a *five*, poor dumb sonofabitch."

"Maybe he's only violent when he's drinking," I said.

Gary finished the bread with the last bite of meat loaf as he said, "The twink is bad news, any way you cut it. Shoveling zoo doo is exactly where he belongs."

*   *   *

Debut House is on Hollywood Boulevard near an old theater heretofore host of the splashy movie premiere; a little beyond is the famous lingerie house, Frederick's of Hollywood, where in the seventies you could get garter belts and crotchless panties and all manner of sexy stuff now sold right out in the open on the carousels of Robinson's, amid the flannel pj's and Ninja Turtle sleepers.

It was Christmas Day. There'd been no traffic on the freeways going north. My jacket was off, my window half down, and I had a tape of western birdsongs playing. I was up to the mewing sounds of the tiny California gnatcatcher, which nests in coastal scrub but is now practically extinct from housing overdevelopment. Then came the deep *chuh-chuh-chuh-chuh* of another endangered bird, the cactus wren. A heavily spotted bird with a downward-scooping bill and a white eyebrow, it hides in the underbrush, sort of growling. I was privileged to see one once when I was walking Farmer outside Capistrano, in a wash. I studied it without knowing what it was, made mental notes, then looked it up later in *Peterson's*.

The hillsides were almost totally brown from the drought, but otherwise it was the kind of day people see on TV and give as reason to move to California; a day bright and clear, and I thought how nice it would be to keep going all the way up to Santa Barbara. A beautiful, perfect day for hunting Annie Gwendolyn Dugdale, mother of Phillip and Roland G. Last known address: Debut Halfway House, Hollywood Boulevard, Hollywood. Next to Frederick's.

Carolyn Snyder was a pleasant woman about my age, maybe upward, with a trim body and earnest eyes.

When she talked it was as though you'd brought her a great problem to ponder, her eyes worried and far away.

She was leaning one hand on the door frame, a blonde spear of hair drifting down the right side of her face. All I asked was, "Do you have an Annie G. Dugdale residing here?"

Carolyn was responsible for seeing that twelve ladies had enough soap for the washer, sheets for the beds, and access to doctors and counselors. Early on in the conversation I told her who I was and where I worked.

"Annie's in trouble, then," she said.

"I just wondered was she here today by any chance. Just to talk to her."

"They're like children, you know," she said, shaking her head slowly. "They're good for a while, you think you've done something; then they leave. Oh, they come back—usually, anyway. Sometimes they're not even using. They just disappear," she said, shrugging, looking at me now with a pleasant expression. "And then they show up again. I ask them where they've been and all they do is get quiet and smoke. Or yell. Sometimes they yell. They'll say—oh, they'll say I don't have a right to treat them like kids, stuff like that."

I nodded, knew it was necessary for her to tell me about this life. I glanced at the window of the store next door, a plaster-of-Paris store where you buy chunky objects bare and paint them ugly colors. Rust rabbits with turquoise ribbons were clustered in a corner, their beady, hard eyes looking our way, and in front of them, a green chipmunk with a tiny Christmas wreath on its tail looked poised to run.

I said, "So Annie isn't here today?"

"I'm afraid she vanished last Friday. I don't think she liked having to keep house," she said, and smiled for the first time. "She had kitchen duty for over a month, but that's because one of the girls had bad dermatitis and couldn't get her hands in water or rubber gloves, and the other women had had their turn. She managed to wangle out of it the month before, so I stuck her on it. That seemed fair to me, doesn't it to you?"

No argument from me. "What does she look like, would you say," I asked.

"Oh, kind of heavy. Her hair won't do much anymore, she keeps dyeing it. She's . . . let's see if I can remember . . . about fifty-five. Yes. She's fifty-five August sixth. You can come in, see my records, if you like."

She nodded over her shoulder, and in the hallway behind her, I saw a woman—a dim silhouette, actually—start to cross the hallway, then stop and look our way, two holes where the eyes would be, a short line of nose, a scallop of chin. She moved on as I stepped in, and then a burst of laughter came from the room she entered, and I heard other women's voices, and caught the heavy scent of what was probably a Christmas bottle of perfume.

Carolyn led me into a waiting room, a sun room, my mother used to call it when we lived in a house in Northern California for a short while. But that was where you'd face an acre of mountain laurel and sage, not a grimy, too-long-between-rains Hollywood, U.S.A., street.

I sat on a brown couch and studied the philodendron tendrils that dangled from a green plastic pot over the window, the roots spidering out of the holes in the bottom. Under my feet was a faded Indian rug, fringed on the ends. A pressboard coffee table sat in front of me.

What Carolyn brought me was semiuseful. She handed me a folder and said she'd be right back.

Annie had been there two months this time. Three years before, she'd spent six weeks in Debut. Twice before that she'd been in halfways: one in Oklahoma City in 1972 and one in Reno, 1983. This was all information volunteered, in her own handwriting, on the paperwork. After the printed words, "Substance abuse?" she had written, "Booz and Speedballs."

Carolyn came back in with a tray of coffee and cinnamon rolls. "There's plenty, and I'm glad to have the company," she said, almost whispering. Then she sat beside me and cranked her head to read the file along with me.

I said, "Seems she's had problems quite a while."

"She goes on binges." Carolyn was tearing at her cinnamon roll, eating as she talked. "I think it's harder for Annie's type. They can go *years* without taking a single drink, but when they slip, they slip big," she said. "Annie said she wasn't really an addict." Carolyn raised an eyebrow. "We were working on that."

"She wrote down speedballs," I said.

"What's that again, exactly? I have a hard time keeping them straight." Her face was scrunching up. In another life we could've been talking about kids and PTA and husbands who don't appreciate us.

"Coke and heroin, cooked. How was Annie with the other women? I mean, how did she get along?"

"She accused people of taking her stuff two or three times.

Say, you wouldn't like to come back for Christmas later? Haven House, over in Brentwood, invited us over. It should be *real* nice. Two twenty-five-pound turkeys and I think a ham. You're welcome."

I said, No, thanks, I had to be going. Her face fell, and I thanked her again for her time and graciousness.

Walking back to my car, I looked up at the tinsel decorations strung across the street, the red and silver strands winking as they rippled, no one but me and a raptor-looking man behind the steering wheel of an older Rolls-Royce, stopped at a light, to appreciate them.

It wasn't till I'd passed Wilshire on the 405 that I thought about Phillip Dugdale again, how he had sat with his slicked-back hair in the interview room, glaring at the detective, not giving him any more than he wanted to.

I popped in the bird tape again. I kept having to rewind it and relisten, losing track of which song was which, thinking about the faceless man announcing the burrs and croaks and trills in his monotone voice. Who was it who'd go wading in a marsh, or pushing back tick-ridden branches, microphone in hand, to record this gab of nature for posterity?

Gary had mentioned that Phillip lived in Carson. Carson was next to Long Beach and sort of next to San Pedro, where Roland worked. I pulled off the freeway at Wilmington near Spire's, "The Pinnacle of Eating." There were phone booths outside, but I went in to call Patricia's number again, it being cheaper than from my car phone, and I could get another cup of coffee. I dialed; no luck.

I borrowed the phone book and went to the counter to sit, opening it to "Taverns." Asked the waitress for coffee and three dollars' worth of change. Said to myself, Here goes nothin'.

CHAPTER
29

The Goodyear airship floated in the distance ahead like a whale quietly intent on warm waters. A man in the restaurant told me I could take Wilmington Boulevard south to Sepulveda, and Sepulveda east to Long Beach if I didn't want to get back on the freeway. I'd spent thirty minutes dialing the numbers of drinking establishments in the Carson/Long Beach/Wilmington area, found several open, and asked if anyone who worked there was named Judy or Jubey. I didn't complete the list, though, because my coins kept not wanting to stick in the machine, rolling on through to the coin-return slot so that I had to try three or four times to make just one call. "The ones outside are worse," the waitress told me as she rushed past to take a bathroom break. So I decided to travel.

I was now in an industrial area, surrounded by mute and towering constructs I knew had to have been designed by human beings, built by them, presumably tended by them, yet inhabited by none. Rusted trucks were parked in gravel lots, but nothing moved. Here I could go see Dark Man, mutilated and on the run within the channels and walkways of these abandoned hulks, see him slipping under the colored pipework: blue where the boiler steam travels, orange where the effluent flows, white where encapsulated electrical cables join with yet other conduit to form geometrical mazes, and say, Hey, Bud, how about a game of poker and a beer? We could sit there in the shadows together, one across from the other; and he would like that because I would show respect, and would not ask to see his face.

I drove along Wilmington like the man said, then onto Sep-

ulveda Boulevard, where my car rattled over asphalt ribbed
from the weight of hundreds of tanker trucks, and saw one
coming at me jiggling too, despite its weight, and wondered if
it would stop at the stop sign like I had. The driver had a
beard, and I could see his jaw moving and his white teeth as
he chewed gum, but I could not see his eyes for a dark baseball hat he had pulled down low on his forehead. I rolled
down my window and moved through the intersection as he
made a right turn, and heard *boo-boo-boo-BOOM*, the sound of
classical music thundering from the cab.

There was a long stretch of chain-link fence corralling tank
farms, metal windbreaker slats woven in the link, and on top,
three-stranded barbed wire to keep out anyone who decided,
for whatever reason, a tank farm is a good place to be. The
barbed wire was supposed to angle *out*, toward the street, but
on one side of the road the wire angled in toward the yard,
maybe to contain the workers, but at any rate I hoped the
supervisor on that one didn't get a raise.

Sepulveda became Willow when I wasn't looking, and I was
in civilization again. I passed a cemetery right there in town,
with real headstones, upright, not flat for mowers. I passed a
twenty-one-minute Laundromat, a war-games shop, and then
a joint with a woman's nude silhouette in red and the words
HARDBODIES—GIRLS, POOL, FOOD, BEER, but today it was closed.

Graffiti coated the WELCOME TO LONG BEACH sign. Good, I
thought—I'm in the right territory. I knew about the troubles
Long Beach was having, with a small number of police and a
massive and rapid increase in crime. This year in Orange
County we had 170-odd homicides, the most in our history,
and I could not even imagine the chore L.A. County cops
faced, some 700 or so homicides to investigate. To top it off,
the coroner's office was receiving young Cambodian men of
the Hmong tribe, dead of mysterious causes. They'd go to bed
at night, wake up dead in the morning; and trying to trace
their medical backgrounds was impossible because the Hmong
have no written language.

While I waited at a signal, two men, one black and one Mexican, rolled a white dented VW up an incline to my left to
reach the intersection. Ahead I could see a few people drifting
in and out of doorways, and as I slowed at one corner, an

older boppin' black man, silver watch chain draped across his vest, black beret shading half his face, and an earphone wire running into his shirt pocket, stood waiting to cross at the light. His beard was swept neatly with gray, and as our gazes met, he nodded deeply. I nodded back, some acknowledgment passing between us, he and I alone in our irrevocably separate worlds.

I turned onto Tenth, not wanting to get too close to the Queen Mary and Howard Hughes's Spruce Goose, places where Roland and Phillip Dugdale would surely never be, and I got lucky. In my rearview mirror I saw a woman with dark hair walking down the sidewalk, wearing a pink blouse, black shorts that pinched her plump legs, a black cowboy hat, and high heels. There must be a bar around here somewhere. I circled and parked in front of a closed restaurant with Oriental writing on it, looked around, got out, locked my door.

The bar was there all right, in the direction the woman had come from. There was no name above the open door, a door that looked like my father's padded and buttoned office chair, but locals wouldn't need a name; it would be called Freddie's or The Club, or some such, and that's all you'd need to know.

It had been a long time since I'd been in a place like that, a bar-bar, not a watering hole for cop-a-roozies. Peanut shells covered the floor. There was a silent jukebox in the middle of the back wall, a wall made of huge dark beams like telephone poles. I walked past three customers seated at the bar and stood waiting for the woman behind it, who was kneeling down on the duckboards trying to stuff bags of chips into a cabinet under the counter. I heard her swear when they wouldn't all fit in, the slippery little devils plunking down by her feet. She then picked up the bags and shoved them at an angle deep into the recesses behind another door. When she stood up, I said, "Merry Christmas."

"What'll make it merrier?" she said, lifting her head so she could see through her glasses, which had slipped a little down her nose. She wore a man's white shirt with the sleeves rolled to the elbow, and her graying hair was done up in a bun on top of her head.

"How 'bout a Coors?"

"You got it."

Behind her, fake snow was blown onto the mirrors in waves just above the bottle necks. I hoisted onto a stool, glancing down to where the men sat, and found them watching me; but then they turned their heads back into profiles and began to sip their drinks.

I said when she came back, "Your name wouldn't be Judy, would it?"

"I hope not," she said, and smiled. "The last Judy I knew had five kids and another in the oven." Her teeth were the color of weak tea, but her lips were pretty and her skin was perfect. She went down to the three men and pincered some empties, then came back my way.

"Would you happen to know of a bartender around named Judy? Or maybe Jubey?" I said.

"If you're lookin' for a job, honey, this don't look like the place for you."

Three times I asked the question that afternoon, in three bars along Alamitos Street and Anaheim Street. I told myself it was pointless, but I couldn't stop; told myself you get a lot of information just nosing around. As a cop, you see things that don't look right, so you stop and ask a question and find an arrestable situation or people needing help. But it was seven years since I was a sworn and had a *duty* to go nosing. Maybe I had too much time on my hands. After bar number four, I did give up, and headed back toward the freeway, past the few remaining oil rigs that at one time numbered in the thousands along the Pacific coastline.

Almost to the on-ramp, I checked my gas gauge and got a chill: The needle was on "E." I never let my car drain that close to empty. In college I drove a clunker to night classes, and one time I read about a woman who ran out of gas at night, so she trudged off for a gallon. On the way back two men poured her own gasoline over her and set her on fire. The only reason anyone knew what happened was that this creature from the black lagoon came walking into a liquor store, went up to the clerk, told her story, collapsed, and died. That was when I bought my first gun.

I pulled into a Unocal station. After paying, I asked the attendant in the glass booth if I was still in Long Beach.

"Signal Hill," he said. The whites of his eyes glowed in a nest of dark lashes.

"Signal Hill? I didn't even know we had a Signal Hill. Do you know if there are any restaurants around open?"

"Take Cherry," he said, and waved an arm eastward.

"Do any of them have bars, do you know?"

His eyes shifted left a moment, thinking, My, these American women are something else, I guess, and I found myself giving the guy a stupid story, saying I had an uncle who worked at a bar around here someplace I was trying to find. By this time I was really feeling dopey and discouraged, thinking, You do not know what you're doing, Smokey, get the fuck home; nobody's working but the poor immigrants who don't know how to stop—and you. Instead, I passed over the 405 again and drove north along Cherry. One more try.

I came to a low building barely recognizable as a restaurant, and stopped. When I got out of the car, the pungent aroma of eucalyptus reached me, and these tall trees had no beetle chewing them to death. Despite the gray overcast here and a chill dampness in the air, the scent lifted my spirits a little, and I set off toward the front.

Inside was a patio off to the right, enclosed with turquoise plastic slats. A woman in a plum-colored waitress uniform sat at one of the tables there, working a crossword puzzle. Overhead, a heater was on, blowing warm air her way. I asked if it was all right if I sat here. She said, "Sure, I'll get you some coffee."

"I'm surprised anybody's open today."

"Yeah, well, we get the aerospace people, you know."

If I bobbed my head while I looked through the slats so that the letters on a distant building joined, I could make out, HOME OF USAF C-17, and then, DOUGLAS AIRCRAFT COMP . . . with the rest obscured.

The waitress came back with a cup and a pot, saying, "They take the week off between Christmas and New Year's, but we always get some who keep working. They come in early as six, six-thirty. Not me, boy, if I had the time off." I read her name tag: It said FRIEDA.

"Me either," I said.

"It's probably the computer types," she said.

I said, "They do get engrossed."

"And the managers. We get them all the time, the ones not too friendly, sit there reading their papers and don't look you in the eye." She was standing with her pencil poised on an order pad.

I smiled, looked her in the eye, and ordered a burger.

When she came back with water, she said, "Now, the ones I like are the oil hands. I tell you, some of them are funny, those oil people. They do love a joke." On the heavy side, Frieda was still attractive. Not so many years back the boys would've said, Now, there's a blouseful.

From a room behind the main room and within earshot of the patio came the sounds of a football game and a male voice yelling, "No, you dumb shit, don't go that way! Oo, ma-a-n."

Frieda looked over her shoulder and shrugged.

I said, "You wouldn't happen to know of anyplace around with a bartender named Jubey, would you?"

"Just a minute," she said, and walked away, into the back room. She came back with a black man with a receding hairline and a thick mustache. He was still wiping his hands on a towel when he came up to my table.

"This lady here wants to know if we know anybody by the name of Jubey."

Putting the hand with the towel in it on his hip, the man said, "Hi. I'm Avri Rousseau."

"How do you do?" I said, liking his name, his African look. "Merry Christmas."

"Thank you. You want to find somebody named Jubey?"

"Yes," I said, stunned that there was any response at all to the Judy/Jubey question.

"What for, may I ask?"

"Oh, well, uh, I think he knows a friend of mine."

The man leaned against one of the chairs and cocked his head at me before saying, "You a process server, now?"

I laughed, shook my head. "No way. Really. I'm just trying to find a friend I think was in his place. She telephoned me. I heard music in the background, like at a bar, and someone call a name that sounded like Jubey, or . . . or Judy, and then my friend and I got cut off, and it's really important I find her—"

"On Christmas Day."

"Well, she didn't call me *today*. She called the *other* day."

"She could call you back."

"Yes, sir, I know that. But she seems to have some sort of problem."

"That's my brother," he said. "Can't be two people by the name of Jubey, now, can there?"

I had to agree that'd be unlikely.

He pointed out toward the direction I'd come. "Go down Alamitos till you pass Seventh—"

"What city would I be in then?" I asked.

"Long Beach."

Not bad, Smokes. Right city anyway; wrong bar.

And then he told me the address of Jubilee's Saloon.

"He may not be there today, though. He was going to take his kids to the river."

I said, "Gee, I looked in the phone book. I didn't see—"

"He took the place over last month. Don't think he'll make a go of it, though. Today, for instance. He takes his kids to the river. You can't be going to the river when there's people want to get out of the house, away from the relatives, go to a nice bar and relax."

This was nearer the waterfront than I'd gotten on my first trip. The sign outside read THE OASIS, and the one on the door said SHOVE.

Inside, the jukebox was on and vibrating, a male voice asking if his girl would ever get tired of hurting him. Behind the bar was a man who looked like Avri except that there was no gray in his hair and his skin was mocha-colored. At the stools, four men: two Asian, one black, one Cauc. Two other Caucs with Fu Manchu mustaches and ponytails were playing pool in the back, sending a pod of balls cracking just as I stepped in. Fu Manchus usually mean Aryan brotherhood, and I wondered what they'd be doing in there.

Men look at a woman when she walks in a bar in two ways. The drunker ones stare; they reel around on their bar stools and follow your every move. I can outstare most of them, get them to the point where they snort, as if to say, "Shee-it, I bet she ain't a good hump anyway," and then they go back to their beer. The second way, they glance over but pretend they don't even see you, at least for awhile.

I walked to an empty stretch of the bar and stood, waiting for the bartender to come down, and when he didn't right away, I hefted up on a stool. One of the men down the line broke away, went to the jukebox to choose a song, and, as if choreographed, the second one came over and sat one stool over from me. *Then* the bartender came down. His eyelids seemed thick, and one eye was bloodshot. I said, "Are you Jubilee?"

He said, "All day long."

I ordered a beer to give Jubilee Rousseau additional reason to be open on Christmas Day.

The minute he moved away, the man next to me swiveled on his stool, looked me over, and said, "Hel-lo, Heaven." His face was pinched and speckled unevenly with beard.

"Sorry. I'm here to do business with Jubilee."

Three or four expressions passed quickly over the man's face as he considered each possible retort. Then he simply got up and swaggered, the way men do when they've just told someone off, back to his stool and his buddy, his pal-o leaning out once to look at me with a grin on his face.

When Jubey came back with the beer, I told him very directly that I was worried about a friend and was looking for her companions.

"Are you a police officer?"

And, of course, I could look him square in the face and say no.

His shoulders relaxed, and he leaned on the bar next to me but kept his body so he could see the others. I had the feeling the posture was not just to see who might flag him down for a drink. His voice became soft-spoken then, and he asked me, "How come y'all are not out with a boyfriend on Christmas Day?"

"Dumb, I guess."

"Now, I don't believe that." He hadn't asked it in a salacious way, but as a family man might.

And then we talked variously about his patrons, how well he knew them, and if he remembered a tall, pretty redhead in here last night; then about what was happening in the Gulf, about tough times ahead for everyone, about the weather and the water police.

Because he couldn't help me, and that was the bottom line.

CHAPTER
30

The week after Christmas was extremely busy, lots of tox testing from all the drivers who'd soon be paying lawyers before they paid their Visa bills.

I was in the robot room working with Chris. I'd spent all day entering data into the computer and trying to print it out, but the paper kept jamming, and it seemed I was spending more time fooling with that than producing anything. I went back to my desk for a chocolate-covered peanut and a tea bag, when the phone rang.

"This is Rowena Dwyer."

"Well, hello."

"I wanted to call you yesterday," she said. "I wanted to call you *Christmas*." She sounded funny, but I couldn't put my finger on it. There was a hardness there, and a breathiness, as though she were taking a drag on a cigarette and exhaling. She said, "I don't have your home phone number."

"No. It's not listed."

"That's smart, I guess."

"Are you all right, Rowena?"

"What do *you* think?"

Chris Cummins stepped out into the hall as though he were looking for me. When he saw I was on the phone, he went back in.

"What can I do?" I said, thinking, If she just wants to talk, I'll talk.

"It's not working for me," she said, pausing for only a moment. "I know that's not your problem."

"Have you talked to the detectives at all?"

"Oh, yes." And then I thought I heard a soft sobbing coming from her. I didn't know what to say, so I waited a second, and then she added: "Oh, God, I'm drunk," and then more sobbing, her voice cracking when she spoke again. "I'm sorry. I bet you've never been drunk, have you? I shouldn't be calling you. I'm sorry, so—"

"You want my home phone, Rowena? You have something to write with? It's kind of hard for me to talk here."

"Let me see," she said. I heard more sounds, some sniffling, her blowing her nose. Outside my work area, people passing by were talking loudly. I put my hand up over my other ear. Rowena came back on the phone and said, "Okay. Here I am. Smokey? I know your name is Smokey. I heard."

"Yes," I said, and started to give her my home number.

"Just a minute. I have to tell you something."

"What's that, Rowena?"

There was a long pause. Then she said, "What?"

"You were going to tell me something."

"I was. . . . Do you have a mother?"

"My parents live in Florida."

"Oh. I'm back home. Did I tell you that?"

"You're in Wichita, then?"

"Uh-huh."

"Can I help you with something, Mrs. Dwyer?"

She said softly: "Oh, there you go again."

"I'm sorry—I should be getting back to work, Rowena."

"Wait," she said. I could hear a raspy sound through the receiver, like a wheezing, and then she said, "I loved that boy so . . . much." Her voice was soft and I had to strain to hear it.

"I know. I know you did. Rowena?" She was still there, I knew, but she didn't answer. "Rowena, where's your husband? Where's Mr. Dwyer?"

"Who knows? I don't care. The sonofabitch. I wanted him to get a private detective. I wanted him to go after this, and he won't do it. He says leave it alone. He says it won't bring Jerry back. I'll hire the goddamned detective myself. That's why I'm calling you: I want you to tell me the name of a good detective, not one of those other ones. Can you do that for

me? I have the money. I was going to send it to Jerry for half
a car. For Christmas."

Now was not the time to argue with her. I knew that from
home experience, both parents.

I got her to give me the number in Wichita where she was,
and told her we'd talk soon. Somehow in doing that, I wound
up not giving her my own phone number, and later I thought
it was probably for the best. I am not a very good vessel. People's
woes pour into me, my sides burst.

Chris was struggling with the printer when I came back. He
said, "This thing has a vendetta against me. When's Stu going
to get the new equipment?"

"Don't ask me. I only work here," I said.

We wrested the paper out and set back to the job of processing
the dozens of samples lined up on the counter, Chris
feeding the Robert, and I building charts as he read data off
to me. At one point I turned in my chair and said, "People
do persist in killing themselves, don't they?" and Chris said,
"Less people to get in my way at the Meadows," meaning an
outside concert stadium south of the lab, in Irvine.

"You're such a sweet guy, Chris. I don't know how I ever
lived without you."

"That's what my wife tells me every day."

And I was right. People kill each other on the freeways, on
the side streets, on back roads where the only other vehicle
around is a tilted belly-dump earth mover perched on the
shoulder; and we sit here handling their fluids like it was
something delivered from a drugstore.

The week was going to be a bitch. As if in verification, Billy
K. stood outside in the hallway telling the new girl that by
noon on Christmas Day the coroner's had six more stacked up
in the cooler.

Contemplating this, and despite the fact that Chris could've
used my help at the spectrometer all day the next day, Friday,
what did I do but type up a request for vacation. Because in
my mailbox when I got home Thursday night lay a postcard.

I had gathered up the mail and put it on the counter, and
then, while putting groceries away, I'd slid a couple of pieces
of mail over, glanced at them, put something else away, poked
a finger at one or another to read the envelope better, put

something else away, and then I came to the card. It had on its front a cartoon picture of a beavertail cactus—*opuntia basilaris*. Its spineless gray-green pads resemble paddles, or beaver tails. I flipped the card over. There was no message. I flipped it to the front again.

It advertised the Beaver Tail Inn, North Las Vegas, Nevada. The cactus had a smiling face and wore a pink bloom on its head as if behind an ear, and its pudgy arm waved us toward the miniature motel in the background.

I looked again at the back. Unless it was written in disappearing ink, there was indeed no message. Yet the card was addressed to me, in black felt-tip pen. I did not recognize the writing. The edges of the card were yellowed. "Beaver Tail Inn, Lake Mead Blvd. and Comstock," is all it said in the left corner, and there was a phone number with a 702 area code.

Taking it into the living room, I studied it some more. When had I seen Patricia's handwriting? In August she'd sent me a birthday card. But I don't keep cards. When else?

I dialed the number. "The number you have dialed is no longer in service."

Two times I returned to the card while putting my groceries away. I took it up a third time, sitting at the counter in my kitchen, staring at my bird calendar for the new year. January's picture was a long-billed curlew standing in water. We have curlews in the bay. Their call is a plaintive *cur-lee*.

I looked at the postcard again. And said to myself, "This is from Patricia."

I could go to the lab and do a fingerprint run. But that would help only if Patricia had had her fingerprints rolled in her lifetime. What are the chances of that? Then I thought, Well, if she has a tattoo and she hung with a felon, maybe . . . Cops check people out all the time: the wife, the girlfriend, the son's girlfriend, the daughter's latest, the new second-job business partner. You're a cop, you're a paid paranoid.

But it was six o'clock, I knew Betty and the other Print people would have gone home, and I really didn't want to mess with their computers. They'd probably changed passwords a dozen and a half times since I used the system anyway.

I slipped the postcard in an envelope and tucked it in my purse, then got in my car and drove to Huntington Beach instead, to check if Patricia's car was there, or to annoy her landlady again.

"I don't know nothing about her, and I don't like being disturbed at night," she said. Lawrence Welk's family was singing "Walking in a Winter Wonderland" on the TV as she shut the door.

When I got to the lab Friday morning, I phoned Patricia's place of work.

"She doesn't work here anymore," a woman told me.

"Since when?"

"I don't know. This is only my third day." Behind her, phones were ringing.

Last ditch, I asked, "Could I talk to Annabel Diehl, then?"

"Who?" she said.

I said the name slowly, spelling out the last name the way I thought it would be. The woman put me on hold. When she came back, she asked me who it was I wanted again, and then, with phones still sounding in the background, said, "There's no one here by that name."

On my way to Stu's office I saw Bud Peterson in the hallway and asked if I could run something through the Printrak. He said, "You can, but I hope you don't want it anytime soon."

"As a matter of fact, I sort of do."

"Rots o' ruck. They picked *this* week to Beta-test the ProFile system," he said, referring to a computerized mug-shot program that would blow all the others out of the water. "Nobody's access time is better than three hours."

"You're joking."

"I'm kidding you not," he said, and left, the usual deadpan expression gone from his face, replaced by a slight panic in the eyes. He wanted it, he got it: his jump up the management ladder.

Stu Hollings wasn't thrilled. The only thing was, I'd been with the lab four years and hadn't used up four weeks of the eight for vacation that I was entitled to. He'd been the very one who, when he came in new to his position, called me in one day and seriously urged me to use up my accumulated vacation—the department's new policy was to clean excess days off the books. Now he was reminding me I'd been out six weeks this year. I wasn't going to defend my medical. I stood there, not commenting. And then he said, "You took a half-day vacation not too long ago, if I remember correctly." He started turning pages in a blue three-ring binder.

"You don't need to look it up," I said. "You're right. I did." He looked at me, waiting. "This is an emergency. I need the time. I wouldn't ask if I didn't."

"A family emergency? Well, then, of course."

"No, it's not a family emergency. I don't like making up false excuses. Why can't we just say it's an emergency of a personal nature? What's the difference if it's family, medical, or a UFO sighting, Stu? Look at my record. You'll see I'm not frivolous." I said this kindly, smiling, saying, Come, let us reason together.

Both hands were laid on his desk near the binder as he sat peering over his wire glasses, his Wilford Brimley pate gleaming from the fluorescent lights overhead. He said, "I don't like to be told these things."

I was standing politely near, but not too near, his desk. One hand was still on the door handle behind me as a brace. I said, "You want me to lie then."

"No, I want you to tell the truth. Of course I want you to tell the truth."

I took my hand off the doorknob, and I shouldn't have, for the gesture I used then was palm out, like a traffic cop. He frowned. I said it anyway: "Some things are private."

"We're overloaded here. This is not a good time."

"One day. That's all I'm asking for. Monday. I'll be back Tuesday morning."

"No deal."

To Joe I can say fuck you. To Stu, if I wanted a job when I came back, I'd better bite my tongue till it bleeds. Okey-dokey, I'd phone in sick from Las Vegas, if that's the way he wanted it, the world-class idiot.

Before I left, I went into Joe's office, closed the door, and sat down. He was "staff" now, not a supervisor, but so well regarded he got to keep his office. He'd taken the whole week off except for today. I thought that was odd, and asked him about it when he called me that first day back after Christmas—why not take the whole week? "Because I'll miss you too much," he said. He told me he'd spent Christmas Day with Jennifer and his son, David, and I felt a little pang but didn't say anything. When he asked what I did all day Christmas, I told him I slept.

I said, "What do you think of Stu Hollings?"

"I think he's fine. I think he's doing a good job. Why?"

"Oh, nothing."

The muscles around his eyes relaxed, and he put both hands together in a prayer gesture and laid them against the side of his face, his elbows on the desk, as he looked at me.

I said, "I came in to tell you I'm going to take vacation, starting two hours from now."

His chair squeaked badly as he leaned back.

"This office is intolerable without you," he said. "You can't go."

"I haven't seen you all day. How can you say that?"

"I was looking forward to a weekend maybe—"

"There will be weekends."

"It's one reason I spent the last few days with David. We saw some real wonder wagons at the Coliseum."

"The car show?"

"How 'bout a Benz for fifty-six thousand to run around the mud with? Station wagons with four-wheel drive," he said, shaking his head. "The Benz, even without a turbocharger, rates with an Audi two hundred Quattro. Oh, I'm sorry. I don't know if you're into those things."

"I don't like to window-shop. Can't buy, don't try's my motto."

"I should have been married to you the last twenty-five years. Now, tell me, where are you going without me, you heartless female?"

"I have some business to take care of."

"Business."

"Well . . . yes. Plus I need to get away awhile. I thought I'd go see a friend in Northern California. Clear my head."

"Not of me?"

"Don't be silly."

"That's one I don't remember ever being accused of."

"Joe," I said, thinking about how I was going to say this, then just saying it: "I almost went out to see Phillip Dugdale."

"Oh." All the cheerfulness went out of his face.

"See what I mean, then? I need time off."

He came out from behind his desk and stood me up out of the chair. "You didn't, though."

His presence felt wonderful, but I warred with myself. I looked down. "No, I stayed put." A lyin' little shit-titsky, that's what I was becoming.

He kissed me lightly on the lips. "You do what you need to. Vacation sounds like a good idea. I'll miss you, but time away is good. If I'd listened to Jennifer, maybe I wouldn't have had my heart squeezing stones a while back."

"It makes me kind of uncomfortable kissing in the office," I said, pulling away. I had no problem with office romances, as long as they were discreet. Where else are busy people going to find each other? But I said, "I mean, is that okay?"

"Of course. You're right. I'll cool it." He sat on the front edge of his desk, hands gripping the edge. He seemed bemused.

I moved to a chair in the corner, the back of my leg touching it for support. In the pocket of my green rayon jacket was a stubby pencil convenient for fiddling with; I pulled it out and tested the wood with my fingernail. "I want to talk to you about something," I said.

"Shoot."

"I am super-worried about Patricia. She's seeing one of the Dugdales."

"I know. You told me that. Several times."

"But Joe, listen to this—she left her job. I phoned there this morning. Joe, she would have *told* me."

Thoughtful for a moment, he said, "People go south on you once they get involved with somebody. I've got friends once they're married you never hear from. I'm not so good about that sort of thing myself."

This was different, with Patricia, I told him. I said, "You don't think it's a pretty drastic—well, at least, a significant thing to do, leave your job? I mean, you usually think it over, talk it over with somebody first. She was happy there. Three weeks ago she was telling me she was making major bucks. She was doing well. Do you think I should go see her employers? Her *former* employers?"

"Absolutely not."

"I mean—"

"How would you feel if she came to your place of employment, asking questions about you? Low marks on judgment, Smokey."

"Even if she's gone? How could it hurt?"

"You don't know the details. I just wouldn't do it. You asked for my opinion, I gave it to you."

"I could ask in a way that wouldn't jeopardize her."

"It's a good thing you're not working for me," he said.

"Now, what does that mean?"

"High on creativity, but I'd say sometimes low on judgment. That's how I'd mark your performance evaluation."

"Oh, thanks." I was genuinely hurt, but I couldn't show it. "What about initiative? What about quality?"

"Quality, yes."

He stood up from the desk, put his hands on my shoulders, and pulled me to him. "Yes, yes, and yes."

Up my arms went, around his neck. I kissed him. In the office.

When I went out of there, his scent still fresh in my senses, but his words also, I thought, I wonder if I could get along with him, all day, all night.

I packed that afternoon so I'd be ready to leave early Saturday morning. I packed stuff for a week, even some semi-nice clothes, thinking maybe if I got a cold trail in Vegas, I'd go on up to San Francisco and see an old friend. Then I was twirling my thumbs. What do I do now, between five-thirty and five-thirty?

I took a chance that Yolanda, Raymond's girlfriend, wasn't home from her day-care job yet, and called his house. He'd been doing overlap shifts during the holidays, logging extra hours because Yolanda was really putting the muscle on to get married and he needed the extra dough if they were going to do it, so I wasn't sure he'd be there, but he was.

"Ray," I said, "look, I'm sorry if I shouldn't call—"

"No problem at all, Smokes. Yolanda and I, we had a talk. She's cool now. She's got it. Friends, she says. As long it's just friends and nothin' else."

"I won't ordinarily call anyway. Not everybody can understand."

"You in trouble, hon?"

I said, "Ray, what do you think of accompanying me to Carson tonight?"

"No can do. That's why I'm getting to work overtime—they need me out there on the highways and byways. It's going to be party time till New Year's. Besides, that is not a smart thing to do. That is not a kinder, gentler city. There was a freeway shooting out there off Wilmington just last week."

"I want to find Phillip Dugdale, Raymond. Listen, his brother's gone from the apartments, moved out, and so's Patricia. Well, she hasn't moved out, but she's left her job and I can't get in touch with her, and I'm telling you there's something walla-walla going on."

"Why don't you wait till tomorrow? Maybe I can get away then."

"Tomorrow I'm leaving on vacation. To San Francisco." I didn't tell him about the postcard.

"Boy, one operation and you figure you like it out there in the world, huh?"

"Don't give me a bad time, Raymond."

"Hey, I gotta run, babe. I just got out of the shower. Call me when you get back, huh?"

"Absolutely. You be careful now, Raymond."

"You're the one going out there in a little Jap car."

It was going to be a long night. I turned on the news while eating a microwave dinner. Protesters in Irvine were carrying signs that read PEACE, DUDE.

Afterward, I went to the bedroom, reached inside a fireplace I never use, and removed my .38 Colt revolver with the stainless-steel barrel that I hadn't cleaned in a long time. I sat on the bed, a newspaper spread out and the kit with the Gunslick, cotton patches, and cleaning rod in the middle. The gun

seemed heavy as I lifted it. I gave away a two-shot derringer
backup when I left the force, and now I wished I hadn't. At
the time, I thought it was a silly little gun, a .22 single action,
which I never liked, but Bill had given it to me, telling me,
No, no, a twenty-two's all you're going to need in a situation,
close up. At least I could carry it in my pocket holster, and
did. I could cock it in there and it would look like I was grabbing a ring of keys. Wearing an ankle backup didn't work too
well with women, at least not for me, and wearing it Texas
Ranger–style, tucked in a weak-hand holster in the small of
your back, always seemed awkward to me. I gave the .22 to a
copper since transferred to Michigan. She invited me to her
house for dinner, and I paid her back with that. Her mom
stopped by as I was leaving, and I remember her saying, "Are
you a lady policeman too?" Yep. We were lady policemen.

Closing the cylinder, I worked the action. Wow—stiff. I
stood up and took the stance. In the mirror, the gun wavered.
Out of shape, Smokey. Way out of practice.

After cleaning the Colt, I slipped it into its rug and found
space in my suitcase, then went to the living room to look at
the reflections over the bay. The light was off and I left it off.
I walked to the window where the gifts were stacked, and
pulled back the drapes. Moonlight made the gold paper on
the gifts glisten. I hadn't even given Ray his Mustang. The
paper banner with his name on it was still taped to the antenna.

Out on the bay, white ripples scalloped the surface of the
water. It might have been a painting on black velvet, the saltgrass backlit, the outline of ragged pampas off to one side.
Below my apartment, a car's headlights came on, and a pos-
sum's eyes lit up red in the near brush.

Maybe I'd go knock on Mrs. Lambert's door, see if Farmer
wanted to go for an early weekend walk. Farmer and I, we
think well together.

CHAPTER
31

It isn't that Californians love to drive. We just *drive*, like we just brush our teeth.

Still, it surprised me that there were so many cars on the freeway before the light broke Saturday. Weekdays it's bizarre: You can get on the freeway at 4:45 in the morning and see thousands of taillights shrinking in the distance. Farmer would love it, all those little red bunny tails inviting chase, except to him the red might be Garfield-the-Cat-orange, and Garfield himself might be yellow. Joe and I had an argument once about whether dogs could see color. He called his vet to check. The vet said no. But I remembered reading somewhere that they do, so I called Washington, D.C., and found two scientists who said, yes-indeedy, dogs do discriminate colors, just differently from you and me; and so I collected from Joe a high-priced lunch at the Boardwalk, ordering wine as well.

I was thinking this and then wondering if I'd have a job to come back to, if I'd be having lunch with Joe at the Boardwalk ever again and be making bad jokes about Glop in a Crock-Pot. With county cutbacks in the offing, they could trim a Smokey Brandon and not miss her a bit, though they wouldn't gain much from the saved salary.

As my six-cylinder whined up the El Cajon Pass, heading into Victor Valley, the L.A.-syndrome shackles began to fall off, but as I approached Victorville, I thought of the license plate on the Bronco parked at Patricia's apartment complex, which I later learned did belong to Roland, and wondered why a guy who lives in Huntington Beach, formerly of Garden Grove, would buy a car in Victorville.

A gray Taurus kept pace with me, I noticed, and I remembered that when I left the lab Friday night, a gray Taurus kept making all the turns I did, even down my street and into my lot, and I thought, Hm, here's a guy maybe I could carpool with. I could carpool with him all the way up to Vegas, it seemed, if that was the same guy. Picking up speed to test him out, I was flying, and so was he. Then he surged ahead of me and around a big truck and then I saw later he got lodged between two of them and couldn't pull out for a third one on his right. Ho-hum.

I drifted right through, or rather, over, Victorville, the city getting so upscale it has its own massive discount stores and a Holiday Inn I could see from the freeway, and a more unattractive shade of turquoise it could not be.

This is the territory of ugly names: Victorville, Cleghorn Road, Barstow. And out of Barstow, Boron, not the place of covered wagons and Ronald Reagan advertising for Twenty Mule Team Borax, but the locale of a federal prison camp, where, I was reminded, I had a relative. The camp was a former radar tracking station. Now it houses five hundred or so inmates, one of them a cousin on my mother's side, Daniel Cross, a man I've never met. Last time I talked to her, she told me Danny, as she calls him, wound up there on a drug-related charge. I thought, driving by, I should go introduce myself. But why? It's not that I condemn people who get in trouble, not the way some of my copper buddies do who're absolutely hard-ass on all miscreants. Who say arrests are a way of life for these people, that the jug's just another word for a change of scenery. I hadn't quite reached that point of belief, but the work does give you a different take on life, and even that changes: First you hate 'em, then you cry for 'em. Then you hate 'em, then you befriend 'em. Then you hate 'em. Then you hate 'em. I knew there'd be types in there who'd hold a guy down and pour a strip of nondairy creamer on him, touch it off with a lighter. It burns like napalm. I wouldn't be stopping there today.

The landscape became less desolate soon, between Barstow and Baker, and I took pleasure in the soft rust colors of sandstone crust and the deep blue shadows stairstepping down the craggy ridges in the near distance. In the far distance, the landscape softened as though a painter had swept a brushful of milk over the canvas to plead away the harshness. Slight trees at roadside knuckled with parasites. In the slow-vehicle lane next to me, a truck laden with pipe crawled toward Halloran Summit, and just ahead of it, a silver tour bus loaded with Vegas bettors droned on, and as I pulled away approaching the ridges, I saw the broken black stone left by the glaciers, and the bleached sand that had swept up the sides of the mountains from the valley floor in lonely drafts.

Ten miles before reaching Baker is Zzyzx Road, as in *eye* and *six,* and down it to the east about five miles is the Desert Studies Center. A zealot of one sort or another squatted the land many years back and built a spa, hotel, and church that were in operation till the BLM—Bureau of Land Management, a big honcho in these parts—confiscated the buildings. I knew about this because Jeri Landsforth, our forensic anthropologist, taught a class in insects there two years ago. Who knows, if our department had had the training dollars then, maybe I'd be pushing around insects with tweezers the size of knitting needles today, or out in the brush bothering birds. Joe S. told me, my first week in the lab, You'll get one-sided here. Have a life apart from this, he'd say. Get involved in your community. Be around kids if you can. Enjoy your family. Join a baseball team. Play badminton or racquetball or bingo. If I were out of Building 16 more often, maybe I wouldn't get "possessed."

By the time I reached Baker and stopped, the temperature was warm enough to be summer in most other places of the world. In the last week of December the so-called Yukon Express had made noble attempts to break through the desert heat, but failed. My body wouldn't have dry skin where I didn't know I *had* skin if the storm had made it this far, because it would've pushed through to California too. Orange County was into big-time drought, at the same time that land developers were spilling millions of gallons of water on graded land to keep the dust down, and cities were setting up the Water Police and cajoling us to take sixty-second showers. No thanks. This citizen is going to order water every time she eats in a restaurant too, so there. Put me in jail. Then release me in fifteen minutes.

I drove up to Bun Boy and saw it was boarded up, then

wheeled back to the omnipresent Denny's, where I parked under the inadequate shadow of a palm and stood by my car to
remove the long-sleeved denim shirt I had on over my white
T. The bumper sticker of a car parked next to mine with the
blue-and-black plates from Baja California read: NO A LAS
DROGAS! So—some Mexicans don't like drugs any better than
we do. One time Raymond asked me to go blue-shark fishing
in Mexico, before he moved in with Yolanda. I wish I had.
But I was sick then. He brought back a seventy-pounder,
showed the pictures around, and said, "Is that an ugly thing
or what?" I said, "Which, the one standing on its tail or the
one beside it?" and he said for someone who chickened out,
I sure sounded jealous to him.

Inside, after taking care of business, I ordered a coffee and
bagel, then sat imagining how it would be to take a vacation
with Joe. Hours to talk with him, to ask what he was like as a
little boy, what he wanted to be when he grew up; what his
parents were like. To ask who his best friend was in grammar
school—those kinds of questions. I wondered about things like
who did Joe vote for in the governor's race, and I was afraid
to find out. And I wondered if he and Jennifer ever wanted
more than one child. That night in his apartment, after we'd
finished the first time, he laughed and said, "An old man with
a weak heart has just been seduced by a woman with none."
I said, "Wait a *minute*. Who was it who kissed who right on the
ever-lovin' lips in the *office*, huh? You started this whole thing."
And then I asked him when was the first time he ever thought
about me, and he said, "That's naughty." I pressed him, and
he looked like he was thinking, and then said, "What'd you
say your name was?"

In a quieter moment, he dragged a finger over my still-fiery
scar and called it my evil grin. That thought, while I sat there
in Denny's, led me to thinking about how else Joe would make
love to me—in the bathroom, in the kitchen, in a car, in a
sleeping bag, one of my fave fantasies, like, Oh, we're lost on
this big bad mountain and only one sleeping bag between us,
tsk, tsk. And after that, thinking I'd like to see him watching
a movie. I'd like to watch him working on something at home,
and cooking something I'd never eat.

And before I knew it, I was thinking of Patricia, her telling

me not only in Chi-Chi's but another time, when it had been
a long spell between interests for me, that she was going to
have to get me some serious action. Patricia with the purple
earrings and the tease in her eyes—strong, sure of herself.
The only time I didn't see her sure of herself was the time I
took her to the jail. The only time I didn't *hear* her that way
was on the telephone when she told me Phillip had done
something with or to a girl; oh, and yes, when she said someone'd been in her apartment. How did my friend, Patricia
Harris, wind up with Roland Fuckhead Dugdale, who looks
like Chuck "The Rifleman" Connors, that's who.

I slipped the Beaver Tail postcard out of my purse and studied it some more. Cactus waving "Y'all come" on front. Could
be a whorehouse. Beaver Tail's suggestive. Nah. Whorehouses
are lying low these days, done in by AIDS or the IRS. The regular houses were more out in the hinterland, in Nye, not in Clark
County, where Las Vegas is. Nevada's big cities outlaw prostitu-
tion, so the houses string out along the arteries. Nye, eerily
shaped like a mushroom, is close enough for Nellis Air Force
boys to pop over for a poke. At the stem end of the mushroom
is the Nellis Nuclear Testing Site. Pick your poison.

I turned the postcard over. Definitely *my* address, my name:
Okay, Smokes, stare close. Maybe your powers can read Patri-
cia's whorls, loops, and arches right there on the postcard's
blue sky, spelling out her name in fingerprint language.
Maybe you'll turn a cactus wrinkle into a scrawled line of text.
Like a message in a bottle."

I put the card back, dredged the last of the coffee, and sat
waiting for the check. Patricia's voice moved into my memory
again, telling me someone left the milk carton open in her
apartment. Someone threw egg on her car. Saying, "Smokey,
something completely weird is going on."

My face flushed. I didn't want to think about it. It was clear
now that I had been so afraid for her at some unarticulated
level, I had let the episodes slip right out of my mind; as if
criminal things won't—can't—happen to people close to you,
because your very presence in that person's life is stop-order
enough. Jerry Dwyer? True, we weren't close. But he was "in"
my life, and I in his. We traded jokes and regarded each other
in that watchful way when you have an interest in someone

but can't fulfill it due to a whole car-lot of differences. Jerry, the kid with the morning full of smiles.

The waitress bid happy trails to me, and while I walked back to my car, I said to my mental picture of Patricia: I'll be there, *amiga*. I'm coming. Hold on.

On the frontage road leading back to the highway, I saw the gray car again in my mirror. Nuts, I'm flipping out here, I thought, but I pulled across the road into the dirt lot of the fire station, and then I saw it was a one-horse police station too. How convenient. The Taurus went by. I circled back up to the road and picked up speed again.

From Orange County, figure five hours to get to Vegas. Barely anything in that long trip to break the fundamental monotony of the highway as it ribbons through sandstone, limestone, dry lakes, and lava beds, except the game of spot-a-cop-before-a-cop-spots-you. Yes, Samantha June Brandon does break some laws, shame on me. I try to put a cap on it, though. Honest, I do.

Ahead, a dust devil danced across the flat land, and even with my air conditioner on, I could hear the rasp of grit-filled wind as it broke across my windshield, and I slowed, and noticed for the first time the pale-green bushes on black wood poked up behind wire fences strung as far as the eye could see. Everywhere, wire fences. Not a place to pull off the road and shoot at tin cans anymore.

A dark mound loomed in the highway; roadkill, no doubt. I was coming close when the humped shoulders moved and a turkey vulture lifted off from the meat, his bare, red, and wrinkled head like a raw drumstick. A glance upward showed me two more of the birds riding thermals, tilting unsteadily, their six-foot wings pitched to a dihedral; that is to say, a shallow V. Not a cop in a 'copter, just the graceful birds cleaning carrion for us. I've often thought, if the digestive systems of buzzards, call them vultures, destroy whatever malignant bacteria fester in ripe meat, then let us bottle that stuff, add a solvent here, a distillate there, press the jar mouth against diseases that attack human beings, or against the rough hide of a society that murders its own; clean its carrion.

CHAPTER

32

Bonnie and Clyde's bullet-riddled death car rests in the lobby at Whiskey Pete's. At the Prima Donna casino, across the highway from the "Death Car," as it is billed, stands a Ferris wheel you can ride. Up the road a little is Kactus Kate's, and beyond that the Gold Strike, behind which is nested, in this bleakest of terrains, the Sandy Valley Correctional Center, a medium-security state prison with rust-colored blockhouses and beige guard towers that stick up on the north and the south boundaries. Rectangular slits at the top of the towers look like the eyeshields of welder's masks, only from the highway they seem to stare not at the yard, but at you. Guys at Sandy can look down at the Gold Strike and plot escape long enough to blow quarters down the chutes for the ten-thousand-dollar prize and then ride, man, outa there. I'd forgotten what Nevada could mean.

Here, in another life, I was Dusty Rose, and then I was Smokey Shannon. Alias Samantha Montiel or, rather, the other way around. My hair was red, my legs were long, my costume was less than I now wear to bed.

Fifteen years ago, Stretch Jones and I were on our way to San Francisco—'Frisco, we called it, but San Franciscans hate that. It was the middle of November. I was recently out of high school, working a couple of different jobs at local stores and trying to decide if I could avoid taking a job with my dad in his bookbinding business much longer, or if I should go on to college, as my biology teacher wanted me to. I'd been living more out than in at my parents' in Camarillo, a sleepy little town about fifty-five miles south of Santa Barbara. The day I met Stretch I'd just hopped out of my boyfriend's car after an argument and went hitchhiking up 101 in the rain. Not too far up the road, this guy in a yellow VW stopped and asked me if I needed a ride. I said no. But about a half-mile farther I came to a coffee shop and went in. There he was at the counter in his dry denim jacket and goatee, the same guy as in the Volks, sipping hot tea and eating a burger. He looked a little like the pictures of Ichabod Crane in schoolbooks, if Ichabod Crane wore denim and love beads. We talked a little. He had a quiet sense of humor and sad brown eyes. When it came time to pay, he dug with two fingers into his pocket, checked his wallet, and came up short. I bought the burger and invited him home.

A few days later we were on the road, headed north to check out the Haight because that's where it was happening. In my heart I had misgivings, because I didn't want to do heavy dope, and the pressure would be on in a big way there. Peyote and other psychedelics were available everywhere, including my mom and dad's own middle-class abode, but I thought it would be worse in the Haight without my natural parent/child rebellion to account for abstention. Stretch got an idea we should go to Nevada and gamble, see if we could get a stake. We got as far as the city of Jean, just over the border. I said, If we're going to do this, let's hit the big casinos where they'd have more money to give away. There was a billboard I'd seen announcing Debbie Reynolds at the Desert Inn, and I thought, Wow, despite the fact that Debbie Reynolds was not what a teenager in my set would consider cool. The year before, I'd seen Valerie Perrine in *Lenny*. What a wonderful thing, I thought, that you can be a showgirl like her or Goldie Hawn, then switch careers.

What happened instead was that we escaped Jean, arriving in "the city without clocks" at about three. We wound up stopping at the first tiny casino outside the Strip, a place with wagon wheels in the front yard, and it was all over. Stretch, with his black headband and feather earring, drinking Jack D at the slots and telling me in his honey-smooth voice, You go do your thing, and I'll do mine. It's cool, baby. It's cool.

So I did. The only problem was, it was Stretch's car and only *my* knapsack and blanket. I went back into the place twice to try to reason him out of it, the last time telling him, Okay, I'll leave the blanket; what'll happen if you have to sleep in your car? And then coins came avalanching out of his machine, and after a good deal of whooping and smooching, he looked at me one solemn second, took up a handful of coins, using the other to pull out the right front pocket of my jacket, and poured the fistful in. He did that till I felt like a kangaroo with ten babies, and then he said, Oops, you're listing, sister; and added more to the left.

I walked up the Strip and applied for a job at the next casino, but was too dumb to lie about my age. I did that several more times, not missing souvenir shops and even one gas station, and I knew I should be lying, saying I was twenty-one, but I thought they'd laugh me right out of town. It was getting dark, and I was blue to the bone by now and a couple of miles away from where I started, and both mad and scared. Outside a drugstore, I saw a girl washing windows and asked her some questions. She looked me over once or twice and said she was going to a part of town, that had a lot more chances for jobs; she'd be off soon, and she'd drop me, if I liked. That night I stayed in a motel in North Las Vegas, paid for with slot-machine nickels.

The next day I walked up and down sidewalks, going in every furniture store and carpet place, every bakery, every newsstand hole-in-the-wall, looking for work. I can tell you grit sticks to your teeth when the hard wind blows. There's a neat little three-pronged sticker that jumps right in your shoes, called devil's weed for good reason. People told me Las Vegas suffered the worst flash flood in its history four months before, and sweeps of flood deposit were still visible at the roadsides; still, it didn't flood away those stickers. But I was young, and I wasn't worried. It was fun.

Then one day I found Cipriano Rycken, sole proprietor of Randy's, a good-time place that, well, employed young women who liked to dance and didn't mind taking off their clothes.

Cipriano—or Cip, pronounced "Sip"—was a nice man with quiet ways, the kind of man you'd expect to be running a restaurant or a lumberyard, not a strip joint. A beige canvas apron was tied around his waist when I first saw him, and he was carrying a pickle jar out the door of his place. Holding the jar to the light, he glanced at me once and went back to inspecting whatever was in there. I waited, thinking maybe they could use a dishwasher or even a waitress inside the establishment, because I assumed Randy's was a café, there being a nice big window with geranium plants in front and a panel wall just behind and no sign to announce it as a topless, the reason being, I learned later, he was having one repainted. He wore green snakeskin boots, and I guess I was studying those when he said, "Look what my cat was playing with." He lowered the jar, unscrewed the cap, and I looked in to see this amber-colored creature trying to grab a toehold on the glass. I jumped back, and he laughed and said, "Girls don't see the beauty of these things. It's just a little old scorpion. Long as they don't whap you on the skull or face, you're okay. Look at this, how he's got a couple eyes on the top of his head. Cute little devil, don't you think?" I looked again, but skeptically, and he said, "He's got four or five more on the side and he's still blind as a bat." Then he grinned at me and put the lid back on, and that's when I asked him for a job.

I told him I was eighteen, and he said, "Can you wait tables?" . . . "I don't know." . . . "Can you smile and look pretty?" I did, and he let me in, let me wear my own clothes and not a uniform, and told me, don't take no lip from no*body*. Just come and tell him, he'd straighten it out. I worked three weeks as a waitress.

I stayed almost two years.

My name was Dusty Rose. I wore black stockings with seams down the back and a pink suit jacket that was longer than a miniskirt. The jacket was an old one of Cipriano's; he was narrow enough in the shoulders for me to make it work. I wore a pink camellia in my hair. I learned to use makeup.

Frazier Baldwin, the most beautiful woman I've ever seen, taught me how to dance. She was a mix of White, Afro-American, Choctaw, and Thai. She told me she was "Thai dyed." And telling me this that first day I met her, she smiled, and the history of all that was calm and lovely in the world beamed into that room. I am not gay, but I fell in love.

She was tall to my short, dark to my light, centered to my randomness. She wasn't on dope, and she took a special interest in me. Frazier was the old lady among the rest of us: twenty-six, with a six-year-old son her mother took care of while she worked. I watched Frazier as a student would a master teacher. Not in a hundred years would I ever match that: the concentration so fierce on her face as she danced. I could see a bead of sweat trickle down next to her ear as I stood in the annex watching. To me it looked like a diamond. She did a flamenco wearing a shiny black hat and sleek rip-away pants. She dropped her top early in the dance. Her breasts were rather small, and after a while you simply forgot the top was not on, and so did the audience; you could tell, because when she'd finish there'd be this grand hush, and the calls from the back sounded different, respectful, and always at least one guy would stand and give an ovation.

Frazier was good to me, bringing me to her apartment several times, giving me clothes. We took her little boy to the donkey rides. He cried. I gave him money to play a kid's kind of roulette. Then he was happy. Frazier also lectured me, saying this was okay for a while, what we were doing, but I had to go to college. You listen to me now, she'd say, and you won't be sorry.

The last time I saw Frazier Baldwin, she was waving to me as she went out the door the second day of my new act. She had helped me with that too, watching the first night to tell me what I should be doing next, and when. She gave me her kid's toy machine gun to use, the kid with the perpetual sour look on his face. She was on her way with him to Houston, to join a dance troupe there. "The hat stays down," she said. I said yes. She said, "Don't forget what else I told you, either. You save your money. You go to college." I never promised her I would.

I changed my name to Smokey Shannon, then shortened it to Smokey, period. Cip put up an eight-by-ten photo of me, in the window above the geraniums. Time does funny things to you. I think most people are basically the same all their lives, the same person. But I'm so many me's, I'm going to have to start a color-coded file. Third up each evening, my act went like this:

There'd be a flat, white movie screen set in the middle of the stage between partially drawn drapes. I'd be in silhouette behind it, in a trench coat and fedora, my hair tucked up underneath and a cigarette hanging out of my mouth. Cipriano's nephew, a boy of fifteen named Buddy, would throw smoke down. Then he'd pull the screen up and draw the drapes back, all this while the intro to Santana's "Evil Ways" played on the stereo behind us.

I'd step out, head down, fedora brim resting on the bridge of my nose, hands clamped on the stock of the gun between my legs. The gun served as a pivot as I danced and played with it in ways not too hard to imagine, until Buddy would move in, like a version of Rudolph Valentino, wearing Frazier's black hat and braided vest, and receive the gun from me, and he'd then rush backstage and cut the music to "The Game of Love," where we would learn just what the purpose of a man was, and the purpose of a woman. Off would come the trench coat.

The bra was black, the garter belt too. Bra came off, gloves stayed on, anchored by rhinestone bracelets. I wore a gray leather skirt I bought in Mexico one bad weekend with another dancer and her boyfriend, and over that I draped a belt of silver bullets. A few more beats, and then it was time to "drop trou" —off with the skirt. It slid off over gray high heels I sequined myself. Down to the basics then: sequined G-string, nothing on top but hat and gloves. You can do all sorts of things removing gloves.

"The hat stays on. The hat stays down. Do it this way," Frazier had said. I got good with the hat; it kept the stage light out of my eyes. Five years later Randy Newman came out with "You Can Leave Your Hat On," and I grinned when I heard it, the guy in the song telling the girl to get up on the chair, do her dance, but she could leave her hat on. When that song came out, I thought about going back to Randy's, see if I still had the touch, but I was checking groceries in Napa then, and quite happy to be doing it.

Then Buddy would cut to "Poke Salad Annie." I needed something I could let my hair down—literally—to. The grunt. That's where. The whole song's a humid, Southern, sexy sound; it was right for it. I'd turn

my back to the audience, pause, and then lift off the fedora. The hair would fall to my waist, and would get
some noise from the audience.

Time for fun then. This is the part I liked best. All
disguises gone now, I could be myself; look out at them
and smile, come close, like the girl next door, and celebrate. Leave 'em happy, not just horny. I could see their
faces, usually young—not like people think: old men with
hats in their laps, doing things under there with one
hand. These guys, their faces would be tan and their
foreheads white—air force tan. They'd be smiling, their
eyes would be shining in the light. They were out for fun.
Only once in a while would there be one who was sad or
angry-looking. He'd be sitting out of the light, back farther, his hand raising with his drink more often than the
others. I remember one very handsome man, not an air
force type, who chilled me—it was the only time I was
afraid the whole time I worked there. He had a full head
of long, curly, blond hair. His shoulders were massive.
He always wore a white T-shirt under a leather jacket,
summer or winter; maybe he was subject to colds. Every
Wednesday night he came in, when it was slow, and
sometimes he'd be alone, but usually he'd be with a
buddy. They'd sit at a rear table and play cards as if this
weren't a strip joint, as if they were in the park in the
sunshine at a picnic table or at a dining-room table, and
only when Frazier would come on, and later when I
would, did he swivel his head over to look. Even then, I
knew it was an act, that aloofness, but I couldn't figure
out why. I took my break once at the same time this guy
was leaving, stepping out back for some air. He left on a
Harley, turning his square jaw to me for one brief moment as he rotated the handgrip to rev up, his jacket
shining under the light like it was wet. Then he said, in
a very deep voice, "See you later, sweetheart." He came
in two more times, and then he was gone. Cip told me
he was a family man.

The last number in the act was a song I loved the very
first time I heard it. Later, after Bill died, it would bring
tears to my eyes whenever I heard it, and I usually
turned the radio off. It was "I Can Help" by Billy Swan.
I can still sing it, know every word—except in my act I
changed the male words to female. It goes like this:

If you got a problem—*don't* care what it is—
you need a hand, I can assure you of this: I can
    help.
I got two strong arms, I can help.
It would sure do me good
to do you good.
Lemme help.

It's a fact that people get lonely, ain't nothin' new.
But a woman like you, baby, should never have the
    blues.
Let me help. I got two for me

Here I would point, let us say, not to my arms.

let me help.
It would sure do me good
to do you good.
Lemme help.

When I go to sleep at night you're always a part of
    my dreams.
Holding me tight, telling me everything
I want to hear.

Don't forget me, baby. All you gotta do is call.
Ya know how I feel about you, 'f I can do anything
    at all,
lemme help.
If your child needs a daddy, I can help.
It would sure do me good
to do you good.
Lemme help.

At the end of the record there were whistling and
whoops in the background. My little buddy Buddy would
hike the sound up at that point, the kid into it, sending
out a whistle or two himself so the audience would pick
it up—and they would.
    I liked that.

CHAPTER
33

As Yogi Berra once said, "It was déjà vu all over again." Along Lake Boulevard there were still more telephone poles than trees, and among the bait-and-tackle shops, boat lots, and cement houses with weedy yards were patches of mobile-home parks. I'd come into Vegas the back way, through Henderson, which is just a few miles southeast of town.

I stopped at a Travelodge and paid for a room. It was only two o'clock but the sky had turned dark, shoving a coolness down, and in a couple of hours more it would be nearly dark and I'd need a place to come back to.

When I parked at the motel, I made sure I could see my car from inside. Though the Colt was safely nestled between my socks and my turtlenecks, you can punch a trunk lock in nothing flat and have free binocs, suitcases, clothes, cameras, tire tools, down to the carpeting, if you're greedy. It had been a long time since I'd worried about a gun.

I paid my money, not nickels this time, to an Iranian whose attention remained fixed on the Lakers game playing on a tiny black-and-white. He stood up to bring me a guest-information card, sliding it to me, asking, "One night?"

On the way out, I'd barely passed under the open stairway when a guy with a fortyish face came around the corner with a beer in his hand and said, "Hey." His jacket covered a blue shirt open to his breastbone. I didn't figure he was talking to me until I was several steps beyond and he said, "You, with the earrings."

True, long earrings, kind of Indian style, were dangling from my ears, but I'd forgotten about that. He was propped against an open door, presumably to his room. He said, after taking a sip from the can, "I'll bet you and me could party down real fine." In the V of his shirt dangled a silver dollar on a gold chain. Cool. Real cool.

I headed for the Thrifty's next door, mad at myself for letting him make me stop, hoping he'd go back into his room and not see which car I was going to get into. Then thinking, This is nuts; wheeling back, glaring him down as I walked to within ten feet of him and said, "Why don't you just go on in there and mind your own business, Slick?"

His tongue flipped a gray ball of gum across the cavity of his mouth as he grinned at me. "Sassy lil' thing, aren't ya?" he said.

I kept my voice level, almost quiet. I said, "When's the last time you been arrested?"

He pulled up, held my gaze for one second. Then rotated his shoulders, the rest of him following, right into the room, quietly shutting the door behind him, as if I'd never been there at all. You can put the fear of God in with that question. You don't even have to be looking in their eyes when you ask it. They know you're a cop.

This incident coming so close on the heels of my reminiscence of my time at Cipriano's, as I crossed to my car I felt ashamed. Sure, I was young and stupid then. I also felt I was equal. We were all there having a good time, doing something a little naughty, nothing to hurt anyone. Our bodies were fun; sex was fun; booze and music and a tin of reefer were fun. Fun. Only much later did I come to feel like prey—as now—and did I come to have respect for consequences. How'd I get to be a cop with that history? I can say only that I told the truth. I didn't lie. They hired me anyway. There's no way that that would happen now. Now you have to be cleaner than squeaky.

As I drove away from the Travelodge, I slipped the earrings off and put them in my purse on the passenger seat. Then I wondered why I did that. What's wrong with earrings? Guys wear them. At a light, I put them back on. It's a damned confusing world.

Two black jets passed overhead, so close their wings seemed fused. My stomach turned for them, guys younger than I mayhaps, guys getting ready to see duty in the Gulf. Do good is what I wished. Don't fall asleep.

Traffic slowed to a single lane to squeeze by road crews, and I could watch the jets come around in a flat circle and then take off straight up, the cloud cover broken now and the sun's last rays painting the sky orange.

I passed a military-surplus store, the Circle K, the Moose Lodge by Pecos Road, and the Messin' Around Bar, a concrete box covered in plywood. I drove past the address on Lake Mead Boulevard where the Beaver Tail Inn was supposed to be, passing a storefront window with red lettering on it that announced COMPASSION REVIVAL CHURCH, only the letters spelled *chruch* and compassion was missing the *o*.

When I could deny it no longer, that there was not a motel named Beaver Tail on Comstock and Lake Mead, I pulled over to the side. I was near a trailer park. The manager was up front, a sign in the front window to tell me. Inside, a man was busy scratching his back on the frame of the window, weaving back and forth. I could hear a TV or radio on. A tiny bell tinkled as I opened the wood-and-wire gate across the path, bringing the man to the door. He swung it and its screen out at the same time.

"Can I help you?" He was tall enough that he had to bend forward, one hand still on the door. He looked like a high school teacher, clean blue jeans, wire-rimmed glasses, tan socks without shoes; the kind of twenty-nine that has the hair halfway up the skull.

"I'm looking for a motel, actually. A Beaver Tail Inn supposed to be around here someplace?"

"No, don't think I ever heard of it." Then, turning back to someone inside, he said, "Lizabet, you hear of a Beaver Tail Inn?"

There must have been a negative, because he called back into the trailer a little louder: "Mom?" and then, "Excuse me," stepping back inside, both doors swinging shut again.

His shirt went by the window, and then a youngish woman with brown, curly hair stood up from wherever she'd been sitting to look out at me. She was smoking and chewing gum, and she looked ghostly through the window screen. She said, "Used to be one here. Before they put the trailers in. I don't know its name, though." A figure passed behind her then, followed by the man, and then the two doors opened and a gray-headed woman in a blue-and-white polyester blouse with wide collars and blue pants not quite matched to the blouse framed herself in front of the man. "There used to be a motel here by that name," she said, her voice cracking. "I've had this place eight years now. It was before that. Who you lookin' for?"

"You mean the motel used to be here on this spot?"

She nodded, clearing phlegm, coughing.

Her son said, "You're not looking for a place to stay?"

"No. I . . . I just found a room key I was going to turn in," I said. I had no idea why I told that story, and thought it must have sounded inane. Who turns in room keys? If you're a good citizen, you drop them in a mailbox; if you're not, you use them.

The mother was saying something to me after I said thanks anyway, about how there were two, three vacancies at the back of the lot if I was interested; and I was smiling, waving, as I walked back down the dirt path to the gate, saying, Thanks, sorry to bother you; the guy still hollered in the doorway, both hands up overhead now, and the woman named Lizabet framed sideways in the screened window, her cigarette hand arcing away from her mouth, and her chin lifting.

On Main you can get married at a chapel and have the flowers, tux, license, rings, and apartment all in one, then step out on the sidewalk and buy yourself furniture at any of about fifty stores, the brass lamps and vinyl chairs sitting outside under a blanket of car exhaust.

Ahead, I saw a sign for NUDES ON ICE and decided that was quite a concept. "Boy-lesque" was playing at the Congo with Cook E. Jarr and the Krums, but I thought I could pass on that too. If Patricia were with me, though, she'd go for it. Wouldn't she? Patricia.

Randy's was still there, a slot between a bail bondsman and a furniture store whose windows were covered with bubbled-up cellophane sun shield. Across the street, the pawnshop's roof sign said: LOAN—SELL—BUY—TRADE, and, on the win-

dows beneath, I read that I could get ANTIQUE JEWELRY, GOOD
GUNS, CAMERAS, AND MORE.

There were no geraniums in Randy's window. What replaced the dark-wood paneling was a yellow painted wall with
a big clock made out of a wagon wheel in the center, and a
bunch of old Nevada license plates tacked alongside, the significance of which was not apparent.

I parked in back, thinking for one moment about my gun
in the trunk, and then walked around, stepping nearly out
into the street to read the name again, to be sure it was the
same place. Not ready to go in, I dodged a cab to go across
the street to the pawnshop, where I stood for a few minutes,
staring at hinged boxes of dusty finger rings yawning open in
the window, a banjo standing above a set of drafting tools,
and a china doll whose face had checkered from time. The
doll wore a green-velvet 1890s dress, spread out over her stiff
legs. I kept looking at the doll, not knowing why, and then
the picture of the Vietnamese woman in the doughnut shop,
the one with the stubby legs and the white/red towel over her
head, rushed in, and I pulled up, crossed the street again between two trucks to the doorway at Randy's, and went in.

The place was not at all what it was before. There were
fluorescent lights in the ceiling, but not all of them were on,
as if the owner were conserving. The stage had been carpeted
with a yellow-brown paisley pattern and was now an upper-
level eating area, where, I assumed, the barbecue sandwiches
advertised by signs tacked onto the floor-to-ceiling stanchions
were served to parties of more than one woman from L.A. At
a table sat a paunchy man and woman both in tan knit shirts,
the woman without her false teeth in. She laughed, and it was
a deep diaphragm-evoked sound that was strangely soothing.
Two tables away, a man with huge deformed knuckles polished to a gleam held a white-bread sandwich in both hands,
his left cheek knobbed out with something already in his
mouth, and when she laughed, he smiled too.

My gaze then fell on a man to my right who'd been
hunched over so that I barely saw him at first. He was young
and thin, with a diamond-shaped face and very long, very
black hair he flicked aside as he looked up. Cochise, except
his skin was very light, as if he stayed inside all day. His hand

was still on the infant carrier in front of him, the baby inside entirely pink, without a shred of hair. I smiled at him, not a thing I often do. His full lips pressed together, and then he looked away.

I went over to the bar and ordered a coffee. "Put a little whiskey in it too, will you?" I said to the man. He was old, maybe sixty, with a flushed complexion. His close-cut brown beard and mustache seemed painted on.

"You got ID?" he said, and he wasn't smiling.

"Thank you," I said. He still didn't smile. I brought out my license. He looked at it, then moved away down the bar and came back with the cup and plopped it down, sloshing some liquid over the side. He said, "That'll be five-fifty."

"Five-fifty?" I said. "Isn't that a little steep?" Something else was going on. "You always this friendly," I said, "or you just having a bad day?" I'd pulled up my purse and unzipped it, complying.

He moved directly in front of me and stood with his thumbs tucked in his back pockets. Keeping his voice down, he said, "No business here, lady. This ain't that kind of place."

"Excuse me?"

"You heard me." And he turned his back to me and walked down the strip of black-rubber flooring behind the bar.

I drank my coffee in peace and didn't let it bother me. I needed information. I could wait. When the time came, I did have to walk all the way down to him though, but I didn't wait for him to finish futzing around. I said, "Do you happen to know where I could find Cipriano Rycken? He used to own this place."

It took him half a second to answer, and this time I didn't see quite so much hostility. "Did you look in the phone book? There's a phone book over there," he said, nodding toward the hall.

"No, sir," I said, "I didn't."

I started away, and then the man said, "He won't be in there." He loosened up as much as he was going to as he told me I'd find Cipriano in Saint Rose, in Henderson.

"What's that?" I said.

"A rest home."

Rest homes are for old people—real old people. At eighteen

I thought of Cip as "older," but older as in forty, forty-five, not a gray hair in his head; though now as I thought back on it, the hair, yes, had been too black. But Cip was appealing in his own way if you were into father figures, and certainly appealing enough to be married to a pretty woman with perfect skin, I remember that, having met her once or twice. I couldn't recall her name, though Cip talked about her often enough, seemed to be in love with her, the mother of his baby girl. Her picture had been on his desk, a wheat-scrubbed look to her. She'd been, he said, a dancer—not in a topless place, but onstage in one of the biggies—before they married. He was always talking about the casseroles she made him, patting his nearly empty shirt and saying she was making him fat.

"He hurt his leg," the bartender said. I looked at him curiously, wondering how many quarters I'd have to put in his mouth to keep him talking, when he added, "He's my brother-in-law. He usually lives with us."

I thanked him for the info, intending to leave, when he came out from around the bar and walked with me toward the door. He said, "You're not a friend of Kirsten's, are ya? From California, you a friend of hers?"

"No, I'm afraid not," I said.

"Oh," he said, nodding.

"Is that his daughter?"

He nodded again. His jaw went tight, and then he turned and walked away toward the table with the tan shirts at it. The Indian-looking man with the baby met my eyes, then quickly looked away as I opened the door to go out.

At a corner of the parking lot, conspicuous because there weren't that many other cars around, was the Taurus. "God-*damn*," I said to myself, furious that someone *was* pinching my behind, all the way up from Orange County. "You fucker." Keys in my hand and rage filling my throat, I made a beeline across the lot, walking fast, and sure I was going to yank the twit right out of the driver's window by the hair. When he saw me headed for him, his elbow pulled in and he sank back as if he expected a blow, and the mirror of his sunglasses wavered and flashed.

"Get out of the car!" I yelled. He looked bewildered, so I said it again: "Get out of the car. I want to talk to you."

The door opened. I knew he could have a gun. But something about him told me that that was not likely.

He stepped out, and a waxed-paper wrapper fell to the ground near his black shoes. His socks were white, the pants gray, the knit shirt a deep rose. He had a nervous smile on his face, and he stuttered, "I . . . I . . ."

"Who *are* you? Tell me right now."

He shut the door and let his hands fall.

I said, "Take off your glasses."

"Listen, I'm—"

"Do what I tell you, you creep, or you're going to be kissing concrete."

He let a puff of air out his nose and turned his head—the start of a laugh—and I knew it was ridiculous too: I wasn't going to flatten the guy, wasn't sure I even knew how anymore. I took a step forward anyway, and said in a more normal tone, "Who are you?"

The man's pointed chin raised while he removed his glasses, and I saw a white scar on the red neck near the Adam's apple, like maybe a thumbnail had dug in there once. He'd composed himself by then. "My name is Lionel Crowell, and I'm a licensed private investigator."

"Shit you are."

He pulled his wallet out and opened it. I took it. It was a California license.

"What do you want from me?"

"A client is seeking information."

"Now, that's big news. What information? Where do you get off following me? Why not just come up and talk to me?"

He shrugged and wagged his head. "Is now a bad time?"

Too much. I had to laugh. Once I let down, it occurred to me: "Did Rowena Dwyer contact you?"

"I don't ordinarily give out my clients' names."

"You're not supposed to be following *me*, you dumb shit," I said, smiling and shaking my head. He wasn't even supposed to be wasting gas trailing someone out of state, and I figured he must be a few points low on the scale, and said, "What the hell, buy me a drink."

I eventually dumped Lionel Crowell, pointed him home the way you would a blindfolded partygoer holding the tail of the donkey, and vowed I'd call Rowena Dwyer as soon as I could and tell her not to pick her PIs out of the phone book. He'd meant no harm, but he was a history teacher whose wife stepped out on him, he said, and so he decided to try this profession. On the way out of the casino we went to, he dropped three quarters and won four-hundred, so what do I know?

CHAPTER
34

Cipriano was in the bathroom when I came in. The nameplate on the door outside told me this was the right room: CIPRIANO RYCKEN and STEVEN NEFF. Steven Neff was the old man dressed in brown in the wheelchair next to the perfectly made bed with the woven bedspread, white horses rearing on a pale blue background. Parallel to that bed was another, with a green bedspread, an empty wheelchair beside it. On the high table next to the bed three decks of Diamond playing cards were stacked atop some magazines.

"Excuse me," I said to the man. He was looking across the room, out the sliding-glass doors that led to a veranda. A badly pilled brown throw lay across his lap. A moment later, his eyes locked on my face. I smiled and said, "I'm looking for Cipriano Rycken."

Then I saw that the old man had a small purple stuffed dog sitting in the crook of his arm. Mr. Neff's blank blue eyes and the dog's stony black ones held on me, no answer forthcoming. I heard water running in the bathroom. As though a spell had been broken, Mr. Neff's expression changed, and I tried again: "Is that your dog?"

"Yes," he whispered slowly.

"He's a great-looking dog."

The man's head dropped to look at it. "Yes," he said again.

"I'm going to wait here, all right? For your roommate." I smiled as pleasantly as I could and got out of the way of a yellow-skinned black woman who came in to empty a wastebasket. As she straightened up, one hand at the small of her back, she looked outside where pink roses from the veranda stretched close to the glass and shone like cups on stems. "Gosh, aren't those beautiful?" she said. "Looks like we're finally going to get rain. That'll be nice, won't it?" The basket in her hand, she turned to the patient and said, "How you doin' today, Mr. Neff? You doin' all right?" and the old man looked away, toward the roses, with a forlorn and lonely or maybe just bewildered expression on his face, as if he were trying to remember the word for those flowers.

She left, and I went to the bathroom door and said, "Cipriano?"

I heard a muted, "Yeah?"

"Come on out here, or I'm coming in."

In my mind, Cipriano was still forty-five-ish, slender, with a mass of black hair on his head and a bunch more sticking up out of his shirt in the back. He had most of the elements for being handsome, but he wasn't quite, though now I couldn't remember why, and despite that lack there was about him a look of worldliness that I had found compelling. I'd kid with him, making suggestive remarks, and he'd do the same with me, though I was certain he'd never violate the relationship with his wife, nor did I want him to. Such self-sacrifice on my part was not so noble as it may sound, nor was it that I understood what marriage meant. I just didn't want to disturb or disrupt a man who had been good to me. There were days I thought all he'd have to do would be to crook a finger. That was when my body was separate from me, with a will of its own, the head minding its own business, the body saying, Kiss me, you fool. I loved men and I loved what they owned; not material things, but their own clunky, solid, purposeful, and peculiar energy. My desires were not so different from what most men and women of vigor want: a deep drink of the opposite sex, not in one flavor only. I wanted every man at least once, and a few more than once, and I didn't much care what they looked like as long as they weren't mean. Their mystery is what I wanted: all they knew that I didn't. Their special awareness of the world, their privilege, their special language. By rubbing against hairy skin long enough, hard enough, I figured one day I'd ease into the pores, osmosis perfected, ease out again, both of us the wiser; then go on quest to find one I could swallow, whole.

Inside the bathroom there was utter silence for a long while. I said, "You can hide but you can't run. On the count of five, Cipriano."

"Who is that?" His voice boomed out at me.

"It's either a bounty hunter or Marlene Dietrich. You have to come out to see."

Silence.

"No—make that Rita Hayworth. Rita Hayworth." I remembered now, she was his favorite.

The water trickled again and the pipes whined off. "I know that voice somewhere." There was the rattle of the door handle long before the man emerged. I was standing with my arms crossed and one ankle laced over the other, leaning against the wall. Would he recognize me? My hair was short, it wasn't red, it'd been fifteen years and I was probably a long history away down a row of babes Cipriano had hired and fired, pampered and protected. If I could have planned for this moment, I would have dressed up, come feminized, wearing at least a dress; maybe brought a plant, or, better yet, a flask and a copy of *Playboy*.

He came out. Older, God, and smaller, wearing gray slacks and a gray plaid shirt, brown slippers on his feet. Wearing glasses. His forehead was spotted both brown and purple.

He looked at me steadily as I said, "Hey, big fella, I can use a little help."

"Shit-bones," he said. "What in hell are you doing here, Smokey?" And then he shuffled over and grabbed me in a big hug, and I felt how bony he was and how bent for a man who used to be a full head taller than I. He patted my back as if he were not too sure this was at all okay, swatting with the palms only. Then we pulled away, and as we walked to his side of the room I said, "Shit-bones yourself, Cipriano. What in the world are *you* doing here? You don't belong here."

As he sat on the edge of his bed, he motioned for me to take the chair. "Nothing wrong with me a little privacy wouldn't cure. I don't mean you." He told me how he had phlebitis and fractures of the right metatarsal all at once, the foot injury from a hefty woman treading on him at a Veterans of Foreign Wars dance. He told me how he didn't like his sister but he liked her cooking; so he'd come here to the rest home once in a while for respite, manufacturing some ill or another, and then, when he couldn't take that any longer, he'd go back home to his sister's.

"But why don't you live alone, then?" I wanted to ask about his wife and daughter. In some places, and not just New England, you wait for people to tell *you* about the deeply personal things. You ask *around* the subject.

"Aaah," he said, with a wave of his hand. "That's no good. Hear your own voice bouncin' back at you from the walls. No, that's not for me." A look came to his eyes. "Now that *you're* here, I'll come live with you."

A voice from behind us said, "His name is . . ."

I looked around. Mr. Neff was going to tell me his stuffed dog's name. His long spatula fingers rested on the dog's head. As soon as my shoulders shifted around, and Cip turned his attention upon him, Mr. Neff forgot, and the bewildered look reclaimed his face. I said, "What is it? Your dog's name? He sure is pretty." But Mr. Neff was far, far away. His eyes followed my face as I stepped over to him and patted the dog's purple head, saying, "Yes. You sure do have a mighty nice dog there," and then I returned to my chair.

"There's only so much you can take of that, too," Cipriano said.

Cip could walk, but he said he'd better take the wheelchair. I wheeled him down to the community room, where the big TV was playing in the corner, five wheelchairs in a row in front of it, all occupied by women. At the long folding tables other men and women sat plucking at the blankets in their laps. Some of them rested their heads forward on the table, asleep, mouths open. Others were backed up along the wall by the windows, heads lolled back, mouths wide. I said, "Cipriano. This can't be good for you here."

"It's okay. I pinch the nurses."

"What're you doing New Year's? You want to go gaming?"

"If you're in town, we'll do it," he said. Then he pulled me down by my jacket sleeve and whispered in my ear: "Can you cop me some nookie with a cute little blonde?"

"Cipriano Rycken," I said. "I don't remember you talking like that before."

A satisfied smile crossed his face.

Eventually we got around to my story—what brought me to Vegas: the strange postcard with the waving cactus, my missing friend, my friend's current companion. When I said I thought the guy was a serious threat to society, Cipriano's glance went elsewhere and he did something inside his cheek with his tongue. "I guess I'd better tell you what I've been up to since I left you, Cip."

We'd gone over near the windows, and now I sat facing him. It felt both strange and natural for us to be here like this. This would be the way it was if I had a grandfather. We'd sit in the window light and he'd ask me how I was doing in school. He'd tell me how it was in the old days. But this was Cipriano, and he had a wife and child I didn't know, and ran a club of dancers, or did.

"You cut your hair," he said.

"Yes, yes, I did. It showers easy."

He looked at me a while longer, then said: "You got kids?"

"No."

"You ain't gay, are you?"

"No, Cipriano."

"I only ask because of the stuff going around."

I thought for a few seconds before I said it: "You ever hear of DES babies, Cip?"

"Don't think so."

"Diethylstilbestrol. My mother took it so she wouldn't miscarry me. It gives some people cancer. Not me, but other things. So we jerked the plumbing."

He thought about this for a while, then said, "You in show biz?" He wanted to make me feel beautiful.

"Well, let me think about that."

There it was: the half-smile, the crink that always made me think he knew more than he was telling or than I could understand. And then the whole smile opened up, and I noticed for the first time the teeth that were too white, and wondered if they'd always been that way. "Lemme guess," he said. "You got religion."

"Of a sort," I said.

"Like I got three sets of the family jewels." His head cocked at me like a wise rooster.

"Let's say I have a kind of work that lets me feel I do some good once in a while. The county pays me."

"For what?"

"For figuring out things. Putting puzzle pieces together. Actually, I work for the sheriff-coroner's."

I could tell Cip was not sure how to answer, or if I was kidding. First I told him what I'd done after I left his employ, from grocery checker to cop. While we talked, nurses hustled to and fro through the great room, their voices loud, their laughter hearty enough to assure you life goes on. They'd stop and speak to a patient, or pick up a toy off the floor to place it back on the lap that lost it, with a pleasant word, and it crossed my mind that this is not at all what I expected in this place.

My old boss remained quiet as I explained what a forensic specialist was. "A lot of it's just paperwork. Peering into microscopes, typing blood, that sort of thing," I said. I don't know why I didn't want Cipriano to hear how direct the work can be. Nor did I tell him how, after a few months on the job in Oakland, I had to go to a police therapist for six weeks to try to find a way to stop re-creating the last few moments of a victim's life: If he'd left one minute before. . . . If she only said (blank) instead of (blank). . . . If they hadn't used lighter fluid. . . .

Cipriano said, "You see dead bodies?"

"Sometimes."

He thought about this awhile and then backstepped to the police work. "I can't figure you a cop."

"Why not?"

The cheek flowered out again before he spoke. And when his cheek collapsed, the flesh around his mouth settled down like ears on a beagle, and his neck became a long fin. "A woman cop," he said.

I said, "There's lots of them now."

"I never liked cops much myself," he said, looking out the window. We spoke then in that measured way people do when they're trying to figure each other out, or the way married people do when they're having a *serious* discussion and they're trying not to trip the trigger.

"I didn't know that, Cip. I guess I should've."

His head gave a slow nod. He said, "You couldn't stick with it, huh?"

"Couldn't stick with it."

He lurched forward to start the wheel of his chair, headed for a table about ten feet away, where a water dispenser stood. He glugged a Styrofoam cupful, then raised it in a gesture to offer me some.

"You always told us no drinking on the job."

He smiled. "So this is a job? I ain't dead yet."

I looked at him, saying in the shake of my head, Of course not, adding, "So you never heard of that motel? The Beaver Tail."

"You believe women ought to go to war?"

"Cip, are you going to answer my question or not?"

"Yeah, I heard of it." He told me then. He knew the owner. Ralph Polk. The motel burned down a few years ago. "He's in Overton now. He was making flies, you know, for fishermen. People bought his flies, they went away home with fish in their *shoes*. He had one I bought from him he called Miss Piggy would call every crappie in the lake to dinner. Then for some reason he gets this harebrained idea he's going to find oil the other side of the lake. Wants me to go in with him on a rig, bring it up from somewhere in Texas. I told him not no but hell no. He says, 'You don't know luck when it lays down and begs.' 'Bring me that luck shined up with oil and I'll lick it clean down to the bone,' I says. 'Till then, don't bother me.'"

I waited for the smile, but his face was washed of humor. "Cipriano?"

He was sitting with the chair swung outward now, toward the door that led to the front desk, where a delivery person was causing a commotion with whatever package she brought. Across the way, in the doorway that led to another hall, Mr. Neff was attempting to enter the great room, but his chair was lodged against a woman's who was dressed in a bright-red sweat suit, trying to enter too. She kept saying, over the noise of the TV, "Just hold on there. Just hold on." I popped out of my chair to help, when Cipriano called me back: "They'll get it," he said. "We're always having traffic jams." And they did.

He felt my eyes on him. When he turned, I asked, kindly, I hope, "How old are you, Cipriano?"

"Seventy-two."

"You mean you were an old geezer when I met you way back when?"

"That I was."

"You coulda fooled me." I leaned over, gave him a kiss on a brown spot the size of a thumbprint, and told him I'd try to see him on the way back through, probably tomorrow. I asked him just how I might find Ralph Polk in Overton.

"It's not that big a town," he said. "Ask in the hardware." As I was leaving, he said, "What else were you going to ask me? Before."

He was sharp. He may not have been exactly the man I remembered, but he was a man with eyes and maybe more heart than I wanted to give him credit for.

"I don't know," I said, then looked around the room of rag dolls and said, "Yes, I do." I walked back and stood before him, but not so close he had to look up, the way I don't like to look up to people who are too tall. I asked him this, and the question was almost as much a surprise to me as it was to him: "What is it makes you happy in life, Cipriano?"

"Me?" He'd wheeled himself forward, and I tagged along. Halfway through the wide door near the nurses' station where several women in white uniforms had collected to witness the opening of the package, he stopped to give a proper response. "A good shot of JB whiskey," he said, "and Ethel M chocolate, preferably at the same time." He looked up at me as if that were the God's truth, and then said, "And now I'm gonna see which of these fine ladies is going to give me some." And then he winked and said, "Forget that other I told you."

"That other?"

"Yah. Nothin' but trouble, those." To be sure I got it, he added, "Women."

I gave him a thumbs-up with that, and once again started to leave. I saw his reflection in the double-wide doors. He'd come to say something more. "Smokey? You know what else I got?"

"What else?"

"That goddamned Yuppie disease. Chronic fatigue syndrome. You ever hear of that?" He wheeled up closer to me. "Listen, I still had all my hair until six months ago. Now it's comin' out every which way. Everything hurts. I get fevers, and I don't sleep well at night."

"That's awful, Cip."

"Those peach-fuzz doctors take one look at me and say it's everything from arthritis to phlebitis to sluff-off-itis. I say it's chronic fatigue syndrome, you know why?"

"Why?"

He held up his hands, thumbs tucked in the palms as though I'd asked him how old he was and he was saying eight. "I lost my fingerprints. Now, there's one for ya. Goddamned doctors think unless they say it first, it can't be true. I tell 'em, they look, scribble some shit, charge me sixty bucks, and it's good-bye."

I leaned down to see, holding his left hand in my fingertips. "You can't see it here," he says. "The light's no good. But take it from me, they're gone."

The light was good enough. The tips of his fingers were cold. They had longitudinal wrinkles in them, a chill in the room pulling them to corduroy. I gently pulled the pads on two fingers taut. "Smooth as a baby's butt, Cipriano. Now, how would you notice a thing like that?"

"How would I notice you drive a white Jap car?" he said. "With the paint off the right rear fender."

CHAPTER
35

Driving away from Saint Rose, I thought about the last thing Cipriano had said: "Maybe I'm just making it up. Who needs fingerprints, anyway? Maybe I'll become a safecracker."

How could a thing like disappearing fingerprints be known somewhere in this world and the Orange County Crime Lab not be privy to it, not issue bulletins about it? Then again, any thief with CFS might be too tired to burg, so there ya go.

I thought of Annie Dugdale not wanting to do her share of kitchen duty, which included dishwashing, and remembered that people who have their hands continually in water often lose their fingerprints. What, then, about Phillip Dugdale, cleaning brushes with solvents after painting a house? Do deep-sea divers have fingerprints? Sure they would; their hands are encased in heavy rubber gloves. Maybe I should get in my car and go home, save my money, my job, and my self-esteem. Patricia was probably back home, full of explanations, rife with apologies for having worried my little head. Probably selling real estate overlooking Emerald Bay, a millionaire by now. And maybe Forrest Sinclair had confessed to a few more murders while I was gone.

Cipriano told me to go back through town and take I-15. I said, That's okay, I'll take the scenic route.

When I left, the sky was cast with peach and crimson at the horizon; the day would soon be shutting down. Saturday night, Ralph Polk could be out. He could also be home eating baked beans and watching *American Gladiators*.

The road out of Henderson spilled quickly into craggy sand- and limestone formations. Like fired copper from the sun, a table rock and a spire next to it glowed incandescently, while neighboring boulders were as black as if the rocks themselves had burned. In the rearview mirror were the trillion lights of Vegas, a desert aurora borealis.

A few miles off Boulder Highway, a long, tapered sluice of Lake Mead came into sight. These waters form a meandering, inverted Y, like stress lines in a wound. One arm inches along the Arizona border, another struggles north toward Utah, and the leftmost tentacle stretches west toward Vegas and south toward Needles, California. The Virgin River and the Muddy, and the great Colorado back up a hundred miles behind Hoover Dam to form this giant reservoir that feeds the power plants that light up Vegas like a golden eye.

I'd driven half an hour and came to a valley set in shadow, a long string of charcoal mountains in the distance tapering toward the lake. As I pulled into one of the bends crossing the valley, the gray shape of a burro materialized over a rise, head first and weaving. I slowed and stopped and so did he, and we peered at each other for the longest time, he chewing whatever life this barren land would give up, until I let off the brake and rolled on.

You'll come to the silica plant, Cip had said. You'll see rail cars there, on your left. Eight tenths of a mile from there you'll hit a big dip. Don't speed: It goes from fifty-five to twenty-five real quick before that gully, and there's one cop with nothin' to do but spy California plates like a spider spies an ant. You pass the Eagle's Nest and the restaurant. Let's see . . . there's the supermarket. Oh, hell, I don't know. Across the street there's a pizza place where the teenagers hang out and play those noisy shoot-em-up games. Well, the movie house is on the corner. Turn there.

What's the name of the street, I'd said.

You don't need the name.

Okay.

Go down the end. Knock on the door even if there's no light. He'll open up.

Cip was right: No light at the trailer. I knocked anyway. A light came on, and then a bare lightbulb outside the trailer.

"Sorry to bother you," I said when a man in blue bibbed overalls came to the door. "Are you Ralph Polk?"

He turned to look at a custom tag under the window that read R.M. POLK, in scrolled letters. "Yep, I guess that would be me. What can I do for you, little lady?"

"I'd like to talk to you about a business you owned. Cip Rycken gave me your name."

He told me to come in. I sat on a brown couch at the front of the trailer, and saw through a window the shed out back. Light from one of its small windows threw a yellow glow onto the bushes.

"Well, now, I had a lot of binisses. I got a lot of binisses *now*. Which one you interested in?" His eyes were ringed in puffiness, his broad lips purple, and his backward-waving hair sat too heavy on his head. He turned on the fire under a teapot and then sat down at a table.

"The Beaver Tail Inn."

He waved a hand and expelled a puff of air as if to say, Oh, that old thing.

I said, "Cip told me it burned down."

"Yeah. Nineteen eighty-five." He got up and removed a tin box from overhead, above the double stainless-steel sink. "Damn thing was a money loser. Utilities ate me alive." He brought the box over to the table and set it down and began to unload loops of wire, scissors, a pocket knife, sheets of hobby-store metal, and a squat jar of colored feathers compacted against the glass. Before he sat down again, he said, "Want some tea or something? I'm a tea drinker myself, but I got a V-eight and one bottle of beer."

"Nothing, thanks."

He sat down. "I should have arsoned it, that place. Some people think I did, but I didn't. That's not a very charitable thing to say about a person, do you think?"

"I guess people like to speculate."

He nodded, smiling. "I swear the school superintendent fired his own boat down at Echo Bay two weeks ago, and I don't have a bit of proof on that, now, do I? Goes to show."

"Mr. Polk, would you know how a person might come by one of the old postcards from your motel?" I retrieved the card from my purse and handed it to him. He turned it over a couple of times, just as I had when I first received it, and just as I had a dozen other times.

As he looked at the card, a grin pulled the purple lips tight. "I *will* say I had some good parties there. I'd roast a pig right in the ground, throw in some corn wrapped in aluminum foil. Invite people over. I got a girlfriend or two out of it, once they knew where to come. One time I put up a whole passel of women headed for the Valentine Ranch up out of Carson City. You wouldn't know about that, would you? Their car broke down, see, and I was coming back from towin' a fella up to Indian Springs, and there they were, waiting alongside Ninety-five for a kindhearted soul like me."

The humor went out of his eyes when he focused again on me. "How'd you say you know Cip Rycken?" Only he pronounced it *Rick-en,* instead of *Rye-ken.*

"I used to work for him."

"Work for him . . ."

"I stripped," I said.

He stared at me awhile, and gave a little grunt before he said, "Well, now. You never do know, do ya?"

"Nope. You never do."

He got up and poured himself a cup of hot water, put in a tea bag, and returned to the table after offering something to me one more time. Then into the glass jar went the tweezers, to pull out a tiny red feather. From where I sat I could see knuckles and fingers, but not what went on between them.

He said, "Where'd you get that card?"

"I have a friend. I think she sent me this card."

"People could have those cards. Like, you know, people take towels when they don't need 'em. But that's a long time to be holding on to a motel card don't exist no more. How come your friend wouldn't—?"

"I don't know. I think she might be in trouble. How do you think somebody would have a card like this?"

"Only other place I know would be my motor home. I got a bunch under the bed in a shoe box. I don't know why I keep that junk."

My expression must have shown disappointment and fatigue, because his own changed then as he asked me, "See this here little feller?" He held up a tiny bright-yellow feather. "This is gonna catch me a mess o' trout after they restock the lake. The dry spell about sucked up all the water, and the striped bass about cleaned out all the trout, so all that's left is catfish, and I don't eat 'em."

I stood, saying, "I'll be on my way, Mr. Polk. Thanks again."

"You might want to come out to my drill site." He stood now too. "There's a host of minerals out there, Miss. You want to invest, I got the opportunity. I'm sittin' on a leaky oil fault, down about four thousand feet. High-gravity oil and methane gas, and I'm gonna get me some. Goddamned Iranians and Iraqians and all them other towel-heads don't need to think they got it all, uh-uh."

"Let's hope you're able to make it work," I said.

"You might want to take a look out there tomorrow, like I said. I'll give you directions. I can't go out there myself tomorrow, because I'm a deacon at the church and it's my turn to count money."

"That's quite all right. I appreciate it."

"You by yourself?"

"Yes, sir," I said, my hand on the door handle.

"We had a real cold wind last week. Raised waves so big on the lake it sank a houseboat."

"Is that right?"

"That's a pretty nice drive around there. I wish I could go with you. You wouldn't want to wait a day?"

"I'm afraid I can't make it. I'm sort of on a schedule."

"Uh-hm. Well, if it rains, I wouldn't chance it. The whole geography can change in a day's worth of rain." He sat down again at the table, and from a square tin he took a black fish-hook and began fidgeting with a thin wire I could barely see and another feather. And then he said, "I wouldn't mind you going out though, if it don't rain."

His gray, rheumy gaze was direct, and as he blew across his tea, I knew there was something else he was going to tell me. I said, "Why is that, Mr. Polk?"

"'Cause there's two fellas I got out there helping me guard the equipment. One of 'em's married, and the lady seems a bit queer to me. Maybe she wrote your postcard for ya."

"There's a woman out there?"

"There's two women out there."

"Who are these people?"

"Oh, a family kinda down on their luck."

"How old, would you say, is the woman you're talking about? The one—"

"I'm not too good with ages. I'd say . . . oh, hell, I don't know. Childbearing. She'd be childbearing age. Twenty-five, I'd say. Deutsch is the name. The other one, whew, I wouldn't kiss her in the dark with a blindfold. But boy, I can tell you one thing, I wouldn't mind having 'er around when I need some muscle. She's one big galoot."

"Is the young one named Patricia?"

"That I don't know. I don't always hear so good, or maybe I don't pay attention. Now, the kid with the heartbreaker smile, that's Ronnie. My little niece got near blown off her feet she saw him in town. She's sixteen—girls that age, you put their brains in a hummingbird's noggin, they fly backward. The other fella's a real sharp guy. He knows people back in Texas, a whole bunch of 'em outa work with layoff money to spend. He's going to help get up some investors. Sure you don't want to get in on this, now?" he said, and grinned at me.

"This fella—is his name Phillip?"

"Phil, yes. How'd you know?"

CHAPTER
36

"Smokey, you are one nutty motherfucker."

"Go easy on the compliments, Raymond. Can you do it?"

I was talking on a pay phone outside the Overton drugstore. Standing a few feet away was a Mexican man in a blue quilted jacket and jeans, waiting to use the phone too.

Yolanda had answered. When I asked for Raymond, she handed the receiver over without a word.

"You know I can't."

"You don't have to take your Mustang, if that's what you're worried about. And I'll pay your gas."

"I got a hot-pursuit car goes a hundred and seventy in seven seconds and you think I wouldn't open it up in the desert if I could?"

I sighed. "I know."

"You know what you should be doing, don't you?"

"Yes."

"Let local law enforcement handle it."

"You *had* to say it out loud."

"It's hard not to." His voice went soft. I knew he wanted to say something more, something like, "I'm concerned about you," but with Yolanda there, he couldn't. He said, "Did you get your buns beat when you were a copper, Smokey? Like, a lot?"

"Shit, Raymond, I'm tame. We had *cowboys*."

"You got no license to be a cowboy, dear."

"That gives me even more freedom, then, doesn't it?"

"What about those other suspects, what's their names?"

"They didn't do Jerry Dwyer. I know it. I don't want to talk about it. Ray, the Dugdales are *out there*."

"Hey, sweetie, why don't you go drop some coin in Vegas and come on back here and let me feel up your legs."

"Raymond!" I found myself whispering as if I were the one having to keep my voice down. "Where's Yolanda?"

"She went down to the laundry."

"Well, cut it out, Raymond. I feel bad enough about calling you at home, disturbing her."

"You're playing cop, Smokey. You're not a cop."

"There's nothing to get the cops involved with, Raymond, except to alert them to known felons tootling in their territory, and I'm sure they've got enough of their own to give away at raffles. Work with me, Raymond. Help me. I need some ideas."

The Mexican man walked all the way down the side of the building to the dark lot in back. From the way his elbows moved as he stood there, I knew he was urinating.

I said then, "At least I brought along a whacker."

"Now, listen up, pal. I know you can take care of yourself, but don't go doing anything stupid. Leave that thing where it belongs. You—"

"Why Raymond, I think you're mimicking me. 'Leave that thing where it belongs.'"

He laughed, but homed in again: "I'll tell you what. Why don't you let me see if I can find a buddy who knows someone on the Vegas force, just to have somebody to call in case anything gets funny."

"No, don't bother, Raymond."

"It's no trouble."

"Of course it's trouble."

"You were going to ask me to drive three hundred miles ten minutes ago."

The Mexican came back. Now he stood on a concrete bumper, hands in his pockets, as he looked at me. I put up one finger to tell him I'd be done soon. At the curb, a man got out of a car on the passenger side and headed toward the front door, passing close to me. He was grossly fat, with long brown hair arrowed down onto his shirt. He had a beard and the blackest elbows I'd ever seen. Not work dirt, but forever-there dirt. When he glanced back, I felt a strange needle of fear.

When I hung up, I was going to go directly back to Henderson and come back out in the morning. I was going to go out the quicker way too, through Logandale, and not be driving alone in that dark country in a car that had a ninety-thousand-mile reading on the odometer. But when there's a blip in your nature that compels you to think that if you do just one more thing—check one more fingerprint card, study one more photomicrograph to compare this screwdriver with that doorknob; or, as a cop, compile one more plastic sandwich of transparencies for an "artist's rendering" of a suspect, or run one more vehicle ID number through the VINSLEUTH system while your FBI buddy is yawning and rubbing his eyes, this at three A.M. when your shift ended twelve hours ago—you think that somehow, somewhere, you'll come up with something like a hit.

That same nature made me take one more turn back through town, where I saw a square-grilled vehicle parked deep behind the bar, red neon light from a rear window coating its dark sheen. A big flatbed truck was sticking out into the narrow driveway at the side, so I drove slowly up over the curb and into the lot until my headlights reflected off the white plate of the vehicle, the plate with a tin frame around it that said it was from a car lot in Victorville.

Inside the Eagle's Nest were about fifteen people, mostly on the old side. I looked for someone tall, someone blond, call him Ronnie Deutsch or Roland Dugdale.

At one table a young woman in a black loose-weave sweater and a black flower tucked in her white-blonde hair was speaking to a guy with hair so short it looked as though he had a bald spot in the back of his head.

The waitress, a girl who didn't look old enough to be serving drinks, said, "Diet?" and set a glass in front of the woman and slid a bottle of beer to the man. The woman in the black crocheted sweater laughed and switched drinks, saying, "Why do they always think the *women* take the diet?" as if the waitress were not still standing there.

When the man reached out to pay the waitress, I saw what I first thought was a yellow bracelet coiled along his forearm to the elbow. His profile showed a hook to the nose and a ridge of mustache. An odd feeling grew in the pit of my stomach.

I stepped up to their table, and in those few steps I could see that the bracelet was a snake inked among the black hair, and on the other arm there was a green peacock.

"Excuse me. I wonder if you could tell me if you all are from California?"

Phillip's face fell slack, and then recomposed. He pulled a chair over from another table and said, "Take a load off."

"Thanks. I might need a ride back to California. My car's giving me trouble. I'll pay," I said.

"I'd like to help you out, but I'm going to be here awhile," Phillip said. "I'm curious, though." He was smiling. "How'd you know I'm from California?"

"You look different," I said, and nodded toward the patrons at the bar.

"I see what you mean," the girl said, getting a smart look on her face. "I'm from Phoenix," meaning Phoenix was definitely more cosmo than this hick town.

"You know of a place to stay around here, then?"

"There's a motel down the street. Two, in fact." His eyes held directly on me without blinking.

"Where you from in California?" I asked.

"Beverly Hills."

We all laughed. Fake it, Smokey. I said, "Me too."

He said, "Goddamned small world, isn't it?"

The girl from Phoenix said, "You could probably stay at my aunt and uncle's. They got a place out on Overton Beach. I'm staying the week—they take care of my little boy."

"I'll do just fine."

"We ought to get you something to drink," Phillip said. "I stay off the sauce. This is as high as I get." He took a swig of his diet. "You don't love me now, you miss out."

Now he was looking at the blonde and she was smiling back, running her tongue halfway around her mouth. Her upper body jerked, and I imagined the arch of her foot sliding up Phillip's shin, her flexing toes going for the groin.

Phillip gave her a deep wink so I could see it, and then, as a rap song came on the box, and someone at the bar said, "Turn that shit off," and someone else said, "Right, turn that junk off, Mackie," Phillip put a finger under my chin and said, "How's our little cop-ette from L.A. today, Miss Brandon?"

The girl from Phoenix said, "Oh, wow."

Phillip dropped his hand, wagged his head at me, and said, "What's your next move, Suzy?"

CHAPTER
37

"Where's Patricia Harris?" I said.

"Now, you think we've gone and done something to your friend, don't you?"

"That's about it. I'd like to know how your brother just happened to move into her apartment complex."

"Hey, it's a small world."

"Cut the bull-puckey, Phillip."

"Your friend has got a mind of her own. I noticed that."

"Where is she?"

"Her and Roland are home watching TV, I guess. Countin' pinto beans—hell, I don't know, I never been married."

"What do you mean, married? She couldn't have gotten married."

The girl with the white hair was flicking her eyes back and forth at us, hanging on to her beer. The skin above her breasts was flushed, and her nose had a damp sheen on it.

"Where is she?"

He said, calmly, "She's the other side of the lake. We got a claim out there we're guarding for a man, make sure thieves don't run off with the equipment and sell it to Jackson Drilling. Look, honey, don't imagine trouble where there isn't none. She's doing just fine."

"Aren't you supposed to be reporting to somebody?"

"That's the wonderful thing about this country, you know it? Man makes a mistake, he does his penance, he's free to go friend-up the beautiful women." He hung his gaze on the girl again, and smiled. She looked at me with a hard glare.

*   *   *

I went back to Henderson to the motel, and slept. It was
pointless for me to try to find the spot where Ralph Polk
parked his motor home in the solid blackness around a giant
lake in a country of wild burros.

The next morning I went the short way to Overton, and
stopped in at the restaurant before I headed out for the other
side of the lake. I had pancakes and wished I hadn't. When I
went to pay the check, the man who was framed in the long
open window behind the woman who took my money said,
"You hear Leon got his water truck fixed?"

She answered him without looking back. "No, I didn't hear
that. That's a good thing."

The man moved back and forth, doing things at the grill.
He said, "Ronnie Deutsch bailed him out."

She nodded and was toiling with the till, my money in hand.
She asked me, "You have anything smaller?"

I shook my head. "Ronnie Deutsch?"

"Yeah, you know him?" she said.

"I think so."

"Good boy, that Ronnie."

I said, "I met him once when I was passing through a while
back. If that's the one."

"Must be another Ronnie Deutsch. This one's not from around
here." Her glasses slipped from her nose and fell onto her chest,
dangling from a red cord. Her ash-blonde hair was pulled close to
her head so that she looked like a post with features.

"He come around a lot?"

"When's the last time Ronnie's been around, Myron?"

"Huh?" the man at the window answered, the arms going
wide and back again like a man at a piano.

"Ronnie Deutsch. He's been around when? Wednesday?"

"I saw him this morning."

I spoke to the cook directly then, over Mrs. Cook's shoulder, till she handed me the change and stood away. "He was
in this morning, here?"

"He's over the hardware store right now."

"Can you tell me . . . did he have a tall, pretty redhead with
him?"

Myron did something back there that sent up a lot of steam.
The woman moved away to clean a table. Myron came back
to the window with a smile on his face. He looked at me as he
patted something I couldn't see, *pat-a-pat-a-pat*, like a tortilla
maker, and said, "Not yet. But, then, it's only eight-thirty."
Then he laughed a phlegmy laugh, until he had to cough and
turn away from the window. "Gimme a cigarette, Mavis."

"You got half a lung left, you want a cigarette."

"I don't have half a lung, I have two good lungs with a
tickle, and that's the God's truth." He winked at me and said,
"Woman's gonna be the death of me yet."

The hardware store looked like a warehouse, covering many
hundreds of square feet. It was loaded up with everything from
clothes to chainsaws. I completed a quick round of the store and
didn't see Roland, didn't see Patricia. I took another tour and
dawdled at the hammer rack, thinking maybe he was having
keys made in the back, or a screen cut or a pipe severed.

On my way out, I stopped at the cash register and asked a
man who was sticking price tags on silver bolts, "Was there a
man in here a while ago, tall, light hair?"

His left top incisor and the tooth next to it were a dark
silver; at first I thought they were missing. He wore an or-
ange-visor cap with a fish emblem on it. He said, "You're my
first and best customer, doll."

An older man in a gray shirt pulled up from kneeling at
the bottom of one aisle, hung a plastic packet on the peg-
board, then turned to me and said, "We got a real good buy
on Christmas lights." Only these two in the store.

"People in the restaurant said they saw Ronnie Deutsch in
here. You know him?"

The older man said, "No, ma'am. I don't. But if he comes
in, I'll sure tell him you're lookin' for him."

"That's okay," I said. "I think I have the wrong person."

I took a packed dirt road around the lake. At times I could
go only twenty miles an hour where storm runoff had cut new

rust-colored channels across the road. Several times I thought
I was lost. I passed a dead tree up on a low rise, and sitting
on it was a golden eagle, eye turned toward whatever morning
menu scurried from one hole to another. And then nothing
more for many minutes but the bleak landscape of alkali-
crusted soil.

At a long curve of road, I came upon a bustle of dust from
a lumbering, yellow, older Pontiac ahead of me. Just as down
south, you're supposed to pull over when the person behind
you doesn't have an Old Fart's license and wants to go more
than ten miles an hour.

I was pretty close on his bumper when his brake lights came
on, and then he came to a complete stop. He was slouched
down, wearing a brimmed hat. It passed through my mind
that this was Lionel Crowell, the pseudo-PI again. And then
it passed through my mind that whoever it was would get out,
pull a pistol, and whack me. Before leaving the motel that
morning, I told myself, What if I run into a rattlesnake? I
reached for the Colt I'd taken from the trunk and slipped
under the seat.

What piled out was a sight I wouldn't have bet a million
against a dollar on: Cip Rycken, in a floppy hat, gray shirt,
and purple suspenders clamped onto gray pants. My eyes
went automatically to his feet, to see what sort of miracle shoes
a guy with a fractured metatarsal and phlebitis would wear,
and saw thick white socks and brown leather bedroom slippers. In my paranoia, even though this was Cip, the man
who'd given me a job when I desperately needed it, who
nursed me a few times when I was physically ill and a few
when I was emotionally needy, this man might be the man
whose turn it was to put me under. Who knew, in this world?
I slid my jacket onto my lap from the passenger's seat, over
the gun.

He came up, leaned close to the window, and said, "Why
don't we just go in one car?"

At that moment I could hear my Bill's voice telling me—the
both of us sitting on our bed with the one slat that kept falling
down, and me in a literal sweat because I'd scared myself on
duty that night, almost blowing away a guy who'd been trailing
me the day after we'd testified in court and sent his buddy to

piss 'n' puke dinners for seven years—Bill telling me, It's all right. Think that way and stay alive. Stay alive. He said that to me again that last night in the hospital, his forehead a mass of clear bubbles. It was just after I thought the fever'd broken. I thought, Oh, boy, we're on the way up, here. I was tipping the water pitcher, which was filled with ice, to wet the wash-cloth I would put on his head, when he called me in a whisper to come—it's what he said: "Come." I had both hands on his shoulders and I was leaning over him, willing him to be all right. He said, "Smokey." Yes, yes, I said. He said, "You stay alive." And then the pupils of his eyes widened until there was barely any retina left.

I followed Cipriano until we came to a turnout, and as he was climbing in with me, I nudged the Colt I'd returned to the floor back underneath the seat with my heel because it had drifted forward. His eyes flicked to it and then up to my face.

"You think we'll see bison, dearie?"

I smiled, and pulled away, glad he was with me. The sun was out, and the sky was clear, and the air just the right amount of cold.

We started out again in this drear land and I said, "You sure you're not taking me somewhere to have your way with me, Cipriano?"

He said, "This stick hasn't dipped for a long time, Smokey, but thanks for the thought anyway."

He offered me a piece of cinnamon gum. Its sweet smell reaching me, I recalled the smell of my home in San Jose where I'd gone after leaving Cipriano's employ and before be-coming a grocery-store checker. In that rented bungalow, I'd stashed bundles of cinnamon sticks in closets and drawers. Cinnamon must have been in that year. When I smelled that fragrance, I felt a loss at who that girl was, the one who had wanted to settle down and study painting and wildlife and wound up probing dead bodies.

I said, "Tell me what you know about Ralph Polk."

"Ralph's been stuck out here a long time, long before this oil thing came up. I'm beginning to think he's gone a little round the bend."

"Does he have any kind of criminal record?"

"Ralphie? Naw-w."

"By the way, how'd you spring yourself from the rest home?"

"Walked out the door. Got tired of restin'. Hey . . ."

"What?"

"How come you don't smile anymore?"

"Whose life do you have to make miserable when I'm not around?" I said.

We were into hillier terrain now. There were a few Joshua trees and creosote bushes, and the earth was striped with rust and gold and gaining a few patches of green.

"Who would ever think you could put a lake on top of this land and it would stay there?" I said.

"You know where we are now? We're southwest of Mica Peak. You can go across these hills and see shards of mica laying in the gullies like kids been down there breaking bottles."

We sank into a wide wash, rounded the hill to the far side, and arrived at a sickle-shaped cut in a low cliff face. Nested in the cavity was a white-and-tan motor home. Off to one side were two goats behind a wire-and-wood fence, idly sweeping up alfalfa. Our tire noise did not keep the goats from their appointed munching, though they did raise their heads and stare with wary eyes.

On the other side of the goat pen sat a long, flat-roofed plywood shed. I saw no Bronco. I saw no other vehicle of any kind. I cut the ignition and we both just sat there, staring ahead.

"Cip, I'd better tell you something else about my friend Patricia. She was seeing a guy who'd been in the jug for robberies."

"If you threw a stick in a prayer meeting, you'd hit a couple with some history," he said. "What's a girl to do?"

"That's a little tough for me to buy into."

"You always were a hard-nose," he said.

"I don't know how you can say that."

"The other girls never gave a shit."

"What about Frazier? She did."

"Yeah, she did. She was different, like you."

"Listen, Cip—I'm pretty sure one of the guys helping Ralph

out is her guy. And this guy's brother, Phillip, is bad news too. These are not reformed people."

"Seems to me you don't even know for sure these people are the ones you're lookin' for."

"You're right. I don't. What would *you* do if you thought a friend sent you that postcard, and the postcard traced to here? What would you do?"

"I'd wait for another postcard."

"Fine. Well, that's not me."

He reached over and patted my hand and smiled at me.

I sighed and said, "So, what do we do, walk up and ring the bell like the Avon lady?"

After thinking about this awhile and looking out the window toward the fence and the goats, he said, "Ralph Polk never did have any sense."

"I saw Phillip last night. In the bar. He was with someone, a pretty girl from Phoenix named Constance, and it seemed, you know, okay. I'm not saying I have this figured out. I could be wrong all the way to Minnesota. You follow me?"

He nodded, thoughtful.

I said, "It doesn't look like anyone's here."

"The old lady's in there," he said.

I'd forgotten about the mother. "How do you know?"

"Ralph told me. He said she don't do nothin' all day but sit and smell up the place. He's not too happy she comes along with the deal."

"They can't all live in there." I was estimating the length of the trailer at maybe thirty feet, then assumed the shed wasn't just an equipment shed but a domicile as well.

I'd seen plenty of living arrangements like that when I was in Oakland. There'd be a shack with a slanted roof attached to a backyard fence, the height no greater than a Doberman, yet some lanky tweak would come unfolding out from it, three of us yelling and waving big bad police specials at him. They can get in tiny places. I was after one jerk once, saw his hind end and sneakers go out the bedroom window. My partner looped him back into the house. We were all over that place for an hour. The rest of the family was huddled in the living room under watch of another badge, two preteen sisters sitting on the couch with their mother, sniffling, and the badge trying to ask them about school to divert their attention. I could not believe we couldn't find him. I mirrored the attic space twice, finally crawling up there myself with my flashlight and gun, feeling very exposed the whole time, finding nothing but rat shit and spider webs. I looked under every bed twice. Ready to open the dresser drawers and look for him, I walked out on the back porch and saw a refrigerator about five feet high, the enamel worn off the edges. Something made me go over to it and open the door. There he was, one little raggedy-ass wimp we put away for, unfortunately, only five for murder and CCE—continuing criminal enterprise—and the tweak smiled at me and spit. It caught me under the chin. He was lucky he had an intact forehead when he walked out of there, but he did have one or two stretched finger tendons from application of our own brand of pain compliance. That, as I explained once before, was not the real me. That was someone named John Wayne.

We got out of the car and went up to the trailer. Cipriano knocked.

The door opened immediately, *wham!* slapping on the trailer skin, making me jump. What I saw then is hard to describe because I don't think most people would believe me. This thing stood before us, about six feet tall, two-fifty. It wore baggy khaki pants and red bootie-type slippers with leather soles. It wore a tan shirt with short sleeves. And running down the length of the arm that held back the screen door were lakes of oozy red and pus-filled lesions. Her face was tinged a sort of orange and there were brown circles under the eyes; the eyes blue, the eyebrows yellow. Brown curls jutted out under her ears like boar horns. The thing spoke. It had no teeth.

"Who you lookin' for, bub?" it said.

Who you lookin' for, in a female voice. This was Annie Dugdale.

CHAPTER
38

Cipriano's posture changed. He grew taller. His voice grew younger traveling the distance between where we stood and the trailer door. When he removed his hat, his dark hair sprung out like foam. He said, "We're wondering if you have a gallon of water." Smiling at Annie Dugdale with the kind of twinkly eyes he reserved for his best girls. "These kids," meaning me, "don't know how to take care of cars no more."

She went back inside and brought out a white bleach bottle without the label, dark smudges around the neck.

"Oh, we can't take that." I'm thinking, Why not?, when he adds: "That's your drinking water."

She said, "Go on and take it. There's more where that came from."

He stepped forward and took it from her, thanking her, and then put his hat back on and touched his finger to the brim.

She said, "You want some coffee? I just made a pot."

We went inside. I had the same cramped feeling I'd had in Mr. Polk's other trailer, only this was worse. Things were crammed deeply into the compartment above the driving area. Latches to the overhead cabinets were unlatched, and half of a potholder leaked out from one. On all the flat surfaces, including the stove, were coffee cans and salt-and-pepper shakers and casino ashtrays and decks of cards, along with a TV guide and a paperback book whose cover was off, and another one whose cover I could see, by Michener. Part of the claustrophobia came from watching Annie, the top of her head just inches away from brushing the ceiling.

We sat on the bench at the table, watching the giant woman get mugs and pour. I looked for resemblances. This didn't look like it could be the mother of Phillip and Roland; both of them were decent-looking.

She said, "You take sugar?"

I shook my head no, and Cipriano said, "Please."

Annie said, "I got sweetener."

"That's just fine," he said.

She returned with the mugs, squeezing in behind the table. The lips that guarded no teeth looked like the pale underbelly of a fish. Above them there was a shadow of brown mustache, and along the side of her face where the light hit, a sandy forest of hair. The yellow eyebrows, I guessed, came naturally.

I saw Cipriano's eyelids drop briefly, his gaze taking in the graveyard of Annie's crusty arms. When I looked again at her, her eyes were set on mine.

She said to Cipriano: "What are you doing out this way? Prospecting?"

"I know Ralph Polk."

"You do, huh?" She held her cup of coffee with both hands, completely obliterating it.

Cipriano said, tearing the packet of sweetener, then stirring the coffee with a tablespoon she'd brought him, "Maybe he's got some oil out here, what do you think? Think maybe we can pull up some money from this old parking lot?"

She smiled and patted the front of her shirt looking for cigarettes, then rose and went to the sink, where the pack was resting between two water glasses. "You got money in this?" she said.

"I sure do." He glanced sideways at me, and I shook my head and grinned, not knowing whether to believe him or not, but thinking, Yes, he probably did, the old fart.

I touched a finger to the bottom of the faded turquoise curtain near me. The cloth was stiff and moved easily forward so that I could see, in the deeper cup of the sickle, a green pickup truck, two bales of alfalfa in its bed, one up, one down. I kept staring at it: It can't be this easy. It's *there*, by damn, it's *there*. And looking harder, taking in the lines of its rounded fenders and top, I saw through the dusty windows a red baseball cap on the dashboard—a red *bazeball* cap—and felt my face flush.

I dropped the curtain as Annie was saying, "Not many people out this way. It gets a tad lonesome." But she was looking at me, blowing smoke up to the ceiling.

Cip was saying, "You ought to come into town once in a while."

"I'm not much of a one for gambling. I like a sure thing," she said.

"You're a wise woman," he said, and took the first sip of his coffee while she could think about that. Then he said, "You probably didn't invest any of your hard-earned money in Ralph Polk's scheme, neither."

Her eyes, small and empty, flitted to me once, then back again to him. "I don't like all that hustle in town," she said. "I like the peace and quiet." As she hoisted her cup, her lips took on a life of their own, like an elephant seeking a peanut, but she kept looking at Cipriano, sizing him up for dinner or bed, I couldn't tell which.

"Maybe we should cut to the chase here," I said, speaking for the first time. Cipriano flicked a glance to me but said nothing.

I heard a soft *sniff* as Annie touched her nose with a finger. Pack my nose, shoot my veins, fuck it. When my septum disintegrates, stick me between the toes, in the stomach, the groin; hell, I got skin to spare.

I looked at her and said, "You know, I came upon a girl in jail once was shooting herself up in the blue vein of her breast with a needle she would not surrender till four officers pinned her down."

Annie's stare could've knocked over a silo. She said, to her credit and to the point: "You're looking for Roland." Her small eyes leveled out to me, and she smirked. "He's over the hill."

"A lot of us are," Cip said, still quick, not sure if this was the way the conversation should go.

Annie propped both elbows on the table, her cup at the pinnacle.

"He's drilling out some old pipe." She sipped her coffee, and then, without taking her eyes off Cipriano, she tipped her head a little toward one shoulder and yelled, "You gonna come out and meet our company?" She turned her eyes on me, and the gap that was Annie's mouth spread to show fences of pink gums.

A door opened down the, quote, hallway. The foundation shifted as someone stepped out, the door blocking my view. I realized then that it was the bathroom. And in there was someone who'd been watching us the whole time we were parked like two dumb nail kegs in the front seat of my car.

"Well, well, well, well," Phillip said, coming toward us. This time the tattoos were covered with a light yellow flannel shirt, his jeans dirty brown at the knees.

He pulled up opposite us, sitting on a director's chair with a leather sling, near the door.

I felt trapped and wanted Cipriano to slide out, but he just sat there, his hand on his coffee mug but his thumb jiggling up and down and his right knee moving.

"Didn't I tell you last night your friend likes my brother? I don't interfere. Neither should you."

"Is she here?"

"You want to see her, she's in the add-on." He made a motion with his head in the direction of the shed outside, and then stood up.

Cip slid out, and I followed.

"You stay here," Annie said. She was up now, gripping Cipriano's arm.

I felt my first surge of adrenaline. "You don't order him around."

"He can come, Ma," Phillip said, quietly, and stepped through the doorway, and down. I went out too, expecting Cip to follow.

Annie piled out of the trailer, entirely avoiding the grated iron step, taking one giant step for womankind. "Fuck you," she said.

I looked back and saw Cip hanging in the doorway. He said, "I'll stay here," and waved a hand.

Now that I was out in the open, I thought I heard the sound of a TV coming from the shack, and noticed for the first time a small white dish antenna on the slope above the shed. Annie was standing with both arms out from her

sides like a cowboy ready to draw or a man whose lats are too
big.

"Fuck you too," Phillip said back.

He was saying "fuck you" to his mother, and it sounded
more like a ritual between them than anything else, until Annie came forward and slapped him on the upper arm.

"Fucking *ding*," she said.

Phillip put up both palms as if to say, Okay, stop, but she
came at him anyway, grabbing him by the shoulders and shoving him. He shoved back, the both of them clinging and pushing in a push-me-pull-you affair. Scorpions mate that way, the
male grasping the female by the jaws and pushing her back
and forth till she deposits her eggs in the sand, then fertilizing
the eggs as he passes over them again and again.

Phillip began to laugh, saying, "Ma, goddamn it, cut it out."

She dropped her arms, said, "Ah, ya little shit."

Cip stood in the doorway watching this special brand of
Dugdale Dozens, shaking his head once as if to say, Jeezuz
Christ, then bringing his hands to his elbows as if holding
himself in.

CHAPTER
39

Annie held back while Phillip and I walked to the shed. I could definitely hear the sound of a TV now, an odd sound out here in the blankness, and disembodied. The door was cut square in the middle of the gray, weathered, and peeled plywood, and above the metal cabinet handle was a slotted hasp and plate screwed into the wood, with an open padlock dangling by its shackle.

I said, "Why don't we just have Patricia come out?"

"Sure. Call her." Phillip opened the door and called in: "Company, folks." A powerful smell reached me, of stale beer, hair spray, dirty dog, or sour breath. He stepped in, saying, "Here," and motioning for me to follow. Opposite me there was a window covered with a sun-hollowed curtain with clumpy threads hanging at the bottom.

"Somebody here to see you, Patty," he said, and moved back. From the side of the door, I looked in.

On the right was a mattress resting on the floor, two blankets curled around each other on top of a dirty sheet, three pillows in a pile in the corner, the top one upright, like a mock person.

I looked left and saw, at the end of the shed, two women. One sat on the floor between a laminated coffee table and a couch upholstered in a fabric of brown roses on a white background. The one on the floor was Constance, the white-blonde girl in the black sweater I'd seen with Phillip in the Overton bar. She had on different clothes—a pink knit shirt and jeans—and a smile played across her lips when she saw me. She was smoking and picking at her fingernail polish.

Next to her on the table was a silver can of beer. Opposite, against the wall, the television was playing a Cary Grant/Audrey Hepburn black-and-white movie, Hepburn getting the chance to see how rapidly she could talk, Grant dressed in a suit and hat, looking bumbled.

I saw the other woman hitched under a dark green blanket on the couch, her knees up; looked straight at her, and glanced again to my right to see if I had missed Patricia when I first stepped in.

"Smokey-y-y."

"Patricia?" I stared at her and went forward, glancing back at Phillip, who was staying his ground.

"What are *you* doing he-e-e-re?" she said. Her hair was brown now, not red. It hung around her face, her face not completely visible because of the blanket and a thing around her neck that looked like a cervical collar or maybe a dirty towel, hiding her chin up to her lips, until she shifted so she could see me better and threw the blanket back. She wore a gray sweatshirt and black shorts. Red dots, many of them, stippled her face. And she was wearing glasses. I'd never seen Patricia in glasses. No way would I have believed it was Patricia if it were not for the little-girl softness in her voice. It hadn't been five weeks since I'd seen her. How could a person change that much in that short a time?

"Patricia," I said. "Are you sick?"

"I have the mea-a-sles," she said.

"You're stoned to the gills."

"Have *you* had the measles? No? Uh-oh. Your balls drop off," she said, and giggled, "or something. That's what Roland says. That's what happens when you didn't have the measles as a widdle kid."

I looked at Phillip, furious that Patricia would be here, furious that she would be like this. I moved toward her, intending to yank her up and pull her out of there, though Constance was in the way, and so was the coffee table.

The light changed then, and I twisted back, thought it was Phillip coming for me. But it was Annie stepping in. In her hand she had a chrome small-bore pistol that she held at gut level so that it looked like a silver button in place of a brown one on her tan shirt.

Phillip said, "Ma. Put that away. You nuts?"

"Shuttup. *You*"—meaning me—"get the hell over there." She was pointing to a spot at the end of the table in front of the television.

I complied, bumping the table with my leg and tipping the beer can off. Constance caught it and said, "Oh, wow."

Annie told Phillip, "Shut that thing off."

He flicked his eyes at us both and then slipped behind me and punched off Hepburn and Grant, pressing my elbow with a thumb and two fingers at the same time, and I wondered what that meant. I heard, or rather felt, a bump on the wall. The goats were displeased.

Annie transferred the pistol to her left hand and took her long reach to the wall, *whomp-whomping* against it, and the soft bumping from the other side stopped.

"This is real smart," I said.

"Shut your mouth. What do you think you're doing coming around my family? I know who you are. You got no right poking your nose in our business."

I wondered where Cipriano was.

"You don't want to do that, Ma."

"*Fuck* you," she said.

"Calm the fuck down, Ma. Put the gun away. We're not doing anything here. She's just checkin' on her friend."

Constance's eyes were wide open now. She said, "I'd like to leave, please."

"Go get Roland," Annie said. "Get him."

Patricia was watching the whole thing with no more expression than she might have had if she were choosing between two skirts.

Phillip putting up his hands to placate his mother, shaking his head. "Sit down, Constance," he said, and she did, and then, to his mother: "What about the guy? Get it together. Hey, we'll chill out. Play some cards. Have a fuckin' party. Didn't Roland bring up some steak?"

"She's the one, goddamn it," Annie said. She was rocking now from foot to foot, the top of her hair snagging on something on the ceiling, but she didn't notice or care.

"She's the one what?" Phillip said. He bent his knees and shoved his butt onto the table, laying his arms on his knees.

He faked a yawn and worked his shoulders, the mowed head dropping down on his chest and rolling back and forth.

Annie drew up a gray wooden chair from against the wall, turned it backward, and sat in front of us all, the gun arm pointing down, the other across the top of the chair where she rested her chin. "I'd like to know what we do now," she said. "You got any bright ideas. You know who this one is, don't ya?"

I had stepped back and took a seat on the couch arm.

"So fuckin' what? She works for the county, that's all. She's harmless. Okay, let's kick her *and* her friend out, get back to normal here."

We heard the bumping again, the goats against the fence posts and the shed, disturbed from whatever psychic tremors were dancing in here. Annie's attention left her son's face as she listened to the bumping as well.

Phillip's voice conciliatory, his manner smooth, he said to his mother, "Everything's fuckin' A here, ay, Ma?" He turned his head to me and said, "Everything okay with you, sweetheart?"

"Wonderful."

"Where's the other guy?" he asked his mother.

"In the head."

"What'd you do to him?"

She thought a minute. The beginnings of a smile moved the mask that was her face up and back, a wave of flesh smoothing her brow and causing her two big ears, which were exposed, to move backward with her scalp. She brought the back of her gun hand to the side of her face, and said, "Kissed him," and laughed.

I said, "That better be all you did."

We heard the bumping again, and then a louder sound, almost like a crash. And then another one as Annie was getting up out of her chair, and I recognized it as the sound of the trailer door smashing against the side. I jumped up and moved past Phillip *and* Annie, but she grabbed me by the back of my shirt and yanked, and then I saw the yellow flash and Phillip reaching for me. I threw a shoulder onto him, and we stumbled about a bit, and I heard Constance yelp and Patricia make a sound like a little hum.

Outside, Annie was striding to my car. I saw the door was open on the driver's side, and then saw the back of Cip's shirt and purple suspenders rising from the interior like a humped whale.

"Hold it," I yelled, and as I did, Cip dropped down again.

Annie turned—God help me, why?—or she would have shot him then and there. And how did I know that? At this moment I can't say; but I did know it, as sure as if I'd read it in a police report after the fact. And what plan did I have for what I would do next? None. There was this woman, turning in her tracks, a look of sudden calm on her face, raising the pistol, and I thought, as if my body were separate from my mind and another part of me were watching, She's going to shoot me, even as she tried.

The gun went off like a firecracker and I heard the round smack into the plywood behind me. I'd heard that sound before, in a bedroom in Oakland, a housewifey type ruining my day. Behind me, one woman's scream and then both their voices; Phillip's voice, too, shouting, "Ma," and then another pop reverberated in the solid air.

If I was shot, I did not feel it. It seemed as if I were walking up to her as I might any person on any other steady, imperturbable day. When she was almost upon me, or I upon her, I don't know which, my left arm snapped up and out, clamping her at the elbow, while the heel of my right hand slammed under her chin as I fairly leaped upward.

Her arm tore from my fingers, as her brain bounced like a handball on the backstop of her skull.

Annie planed out as she went down. Actual dust flew.

The weapon landed two yards away, and I scooped it up and went to see what happened to Cipriano, popping out the magazine as I went. Over my shoulder, I saw Constance and Patricia huddled together, crouching, and Phillip kneeling over Annie. Annie would be out for a while. Unfortunately, she wouldn't be dead.

I opened the passenger door and set the pistol, which was a Raven .25, a "purse gun," inside on the floor, slipped the magazine in my hip pocket, and slammed the door.

I walked to the other side. There was Cip, facedown, one arm under and one arm out. He was cyanotic, which is to say blue, and he was jerking. My Colt gleamed as it lay on the dirt under the car. Cip must have gone for it! What could have gone wrong? He couldn't have been shot.

Yelling his name, I tugged at his shirt and pants and rolled him over. There was no blood anywhere on him. His neck veins were engorged, as was a vein at the temple. His face was patched in blue and red, his eyes swimming in moisture, and he began to choke. "Oh, my God. Is it your heart, Cip, your heart?" White crusty dirt clung to the side of his face.

I looked over at Phillip, Constance, and Patricia. Annie was rising to her elbows, Phillip aiding her. I yelled, "Help me. Something's wrong here."

Shaken by my own panic, I thought I could not pull his shirt apart, but then the buttons gave. The pulse at his neck was very fast, and as my fingers started to drag away, I felt the beat stop, then start again, a dysrhythmia that panicked me further. I rolled him on his side, thinking surely he must be choking on his tongue, and reached inside his mouth to finger free the meaty thing, felt it flex and his jaws move down, and pulled my fingers out just in time. The airways must have been constricting, but from what? He began to quake again, his limbs jerking and flopping.

I stood back, not knowing what to do, and then bent down again and tried to grip his shoulders. Patricia was calling, "Samantha."

When I looked up, Phillip was coming at me, his face mutated to red folds. I heard the word *bitch* yelled loud and clear, and then I said, as if I hadn't, "Help me here! Help me."

Heaving Cip over again, I pounded his back three times, rolled him, pounded again. If there was something lodged in his windpipe, cutting off his oxygen and making him convulse, maybe it would pop out. No change.

Phillip was standing near me. I didn't look up, but I hardly cared what he might be doing. I heard Constance whining, "Oh, please!"

One more thing I tried: Quickly I rifled through Cip's pockets—groin pockets, shirt pockets; slipped my hands to the rear, searching for a foil of medicine, anything, and removed his wallet. Opening it, I searched for an emergency medical card that would tell me what was wrong. Where the bills are kept I found a foil all right; it was a condom.

The voice over me said, "Give him this," and Phillip was handing me yellow pills, three of them. "It's Valium."

What did it matter what it was? He was dying.

"It's Valium," Phillip said again. "That's all."

"I can't give him those. How am I going to give him those?" I yelled, but took them anyway.

He said, "Bite 'em. I'll get some water," and he walked away.

I put the pills in my mouth, crunching them, then spit the mess out into my fingers and pinched Cip's mouth open into a blue flower. I poked the pills in with two fingers. Then Phillip was lowering the bleach bottle over Cipriano, and pinching his cheeks to open his mouth. The water splashed, and yellow bits flowed out and down the sides of Cip's face, but some stayed in as I moved behind him and picked his shoulders up a little and then let him back down. His mouth kept closing and gaping, like a bird's. His eyes were swelling shut, and he seemed bluer. His fingers looked puffy. "Look at this," I said. "What'd we *do* to him?"

Phillip thrust another pill at me. I plugged it in, though it was no easy job, forcing it all the way down with my fingertip and glugging more water down, hoping the disk wouldn't go the wrong way. He choked, and wheezing sounds were coming from him now, and I was heartened. Painful as it sounded, it was at least chest movement.

I changed positions, thinking maybe I could straddle him and do a CPR compression or something if the breathing stopped, when I saw Annie through the car windows, weaving around in the background. I saw Patricia's arms go up to the top of her head and a distraught look on her face.

When I looked down, Cip's forehead and cheeks were turning fiery again. His knees kept rising and falling, his feet flicking out. Crouching down, I was ready to put my hands on his shoulders to steady him, when I heard more yelling and the sound of rapid steps.

Annie Dugdale was grinding around the car toward me. She had something in her hand. And then I saw it clearly: a length of pipe. She raised it above me at the selfsame moment

I scooped up the Colt lying on the other side of Cip and pointed it. I did not yell, "Halt!" I pulled hard on the trigger. The kick threw my hand up, dirt shattered off the underside of the car, and I lost my grip and then recovered. And as Annie turned back from the slight tilt the first round sent her into, I fired again.

I read about a man once, a Jew in Warsaw, in the last days. The ghetto had been razed and most of the people killed or long ago sent off to die in the camps. The ghetto was on fire. The man was on fire. He stormed the line of Nazis that stood in front of his apartment, and the SS knew he was coming for them, not running from the fire. They shot him nine times, and still he came. They shot him some more, until he was upon them, singeing the soldiers and killing them with a knife. The lesson here: That bullets seldom stop a man, not right away. Or a woman.

Annie came on. I twisted in my crouch, this time both hands steady on the Colt, and fired three more times. One caught Annie in the mouth.

CHAPTER
40

Cabbage gleaners are hard at it along Barranca and Sand Canyon. Their sweatshirted forms bend like croquet hoops.

In the beds of pickup trucks parked along the roadway are hundreds of cabbage heads in used plastic grocery sacks. Along the edge of the patch, tall dark-green eucalyptus swing in the wind, their silvery trunks shades lighter than the gray February sky.

I know what the rows look like, after the gleaners come through: At each disrupted bowl of leaves, an empty spot remains, the tough outer leaves that lie on the ground shot through with .45-caliber worm holes.

Today it is cabbage. All year it is cabbage. If you want to know what an autopsy room smells like, it is cream of broccoli soup; otherwise, cabbage. The same drafts that allow a rusty-tailed hawk, its wingtips kinked upward like thick fingers, to scout for rodents over the cabbage patch—these same winds bring currents of scent strongly anew.

It seems late for them to be out, the gleaners, so close to evening. They work the fields southwest of a eucalyptus windbreak along Irvine Center Drive, and across Irvine Center the heavy, dark branches of orange trees in one of the few remaining groves in the county drag the earth; underneath, the fallen orange globes rest like polished stones on the ends of jewelry.

It rained in January, a newsworthy event, and last week. Because of that, the gleaners' shoes will cake with black clay; and after stepping flatfooted to their cars in the dirt lot, they will drive home in their socks so their car mats will not be clumped with black mud. The gleaners are people of heart, who, on their own time and for their own reasons, hack off, dig up, pick, pluck, rake, or rack a harvest of food that would otherwise succumb to weed, worm, and fungus after the paid pickers have been through. Their harvest goes to pass-out programs, that is to say, to soup kitchens and the like, to the homeless whom some forces attempt to drive out.

I know these things because I, too, have gleaned. A four-inch curved knife and two hours on a Saturday is all I need. Saturdays, there are often a hundred people in the rows. Now, when I begin again, it will be Wednesdays, and there will be maybe only eight, mostly retired people or schoolteachers. I am presently on leave from the lab. This time, not medical. The fields are only about five miles from my house, so it is not much of a sacrifice to do this. I do not particularly count myself among the good folk mentioned here. What I will say, it beats a smelly gym; I get my exercise.

October was the last time I came, for the peppers. The peppers are a sight to see. Motorists pull their cars up into the bike lanes along Sand Canyon, Jeffrey, Harvard, and Culver, to sit for a moment and gaze at the feast of color in this colorless geography: orange, yellow, light green, dark green, red. The peppers are lovely.

Sometimes, even when I am not gleaning, I drive this back road for a portion of the nineteen miles to go see Ray Vega at the CHP substation down San Juan way. I cut over to the freeway at Alton to join one leg of the wishbone at the juncture of 5 and 405 called the infamous El Toro Y. There, cars bump like spermatozoa till they find a lane of the six-lane channel to freely flow through. That is, I take the back roads from the lab unless the day is one with high, white clouds in our normally uninspired sky. Those days, or with no bright peppers to see, I'll go two or three miles out of my way down another freeway to take the 405 south, hoping for the sight of a passenger plane coming in for a landing at John Wayne, the beast moving ever so slowly only hundreds of feet above the commuters. I've seen a day-moon balance on an airplane's tail over the freeway, or an orange sun against a lavender sky ride a Cessna's back. I do not mind the other cars then, for the slow traffic is almost an agreement, as though we've for-

sworn erratic speed so that everyone can see this show of odd
gravity. Especially in spring, before the smog and heat sets in,
the skyworks are pleasant. Marine airshows will pull drivers to
the side of the roads, where they get out of their cars and
gawk. People filling their tanks at service stations turn and
look to the skies. Sometimes I have seen, floating over the
white towers of office buildings recently erupted from lima-
bean fields, military sentry planes with radar turkey-platters
on their backs, coming in for a landing. And I have seen the
pregnant cargo planes swim slowly through the skies over
Mexican workers in the strawberry fields, and shuddered
from the jets cracking the air with continuous noise.

The best, the absolute best, though, of these small mira-
cles, occurred one day after I had been to the scene of a
poisoning. I will tell anyone that if he or she—and it is
usually a she—decides one day to kill herself, please do not
use drain cleaner, lye, and the various acids. I would say,
You will die a hideous, grotesquely painful death. Your tis-
sues will spew about wherever you will writhe. You will tear
your fingernails from their beds. You will rip your own lips
off, shit your pants, and vomit black and green fluid. I tell
this for contrast, to explain what I saw at ten o'clock and
what I saw at five o'clock one autumn day.

That hour, on the 405, when there still existed a grassy median between the north- and south-running lanes wide
enough for six cars to line up across it like a police blockade,
the sky at the bottom was a deep tangerine and above it a
purple-blue. Traffic on both sides of the median slowed to a
crawl. I was meeting Raymond for dinner in Dana Point, and
I did not want to be late. The slow traffic must be an accident,
I thought. Then at a wide curve I saw the slow spot, the cars
picking up speed just beyond. No stalled or crumpled vehicles
clutched the shoulders, no Cal-Trans cones were out. My turn
was coming to creep by and ogle, because ahead, with stately
neck extended and one lone staring eye set, it seemed, to car
occupants, there stood a great blue heron, patient or maybe
merely bewildered, I couldn't tell which. Its motions always
slow, it raised one foot as if to take a step, but didn't. What
thing was this, whose four-foot stature and accusing eye,
whose preposterous black plumes thrust backward from the

top like a Boy Scout with a cowlick, could slow a cascade of
metal tonnage to a crawl?

When my car was nearly even, the sun broke one last ray
across the coastal hills like a laser beam striking the bird. It
took wing, thrusting out its neck and yellow forebill, then re-
tracting its neck again into the shoulders for flight. That evening, coming back from seeing Raymond up Pacific Coast
Highway through Laguna Beach, I stopped at a bookstore and
bought my first bird book. My heart would celebrate that
freak of time, forgetting the morning's gruesome visions. I
would remember the dinner with Raymond, and I would celebrate that moment when human beings with every conceivable
background, in every conceivable state of repair and disrepair,
of urgency and dullness, removed from their particular lives
and away from time and corruption for scant minutes to
honor a heron. These are the things we must come back to.
The heron itself, and the people who would pause.

I am on my way to see Raymond again. Once again, it will be
for dinner. Yolanda is East. Ray called her, told her he'd be
having dinner with me, as if to say: See, I'm doing everything
aboveboard here. I will tell Raymond tonight that if Yolanda
is still troubled by our friendship, I won't be doing this again.
He'll protest, and I will insist. Some things you just must give
up for the sake of others. Joe Sanders understands my relationship with Raymond. If there is any jealousy or worry, I
have not seen it. But I will do this as much for Raymond as
Yolanda.

A therapist would say I'm in self-punishment mode, but I
don't think so. I do not feel I should be on leave, and in fact
I was back on the job Monday by noon. After the incident in
Nevada, Stu Hollings and the sheriff himself had me in to
headquarters. This was a big deal, going to the sheriff's,
sitting down across from him in his office, facing his gray
pin-striped suit, his pale yellow shirt and gray-and-yellow
fleur-de-lis tie with the onyx tie tack in it. We rarely ever see

him except in newspaper photos. He spends his days in ways I can't imagine, his nights with politicians and rich people from Newport. Or so we think. Why did I need this? I was already back at work. I felt fine. I didn't need to go talk to the dude. Stu tried to send me to the county shrink, but I refused. We were too busy, I said; I don't need it. "You only think you don't," Stu said. "This will catch up to you, and then we'll have another disability on our hands; in terms of cost, you'll be saving the county money—think of it that way." Stu Hollings, I've come to learn, is not my favorite sort of person. He said, "The sheriff wants you to do this." I said, "The sheriff doesn't even know who I am."

It was not so bad, the meeting with the sheriff. He told war stories about when he was on patrol. He told a joke about the Heiny Lick maneuver, the trick where you bear-hug someone who's choking, and didn't look at me till the last moment, but at Stu. And then the been-around eyes quieted, and he said, "We labor and wait, Smokey. Labor and wait," and I didn't know what he meant then and don't now. When we shook hands, mine disappeared.

Then Stu and I were back on the street, walking to the lab, and I was saying, Sure, I'll take the rest of the afternoon off. And sure, I'll keep the appointment.

That was five weeks ago. I have not spoken with Joe or anyone at the lab for three of those weeks, except for a follow-up call to the woman I was forced to see and try to tell how it feels to whack someone.

Cipriano Rycken is in a coma, the result of perpetual seizure—*status epilepticus,* they call it. The muscles of his body grabbed and ground like a seized motor. Such strenuous action of the muscles brings on fierce heat, hyperthermia, as it is called. He simply cooked almost to death. Cooked, not choked, though he could have done that too. Continuous convulsions over a period of time destroy the muscle cells, sending residue to the kidneys, which clog and eventually fail. He may die.

I thought, when Phillip gave me the Valium, that we had Cipriano. The flailing desisted. The tremors calmed, though he was still blue and gasping for breath. Now he suffers the effects of post-hypoxic encephalopathy, or oxygen deprivation.

Phillip knew what he was doing, shoving me the Valium, but it would've been better if he'd had something injectable. It was an hour's ride to Vegas, Phillip in the front with me, Constance in the back, Cipriano's legs in her lap until he started jerking again. Phillip said, "Sit on his legs," and I said no. I had her get in front, on Phillip's lap. She stayed bent over like that till we reached the freeway; by then the car phone had a cell to lock into, but when we called the paramedics they said we'd be just as quick heading for the hospital ourselves.

Even as I bore down on the accelerator, and the back of my seat was being flailed, and with the wretched couple locked together in the front, still in my mind's eye I could see Patricia in her neck collar, shorts, sweatshirt, and blue canvas shoes walking away from me, looking back as she passed the corner of the shed and the goat pen, as if she didn't know me, as if she were afraid of me. I called to her, but she continued in the direction of the drill site and Roland, clutching at the white thing at her throat.

Annie I left lying on the ground.

In the hospital, I sat in a tiny waiting room with Phillip. I could not supply much information to the doctors. I simply didn't know what had happened to Cipriano. Later I would learn that he suffered anaphylactic shock, a phenomenon most often seen in allergic reactions to drugs or insect bites, but, with Cipriano, undetermined. The body, for reasons not well understood, turns savagely upon itself. I was told it could have been precipitated by an allergic reaction to the artificial sweetener he had used in his coffee, or by sudden exercise, sudden cold, peanuts, or seminal fluid—even that: Imagine, someone said later, the surprise, a guy with his date and the extraordinary earth movement beneath him.

For the moment, the three of us stood in the waiting room, puzzled and afraid, then Constance went to brush her teeth. It escaped me until that moment that she had a purse with her, had managed to keep hold of it through the mayhem across the lake.

The authorities had to be dealt with. I'd made the call to the Las Vegas police as soon as Cipriano's gurney went through the double doors. They were on the way.

But now, in that vacant hour, I said to Phillip, "I don't know why she did that, Phillip," meaning Annie. "I don't." I felt cold and began to shiver and wonder what I did with my jacket. He sat across from me on a brown vinyl couch, his wrists between his knees, making slow washing movements with his hands, and said nothing, but sighed. I said, "I realize you didn't need to come here."

"You're thinking I hate you," he said.

I nodded, or something like it, and stood and went to look at a blank wall.

He said, "You could use a personality transplant."

When I turned to look at him, he was cool, kicked back, legs extended on the floor. The light from a television with the sound turned off was flashing from some sort of explosions in a commercial, and it turned the fine lines in Phillip's face to deep scratches by the ears.

Phillip said, "I want to say something, and I'm only going to say it once, dig? Stay away from my brother. I want him left alone."

"That's up to other people, don't you think?"

"You can do something. To make up."

"Oh, I see."

He sat up and sucked in his cheeks and looked at the ceiling. Then cut his eyes to me and said, "You might look better without that humongous chip on your shoulder, ever think of that?"

"I can't do anything. Think of what you're saying. I don't even want to do anything. My friend is with your brother and she is not right, there's something wrong with her. She's taking drugs. She's not herself."

"No, now you think of what *you're* saying. Your friend is not herself—she's alive, isn't she? You don't know but what she was on the sniff before, now, do you? Roland isn't going to hurt her. My brother is the one who's not himself. He did what he did because of her."

"Because of who? Patricia?"

"Mom."

"You mean the Kwik Stop," I said. "You mean the murder at the Kwik Stop in California."

"I mean my brother—" He broke off, lowered his head, and

pulled his spread fingers through his hair at the temples.
"Mom got us going sometimes. It's not his fault. I can turn
him around, I know I can. Don't expect me to tell anyone else
this, but I am going to tell you what went down that day,
okay? And you are going to keep it to yourself." His voice
dropped. "Dig?"

I gave a quick nod and sat down but didn't look at him.

"And that way we can put a thing behind us. You can quit
worryin' about Patricia, because she's going to be all right. We
have a deal here?"

"You can't seriously think we would," I said.

"All right. I'm going to tell you anyway. It's up to you, then.
But I am asking you not to harass my ass. You can understand
that. I don't think you're a hysterical woman. I think you can
handle this. Can't you?"

"In any other circumstance I'd tell you to get fucked."

"Fine. That's my mom layin' out there in the dirt, no matter
what, Scooter. And it was you put holes in her."

I hugged myself and bent forward.

"You sick?"

"No."

"Okay, then."

And then he told me what happened the day of Jerry
Dwyer's murder. He told how he and his mother and Roland
were going to meet at the Kwik Stop and pull a job. Be there,
or be square, Roland told him. Phillip didn't want to do it. It'd
been years since they clipped a place. Roland said they needed
money to bring up the rig from Texas. We could all be rich
in a matter of weeks, he told him. Phillip said no.

"But you don't argue with my brother," he said. "He's bone-
head stubborn, always was." Phillip wasn't painting that day;
he had a chiropractor's appointment that morning. But he
had no transportation. His license had been yanked, and for
once he was trying to live up to it. He was trying to work the
AA program because it was the only way he was going to save
himself, he said. He walked the three miles to the chiropractor's, the whole time what Roland told him weighing on his
mind so that even after, his muscles did not relax and his
shoulder did not unbind. He took the bus to Costa Mesa,
where he knew Annie and Roland would be waiting for him.

They liked the Kwik Stop because it was close to *two* freeways. "The goddamned bus," he said. "I took the bus."

"By the time I got there, the yellow tape was up." So he walked to the next stop, and waited.

The job went down pretty much as Joe Sanders called it. While Annie was hanging around, Jerry Dwyer accused her of lifting a candy bar. She got mad and Roland couldn't calm her. She said, Let's do it fucking *now*. When the kid saw the gun, he put two hands on the counter as if to leap over, as if he were coming for her. She fired once and he ran, and she kept firing, but it didn't put him down. Roland went for the other gun once the kid got behind the storage-room door; he'd be able to identify them both. Annie couldn't make it again in prison, Roland just knew.

Phillip leveled his eyes at me and said, "Roland is not a bad person. He cares, he really does. It broke him up, what he did. He helps people. What could he do, with her like that? He was protecting her."

"The boy he killed was twenty years old."

"I just wanted you to know."

"That is pure bullshit, the whole thing. Is Patricia in serious trouble with your brother? Is he going to hurt her? You have to tell me this."

"I don't think so," Phillip said.

"What else would you say. Why did I ask?"

"I think she can help him, if we stay out of it."

"She can't help herself across the street. And what about now, with . . ." What about Roland seeing Annie, her big feet cambered out, dead with her boots on in the red Nevada dirt. "What's he going to do *now*?"

"He'll be relieved, believe me. She should have been harder on me. I'm the oldest. She was harder on him."

"He'll kill her, won't he?"

"Of course he won't kill her. I told you."

I looked at him a long time before saying, "She called me from Jubilee's in Long Beach. She said you hurt a girl. Or was it Roland?"

Phillip stood up. He was shaking his head, walking away from me now. I was afraid he was going out.

"Hey—"

His hand was resting on the door, his back to me. The line of his western-style shirt across the shoulders made them look broader than they were. I felt a terrible, awful sadness, and I didn't know who for.

"I did hurt a girl," he said, walking out into the hallway now, stopping, looking down the hallway at some different terrain. The air was better there.

"How?" I asked him.

"I slapped her around. She sat down on the ground outside and Patricia thought it was more than it was." He looked at me with no expression I could discern. Then he said, "I was drunk."

"Which one of you broke into Patricia's apartment?"

"Roland does some shit. He likes to shake people up. He doesn't mean anything by it."

"How'd you know where we lived?"

"Ran your plates."

"How could you do that?"

"If I tell you that you'll know as much as I do, now, won't you?" As he looked away, the expression in his eyes seemed dead or far away. Then he said, "We have some buddies who sell cars. They can run 'em."

How I hated this family. The witch that spawned this.

Phillip moved back into the room, and sat down, and began to talk some more, even as Constance came in, combed and with a new flush to her cheeks. I'd moved to the chair opposite. He said, "No person should endure abuse of any kind." Constance was watching me, the both of them together on the vinyl bench holding hands, a tiny frown appearing between her brows. "And if they do, they're fools."

"It's their own damn fault, is that what you mean? Well, Phillip, what do you think of me? Would you say this 'cop-ette' is a number-one fool? 'Cause if you do, all the fast fred-die ain't out of your system."

"No, ma'am," he said. "I think you're a person trying to do good and came close but no cigar."

I am not the only one on leave. Billy Katchaturian is. His is for infraction of taste, and possibly more, though the bosses are trying to keep it hush-hush. It wasn't Joe who told me, but Trudy Kunitz. She said, "You hear what Billy Katch did?" She was sitting on my desk and swung one denim shrouded leg to and fro, the heel of her sneaker rattling the steel case of my desk, and I wondered if she and Billy ever got together, these two; and decided no, they did not. She said, "With some photos. He's hung out to dry, I think."

I smiled and said, "What were they? Pornographic? All the girls he made it with the last five years, or what?" At the time, I had not even mentally included myself in that number, having put Billy's pillows and white fluffy cat out of mind, though the memory rushed in soon enough.

"He had a show, down at Laguna Beach?"

"Yes?"

"His pictures, all in black and white," she said, spreading both hands before her. She leaned closer. Two tarnished silver arrows fell forward from her hair, swinging from her earlobes. "Splatter," she said. "Every one. Can you believe it? He calls it 'Lifelines.' Is that a crock?"

I'm passing now through Mission Viejo. I'm thinking of what Phillip said to me—about being a person who's trying to do good—and the words comfort me but I wish it wasn't he who said it, Phillip with his piss-poor yellow snake and punctured peacock. Brake lights are coming on. The flow always thickens before Crown Valley, but I know it will open up again between here and Avery.

Roland and Patricia have disappeared. Roland, of course, is on the run for the Dwyer murder, my dimpled and measled friend in tow. I told the Las Vegas police and the Orange County sheriff what Phillip told me, as I'm sure he knew I would, but Phillip is not repeating any of it, just as he said, and the detectives visit him every Friday.

Who pulls the strings? I ask myself. And I asked Joe, each time I saw him before I called a halt for a while: Joe-baby, do you think it's getting any better? Meaning the state of things: the load at the lab; the gang shootings we now just call "Santa Anas"; his knee that hurts every January; the big and the little wars. And he has said he doesn't think so. He's told me that

he loves me. I have not told him back. I do, but I can't bring
myself to say it yet.

On the right side of my vehicle, I hear a high, squeaking
sound. Oh, great, I think. There's something wrong with my
car. I push the button to roll down the passenger window to
hear it better. A symphony of high-pitched yipping wafts in.
I look and look again, thinking there are birds, maybe, on the
wires. But no. In the gully that runs along the freeway are tall
willows, the tops still at a level ten feet below. It is there the
sound is coming from. I finally recognize it: A chorus of
coyotes.

The humans on the freeway above have slowed for this
chilling song. At Back Bay, of course, there are coyotes. They
prevent the meso-predator release of racoons and weasels,
which in turn would eat the eggs of the endangered least tern,
a beautiful white bird with a black crown and an expressive
eyeline, who makes its vulnerable nest in the sand. I've seen
coyotes all the years I've lived in California, loping along resi-
dential streets early mornings and evenings, tails tucked well
down between their legs, no more fear in their eyes than a
wary gang member on his way to a wedding party.

This valley of cries beside the freeway says to me that life
goes on, in all its variety, in all its single-mindedness. Stay
alive, it says. Stay alive.

ACKNOWLEDGMENTS

For invaluable help with the details of criminalistics, my deep appreciation goes to Larry Ragle, retired director of the Orange County Sheriff-Coroner's Forensic Science Services Center and instructor of criminalistics at the University of California at Irvine; and to the staff of the center.

For information relating to law-enforcement protocol and investigative techniques, my sincere thanks to Long Beach police officers Larry N. Chowen and Robert Mahakian; Los Angeles County Deputy Sheriff Scott Anger; California Highway Patrol Officer Gary Alfonso; writer and private investigator Bruce Haskett; writer and former Foster City police officer Tom Arnold; and to Travis J. More and Wayne Apfeld.

For information concerning the creatures and plants of nature, recognition goes to the Friends of Newport Bay; the Environmental Nature Center of Newport Beach; and Rick Weiss of *Science News*.

For additional technical information, I am indebted to my friends Theodore Waltuch, M.D., and Dawn Waltuch, R.N. Thanks also to Ellen Sullivan, and to Ed Keyes of Ed's Sporting Goods, and Nancy Kawamura, of Orange County Harvest.

To my friends in Orange County Fictionaires, thanks greater than words.

My sincere appreciation to the staff and conferees of the 1990 Squaw Valley Writers' Conference for the opportunity of exposure and for sage advice.

Special thanks go to Michael Silverblatt, host of National Public Radio's *Bookworm* on KCRW in Santa Monica, for his enthusiastic confirmation and singular wisdoms.

Without the unswerving support of my family, this effort simply could not have gone forward. To Tom Glagola, Kathryn Ayres, Gerald and Florence Pahlka, and John and Ann Glagola, my deep appreciation for support that involved spirit, love, and personal sacrifice.

For his energy, optimism, talent, and grace, profound thanks to Michael V. Carlisle of the William Morris Agency.

And finally, I am indebted to my editor, Doug Stumpf, for his early faith in me. Without him, I'd still be inserting/deleting/struggling/scrapping and most of all, whining. Deepest thanks to a correctly aggressive, patient, and intelligent man. Thanks also to Erik Palma, Doug's assistant, and to keen-eyed Randee Marullo for her diligent copyediting.

—NOREEN AYRES